ADVANCE PRAISE FOR

Emma of 83rd Street

"The best romantic comedy I've ever read. A sparkling take on *Emma* that would make Jane Austen proud."

—Lauren Layne, *New York Times* bestselling author of *Made in Manhattan*

"*Emma of 83rd Street* is a compulsive page-turner with excellent slow-burn tension. A friends-to-lovers instant favorite!"

—Sarah Hogle, author of *You Deserve Each Other*

"A delightful debut . . . sweeter than candy."

—Marilyn Simon Rothstein, author of *Husbands and Other Sharp Objects*

"Austenites and rom-com fans rejoice: *Emma of 83rd Street* is witty, wonderful, and the best retelling of *Emma* since *Clueless*. I loved every minute of it."

—Sarvenaz Tash, coauthor of *Ghosting: A Love Story*

Emma of 83rd Street

AUDREY BELLEZZA
AND EMILY HARDING

G

GALLERY BOOKS

New York   London   Toronto   Sydney   New Delhi

G

Gallery Books
An Imprint of Simon & Schuster, Inc.
1230 Avenue of the Americas
New York, NY 10020

First Gallery Books trade paperback edition May 2023

GALLERY BOOKS and colophon are registered trademarks of Simon & Schuster, Inc.

For information about special discounts for bulk purchases, please contact Simon & Schuster Special Sales at 1-866-506-1949 or business@simonandschuster.com.

The Simon & Schuster Speakers Bureau can bring authors to your live event. For more information or to book an event, contact the Simon & Schuster Speakers Bureau at 1-866-248-3049 or visit our website at www.simonspeakers.com.

Manufactured in the United States of America

10 9 8 7 6 5 4 3

Library of Congress Cataloging-in-Publication Data

Names: Bellezza, Audrey, author. | Harding, Emily, author.
Title: Emma of 83rd street / Audrey Bellezza & Emily Harding.
Identifiers: LCCN 2022035949 (print) | LCCN 2022035950 (ebook) |
ISBN 9781668008393 (trade paperback) | ISBN 9781668008409 (ebook)
Subjects: LCGFT: Romance fiction. | Novels.
Classification: LCC PS3602.E6476 E46 2023 (print) | LCC PS3602.E6476
(ebook) | DDC 813/.6—dc23/eng/20220909
LC record available at https://lccn.loc.gov/2022035949
LC ebook record available at https://lccn.loc.gov/2022035950

ISBN 978-1-6680-0839-3
ISBN 978-1-6680-0840-9 (ebook)

To our own leading men, Tom and Mike:
Thank you for all our favorite love stories.

Emma of 83rd Street

PROLOGUE

I t was eight p.m. on Christmas Eve and in New York City that meant three things were certain: the annual Woodhouse Christmas Party was in full swing, the residents of East 83rd Street had already deemed it a roaring success, and Mr. Woodhouse was staring at the buffet table in his dining room in abject horror.

"My God, Emma," he murmured. "How could you do this?"

Emma Woodhouse smiled and waved at Mrs. Crawford, who had just arrived and was mingling with the familiar crowd under the archway of fairy lights over the foyer. She didn't have to follow her father's gaze down to the carefully curated array of organic canapés and gluten-free desserts to know what he was glaring at.

"Dad, it's just a cheesecake."

"It's an abomination."

She had anticipated this. It happened last year when he demanded the calorie count for the croquembouche that the caterers had decorated to look like a Christmas tree. The year before that, he had admonished her sister Margo for using real cream on a pavlova. This time, Emma was ready.

"But there's two different fruit platters, too, see? And a vegetable tray on the other end with whole wheat pita bread and hummus."

"Hummus?" he asked hopefully, turning to look further down the table. But then his expression deflated. "It's next to the sugar cookies."

"Yes, but they're *Fran's* sugar cookies."

He rubbed his temples. "Jesus . . ."

"They're in the shape of angels, actually," she said, biting back a smile.

"This isn't funny, Emma. Do you know how much butter is in that recipe?"

She was about to tell him that yes, she obviously knew since they had been making them every Christmas since the beginning of time, but before she had the chance, a hand reached between them and grabbed her father's shoulder.

"Henry, these cookies are amazing! Just amazing!" Mrs. Pawloski exclaimed, waving a decapitated angel in her hand and dusting them with crumbs. "I think this is probably my fifth one! Can you believe it? Of course, it's Christmas so calories don't count, at least that's what I'm telling myself!"

"Helen, please be careful," her father said, taking the cookie from her hand and passing it to Emma as if she would know what to do with it. "The processed sugar alone is enough to give you diabetes."

Mrs. Pawloski laughed, a shrill sound that vibrated off Emma's inner ear. "Good Lord, if that's true, then don't you dare look in the kitchen! That pavlova is going to send me to the hospital!"

Mr. Woodhouse turned to his daughter, his pale skin becoming even more pallid. "Not again . . ."

Emma strained to keep a smile on her face as she motioned them both toward the living room. "Why don't you sit down by the fire and I'll get you something to drink?"

"Tea," Mr. Woodhouse said over his shoulder, as Mrs. Pawloski looped her arm with his and started forward.

"I know," Emma said.

"The chamomile."

"I know."

Emma watched as they disappeared into the crowded room and let out her breath. That was a close call.

She made her way to the foyer, stopping to say hello to guests, to nod and smile and look appropriately humble when they praised the decorations and food. She was good at this. After all, she had years of practice.

That wasn't to say she didn't appreciate the compliments. Far from it. Only that after two weeks of intense planning—which really just came down to managing her sister's vision and her father's expectations—Emma wasn't in any doubt that her efforts would be well received. The decorations—a winter wonderland theme this year that saw white and gold garlands draped over every surface of the four-story townhouse—were perfect. The food—despite her father's concerns—was delicious. There was nothing to do now but accept the praise and see if she couldn't grab a drink and a moment of silence.

She finally made it to the staircase and started down to the kitchen. Their housekeeper, Fran, was walking toward her just as Emma got to the bottom of the stairs, her brow drawn with a serious line, and a full tea service on the tray balanced in her hands. The woman couldn't have been over five feet tall, but that look still made Emma feel like she was six and had been caught sneaking Fran's freshly made blinis to feed the pigeons in Central Park again.

"What's wrong with the cookies?" she asked, looking down at Emma's hand.

It was only then that Emma remembered she was still holding Mrs. Pawloski's cookie.

"Oh, nothing. I just had to run interference between the desserts and Dad." Emma nodded to the tea on the tray. "Is that for him?"

Fran sighed, moving around Emma and up the stairs. "I figured he'd need it before we brought out the pavlova."

"Thank you," she called after her, smiling.

Fran didn't look back, only muttered something under her breath as she continued up.

Emma watched her ascend before throwing the cookie away in the nearby trash can and making her way down the hall to the kitchen. Even with a few caterers still preparing plates of canapés, it was wonderfully quiet down here, and the idea that Emma would have easy access to the champagne, maybe even be able to sit down and take a breath, made her genuinely smile for the first time all day.

The smile dropped the minute she entered the room.

George Knightley was standing by the kitchen island where the bar was set up, frowning down at the row of whiskeys as if they had personally insulted him. He was so tall he had to bend at the waist to see the labels, his dark hair falling forward so he had to run his fingers through it to put it back in place. Of course, it was never in place to begin with, but that only made it look more deliberate. Emma went to school with guys who spent at least an hour every day trying to achieve what Knightley's hair did purely by accident. It was almost annoying.

"What did those bottles ever do to you?" she asked, jumping up to sit on the counter.

He didn't look at her, though a small smile twitched one corner of his lips. "Merry Christmas, Woodhouse."

"Merry Christmas, Knightley."

"The party is a success, as always."

"Thank you very much," she said with a flourish of her hand.

He turned one of the bottles around to examine its label. "I take it he hasn't seen the pavlova yet."

"Why do you assume he hasn't seen the pavlova?"

"Because I haven't heard a scream of anguish from upstairs," he murmured. "By the way, I saw him a little bit ago. He told me the big news."

Emma narrowed her eyes on him. "About the hummus?"

"No, Woodhouse. About you getting into grad school."

"Oh, right. Well, if you thought he was stressed about me commuting three miles to FIT for the past four years, you should have seen his reaction when I told him that NYU is all the way down in the Village. I've already had to promise him a dozen times that I'm not moving out," she replied, leaning over for an open bottle of Bollinger.

Knightley was faster, moving the champagne further down the bar and away from her without even pausing his perusal.

She frowned at him. "I'm twenty-one now, you know."

He ignored her. "So what are you going to grad school for?"

"Art history."

That got his attention. He finally looked up, his amber eyes leveling a skeptical gaze at her.

She lifted her chin defiantly. "What's wrong with art history?"

"There's nothing wrong with art history."

"Then why are you looking at me like that?"

"I thought you were graduating in May with a bachelor's in fashion merchandising."

"And?"

His scrutiny moved to a bottle of Laphroaig as he asked, "Is Prada opening a boutique at the Met?"

"They should. It would be amazing."

The corner of his lip twitched again. "I've just never heard you voice an interest in art before."

"Not surprising, since you never listen when I tell you about anything I'm interested in."

He had just begun to pour some whiskey into a nearby glass when he paused, turning to her with an eyebrow arched high on his forehead. "Is this going to be like the time you got really into gardening and then gave up when six weeks' worth of work yielded one tomato?"

She frowned. "There were two green beans too."

"Or when you begged me to teach you how to play guitar so you could record an album, and then quit the first time one of your strings broke?"

"That blister was on my finger for over a month, you know."

"Or how you saved up for a 3D printer so you could start your own jewelry company, but gave up once you realized—"

She held up her hand to stop him. "Those were hobbies, Knightley. This is different."

"I'm just pointing out that I listen. In fact, I could probably describe every floor of Bergdorf Goodman's—"

"You're welcome."

"—and yet I've never heard you mention art. At all."

She feigned surprise, batting her eyes at him. "Well thank you so much, George Knightley! Yes, I *am* excited to be accepted into such a competitive program, and even though I'm not channeling my megalomania into a start-up that's trying to save the entire planet like *some* people—"

"My company isn't saving the planet. We're just investing in clean tech."

"—I'm sure my work will be nonetheless fulfilling. And knowing that I have your support means so much!"

He stared at her from under his brow, the light above casting shadows over his honey-colored eyes. "Are you done now?"

She thought for a moment before answering, "Yes."

"Congratulations."

She smiled.

Laughter erupted from the far corner of the room, and they both turned as Margo emerged from the hallway with Knightley's younger brother Ben close behind.

"You are so weird!" Margo was shrieking.

"I'm not the one who's never seen *Die Hard*!" Ben exclaimed. "How did we all grow up having a weekly movie night and I never made you watch the best Christmas movie of all time?"

Margo made her way to the bar, doing an awful job of keeping her smile at bay. Emma and her older sister were three years apart and had spent most of their lives being mistaken for twins, but no one made that mistake anymore. They had the same dark hair, but while Emma's was still long and wavy, Margo had cut hers into a stick-straight bob. She had also adopted a pair of thick, black-frame glasses and wore them instead of her previous contacts, so the big green eyes she and Emma shared were now partially hidden. Margo said it was part of creating a more mature image. Emma blamed law school.

"Maybe because *Die Hard* isn't a Christmas movie?" Margo answered Ben, pouring herself a glass of champagne.

Ben stopped in his tracks, mouth falling open. "Are you serious right now?"

"Oh please."

Ben turned to his brother. He was younger than Knightley by only two years, but he was lanky and a few inches shorter, so the age difference looked more like a decade. "George, back me up here."

"What was *Die Hard* about again?" Knightley leaned back against the counter, the sleeve of his navy cashmere sweater brushing Emma's bare leg. She ignored it.

"I don't know," she said innocently, as if they hadn't just watched it together two weeks earlier. "I never saw it."

"Don't worry," he replied, playing along. "I'm sure we're not missing much."

Ben held his hand to his heart as if truly offended. "Sacrilege."

Margo failed again to dampen her smile as she started toward the French doors that led out to the back garden. The yard was narrow but long: large enough for a party and absolutely huge by New York City standards. A few trees lined the back of it and just beyond them Emma could see the Knightley home. Their townhouse backed up to the Woodhouses', their yards adjacent. The brothers had left a few lights on tonight, so the tall windows helped illuminate the worn path between the trees that had connected the two families for years.

Emma and Margo had decided to get outdoor heaters for their yard so guests could sit outside to enjoy the Christmas lights draped over the verandah, but right now, it was empty as Margo made her way outside. Ben followed, coming up behind her and tickling her sides as the doors closed behind them.

"Ben didn't bring a date," Emma said, watching through the windows as the two of them collapsed on a nearby wicker chaise.

Knightley stayed focused on his drink. "Neither did I."

She rolled her eyes. "Yes, but you never bring a date."

"And?"

"And Ben usually does. Even if it's just casual."

"So?"

Emma's gaze stayed on her sister and Ben. He leaned in and said something close to her ear, and Margo dissolved into laughter, barely able to get the champagne flute to her mouth to take a sip.

"So . . ." she pondered, the plan still formulating in her mind. "What about Ben and Margo?"

"What about them?"

Emma turned to Knightley, waiting for him to look up. It took him a moment, but when he finally did, his expression was bored, uninterested.

She wagged her eyebrows at him. "You know."

"What," he said. It was barely a question.

She sighed. "Ben and Margo. Like, *together*."

"Together?"

"Together," she repeated, wagging her eyebrows again as if it drove home her meaning.

He scoffed. "Don't be ridiculous."

"Why is that ridiculous?"

"Because it's Ben. And Margo."

"And . . . ?"

His brow furrowed. "And we've all grown up together. You and Margo are like our sisters."

"But we're not your sisters."

"Semantics."

"Well, I think they're sleeping together."

He had just taken a sip of whiskey and almost spat it across the room. "Jesus, Emma."

Her eyes widened. "What?"

"The last thing I want to think about right now is my little brother and your big sister—"

"Doing it?"

His fingers went to the bridge of his nose as if warding off an oncoming headache. "I'm begging you. Please shut up."

She shrugged and turned back to the window, watching Margo as her head fell back in laughter again, and how Ben stared at the arch of her neck as she did it.

"Well, if they're not sleeping together now, they're going to. It's obvious to anyone who watches them for more than five minutes."

"Then stop watching," Knightley murmured.

She turned back to him. He was looking at her the way he always looked at her, like she was five and drawing unicorns on his algebra textbook again. Mild amusement that really only masked a thin tolerance she was always testing. It was a look that had stopped bothering her by the time she was six, so now she barely registered it at all.

"You just don't want to admit that I'm right," she replied, picking a grape from a nearby platter and popping it into her mouth.

A sharp smile. "Hardly."

It was at this moment that Margo squealed, drawing their attention to the yard again.

Emma smiled. "You were saying?"

Knightley sighed, the kind of sigh that carried more disappointment than he could possibly put into words. "Woodhouse, listen closely, because this is important. I don't know what naive fantasies your brain has concocted, but let me assure you: Benjamin Thomas Knightley and Margo Elizabeth Woodhouse will never, ever be *together*."

CHAPTER 1

Two years later

Ben and Margo were married on a Saturday. It was a small ceremony, with an exclusive pool of guests that fit neatly into the first three rows of St. Ignatius. It was the same church where Emma and Margo were baptized, the same one their parents had been married in so many years before. The priest was the same, too; Emma remembered him being ancient when she walked up to get her first Communion, his knobbed fingers shaking as he handed her the Eucharist, so how he was still standing before them now was a divine mystery in its own right. Still, he made it through the entire mass, reciting the vows and prayers in a mumbled monotone so the only words Emma could make out were the important ones: "I now pronounce you husband and wife. You may kiss the bride."

Margo lifted her simple cage veil and smiled up at her new husband as the setting sunlight streamed through the brightly colored stained glass windows. Ben smiled back, then leaned down to kiss his new wife.

And that was it. Margo Woodhouse was now Mrs. Margo Woodhouse-Knightley.

The reality of the moment hit Emma suddenly, a tightness

gripping her chest, but she kept her rising emotions in check. She knew the tears she choked back must be happy ones.

Right on cue, the sound of the pipe organ filled the sanctuary, vibrating off the vaulted ceilings and echoing throughout the church. The couple reluctantly pulled apart and Margo grabbed the satin length of her wedding dress, practically skipping down the aisle with her hand in Ben's.

The guests chatted happily, slowly exiting the wooden pews adorned with white roses and ivory ribbon at the end of each row. Emma followed suit, her arm linked with her father's while they walked behind Knightley, Mrs. Pawloski, and others making their way out of the church and back toward 83rd Street. It was only the first weekend of September, but as the sun disappeared behind the tall buildings along Park Avenue, there was already a chill in the air. Emma's dark hair was up in a high bun, allowing a shiver to run down her exposed neck. She pulled her silk bomber jacket tighter around her shoulders, thankful for the faux fur lining keeping her warm; her long, mauve-colored slip dress was gorgeous, but its satin material was also incredibly thin.

"Such a sad day," Mr. Woodhouse said, squeezing Emma's arm as they followed the guests toward the reception at their home just a few blocks away.

Emma looked over at him. His thick hair had gone gray years ago, and his dark tortoise-frame glasses were as utilitarian as they were modern. But he looked as elegant as he always had in his classic single-breasted tuxedo and burgundy-colored scarf. Even if you weren't aware that the Woodhouses were one of New York's oldest—and wealthiest—families, Mr. Woodhouse always exuded a refined edge that subtly let you know.

She wanted to remind him that his older daughter was married and happy and that was worth celebrating, but despite her excitement for Margo, Emma knew all too well what her father meant. Today signaled more than just the beginning of a marriage. It meant Margo was really leaving them.

While she and Ben had technically rented a place together over on Lexington last year, Margo had still stayed in her childhood bedroom next to Emma's in the Woodhouse home a few nights a week. But that was over now. The newlyweds had closed on an apartment a few miles downtown. The move felt final, more than even the wedding did. Margo wouldn't be just down the hall anymore. Emma's voice of reason would be gone, and she had no idea how to replace it.

Yes, there was so much joy today, but sorrow too. A gentle sorrow that pulled at Emma from somewhere deep in her chest.

"Don't you dare leave me, Emma," her father murmured, almost as if he'd heard Emma's thoughts.

"Never," she replied, leaning into his tall frame. "I promise."

Her father sighed. "Thank God."

"Besides, I have no interest in ever getting married," she declared. She hadn't realized how loud her proclamation was until she heard Knightley chuckle just ahead. "Something funny?"

He turned to look at her with a wry grin, his cheeks flushed from the chill. It somehow made his golden-brown eyes look even sharper. "Is that right?"

"Yes." She lifted her chin. "Why would I? Being single is too much fun."

"Okay, Woodhouse."

"Excuse me? Aren't you the patron saint for eternal bachelorhood?"

He scoffed before turning back around.

"Why does anyone need to get married?" her father pondered to no one in particular.

The parade of sharply dressed wedding guests continued down Madison Avenue to 83rd Street until they reached the Woodhouses' townhouse. Just beside the stairs up to the front door was a short walkway that led to their back garden. One by one the guests walked through its wrought iron gates adorned with lush florals and vines before entering the yard that had been magically transformed for the occasion.

The two long reception tables were covered with flowers—marigolds and hydrangeas, red roses and rust-toned dahlias—and there were dozens of glowing candles in low hurricane lanterns lining the yard. In the center of the space was a small dance floor with a stage for the band, and the caterer's makeshift bar was over by the French doors leading to the kitchen. All of it was tucked underneath a canopy of sparkling fairy lights that hung from the trees overhead. It was a tight fit, but it was perfect. Everything was.

Well, almost everything. Emma couldn't help but see some lingering imperfections, proof that this was still the yard where she and Margo had grown up. The path through the far trees where the Knightley boys would sneak over from their house was still there, as was the bald bit of dirt in the opposite corner where the four of them had worn away the grass years ago trying to build a fort. And that rose bush by the French doors had never quite grown back after Ben cut down half of it for a bouquet to give Margo on her tenth birthday. But no one else seemed to notice those details. They gaped at the decorations, smiling and laughing as servers began passing around hors d'oeuvres.

"Poor Margo," Mr. Woodhouse murmured, his mantra for the night. "You don't think Ben made one of those extravagant nine-tier wedding cakes?"

"Not nine. Maybe seven," Knightley replied.

Emma patted her father's arm. "Ignore him. I'm sure it will be just perfect."

They were among the last few guests to arrive, and Emma craned her neck to see over the crowd milling about the tables and dance floor. The yard was filled with almost everyone who had been at the church, and Emma frowned in disappointment.

"Looking for someone?" her father asked.

"Ben's best friend. The one Margo's always talking about. Montgomery Knox."

"He's not here?"

"I don't think so," Emma said as she did one last audit of the garden. "I was sure we'd finally meet him tonight. His flight was delayed, so he missed the wedding, but he called Ben and promised to be here for the reception." Her gaze drifted back to Knightley in time to catch his eye roll. "Have something to say?"

"I wouldn't get your hopes up," he replied. "He missed the engagement party, the bachelor party, the rehearsal dinner—"

"Be nice," she demanded sweetly. "His plane is just delayed."

"Right," Knightley murmured, his doubt palpable. "Well if he shows up, I'll be at the bar." And then he turned and retreated into the crowd of guests.

Before Emma could hurl an appropriately scathing retort at his back, a server appeared with a tray of canapés. "Puff pastry and saucisson à l'ail?"

Her father picked one up and inspected it. "You can call it whatever you like, my good man, but these are pigs in a blanket."

Emma donned a placating smile, as much for her father as for the server. "Dad, don't you remember? That's Ben's whole philosophy for tonight's menu. He's reinventing our favorite childhood meals for a modern palate. Comfort food meets gourmet sensibilities."

Her father stared at her, unimpressed. Then he dropped the offending sausage back on the tray. Emma mouthed a silent "sorry" to the server and was about to grab the hors d'oeuvre for herself but was interrupted by Mrs. Pawloski's shrill voice.

"Isn't it all just gorgeous?" she exclaimed, plowing through the small crowd toward them, holding a half-empty glass of champagne in one hand and a canapé in the other. "The flowers and the music and—oh! Have you had one of these yet?" she said, waving what looked like a piece of bread and sending crumbs flying in the process.

"Hello, Mrs. Pawloski." Emma forced a smile.

Mrs. Pawloski threw the rest of the canapé in her mouth. "They're these darling little peanut butter and jelly sandwiches! Except Ben just told me they're strawberry bruschetta with balsamic and almond butter or something. Whatever they are, I love them! Just love them! Margo is so lucky she married a chef! Oh! And these!"

The woman reached out at the tray of another passing server, her armful of bracelets clattering as if to punctuate her point. Emma had hoped that Mrs. Pawloski's jewelry might be toned down today, along with the bright wardrobe choices that seemed to be perpetually stuck in 1998, but no such luck. Her husband Burt had died a few years ago, and instead of the fortune everyone assumed he had stashed away, he'd left his wife with nothing but a mountain of debt. Emma wasn't sure if she'd seen the woman in a new piece of clothing since. But at least tonight's flowing silk dress, a cacophony of pinks and greens and reds faded slightly from years of wear, was a bit more formal. "Oysters! Ben said a chef friend sourced them directly from the Long Island Sound just this morning! There's caviar on them! Caviar!"

Emma worked hard to maintain her smile. Of course she knew about the oysters; she had helped plan every detail of the wedding.

Ben and Margo may have picked what they wanted, but it was Emma who made it all happen, even convincing Ben to swap some of his more experimental menu choices with those more familiar to the families of the Upper East Side.

"Just delicious. Oh!" Mrs. Pawloski's eyes grew wide as she finished chewing. "And did you hear? Montgomery Knox's flight was canceled!"

"Canceled?" Emma was stunned. How had Mrs. Pawloski heard about this before she had? The woman had a sixth sense for gossip.

"Yes! One of Ben's friends told Veronica who just told me. Isn't it devastating?" the woman exclaimed. "I can't believe he missed the wedding and the reception, too! Such a tragedy!"

Emma nodded, trying to mask her irritation. Now she would not only have to wait even longer to meet the elusive Montgomery Knox, but she'd have to hear Knightley wax poetic about being right. Again.

Mr. Woodhouse couldn't feign interest, shaking his head. "Where's the bar?"

"It's right over there, Henry. By the cake!" Mrs. Pawloski was all smiles again, looping her arm with Emma's father's. "Oh, wait until you see it! It's gorgeous! Six tiers! Six!"

Mr. Woodhouse's face blanched. "Dear God."

Emma knew she could lift her dad's spirits once she showed him the selection of organic juices she had ordered just for him at the bar, but before she could mention it, the guests erupted in applause as Margo and Ben walked through the wrought iron gate and into the reception.

"Oh, congratulations! What a beautiful wedding! So beautiful!" Mrs. Pawloski repeated over and over when they finally reached her.

"Come on, Mrs. Pawloski!" Ben exclaimed, throwing his arm around her shoulders. The jacket of his tux was open, and the top of his white shirt unbuttoned. The matching tie was already missing. "Let's get everyone liquored up!"

"Yes, more champagne please!" she cried, thrilled by the attention as the man of the hour grabbed a champagne flute from a nearby server and dramatically took a sip. The rest of the guests joined in the merriment, finding their own drinks from the servers' trays. Emma let out a long breath and grabbed a glass as well, as she looked around the space. It was truly breathtaking. She took a sip of her drink and mentally gave herself a pat on the back. *Well done, Emma.*

Now it was time to gloat.

She placed her jacket over her assigned chair, then walked over to the bar where Knightley stood, his attention on the dance floor as Margo and Ben held court.

He glanced down at her, frowning. "Why do you look so smug?"

Emma nodded to the couple. "Told you so."

A sly grin crept onto his face as he let his gaze return to the dance floor. "Are you seriously taking credit for this?"

Emma only smiled up at him sweetly. Yes, Margo and Ben had obviously been attracted to each other for years, but would Ben have asked Margo to the new Jasper Johns exhibit at MoMA a few weeks after that fateful Christmas without Emma conveniently mentioning that her sister wanted to go? And would her sister have invited Ben to the Mets' opening day if Emma hadn't let slip over Sunday dinner that Margo's firm had box seats at Citi Field? Of course not. Yes, it had all worked according to plan. Emma clearly had a talent for it.

It was a long moment before Knightley turned to look down at her again. "What?"

"Well?" she said, batting her eyes.

He only took a sip of whiskey.

She sighed as if he was testing her patience. "I was right. Is that *so* hard to say?"

"You might want to watch it with the champagne, Woodhouse." He nodded down to her half-empty flute.

"Stop changing the subject. I'm actually a full-fledged adult now, so you can stop with this big brother thing already."

He stared at her. She maintained his gaze, working hard to look cool and collected, but after a moment of silence she couldn't help but begin to fidget under his scrutiny. He noticed, and his serious expression gained a playful edge. "You want me to treat you like an adult?"

She rolled her eyes. "Yes."

He slowly leaned down, pausing at her ear before replying, "Then act like one."

And then he straightened and threw her another wry smile before turning on his heel and walking away.

"Damn it," Emma said under her breath. Knightley: 1. Woodhouse: 0.

No matter, the night was young. Not even Knightley's incessant teasing could derail the evening, because tonight wasn't about them; it was about Margo and Ben. And it was going to be perfect.

With that thought, she threw back the rest of her champagne and began mingling.

It was easy, thanks to the wedding's small invite list. Just thirty people or so were in attendance—Margo wanted to keep it small—and Emma knew almost everyone. There were her father's friends, who were practically family at this point. And then there were Margo's friends from high school, back when Emma was an awkward tween hoping to absorb some of their disaffected coolness by osmosis. They had always been nice to her, but they were still Margo's friends. And since Ben was always over, they had become his friends too. That was the benefit of marrying your childhood best friend: all your friends already knew one another.

The only wedding guests Emma didn't recognize as easily were the ones from Ben's restaurant. As a chef, Ben had an eclectic crew of work colleagues. Some were well-known chefs even her father might recognize, while others were undiscovered food geniuses growing rare microgreens in their basement at a premium. She had met a few of them in passing and knew they could talk for hours about the pros and cons of cooking with different salts, or where the best dive BBQ was in the city, or why you haven't lived until you've gone truffle hunting. But she could barely place their faces, let alone their names.

Montgomery Knox was part of this crew too, but somehow his name was always at the center of the conversation. Everyone seemed obsessed with the enigmatic restaurant investor, despite the fact that he never seemed to materialize anywhere.

"Emma!"

Margo emerged from the crowd and enveloped her in a hug.

"I'm *married*," she said, pulling away but keeping a firm grip on her sister's shoulders. "Fucking *married*."

"Congratulations," Emma replied, smiling. The reception had been going on for barely a half hour and Margo was already tipsy. Despite that fact, she still looked stunning. Her dark hair was styled around their mother's silver barrette that had held her veil earlier, the lace bodice of her Vera Wang gown was maintaining its impeccable fit over her small chest.

Margo sighed, resting her head on Emma's shoulder as she looked out across the yard to where Ben was standing on the other side of the dance floor now, talking with Knightley. "I mean, isn't he hot? He's so tall, I just want to climb—"

Emma cringed. "Ew, Mar."

"No, seriously, Em. Just *look* at him."

Emma rolled her eyes as she let her gaze drift over to the brothers. They were both objectively handsome. Ben was tall, but then, he always had been. So was Knightley. That was really where the similarities ended, though. Ben was lanky, but recent years had broadened Knightley's back and shoulders. And while Ben kept his black hair cropped close to his head, Knightley's was still long on top, so he was always running his hand through it to try to keep it away from his face. But it wasn't just their difference in appearance; it was also how they carried themselves. Ben had always been aware of how he looked and seemed to enjoy the effort required to maintain it; his smile was practiced, his clothes obviously designer. Everything about him was curated. Knightley always appeared perfectly put together too, but unlike his brother, he never seemed conscious of it. He walked with a calm confidence, a sly smirk always present on his lips, and intense eyes that seemed to make women feel like they were the only person in the entire world.

At least, that's what it looked like to Emma. Objectively.

"Just . . . so hot," Margo murmured.

Emma blinked. Right. They were talking about Ben. "Yes, he's very handsome."

"I'm going to have so many of his babies."

Emma laughed. "Okay. But why don't you say hi to the Crawfords first?"

Margo shrugged. "Fine."

As she watched her sister go, another glass of champagne found its way into Emma's hand and soon someone in the far corner announced it was time for dinner.

"Poor Margo," her dad said to himself as he walked to the table. "Her new building doesn't even have a doorman."

"Dad, it's fine. They are just moving to the West Village. Perry Street is not that far down—"

"Don't you dare say 'downtown,'" he replied, cutting her off.

"She'll be over all the time."

"There's no walls in their kitchen, Emma. No walls! It's just this open . . . space."

Emma smiled. "Why don't you grab a drink? It is a party, remember?"

Her father nodded and took his seat, while Emma made her way over to the other side of the table, to the exact spot she had dictated on the seating arrangement. But instead of Montgomery Knox sitting next to her, it was Knightley.

"You look disappointed," he said. His jacket was open and one arm was stretched over the back of her waiting chair. It made his white shirt stretch over his chest like the buttons were working to keep him concealed.

She sat down with a sigh. "I just thought that after thirty years you would have learned to read well enough to find your name on a seating chart."

He chuckled.

"Oh my God, I think I'm already drunk," Margo announced as she pulled out her chair across from them. "Is it too early to be drunk?"

Knightley said no just as Emma said yes.

Margo didn't appear to hear either of them, her eyes widening greedily as she sat down and reached for the full glass of champagne waiting for her on the table.

"Wait until you try the scallops with the fresh succotash," Ben said, joining the table. "You'll love it! Just really clean and simple. I'm thinking of putting it on the menu at the restaurant. I know I can't get local corn all year round, but I can change things up."

"So plans are still moving forward with the new restaurant?" Emma asked, glancing at Montgomery's place card on the table.

"Of course! I found this incredible location in the Lower East Side. Rustic setting with high ceilings and exposed beams; it's great. I'm thinking of doing a modern take on early American dining, tavern-style, with fresh roasts and chowders from local vendors—you know, farm to table. Otherwise, Knox's idea is to do a high-end sushi-taco place."

Emma's eyebrows bobbed up. "Those are . . . very different."

He waved her off. "We'll figure it out. It's about the draw, you know? I'm the food guy, but Knox knows the business side. He's got leads on all the investors and knows how to get everyone on board. And I've got the culinary team all figured out. Now it's just timing and real estate."

Ben continued to outline his plan as the last of the guests found their seats and the din of conversation filled the garden while everyone began their meals. Emma ignored her plate, covertly removing the index cards with her speech from her small bag so she could review them from her lap.

Knightley watched her for a moment before leaning in. "Nervous?"

"No," she replied, placing the cards facedown on the table. "Are you?"

"Why would I be?"

"Because you're giving the best man speech."

"Ah, that's right," he said, as if she had reminded him.

"Oh please, don't tell me you haven't been working on the perfect big brother toast for months now. So where is it?"

He reached up and tapped his temple.

Emma's mouth fell open. "You're kidding."

He shrugged.

"I can't believe you're winging it."

"I'm not winging it. I wrote it this morning."

She rolled her eyes. "Of course you did. Well, mine is *really* good. You're going down, Knightley."

"It's not a competition, Woodhouse." He took a sip of his whiskey. "But if you insist, let's see what you have there. Maybe I could help you out." He grabbed one of her index cards.

"Absolutely not!" she hissed, trying to snatch it out of his hands as he read it, holding it just out of reach. "You're going to steal my sweetest moments! Besides, no one would believe it if you talk about true love and the appeal of marriage."

"And you can?"

"Maybe."

He smirked at her, handing back the card. "Real life is not like the movies."

"I know," she mumbled, grabbing it before he could hold it out of her reach again. She also made a mental note to strike the *When Harry Met Sally* quote from her speech.

"So you're enjoying the wild single life, then," he said after a moment.

"Is that a problem?"

"I didn't realize that was an elective at NYU."

She sighed to disguise her annoyance. "Am I getting shade from the man whose longest relationship is with his dry cleaner?"

"Well, Gladys is very thorough."

Emma scoffed. "Oh, I bet she is."

He smiled. "Seriously though, how are things going? When do classes start?"

"Tuesday."

"And then graduation in the spring, right? So what's the plan after you get that master's in art history?"

"I told you this already, but clearly your memory is going, which isn't surprising considering your age," she said with an overly sweet smile. "I'm applying for an executive internship at the Met."

He watched her intently, finally answering, "Hmmm."

"What?"

"I'm sure you'll get it."

She blinked, surprised by the small swell of pride in her chest. "Thank you."

"The daughter of Mr. Henry Woodhouse of New York's Upper East Side, lifelong patron of the Metropolitan Museum of Art, would certainly have the right connection to score a coveted spot at the Met," he continued. "Don't worry too much."

"My dad's *not* helping me. I'll have you know that I had a 4.0 GPA last year and plan to graduate with honors in May," she replied, her pride quickly swallowed up by self-righteousness. She stood, ready to tell him off and not caring who heard. "In fact, I don't need—"

"Woodhouse, you're up," he interrupted her, pointing behind her.

She turned to find the bandleader, microphone in hand, nodding in her direction. "And now . . . the maid of honor would like to say a few words."

Emma looked back at Knightley, her eyes narrowing on him. Damn it. Now she was all flustered.

He took a sip of his whiskey and smiled at her as if that had been the plan all along.

Oh, it was on.

"Give me that." She grabbed the heavy glass out of his hand and took a swig of his drink before returning it with a thud to the table. She tried not to make a face as the peaty swill burned her throat, instead turning on her heel to walk toward the microphone in the center of the now empty dance floor.

She took a deep breath to calm her pulse and tucked a few fallen locks of her dark brown hair behind her ear, working a smile onto her face before beginning. "Good evening, everyone. I'm Emma Woodhouse, maid of honor and sister of the beautiful bride," she said, letting her eyes skim over the guests. "I wanted to say a few words about the happy couple."

Her gaze found Margo then, tears already lining her eyes. Emma's smile broadened.

"There's no greater feeling than when two of your best friends find love and decide to spend the rest of their lives together. It's even better when one of them is your older sister."

A tittering of laughter went through the yard. Emma smiled. "When we were growing up, you'd think it was always just my sister and I, but it really wasn't ever just the two of us. It was the Woodhouse girls and the Knightley boys. We were always together, and I couldn't have imagined it any other way."

Out of the corner of her eye, she caught Knightley's gaze on her, but she worked to ignore it, looking out into the crowd of seated guests.

"As many of you know, our mother passed away when we were very young, so my sister was always the one taking care of us, especially me. From making sure I did my homework, to practicing the piano, to helping me sign up for college classes, she could never replace our mom, but she was the next best thing. And I only just realized that as much as I always looked to Margo for love and support and friendship, she always looked to Ben. For love, support, friendship . . . and that fake ID sophomore year."

Emma paused as more laughter rolled across the garden. "Today, as they embark on a new adventure together, I wish them all the happiness in the world. They absolutely deserve it."

Tears were spilling down Margo's cheeks now and Emma

laughed, swallowing the emotion that was growing in her throat. "I was going to quote one of our favorite movies here, but I'm not sure it captures what I want to say exactly. So I'll say this: I talked to my sister about what it means to marry Ben and I like her own quote the best. She said: 'It's crazy that the love of my life is the same guy who flushed my Barbie down the toilet when I was five.'"

The crowd laughed again. Emma lifted her champagne glass. "Thank you for always being there for her, Ben. Then and now and forever. I always wanted a brother, and I can't believe I got you. So let us toast to Margo and Ben. I love you both so much."

Sighs and cheers erupted amid the clinking of glasses. Emma returned to the table to find Mr. Woodhouse beaming and Margo trying desperately to save her mascara.

She sat down next to Knightley and threw him a smug grin. "Top that, old man."

He stood, his glass of whiskey in hand, and leaned down just close enough to whisper, "I will certainly try, young lady."

Knightley walked forward, slow and confident in his movements. He stopped at the microphone, raking a hand through his thick black hair as the crowd waited for him to speak.

"Hello, everyone. I'll keep this short and sweet. This wedding is too beautiful to spend much time focused on anything but the bride and groom."

Emma leaned back in her seat and got ready. *This should be good.*

He continued. "Some might say that finding your soulmate is pure luck. Others might call it fate. And then there are those who might suggest you go look right in your own backyard."

Laughter erupted from the guests and Knightley smiled.

"I don't know much about soulmates myself, but I do know this: when you do find that person, your equal in all things, you should celebrate it with all your closest family and friends, just like we are today."

Emma frowned. Damn it, that was a good line.

"Ben and Margo didn't have to look very far for one another. Perhaps they were always destined to be in each other's lives. Though I don't think destiny can take credit for all the times Margo has saved Ben's ass."

Emma jumped when the guests broke into laughter, some positively cackling with delight.

Knightley turned to Ben. "Should I go into the time you set the living room rug on fire and Margo was the only one smart enough to get the fire extinguisher?" The guests cheered. "Or should I tell them the story about that cab ride and the pigeon and how, thanks to Margo, the ASPCA didn't have to get involved? Or maybe about some of those high school parties when Margo practiced her legal skills and convinced the cops no one was home after several noise complaints?"

"You can skip them all!" Ben shouted out with a smile.

Knightley laughed. "Ben, you will leave here today with a wife, one who is warm and loving and for some reason puts up with you." There were more chuckles from the guests. "And Margo, you leave here today . . . with . . . well, a lovely dress and some pretty spectacular flowers."

There was more laughter, even some hooting from amid the crowd, as Knightley threw a glance at Emma.

"You know, I was going to quote Shakespeare, but I think—and I'm sure one of my closest and dearest friends here tonight might agree—that it feels appropriate to quote the classic New York romance, *When Harry Met Sally*, instead: 'When you realize you want to spend the rest of your life with somebody, you want the rest of your life to start as soon as possible.'"

There was an audible aw from the crowd as Emma's mouth fell open. That was *her* line.

"Ben and Margo, I've had a front row seat for years watching your romance grow, and I've seen how you both challenge and support each other, how you find pure joy in one another's successes even more than your own. Do you know how *rare* that is?" Knightley said the last line more quietly, almost as if to himself.

Emma's brow furrowed. *Ah, who is this romantic, and where is George Knightley?*

Then he raised his glass. Emma found herself quickly doing the same, along with every guest who seemed enraptured by Knightley.

"To the happy couple. I think I speak for everyone here tonight when I say it's an honor to watch you both embark on what is sure to be a wild and beautiful ride. You're a very lucky man, Brother. And Margo, I didn't need a beautiful wedding to call you my sister. I'm just glad it's official."

The garden erupted in cheers and applause. Knightley left the microphone and returned to the table, meeting Emma's shocked expression with a grin.

"Well?" he asked as he sat down.

She narrowed her eyes at him. "Plagiarist."

His head fell back as he laughed.

She smiled at him despite herself. She couldn't stay mad after that speech.

The band picked up their instruments and started playing the beginning chords of "Don't Dream It's Over" by Crowded House, as guests started making their way to the dance floor.

"Seriously though, I've never heard you talk like that," Emma said after a moment.

Knightley didn't answer at first. He just looked over at her, cocking his head as he considered her, perhaps waiting for her to say more. She was so used to joking around with him, she wasn't really sure how to compliment him properly, so she turned to humor instead. "So where have you been hiding this sweet side?"

"Who said I was hiding it?"

"Well, that was the first time I've ever seen it."

"Probably because you never looked."

"Oh please. I think at some point over the last twenty-three years I would have noticed."

He raised an eyebrow at her playfully. Or was it condescendingly? She wasn't sure, but she suddenly felt vulnerable again under his gaze.

"I only meant that I've never seen how—" Emma started to defend herself but was cut off as Margo appeared behind her and enveloped her in a hug.

"Look at you! And you!" she said, her words slurring together as she pulled Knightley into her embrace. "My sister and my . . . ah! . . . brother! I just . . . am so . . . I love you guys and . . ." Her voice trailed off as her eyes welled with tears again. "We should all dance right now."

The slow song ended, immediately followed by the upbeat tempo of "Take On Me" by A-ha.

"Knightley's too cool to dance, remember?" Emma said, eyeing him smugly.

"Oh, right. Okay, just you, then!" Margo said, grabbing Emma's hand. "Oh God, I wish Montgomery was here. You could have danced with him! And then got married and had babies and moved in next door to me and Ben and . . ."

She kept talking as she pulled Emma to the dance floor, not bothering to look back and notice Knightley watching them as they disappeared into the crowd.

CHAPTER 2

Well, the band had been a mistake. Of course, Knightley had known it was a mistake weeks ago when Emma told him they were hiring an '80s cover band instead of a DJ. But he had kept his mouth shut. He knew when to pick his battles.

It wasn't that the band was bad. The exact opposite, actually. They kept the dance floor full the entire evening, with Emma and her sister in the middle of it all, swaying and singing and drinking almost as much champagne as Mrs. Pawloski, which was truly a feat.

Knightley took a sip of his whiskey. He was still in his dinner seat, where he had watched the carnage for the past few hours. Now it was midnight and the crowd had disappeared. Mr. Woodhouse had left first, volunteering to walk a drunken Mrs. Pawloski to her home three doors down, and then he'd disappeared inside his own house. Even Margo had long since abandoned the dance floor, choosing instead to watch the action from Ben's lap. The only person left standing was Emma.

That's when, as the band finished the final chords of their last song, the mistake about choosing them over a DJ became clear. Because DJs didn't bring numerous microphones. And they didn't require a spotlight. Both of which were now in Emma's sights as she stumbled onto the small stage and grabbed the microphone from the lead singer just as he was about to unplug it.

"Shhhhh . . . sorry," she said, ignoring his confused expression and turning to point at her sister. "This one, this one . . . is for you, Mar."

Oh Jesus.

"You always took care of me . . . now I . . . now I'm gonna sing our song for you!" she exclaimed as she rocked back and forth on unsteady feet.

Where the hell were her shoes?

Beside Knightley, Ben groaned as Margo squealed and then burst into tears, melting into her new husband as if champagne had somehow transformed this moment into something beautiful.

"You ready?" Emma asked the band behind her.

The guitarist looked at her dumbly, his instrument already in its case. "What?"

She nodded like that was her cue and began stumbling her way through Journey's "Don't Stop Believin.'" "*Just a small-town girl! Something . . . something . . . la la ohhhh!*"

Knightley tried to bite back his smile. After twenty-three years of continual attempts at singing in public, Emma was still awful. Regardless, Margo cheered her on between sobs.

"*Just a city boy! Born and raised in . . . New York City!*" she yelled, turning to point a finger at Knightley.

He met her gaze and found he couldn't look away. Her previously styled updo was a disaster, with dark locks half up and the rest falling into her green eyes and heavily smudged eyeliner. The fitted bodice of her dress looked to be off-kilter too, and without the benefit of her heels, which had apparently been abandoned at some point during the evening, its hem was dragging on the ground.

She was a mess, but a mess by Emma Woodhouse standards was still fucking gorgeous.

The thought landed awkwardly in his mind and sat there, refusing to budge.

He put down his whiskey glass and pushed it away from him. He'd had too much to drink.

After a few more painful notes, Knightley stood up and walked across the dance floor to the edge of the small stage. The corners of his mouth turned up slightly as she continued to belt out the lyrics to him, fumbling over the words.

"La la la . . . cheap perfume!"

"Honey," the singer said behind her, unplugging the microphone to a deafening stop. "I think we have to call it. But that was . . . really great."

"Wahooooooo!" Margo cheered, getting to her feet and almost immediately falling back into Ben's lap.

"Let's go, you," Knightley said, holding out his hand to help Emma off the stage.

She glared down at his smirk, then looked to the singer as if he would somehow back her up, but the poor guy only looked equal parts exhausted and confused.

Emma pretended not to notice. She lifted her chin defiantly and started down the steps on her own, tripping slightly on her dress.

Knightley reached out to steady her, his fingers wrapping around her bare arm even as she tried to shake off his grip.

"Ugh, I'm fine," she said, trying to right herself.

"Clearly."

She got to the bottom of the steps and looked up at him. Her green eyes did a slow survey of his face, as if looking for some hidden flaw along his jaw, his lips, his cheeks. He didn't look away. And he didn't release her arm.

A long moment passed before she sighed, like her search had come up empty-handed.

"Party . . . pooper," she said, tapping his chest with her finger. And then she laughed.

"Having fun?"

"Maybe."

He tried to tamp down his smile again but failed miserably. "I think it's time to call it a night, Woodhouse."

"Oh, *do* you?"

"Yes, I do."

"You're not in charge of me," she grumbled as she almost lost her balance again.

He gripped her arm tighter. "You sure about that?"

She scowled at him. "Do you get off telling me what to do or something?"

He blinked. "I'm sorry?"

"Do. You. Get. Off—"

"I heard you."

"You think you're just soooooo . . ."

"Careful now."

". . . perfect." She whispered the last word as if she couldn't come up with anything better. Damn, she really was drunk. "Why is it so hard for you to admit I know what I'm doing?"

"Yes, you're in complete control," he said wryly.

"Thank you," she huffed, missing his sarcasm.

He chuckled to himself. "Time for bed."

She paused, leaning into his body as if struck with a truly profound thought. "Bed sounds nice."

"You gonna make it?"

She closed her eyes and rested her head on his shoulder. "I don't know."

He sighed. "C'mere."

In one swift movement, he picked her up and threw her over his shoulder, facedown against his back.

"Knightley!" she whined. "I haven't said good night!"

She picked up her head and waved to no one in particular as he walked off the dance floor to the French doors that led to the kitchen.

Inside was dark and quiet as he gently put her down, though he was still almost carrying her as he guided her through the kitchen to the stairs up to the foyer.

The house hadn't changed much since Knightley was a child. Its sprawling rooms were framed with towering white walls and intricate crown molding, all made inviting and comfortable by an eclectic mix of wide sofas and deep chairs. Everything was clad in whites and beiges, too; it always felt bright, even now as he expertly navigated around the furniture in darkness.

Growing up, he had spent more time at the Woodhouses' than his own. But of course he had; the Woodhouse home was defined by its warmth and love and affection. It was everything the Knightley home wasn't.

They made their way up to the foyer, past the dining room to the back staircase. He was careful not to make a sound across the white marble tile, even though he knew Mr. Woodhouse wouldn't hear a thing from his room on the third floor. Emma's room was on the second, along with Margo's, or what had been Margo's. But while Margo's room faced the street, Emma's faced the back garden. Knightley knew because it was directly across from his own.

"I think you can handle yourself from here," he said when they reached the stairs. He released his grip on her waist, but she didn't move from where she leaned against his solid frame.

"You're not fooling me, you know," she said, her face buried in his shirt. "I know the truth."

"And what's that?"

She pulled back from his body, angling her face up to his, even though her eyes were still closed. "That you don't really have it all figured out."

"Is that so?" he asked, arching an eyebrow at her.

She nodded and opened her eyes just a sliver. Her face was illuminated by the watery moonlight through the windows, revealing the dark makeup still smeared across her pale cheeks, the faded pink of her lips. "Yup."

He smiled. "And how do you know that?"

"Because you see me, but don't forget . . ." She leaned in, knitting her brows together as if she were about to share some profound truth. "I see you too."

He blinked down at her face. "Okay."

"Okay," she said with a sigh, her head lolling to the side. Then her expression turned sad. "So stop finding excuses to leave."

Huh. He usually knew what to expect from Emma, but he had not expected that. And he was increasingly uncomfortable with how often that happened. More often, recently. The last few years had flown by in a blur. The small venture capital firm he started a few years before was now one of the most successful in the country. And while he was proud of it, Knightley Capital had taken over his life. Eighty-hour work weeks, red-eye flights back and forth to the West Coast while he set up his firm's second office in Los Angeles—there was barely time to think, let alone notice how the girl who had tagged along with him throughout his childhood had disappeared and left a woman in her place.

His expression didn't reveal his thoughts—he was good at that. Instead, he just cleared his throat.

"Night, Woodhouse."

She smiled and then started up the stairs.

He lingered for a moment, just to make sure she didn't fall on her way up, then turned and went back the way they had come, letting himself out through the kitchen.

The caterers were clearing off the tables when Knightley returned to the reception. Margo and Ben were still there, slow dancing to a song playing from their cell phone. They didn't notice as he walked by them and headed toward the line of trees that separated the Woodhouse yard from the Knightley one.

The path between the two was lit with more fairy lights, but Knightley didn't need them to find his way. A few more steps and then his own house appeared, a wall of windows and steel that did a good job of hiding the building's original brick exterior. And that had been the point, hadn't it? A three-year-long remodeling project to erase the past.

The sliding glass doors opened up to his living room and the kitchen beyond. He used to dread being in his father's house, which had been kept like a museum—dark and cold and filled with antiques that existed only to show off the family's wealth. But after the old man died, Knightley had gutted the entire place. Every piece of furniture was tossed, every floor and corner redesigned to create a more relaxed modern aesthetic. Now it was finished, and no trace of his childhood home remained. He liked it that way.

He left a trail of his clothes along the floor, the stairs, as he made it to his bedroom on the second floor. By the time he sat down on the end of his bed, he was only in his boxers. Christ, he was tired. Happy and a little drunk, but mostly just tired.

His gaze went to the wall of windows that overlooked the backyard, to Emma's bedroom just beyond the trees. There was a time, years ago, when she used to sit at her window and wave good night to him, smiling with her braces on full display. She had thought it a novelty to have that nightly ritual; he had always taken it for granted.

Now, as he stared out at her dark window and the stillness beyond, it felt like something intrinsic to its function was missing. Something that left his own room feeling a bit hollow.

Jesus. He raked a hand through his hair, then down his face, and shook the thought free.

"Definitely too much whiskey," he murmured to himself, and then lay down to go to sleep.

CHAPTER 3

As expected, Emma's hangover was monumental. Thankfully, she had anticipated it. When she woke up Sunday morning, wincing at the bright sunlight invading her bedroom, she reached over to her nightstand where she had already laid out her Tom Ford sunglasses along with a bottle of water and two ibuprofen. When she stumbled downstairs to the kitchen, Fran had a cup of coffee and a contraband chocolate croissant waiting for her, exactly as planned. Emma smuggled both into the media room just down the hall, closing the door and curling up on the sofa to watch an intense marathon of *Love Island*. And it worked. By the time she emerged hours later, she felt almost human.

Well, as much as she could. Did she want to think about how entire sections of the wedding reception were still a blur? No. Or how Knightley managed to get her to bed? Absolutely not.

So as the week began, she stayed busy preparing for her last year of grad school and ignoring the nagging worry about what she'd said or done, until Thursday arrived and it was time to meet Knightley for coffee before heading downtown to campus.

She looked across the table at him now, wondering how much

new ammunition he had on her after that night. If she embarrassed herself, he didn't let on. In fact, he had barely mentioned the reception since. Even now he only stared down at his phone, a bored expression on his face as he waited for his espresso.

They were sitting at their usual table at Vicarage Coffee, a small cafe on Madison Avenue just around the corner from her house. It was the kind of place that was always dark regardless of the time of day, and had four tables in a space that really only had room for three. But it was quiet and cozy and most important, convenient.

"Here you go, Emma," the barista said as he approached with their drinks, barely acknowledging Knightley as he put his espresso and Emma's latte on the table.

Emma smiled up at him. "Thanks, Zane."

He winked at her, a crooked grin on his face as he turned back to the counter to help a pair of women who had just walked in.

"You're on a first-name basis with the barista?" Knightley asked, still looking at his phone. He hadn't bothered to take off his coat, but Emma could spy his suit peeking out from underneath: the navy wool jacket, the silk maroon tie. It was still odd to see Knightley wear a suit every day; it was as if she were watching him play grown-up.

"He's new. I'm just being friendly," she said, offering him a saccharine smile, the one she knew he hated.

Unfortunately, he didn't notice, as he was still scrolling through his emails. "So how are classes going?"

Emma stirred some sugar into her latte and shrugged. "I haven't started yet."

He looked up at that. "I thought you said classes started on Tuesday."

"And?"

"And it's Thursday."

"Yes, well *I* haven't started yet."

He put his phone down and reclined back, his broad frame relaxing into the wooden chair so it creaked under his weight. "Do I even want to ask?"

She smiled over the rim of her mug. "Yes, because it is brilliant. Are you ready?"

"No."

"Okay, so the master's program requires ten courses over the two years, including a thesis. Now, apparently students in the program usually complete six courses that first year, which leaves four courses for their second year, plus all their thesis work, but that just sounds like a lot to ask of someone, you know? So last year I completed *eight* courses and outlined my thesis. Now I only have to do one elective course each semester this year. And since electives are almost always at a reasonable hour, this year will be a breeze. I even managed to limit my classes to Thursdays and Fridays."

He stared at her for a long moment. "You figured this out last year."

She nodded, raising her drink as if accepting applause from the rest of the cafe.

"And now you've achieved your goal of . . . ultimate laziness?"

Her smile flattened. "Yes, Knightley. I overextended myself last year while maintaining a 4.0 GPA in order to be lazy."

"Premeditated laziness, then."

She leaned forward, tapping her finger on her chin and pretending to be deep in thought. "Hmmm."

"What?"

"Just trying to remember why I asked you to grab coffee."

He tamped down a smile and picked up his phone again. "Where are all your girlfriends who are usually attached at your hip?"

Emma tilted her head to the side, trying to recall. "Well, Haydie is still in London for business school, and Raquel has been in Madrid since right after graduation—she just moved into this amazing apartment with her boyfriend. And Lulu got a position as a PR assistant at this fashion house in Paris . . ." Her voice trailed off as she realized Knightley's attention was still on his phone.

It took him a minute to notice the silence. When he finally did, he looked up. "What?"

She rolled her eyes. "Anyway, if I'm stuck here while all my friends are abroad and having these big adventures, the least I can do is give myself a little break in my grad school schedule."

He arched an eyebrow at her. "A little?"

"Yes. As a consolation prize."

Knightley's patronizing expression softened a bit as he watched her, letting a moment pass before speaking again. "He would have let you go, you know."

Emma shrugged, pretending to find something interesting through the nearby window. It was easy to forget sometimes that Knightley knew her father almost as well as she did. Perhaps even better. After all, Knightley was seven when Emma was born and could recall when her father was married to his younger and much more carefree wife. Emma's mother had been the one to take the risks for both of them, and her father had loved her for it. Everyone had.

Emma had been too young to remember when she died, how her mother's unexpected aneurysm had shocked everyone, but Knightley did. Apparently, her father had retreated into himself for months, and when he finally emerged, he was more careful, more hesitant. And so much more protective, like if he tried hard enough, he could learn to control the uncontrollable. At least for his daughters.

"You remember how much he freaked out when Margo got

engaged? There's no way I could have left at the same time," Emma finally replied.

"He would be fine for a few months."

She smirked at him. "You and I both know that's not true."

He nodded, not in agreement, but as a way of not saying anything at all. And really, why bother? She knew as well as he did that talking about it wouldn't change anything. This was well-trodden territory.

"You're coming over for Sunday dinner, right?" she asked, trying quickly to change the subject.

"I always come over for Sunday dinner."

"Just checking you don't have a hot date or something," she said, wagging her eyebrows at him.

"Nope, I schedule my exciting plans for Saturday."

She rolled her eyes. "Well, on *that* note, I'm off. I have an actual class in a few and while I would love to be late, I want to make sure to get a seat in the back so the professor won't call on me. You know, so I can really achieve peak laziness."

He smiled and looked like he had another barb ready, but it seemed to fade as he watched her stand.

She paused, gauging his expression. "What?"

"You're going like that?"

She looked down at where his gaze was locked: her studded raffia Valentino wedges, her gauzy mauve Zimmermann minidress.

"Like what?" she asked.

He shook his head and chuckled to himself. "Nothing. Have a good class. Try not to be too late."

～

Despite any doubts Knightley might have harbored, Emma arrived to class early by a whole four minutes. She took her time getting her laptop ready and reapplying her lip stain as the other students bled in. It was a disparate mix of people, but Emma had expected that. She had also expected that she wouldn't recognize any of them. No, her friends were scattered all over the world right now. It was impressive, really. She had gone from a robust social circle carefully curated over her twenty-three years in Manhattan to . . . nothing. It was just her now.

She pushed the thought aside as the professor shuffled into the room. In only eight short months she would be done. She had a plan, the plan was in motion, all she had to do was what the plan dictated. Simple as that.

The professor made his way to the lectern, the living embodiment of the class itself: drab, tired, and ready for retirement. The hum of conversation died as he cleared his throat, not bothering to even open his worn briefcase as he addressed the half-full room.

"Hello, I'm Professor Goddard. Welcome to—"

The door to the classroom flew open, smacking into the cement wall behind it with a loud thud. The entire class turned as a woman stumbled in. A mess of frizzy blonde hair was held together by a scrunchie on top of her head. It bobbed back and forth as she struggled with a pink nylon messenger bag hanging off one arm and a pile of books in the other. A few books fell to the floor just as the door slammed shut behind her. She scrambled to pick them up, only pausing once she was on all fours and the room was dead silent around her.

She lifted her head slowly, finally meeting Professor Goddard's wide eyes.

"Hi," she said. "Is this Social History of Photography?"

He nodded once.

"Oh, thank God." She sat up and let out a relieved sigh. "I'm Nadine Pittman. I got confused about which side of the park was east and which side was west, so I went to 80 Washington Square Park West and it was just a townhouse, but I still buzzed, and they didn't know what I was talking about, so then I had to ask . . ."

Her voice faded as Professor Goddard's expression darkened, annoyance pursing his lips.

"I'll just . . . go find a seat," she continued, pulling her bag behind her as she clutched her papers and books to her chest.

The professor cleared his throat and continued, launching into a spiel about the syllabus. Emma wasn't listening. She was too busy watching Nadine: how she plopped down in a seat two rows ahead of her, the closest one to the door. How she tried so carefully to situate herself quietly but still managed to make enough noise that Professor Goddard rolled his eyes. How her face flushed as she mouthed, *Sorry*, only to open her backpack and have more papers fall out of it. How she looked close to tears as she searched for her notebook amid the chaos.

Emma sighed to herself, an unusual pang of pity in her chest. There was no doubt about it: Nadine Pittman was a hot mess.

CHAPTER 4

Over the next three weeks, Emma made some important observations about Nadine. First of all, she wasn't from New York. That was immediately obvious. And then there were her shoes. Now, Emma was not a snob, nor would she ever suggest that someone's footwear dictated their character, but by that third week, Nadine's shoe of choice appeared to be a pair of water-stained Uggs that looked like they had barely made it out of 2005.

None of this was out of the ordinary, really. But there was something about Nadine that piqued Emma's interest. She was smart, beautiful, and charming; she just needed some help to realize it.

Of course, pondering the history and social standing of Nadine Pittman was usually an activity limited to twelve thirty to two thirty on Thursdays, something to help block out the droning of Professor Goddard. Which was why it was so surprising when, on a sunny Sunday afternoon as Emma waited for her Uber on the corner of 14th and Fifth, after a visit to the new Jonathan Cohen pop-up shop, she saw Nadine Pittman crossing the street toward her, a cup of coffee in hand.

Nadine hadn't noticed her yet, and as Emma watched her she

was reminded of her father's beloved documentaries, the ones that let you observe animals in their natural habitat while a narrator whispers commentary.

... And here we see the young woman struggling to adapt to her new surroundings. Watch as she attempts to cross the street amid the crowd of locals, a coffee in hand and her eyes up at the street signs, oblivious to the dangers ahead ...

Nadine's Ugg caught the edge of the pavement at the curb, and suddenly she was airborne. Her hands flew up to catch her fall, which sent her coffee flying. The lid came off just as it began its descent, spilling the contents within inches of Emma's four-inch heels.

Nadine scrambled forward, crawling across the sidewalk to the cup as if anything inside was salvageable.

Emma leaned down. "Nadine?"

The young woman looked up with eyes impossibly large, like a deer caught in headlights.

"Did I spill on you?"

"No, I'm fine." Emma offered her hand and helped Nadine to her feet. "Are you all right?"

Nadine nodded, a fast and jerky motion that did nothing to keep her tears at bay. "I'm okay. Totally okay."

"You're sure?"

"Yeah, I just ... I have a job interview at Party World, and it's on 13th Street and Fourth Avenue, but, um, I think I'm a little lost, because after Fifth Avenue I can only find Third Avenue and ..."

Her voice cracked and her chin began to tremble, and Emma knew she had only moments to save the situation. Everyone knew the only thing worse than standing outside the Burlington Coat Factory on 14th Street was to be seen crying outside the Burlington Coat Factory on 14th Street.

"That's because downtown is a nightmare and Fourth Avenue is a myth," Emma said with a smile, carefully prying the empty coffee cup from Nadine's hands as if it were a live grenade and throwing it in a nearby trash can. "You're not far off, really. It's just a couple of blocks away."

"Oh, thank God. I have to be there by three o'clock."

Emma cringed.

"It's past three, isn't it?" Nadine whispered, reading Emma's expression.

Emma bit her bottom lip, weighing the best way to break the truth. "It is . . . but that's a good thing! No one in their right mind works at Party World."

"They don't?"

Emma shook her head solemnly. She had never actually been inside Party World, but she had walked by a number of times and had seen the black lights and sexy nurse outfits in the window. This wasn't even a question.

Nadine's chin began to wobble again, so Emma changed tactics.

"I'm Emma Woodhouse. We have Social History of Photography together."

"I know. I always love your shoes." She nodded down to Emma's pink patent leather heels.

"Thanks," Emma said, smiling warmly. "They're Miu Miu."

Nadine's brow wrinkled like they had suddenly switched to a foreign language. "What?"

Emma was ready to launch into an abbreviated but nonetheless thorough biographical history of Miuccia Prada when a black Suburban pulled up beside them.

Emma held up her hand to the driver, then she turned back to Nadine. "What are you doing right now?"

Nadine shrugged. "Probably going back to the dorm and crying."

. . . Watch as the young woman accepts her fate, moving into the thick brush of the East Village to hide from the world and wait for the cold embrace of death . . .

"Absolutely not," Emma said, the genesis of a plan already forming in her brain. "You're coming over to mine. You need wine and food and I have Sunday dinner in about an hour, so you're invited. It's usually just family—well, our neighbors who have been like family my whole life—but it could use some fresh company."

"Oh no." Nadine shook her head, her eyes growing even wider as she looked down at her coffee-stained top. "I'm a mess. I can't—"

"You can and you will," Emma replied, looping her arm with Nadine's and heading toward her car. This was perfect: Nadine needed help realizing her potential, and Emma had the time. And the closet. "I have clothes. So many clothes. And so much wine! It will be fun, I promise."

"Okay," Nadine replied, though it didn't seem like she was entirely sure.

On the ride from 14th Street to 83rd, Emma was able to fill in the required gaps in Nadine's history. She was twenty-two years old and had just graduated from Ohio State University in the spring. She grew up in Ohio, too; her parents lived only an hour from the university, and she would go home on the weekends to work at their pet store. She saved every cent she earned over those four years to afford coming to New York for graduate school.

"I really want to work at one of the big auction houses someday, and they're all here, so when I got accepted to NYU for my master's, I knew I had to take it."

"Absolutely," Emma said with a decisive nod. "I'm in my second year and can tell you from personal experience that it is the best. Everything in New York is the best."

"You're studying art history too?"

"Yes. I'm going to work at the Met after graduation."

Nadine's eyes widened. "You already have a job lined up?"

"Well, not exactly. They have an internship program for graduates, which I'm applying for. I should have an interview in the spring," Emma replied confidently, brushing her dark hair from her shoulder.

"Wow." Nadine swallowed, eyes drifting back to the car window. "The Met."

Emma had to stop herself from sharing too much: how she spent practically every weekend there as a child, dragging Knightley to gallery after gallery, with Margo and Ben bringing up the rear. How it had been her mother's favorite place once, too—or so she had been told—and Emma would go searching for the paintings her father had loaned to the museum in her honor. And how every time she found them, it felt like she had found her mom again.

An odd emotion swelled in Emma's chest, and she cleared her throat to dislodge it.

"So," she said, turning to her new friend with a manufactured smile. "Did you leave anyone special behind in Ohio?"

"You mean my nana?"

Emma's smile faltered. "No. I mean like a significant other."

"Oh." Nadine's gaze darted to where her hands fidgeted in her lap. "Yeah. Marty. He's my boyfriend. We've been together since ninth grade."

Emma tried to imagine having the same boyfriend since she was fourteen. The longest relationship she ever had was with Jean-Laurent Caron, an incredibly hot and incredibly moody film student from Paris she'd dated during her senior year at FIT. It had been tumultuous and wonderful, punctuated more by orgasms than conversation, but she still hadn't been bothered when he moved back to France after graduation. In fact, she had barely thought about him at all.

"Wow, that's impressive. It must be hard being so far apart," Emma replied.

Nadine nodded. "Yeah. But I've been planning on coming here for a while, so we'll just . . . make it work."

There was something else under the surface of her expression, but before Emma could dig further, the car came to a stop. She got out, already searching through her bag for her keys, so she didn't see Nadine's face as she stared up at the building ahead.

"This is your house?" she asked, her mouth agape.

"Yup." Emma found the gold key ring and pulled it from her bag.

"The whole thing?"

Emma caught Nadine's startled expression, then turned to see what she was staring at.

The house looked like it always did: the neoclassical facade was still white and clean, and the iron banisters along the first- and third-floor windows had only just been repainted black last fall.

"Yes, but we barely ever use the fourth floor. Really."

She walked up the stairs to the black lacquered front door and unlocked it, motioning Nadine inside. The sprawling foyer opened up before them and Emma barely noticed how Nadine gawked at the marble floors or the wide staircase that loomed ahead of them. She just deposited her light blue Saint Laurent quilted shoulder bag on the entry table and started down the stairs to the kitchen.

The smell of sautéed garlic and lemon welcomed them before they even arrived. They found Fran already working on dinner, an array of vegetables and oils spread out on the countertop in front of her.

"Your father says he is going vegan again, but I'm not letting this perfectly good salmon go to waste," she mumbled in greeting.

"Fran, this is my friend Nadine. Nadine, this is Fran," Emma said, leaning against the island and eyeing the platters of food already prepared. God, she was starving. "Can we set another place for her tonight?"

"Of course! Someone needs to eat this," Fran snapped. She paused, catching herself. "Nice to meet you, Nadine." She smiled at the young woman while at the same time slapping Emma's hand away from the basket of freshly baked whole wheat rolls.

"Ow!" Emma protested, grabbing one anyway.

"God help me," Fran murmured, turning away from them to return to the lemon jus.

Emma ushered Nadine upstairs to her room and quickly got to work putting together an outfit to replace her coffee-stained sweatshirt. Yes, all Nadine really needed was the pale pink Alexander McQueen cashmere sweater, but it really didn't go with her pants, so it only made sense to pair it with Khaite cropped jeans and Emma's favorite vintage belt.

By the time they arrived back in the kitchen, Nadine looked like a new woman. And it wasn't just the clothes. Emma had to admit that even without her help, Nadine was beautiful. Yes, her disjointed blonde highlights were obviously from a box, but that was nothing a trip to Emma's salon couldn't fix. And her large blue eyes would really pop once Emma taught her how to do a proper cat-eye. She was gorgeous—she just needed an artist to refine the masterpiece.

Mrs. Pawloski had already arrived and was cackling next to Emma's father at the now fully set kitchen table.

"Dad, Mrs. Pawloski," Emma said. "I'd like you to meet my friend Nadine. She goes to school with—"

"Nadine! Oh, so wonderful to meet you! Good Lord, aren't you gorgeous!" Mrs. Pawloski exclaimed, already on her feet and starting toward them. Emma wanted to cringe when she saw the older woman wearing her usual bouclé jacket. At this point it was so worn and faded that it was barely recognizable as vintage Chanel. Thankfully, Mrs. Pawloski enveloped Nadine in a hug so quickly, Emma doubted her new friend even noticed.

A few minutes later, Ben and Margo appeared, offering Nadine a warm welcome before they all took a seat at the table. Wine was poured and Nadine smiled and, for the first time since Emma had met her, looked truly relaxed. Emma couldn't have been more proud.

"Akron? Ohio?" Mr. Woodhouse asked, staring across the table in wide-eyed disbelief as they began to pass around the poached salmon and sautéed green beans.

Nadine nodded, taking a huge bite of her bread.

The French doors to the back garden were open, letting in the last gasps of summer, which were at odds with a few trees already turning yellow and orange on the edge of the yard.

"Oh, I went to Ohio once!" Mrs. Pawloski said. "Remember, Henry? Burt decided he wanted to celebrate our tenth anniversary by driving across the country, so he bought an RV and we made it as far as Ohio! And I swear to God, the town was called London! Can you believe it? Burt said, 'Now you can tell all your friends I took you to London for vacation!'"

She dissolved into laughter so loud that Emma almost missed the sound of footsteps from the far end of the yard. She looked out just as a tall figure appeared through the trees. His usual suit and tie were gone, replaced by a pair of worn jeans that rested low on his hips and a faded gray T-shirt.

"Sorry I'm late," Knightley called out as he approached.

"Oh, so you *are* alive," Emma replied.

He gave her a placating grin when he reached them, leaning down to give Mrs. Pawloski a kiss on the cheek. Then there was a wave to Mr. Woodhouse at the head of the table and hugs for Margo and Ben before he sat down at the opposite end, next to Emma. It was only then that he noticed Nadine, and the smile went from placating to sincere.

"Hello," he said.

Nadine smiled broadly.

"Nadine, this is George Knightley," said Emma, motioning in his direction. "Knightley, this is Nadine Pittman. She's in grad school at NYU with me."

"Hi," Nadine replied around the bread in her mouth.

"It's a pleasure to meet you," Knightley said. "I thought all of Emma's friends were abroad."

"Nadine just moved here from Ohio," Emma corrected him.

"Ah."

"Were you . . . gardening out there or . . ." Nadine asked, pointing to the yard.

He chuckled softly. "No. I live in the house right there past the trees. Our yards back up to one another."

The lights were on at the Knightley house, so its massive black-framed windows could be seen through the low branches. Nadine gaped.

"Did you get my email about the Mets game on Wednesday?" Ben asked from further down the table.

"Ben, they're four and six this month. They're not making it to the playoffs," Knightley replied with a sigh.

Ben's brow furrowed. "Hey, you don't know that."

As Knightley and Ben sparred, Nadine turned to Emma. Her eyes had gone impossibly wide again, but now there was a smile to match. *He's so hot!* she mouthed.

It took Emma a moment to realize she meant Knightley. *Huh.*

She stole a glance at him as he listened intently to Ben's critique of the Mets' starting lineup, his elbows on the table and his large hands fisted together. It made his T-shirt stretch around his arms, highlighting the sharp definition in his biceps, the roped lines of every muscle. Emma knew he was a runner, but for the first time she contemplated the fact that he went to a gym, that his broad shoulders and toned physique were the result of long hours of hard work and sweat and—

"Is there a problem?"

Emma blinked, suddenly aware that Knightley's attention was on her again.

She darted her eyes away from him and scoffed, pretending to be more interested in her glass of wine than his forearms. "I don't have anywhere near enough time to list all the problems I have with you."

He smirked. "Well, considering your school schedule, that's saying something."

Nadine watched them from the other side of the table like they were the most interesting spectator sport she had ever seen. "How long have you two known each other?"

Emma sighed. "All our lives."

"All of Emma's life," Knightley corrected her. "I was seven when she was born."

"Knightley and Ben were already friends with Margo, so they kind of adopted me."

"Yes, well, we didn't really have a choice," Knightley replied, nodding out into the garden. "There had been a gate up between our yards, but Emma found a way to rip it off its hinges."

"I didn't rip it off. I was five." Then Emma turned to Nadine. "The fence was decrepit, and the gate fell off on its own. I simply stepped over it."

Knightley shrugged as if the details didn't matter. "And nobody ever got around to replacing it."

Nadine's gaze drifted back to the house across the yard. "It looks very . . . modern."

He smiled. "Too much?"

"No!" Nadine said. "I love it. So much . . . glass. Must be lovely in the morning."

"I finished renovating it last year. It had been pretty dark and stuffy, so we opened it up a bit. Tore down some walls, expanded the windows. Even redid the garden." He took a sip of his wine. "We kept the path though."

He said it indifferently, and Emma tried to keep her expression impassive too, not wanting to hint at how anxiously she had watched from her bedroom as the landscapers gutted the entire backyard. She was sure that a new fence would be erected, a new gate installed. But then one day the workers were gone, the project complete. And even with all the changes, the well-worn path still connected the two yards.

It was just about the only thing that Knightley hadn't touched.

"And you all just went back and forth your whole lives?" Nadine asked, looking between the two of them.

"Well," Knightley leaned back and motioned to Ben and Margo at the other end of the table. "Those two were secretly in love the whole time and made us unwitting enablers."

Margo overheard and stuck out her tongue at him.

He smiled again, but it dimmed a moment later when his phone buzzed in his pocket. He pulled it out and glanced at the screen, his expression becoming a grimace.

Emma waved her hand as if to bat the phone away. "I know we'll never convince you to stop working on the weekends, but can you at least put the email away during dinner?"

He didn't look up from the screen as he typed. "Let's have that conversation when you find a job that carries some level of responsibility."

Emma rolled her eyes.

"What do you do?" Nadine asked him, a dreamy look on her face as she stared at him.

"I run a sustainability-focused venture capital firm." When he glanced up from his phone and saw her expression contort with confusion, he added, "We find people who have great ideas about how to save the world and give them the means to succeed at it."

Her brow relaxed as her eyes widened. "Wow. That must be a lot of work. My parents tried to get their town to start a recycling program and just that was almost impossible."

Knightley grinned. "So what are you studying?"

"Oh God, don't tell him, Nadine," Emma said, lifting her wineglass to shield her view of Knightley's face. "Unless you want to be totally shamed about your career choice and the future you have designed for yourself."

Knightley turned back to Nadine. "Getting your master's in art history, too, I take it?"

"Yeah, with a concentration on international sales." Nadine's cheeks flushed. "I know, it's not really applicable to the real world."

"I wouldn't say that," Knightley said, leaning forward on his elbows again. "It's very applicable, particularly now with collectors trying to make sense of new international laws regarding art sales, and museums facing questions about pieces in their collections that were acquired through imperialist channels. I think it's smart."

Nadine beamed, as Emma's mouth fell open.

Seriously?

"Exactly!" Nadine replied, suddenly giddy. "I'm hoping to get a position with one of the big auction houses after graduation. My nana used to take me to these auctions in Cleveland where there were all these antiques. I just love the idea of all these people coming together over these things that have a history already attached." She paused and then gave him a lopsided shrug. "But I don't know. My boyfriend is still back home. I miss him a lot, and he really doesn't want to leave. He's helping run his dad's HVAC company, and I don't think . . ." Her chin began to wobble, and she shrugged helplessly.

"Stop making our guests cry, Knightley," Emma said, waving him off and leaning over the table toward Nadine. "What did I say earlier, Nadine? At this moment you are in the best city in the entire world. And you have me to show it to you. No boyfriend necessary."

Nadine smiled, her tears abated, and Emma sat back feeling very pleased with herself.

Then she glanced at Knightley.

His easy smile was gone and his expression was unimpressed, as if he knew exactly what she was up to.

CHAPTER 5

"Brown?" Nadine asked, her eyebrows knitted together. She was staring straight ahead into the salon mirror at the clear plastic cap over her head.

"Not brown," Emma said patiently, even though this was the fourth time they had been over this. "Balayage."

Nadine mouthed the word to herself again, *Baa-lee-ahge*.

Emma nodded. "Mateo is bringing back your natural color—which is gorgeous, by the way—and painting in some soft highlights to add some more . . ."

"Blonde?"

Emma's head cocked to the side. ". . . dimension."

"Dimension." Nadine repeated, though her brow didn't relax as her attention went back to the cap.

Jolie Salon was a gleaming cathedral of hair care at the corner of Lexington and 83rd, furnished almost exclusively in white marble and chrome. Fridays were usually busy, but it was late in the day, so there were only a couple of other people seated in the sleek white leather chairs lining the wall.

Still, Nadine would have had to wait weeks for an appointment if Emma hadn't called herself, begging Mateo to fit her friend in. And of course he had. Emma had been coming here ever since she tried to go platinum right before high school graduation. She had walked in armed with only a picture of Kim Kardashian's recently bleached locks and the naivete of a woman whose thick dark hair had never seen a developer stronger than thirty. Thankfully, Mateo talked her out of it, and she left two hours later with some well-placed amber highlights. From that moment on, Emma knew that Mateo was a man she could trust.

As if on cue, he appeared beside Nadine again. His white T-shirt was stretched tight across his chest and biceps, showing off an array of tattoos on his arms. His usual smile was missing as he pulled back the cap and considered Nadine's hair for a moment. "God, your hair takes color so well," he murmured, and then he grinned. "This is going to be gorgeous."

Emma clapped her hands. "I knew it! You're going to look phenomenal."

"As if there was any doubt." Mateo put back the cap and leaned down to Nadine's eye level, giving her a wink in the mirror. "Five more minutes and we'll rinse."

She nodded, barely biting back her smile as he turned, leaving them alone again.

"He's so hot," Nadine whispered to Emma a few moments after he was gone.

Even though it was becoming clear Nadine thought this about most men in New York, Emma had to agree in this case. "Totally gorgeous," Emma said, glancing back to where Mateo had disappeared down the hall.

"You think so too?"

Emma turned back to her friend, noting her eager expression.

Oh no. She would have to soften her words so they wouldn't crush Nadine's hopes too much. "And gay."

Her friend's smile fell. "Oh."

Emma thought that fact was clear—what with the perfectly groomed eyebrows and playful winks—but apparently not. Still, she couldn't stop herself from prodding. "Besides, you have Marty, right?"

"Right," Nadine said, nodding, but she looked unsure.

"And you're ... happy?" Emma tried to mask her cynicism but failed miserably.

Nadine's expression blanched. For a moment, Emma thought that she was going to break down in tears.

"Oh God, I don't know! You know?" Nadine exclaimed so loudly that the woman in foils two seats down jumped. "We've been together so long that I don't know what it's even supposed to feel like. And now I'm here and Nana made me promise to start living my life instead of the life everyone else expects from me, but then I still have this old life that's pulling me back and I'm not sure if that's a good thing or a bad thing. Like I'm trying to be two different people but I'm only one person? So which person should I be, you know?"

Emma didn't know. "A happy one, I think."

Nadine sighed, leaning back in the chair.

Emma waited a moment. "Does Marty make you happy?"

"I think so. I mean, he used to. Now we mostly fight about when I'm coming home next."

Hmmm.

"That must be hard," Emma ventured, offering her best sympathetic frown. "But you need to do what's best for you."

"That's what I told him!"

"And what did he say?"

"That I was being selfish."

Emma grimaced.

Nadine's eyes widened. "That's bad, isn't it?"

"I would never just insert myself in your relationship," Emma replied solemnly. "But I will say this: you're in New York City, Nadine. The best place in the entire world to be single. You worked so hard to get here, you deserve to experience it without anything holding you back."

"So . . . you think I should break up with him?" she whispered.

"Oh, I would never tell you what to do."

"But if it were you?"

Emma's lips pursed. This was going to have to be delicate. Very delicate. "Well, if it were me, I wouldn't tolerate a boyfriend who was more worried about his own feelings than mine. You deserve happiness on your own terms, no one else's."

Nadine swallowed.

"But that's just me," Emma continued. "I *like* being single."

Nadine's worry seemed to dissolve for a moment, replaced with confusion. "You're single?"

Emma nodded as she caught her own reflection in the huge salon mirror and turned to the side, adjusting her skirt a bit.

"But what about George?"

Her eyes darted back to Nadine. "What?"

"George Knightley. I just thought . . . I mean, aren't you and him . . ." She left the sentence hanging, punctuated only by a nod that seemed to imply that Emma knew exactly what she meant.

Emma didn't. "Aren't me and Knightley . . . what?"

"Like, dating or something?"

Emma's laugh came out like a snort. "No! No. Absolutely not."

"Oh." Nadine seemed genuinely surprised. "It's just that you two seem so close . . ." It was obvious there was more she wanted to say, but she bit it back.

"We're friends. *Just* friends," Emma continued, ignoring the fact that her heart was now racing. "We've been friends my entire life. He definitely does *not* look at me like that."

"Right," Nadine considered for a moment. "But what about you?"

"Oh my God, I definitely look at him like a friend. Just a friend." Why was her voice so high? Did it sound weird? She tried to hide her discomfort with a laugh, a tittering sound that made the woman two seats down jump again.

"Oh." Nadine's forehead creased as if she was trying to work something out in her head.

"Besides," Emma said, clearing her throat as she struggled for composure. "I think the only way I'd ever get in a relationship again is if it's a forever relationship."

"What do you mean?"

"You know, the relationship you're going to be in *forever*. Like, the *one*," Emma replied.

Nadine nodded, even though confusion still knitted her brow. Emma waited a long moment. "Is Marty your forever relationship?"

Nadine just shrugged.

That told Emma everything she needed to know.

Mateo appeared after a few minutes, stealing Nadine away for a shampoo and conditioning treatment. Then he ushered her back to her seat, flourishing a hair dryer and massive round brush until Nadine's previously frizzy hair was transformed.

A moment later he swung Nadine's chair around, revealing a luscious mass of warm brown waves with sweeping honey-colored highlights. Nadine's mouth fell open and Emma squealed, as much for Mateo's skill as for the glow it immediately put on Nadine's face.

"I don't even recognize myself! This is insane," her friend exclaimed for the fifth time as they followed Mateo over to the front desk. "Isn't this insane? Like, a good insane. But insane!"

Nadine was smiling, a gorgeous wide smile, and Emma couldn't have felt prouder of herself. "You look amazing."

Nadine was still staring at her reflection in the mirror behind the desk when Mateo began pressing buttons on the computer keyboard, cursing in Spanish under his breath.

"I have no idea how to work this thing," he grumbled.

Emma frowned. "Where's Gena?"

"She quit. Got cast in an off-Broadway revival of *Xanadu*."

"Well, that's . . . nice."

He sighed. "It's wonderful, except now I'm out a receptionist and I have no idea what I'm doing. The sooner we can hire someone, the better." He smashed down the enter key again and groaned.

Hmmm. An idea began to germinate in Emma's head. She turned to her friend, who was busy running her hand through her newly acquired soft waves. "Nadine, you're still looking for a job, aren't you?"

Nadine's expression blanched. "Oh God, why? Nana sent me forty dollars for a haircut, but I can put the rest on my credit card if—"

Emma waved the words away. "Oh, don't worry about this. It's my 'Welcome to New York' gift. But Mateo was just saying that they're looking for a receptionist here."

Her friend's eyes lit up. "Really?"

"And you have retail experience, right?" Emma pressed, seeing Mateo's attention now on them both.

Nadine nodded earnestly.

Mateo seemed to consider. "It's just part-time. Mostly manning the phones and scheduling appointments, ringing people up. I would need help with inventory, too, putting in orders for supplies and merchandise. Is that something you could handle?"

Nadine snorted out a laugh. "That's all I did at The Posh Pussy."

Mateo blinked. "Pardon me?"

"The Posh Pussy," Nadine repeated a bit slower, as if he hadn't understood the first time. "It's my mom and dad's pet store. Well, technically the pet store is called Pittman Pets, but then my mom started making accessories for cats—little necklaces and hats, things like that—and those got so popular that they rented out the space next door and opened a shop that just sells her stuff exclusively. Mom even made me CPO."

"CPO?" Mateo asked.

Nadine nodded. "Chief Pussy Officer."

Emma tried not to cringe, but she couldn't help it. She turned to Mateo, bracing herself for a similar reaction, but then she saw a smile on his face.

"Well now, that sounds perfect," he said.

Nadine's smile grew by a hundred watts.

~

By the time Emma and Nadine arrived back at the house a half hour later, it had been settled: Nadine was the new receptionist at Jolie Salon.

"It's perfect," Emma announced as she let them in the front door. "Mateo only needs you a few days a week, which gives you plenty of time to focus on school. And the days you do work, you can just come over here afterward."

Nadine nodded, barely biting back her smile as she caught another glimpse of herself in the large mirror in the foyer.

"Okay, next on the agenda," Emma said, dropping her keys and Balenciaga shoulder bag on the entry table. "Clothes."

Nadine laughed. "Oh, I have plenty of clothes. Nana took me on a shopping spree at the mall before I left Akron. She was so excited about it, too, even got me a power suit. She always says a girl should be two things: classy and fabulous."

Emma paused at the foot of the stairs. "That's Coco Chanel, right?"

Nadine's brow creased as she looked down at her oversized teal sweater. "No. I think we got this at the Gap."

For a moment Emma considered correcting her, but then thought better of it and started up to her room. Nadine followed close behind.

The evening light was dim, so Emma turned on all the lights in her room and sat Nadine on her bed before disappearing into her walk-in closet. She used to share the immense space with Margo—their rooms were adjoining—but now that her sister had moved out, the space was all hers. Emma had been sure she would never be able to fill it with all of her own things, but that had only taken a few months. Dresses and sweaters and skirts and shoes were crammed into every available space, a kaleidoscope of couture that looked moments away from bursting free. Fran had been begging her to cull the chaos, so what better way than to give some pieces to her friend?

"Emma, seriously, I don't need any clothes!" Nadine laughed as Emma pulled a few of last season's dresses from their hangers.

"Are you sure?" Emma asked, holding an emerald-green Reformation slip dress up to Nadine's frame. "Because this would look incredible on you."

"I'm sure. Most of the stuff Nana bought me still has the tags on it. I'm set." Then her friend's gaze wandered to the nearby rack of shoes. "Although those white boots are insane."

Emma turned to see, even though she already knew exactly the pair Nadine was talking about. The white leather Loewe ankle boots were fabulous. She reached up and grabbed them from their perch.

"Then you should wear them on your first day. They'd look amazing with your distressed jeans and that pale blue sweater. The one that made your eyes look so gorgeous? Perfect to make a good impression."

Nadine eyed the shoes in Emma's hands, her face conflicted. "Are you sure?"

"Absolutely." Emma nodded to cement her resolve. "Now, what about these Bottega Veneta heels? My friend Lulu bought them for me in Milan. They dig into the ankle a little bit, but they would look so great with that black sweater dress you wore to class last week."

A half hour later, Nadine emerged from Emma's room with a Bergdorf's bag containing two pairs of pumps and three pairs of ankle boots, and a pair of Chloé sneakers on her feet.

"I know they're a bit small, but you'll get used to them, I swear," Emma assured her as Nadine winced her way down the stairs.

When they arrived in the kitchen they found Knightley already there, standing at the island. He was still in his suit from work, though his tie had been loosened around his neck. His attention was on his phone as he picked at a plate of leftover steamed vegetables.

"Hello, Knightley," Emma said, walking to the refrigerator.

"Hello, Woodhouse," he said, taking another moment to study his screen before looking up. When his gaze fell on Nadine, his forehead furrowed and the fork full of red peppers paused over his plate. "Nadine. I barely recognized you."

Nadine beamed, but before she could say anything, Emma beat her to it. "Doesn't she look fantastic? I took her to see Mateo and he just nailed it. Can you believe that's her natural hair color? Well, I mean, most of it."

"It looks . . . great," Knightley replied.

There was so much pride swelling in Emma's chest, it was like Knightley had paid her the compliment.

"And we got her a job, too. You're looking at the new receptionist at Jolie Salon. She starts tomorrow." Emma grabbed two sparkling waters from the refrigerator and gave one to Nadine. Suddenly, an idea struck her. "Oh! You should stay here tonight!"

Nadine had barely taken a sip of her water. "What?"

"The salon is so close you might as well stay over. You can take one of the guest rooms. Then we can order food and watch a movie down here on the big screen," Emma said, motioning down the hall to the media room. "It will be so much fun!"

"Yes!" Then Nadine's expression fell. "No."

"No?"

"I can't. My roommate is giving me our dorm room for an hour so I can FaceTime with Marty tonight."

"Oh. Right." Emma tried to mask the disappointment in her voice and failed miserably. She could feel Knightley's astute gaze on her from across the island, but she avoided meeting it. "Well, you can always call from here."

"It's okay. I need to start that paper for Goddard, anyway. And if Marty thinks I'm out tonight, he'll ask a bunch of questions and it'll lead to a fight." Nadine pushed her bottle of water away. "I should actually go. If I don't leave now, I'll never make it back to my dorm in time."

"Okay," Emma said, forcing a smile. "But don't forget to wear those boots with your blue sweater tomorrow."

Nadine's forehead wrinkled. "The Lowee ones?"

"Low-a-vay," Emma corrected her. "You can't be nervous while wearing Loewe. It's impossible."

"You're right," Nadine said with a nod. "Nana always says to change your circumstances, you must change your attitude."

Knightley smiled at her. "Eleanor Roosevelt."

"No, her name is Erma Hecker."

His face contorted with confusion, but he didn't say anything as Nadine gave Emma a quick hug and disappeared up the stairs to the front door. A moment later they were enveloped by silence.

There was no reason for Emma to feel disappointed. She had spent the whole afternoon with Nadine and would definitely stop by the salon tomorrow to see how her first day was going. Still, the sudden tinge of loneliness in her chest was familiar and she hated it.

"So, where are we ordering from?" Knightley's deep voice snapped her out of her train of thought.

She turned to shoot him a questioning look. He was staring back, the hard edges of his usual sardonic expression slightly softened. "What?"

"You said you wanted to order food and watch a movie."

A smile tugged at her lips. "It's Friday night. Don't you have a hot date or something?"

"I'm standing here eating a plate of cold vegetables, Woodhouse. What do you think?"

Emma tasked Knightley with ordering delivery from their favorite Chinese restaurant down the block while she went upstairs and changed into her pajamas. By the time the food arrived, she was stationed on the wide sofa in the media room downstairs, wearing her favorite flannel pants and sweatshirt, with a mismatched pair of slipper socks donning her feet.

Knightley set out an array of takeout boxes on the ottoman while Emma flipped through the movie choices, finally landing on the one she was looking for. She thought she had gotten away with it too, but as soon as the opening credits began—a moving instrumental score over sweeping scenes of the English countryside—Knightley paused, an egg roll inches from his mouth.

"Is this a period piece?"

"Shhhh," she said, taking a bite of lo mein.

"It's not one that's been remade a hundred times, is it?"

She ignored him, turning up the volume and cradling her box of food in her lap.

They watched in silence, and it wasn't until the main love interest was introduced—and Emma had paid proper attention to the fit of his nineteenth-century pants as he rode his horse toward the heroine's home—that she turned to Knightley. He was back looking at his phone. "So, what do you think of Nadine?"

"She seems nice." He barely looked up from his email as he answered.

Emma rolled her eyes. "I mean her before and after, Knightley."

He turned to her, eyebrows knitted together. "What?"

"The *transformation*. I've been working on defining her style for a couple of weeks, but the new cut and color just complete the whole look, don't you think? It's like a new beginning for her. I've given her the fresh start she needed."

"You didn't negotiate world peace here. You dyed her hair."

"It's a balayage."

"It's brown."

Emma sighed dramatically and settled back into the cushions. "I think we're getting to the heart of why you don't have a girlfriend."

He scoffed. "I doubt that."

The music swelled and the huge screen filled with scenes of a ball, as the two main stars stared longingly at each other from across the room.

"Here." Emma leaned over and placed her hands on either side of his face, forcing his attention on the television. "Focus. You might pick up some tips."

He watched for a moment, his expression a perfect mix of

confusion and derision. "How much older is he than her? Fifteen years? Twenty?"

"Shhh."

"And how is this romantic if none of these women have any personal rights?"

"Oh my God, shut up."

"They're essentially viewed as property, and you're swooning?"

Emma turned to him and narrowed her eyes. "If you don't stop with the Regency slander, I'm going to tell Fran you snuck salt into Sunday dinner last week."

He laughed, a full, rich sound, and Emma couldn't help but smile. She'd always loved his laugh. Knightley was usually so serious these days that there was a sense of victory when it happened. A joy in something hard-won.

It used to happen much more frequently. When they were kids, Margo, Ben, Emma, and George had caused so much mischief running around the house that Fran swore it caused her hair to go prematurely gray. That was probably one of the reasons she would pile them in this room most nights to watch an array of rom-coms and action films, depending on who wrestled control of the remote first.

"When was the last time we all had a movie night together?" Emma asked after another few minutes.

"It's been a while," Knightley murmured.

Emma canted her head to the side, trying to remember. It had been a regular occurrence for so many years that she hadn't really noticed when they started to taper off. Margo was the first to disappear; college and then law school meant her presence became more scarce. Then Ben was off at culinary school, which led into working nights at the restaurant. But Knightley stayed. Even when he was in college and then after, when he was so busy building his business, he still found time for their movie night. It wasn't until he decided to open the LA office and his trips out there became longer, more frequent, that the tradition seemed to die.

Knightley looked over at her, his expression becoming pensive. "What?"

"Nothing."

"Did you want to call Margo and Ben? See if they want to come up?"

Emma opened her mouth, then paused. Did she want them to come up? They were probably home. And only a moment before, she had been feeling so nostalgic for those lost moments between the four of them that it almost hurt. But now she was struck by a new ache, a sharp possessiveness for this little bubble that she and Knightley had created for themselves. Just the two of them.

She shimmied further into the cushions. "Nope. How about you?"

"No," he said, a slight smile on his lips. "I'm good."

"Good. Now stop talking. They're about to touch hands."

Knightley groaned. "Jesus . . ."

CHAPTER 6

Knightley had been in the office staring at his computer for over an hour. A few emails had come in during that time, but nothing urgent. Updates from his assistant Kate about a few meetings, a half dozen emails with last-minute questions about deals that were still in their early stages. He had answered them easily, and by noon realized he had nothing else to do.

He looked around his office, the windows that framed the downtown skyline, the glass walls that revealed the sprawling office of Knightley Capital beyond, a hive of activity. Everyone out there was busy. But even though it meant that this thing he had built was working as it should, better really, he was left idle.

His phone pinged with a text message, breaking his train of thought. He glanced down at the screen.

WILL

I haven't received an agenda for the Wentworth Hydroponics meeting.

Knightley sighed. Will was a friend, but he was also head of Hampshire M&A, one of the city's largest mergers and acquisition firms, which meant their business relationship often trumped the decade-long friendship.

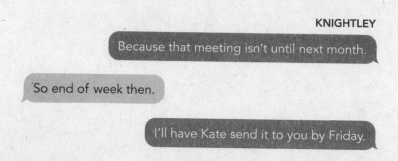

KNIGHTLEY

Because that meeting isn't until next month.

So end of week then.

I'll have Kate send it to you by Friday.

He glanced up at his office, at his empty desk. Then he began typing again.

Want to grab lunch this week?

Can't. I have about two dozen disasters to mitigate by Friday.

Let's grab a bite after the Wentworth meeting when my schedule isn't on fire.

He smiled. Will could feign irritation, but Knightley knew that he thrived on this. They were cut from the same cloth. It had been clear from the moment they met during their freshman year at Columbia University. A friendship had grown there, one built as much on mutual respect as a shared understanding of what drove them: it wasn't about success, it was about creating something of their own.

> Sounds good.

> Hold on. Since when do you have time for lunch?

> I guess I'm better at my job than you.

> Right. Well, enjoy it.

Knightley dropped his phone back on his desk and let his eyes wander to his empty inbox. He should be able to enjoy it. Didn't everyone wish for such a luxury?

But then he corrected himself. Most people probably did, but not everyone. Not his father. George Knightley Sr. used to say that you worked to create more work, and if there wasn't more work, you obviously weren't working hard enough. It was a mantra that had served him well in business, amassing an incredible fortune over the years. It also ensured that nothing else mattered apart from that fortune: not his wife, who finally left him for her yoga instructor, and definitely not their two sons she left behind.

After he died, Knightley founded this venture capital firm as payback. The intention had been to use it to give away his father's money to people and ideas that were making the world a better place regardless of their profitability. Get rid of the entire fortune within a couple of years, and then he would move on.

That was five years ago. And instead of draining the bank, Knightley Capital now boasted some of the country's most successful green tech companies as part of their portfolio.

Knightley stared out the glass wall of his office at the rows and rows of employees hard at work just a few feet from his desk.

Jesus. Maybe his father had won after all.

His thoughts were interrupted by his cell phone lighting up on his desk. A picture of his brother was on the screen.

"Hi, Ben," he answered.

"Hey, do you know how to mount a TV on the wall?"

"No. Why?"

He was answered by the sound of shuffling and scraping, then a grunt followed by a string of curse words. "Because this thing was just delivered and I need to figure out how to get it up before Margo gets home."

"What time is she getting home?"

"One."

Knightley glanced at his computer. "That's in less than an hour."

A pause, and then Ben let out a sigh. "Shit."

"Why do you need to get it up before she's home?"

"No reason."

Knightley smiled. Oh, there was definitely a reason.

"How big is the TV, Ben?"

"It's fine."

"Fifty-five inches? Sixty?"

Another pause. "Seventy-five."

Knightley laughed. "She's going to kill you."

"Not if I can get it up before she gets home."

"And you honestly think that's going to happen? Use your head."

"Wow." Ben chuckled. "You sound just like Dad."

Knightley's own smile dimmed a little. Ben rarely made digs about their father, but when he did, Knightley tried not to take it personally. After all, he had spent most of his life shielding his brother from the worst of their father's criticism and neglect.

Knightley worked to maintain his unaffected tone as he changed the subject. "How's the apartment?"

"Good. Better once I have something to watch the playoffs on besides a laptop." Another grunt. "What's new with you?"

"Same old, same old."

"And how's everything uptown? Margo is worried about her dad."

Knightley sighed, leaning back in his chair. "You two are a ten-minute cab ride away."

"You know Margo."

"Well, you can tell her that he's trying to cut out dairy, so dinner this weekend will be interesting."

Ben laughed. "And Emma has that new friend of hers."

"Nadine."

"Right. Margo said they're attached at the hip."

"Are they?"

Another grunt. "Yeah. I guess she met up with them last week after Emma took Nadine out in the Village to look for a new apartment."

Knightley blinked. How the hell was Nadine going to afford an apartment in the Village? Wasn't she living in the dorms? It was like the hair and the new clothes; all seemingly innocent on their own, but together added up to something that lodged a flare of annoyance in his chest.

"Unbelievable," Knightley murmured.

Ben sighed. "So what's the problem with Emma making a new friend?"

"Nothing, it's just . . ." Knightley raked a hand through his thick hair. "Emma tells her what to do. What to wear. How to act. Nadine's becoming a carbon copy of her."

"And?"

"And that's not a friend. That's a hobby."

"Isn't that just Emma, though? She finds something or someone she's interested in and commits 110 percent."

Knightley leaned forward, his elbows on his desk. "Yeah, but this is different. Emma doesn't need someone who will indulge her. She needs someone to push back, to remind her that you can't just treat people like toys because you're bored."

Ben let out a long breath. "You need to cut her some slack. We've all grown up, and that includes Emma. You have to accept that. You can't just go around judging her actions all the time."

Knightley huffed. "I don't judge her."

His brother chuckled on the other end of the line. "Self-awareness isn't your strong suit, is it?"

"Shut up, Ben."

"God, I wish you hadn't been out in LA when she had that French boyfriend who answered every question with a shrug."

Knightley's brow furrowed. *French boyfriend?* "Who?"

"I don't remember his name. Jean something? I don't know. They dated her senior year at FIT. She ended it around graduation, I think." Another laugh. "I would've paid money for you to have been around to *not* judge that one."

Knightley smiled despite himself. Yeah, he would have had some thoughts on that.

"My advice, Brother?" Ben continued. "Stay out of it. If we learned anything from our childhoods, it's that nothing good comes from telling the Woodhouse girls what to do."

"Fine." Knightley sighed. "I'll try."

"Smart." Another grunt and his brother was back to moving the TV across the room.

A sound echoed from the other line and Knightley knew immediately it was the front door opening. Ben mumbled something under his breath, and then there was the rustle of fabric like he was holding the phone to his shirt as he exclaimed, "Hi, honey! Surprise!"

"Absolutely not!" Margo screamed.

～

Knightley hung up with Margo and Ben still arguing. He leaned back in his desk chair, running his finger along the mouse pad of his computer to stir the screen awake. Just as he suspected, his inbox was still empty, so he grabbed his jacket and decided to take a walk on his own.

The crisp autumn air felt good against his skin as he left the office behind and started up Sixth Avenue. It wasn't long before he had reached 59th Street, a steady stream of taxis and horse-drawn carriages separating him from Central Park. It was mid-October and the trees across the street were a deep shade of red and orange, a bright pop of color against the otherwise gray sky.

He loved this city. The last few years spent bouncing between here and California had been fun at first, but the novelty had worn off quickly. The beaches, the restaurants, the women . . . none of it replaced the fundamental fact that New York was his home.

His cell phone vibrated in his jacket pocket. He pulled it out to find a picture of a manicured hand giving the middle finger illuminating the screen.

"Hello, Woodhouse," he answered.

He knew she heard the smile in his voice because it was mirrored in her own when she asked, "Wait, are you actually happy to hear from me?"

"When am I not happy to hear from you?"

"Honestly, I'm just surprised you answered. It's two o'clock on a Tuesday."

"Yes, well some of us work."

"But are you working right *now*?"

He sighed. She was infuriating, calling mid-afternoon on a Tuesday and assuming he might not be busy. Mostly because he knew she had already deduced that he wasn't. "What do you need?"

"You didn't answer my question."

"At the moment I'm not working, no."

"Good. Because I'm headed to our very favorite place in the world for a little peace and quiet and wanted to know if you cared to join me."

A small smile returned to his lips. "I'll meet you there."

～

Knightley had always loved the Metropolitan Museum of Art. It was a New York institution. The towering columns and limestone facade alone felt like it physically anchored the center of the island. And inside it was a sanctuary: miles of art and sculpture and just . . . quiet.

It was incredible. Truly. But to Knightley, it was always simply a place to go. A safe space that for a long time vied only with the Woodhouses' as a real home. A place to escape when his own became too much.

It was funny, his father spent millions trying to make their house feel like a museum, and Knightley still preferred the real thing.

"I haven't been here in years," he murmured as they made their way through the American Wing to European Paintings.

Though there was an order to how the galleries were laid out, it still felt like a labyrinth, and Knightley forced himself to stop keeping track of their location and just . . . wander. The way he used to.

Emma barely looked up from her pink Moleskin notebook as she made a note from a nearby plaque. Usually when they came here he could count on her to keep his random wandering on track. She never had an agenda or a schedule and would roll her eyes if he even tried to plan the trip. But today she seemed surprisingly focused, notebook in hand and a serious line to her brow. She was even wearing flats.

"Years? How is that even possible? You live half a block away," she said.

He didn't bother acknowledging the comment as he approached a Van Gogh and studied its thick brushstrokes.

They continued on to the next gallery. It was familiar, but it took Knightley a moment to remember why.

"Wasn't one of your mom's Pierre Bonnard paintings in this room for a while?" he asked.

Emma waved him off, focusing instead on the Manet in front of her.

Knightley didn't mind the dismissal, he knew why. Cassandra, Emma's mother, had collected Pierre Bonnard paintings; it was one of Knightley's earliest memories of their house. The brightly colored canvases on almost every wall of the living room, the office, the hall.

They started to disappear when Cassandra died. Knightley had been nine. Over the next few years, Mr. Woodhouse had them removed one by one and gave them on loan to this museum. By the time Knightley was in high school they were completely gone, too painful a reminder of the woman who was lost so suddenly.

Knightley's gaze slid across the light gray wall in front of him.

"They had it hanging right here. *Flowers on a Table* or something like that," he said, almost to himself.

"*Flowers on a Red Carpet*," Emma corrected him, her attention still on the Manet. "It was the one that used to be over the sofa in the living room."

He paused, stunned for a moment. Emma had only been two when her mother had died, and she was barely out of grade school by the time her father had removed the last of the paintings.

"I didn't know you remembered that," Knightley said, turning to look at her.

Emma offered him a shrug. "Of course I remember it. I remember all of them. Mom picked them out so the paintings were like little pieces of herself through the house. They made it feel like it was still her home too, you know?"

He nodded. Sometimes he forgot that while he tried to piece through his memories of Mrs. Woodhouse, Emma barely had any at all.

He wanted to prod her further, but before he could continue, she closed her notebook and started forward again.

"Come on, Knightley. Keep up."

"So what are we doing here?" he asked, following her into the next room.

"Researching my thesis. The proposal is due next week and I'm looking for examples."

"Of what?"

"Influencers."

He blinked at her. "Excuse me?'"

"It's a four-syllable word, Knightley. Not Latin." She stopped in front of another painting.

"You're looking for influencers in European Paintings and Sculpture."

"Yes."

He narrowed his eyes on her. "And what exactly is the topic of your thesis?"

She straightened from where she had been reading a plaque on the wall, a smug grin on her pink lips. "It's called: 'The Birth of the Influencer: Art Patronage from the Renaissance to Today.'"

"What?"

She looped her arm in his, directing them forward as she spoke. "So, you know what an influencer is, right?"

"I'm thirty, Woodhouse. Not a hundred."

She patted his hand. "Okay, then you know how they've built an entire industry around the idea that brands sponsor social media content. Some of these people are making millions of dollars by taking photos of food or beauty products or whatever and posting them. But their careers only exist within that ecosystem. There are no influencers without sponsorship."

"Okay."

"So how is that any different from the patronage of the arts that drove the entirety of the Renaissance? Like, they had the Catholic Church, and we have coconut water, but when you think about it, they're both spending money on imagery created by others that advances their own interests. So why not examine them in the same terms?" She stopped and turned to him. "It's brilliant, right?"

She stared up at him and bit her lip, trying to hide her excited smile as she waited for his reaction. He had to admit, he would have scoffed if anyone else had tried to describe the idea. But there was something about her sincerity that gave him pause. His gaze slipped from her green eyes to her lip caught there in her teeth, and he felt something tighten deep in his gut.

He looked away quickly and cleared his throat. "It's . . . interesting."

She sighed and started into the next room. "I think the word you're looking for is 'genius.'"

He chuckled and followed her.

Another gallery opened in front of them, the walls lined with another array of artwork. Knightley knew this room, if only because of the painting staring at him from the opposite wall.

"I think that's my favorite piece in this place," he said.

Emma stopped, looking up at the painting that held his attention: Gustav Klimt's *Mäda Primavesi*.

It was large compared to the others on the wall, its colors vibrant and almost otherworldly even from across the room. But it was the subject that made Knightley pause, just as it had on every other visit for the past decade: a young girl standing in what appeared to be her bedroom, one hand on her hip as she stared defiantly at her audience. It was as if they were merely her subjects. A small queen ruling over her own small kingdom.

"She's always reminded me of you," he said.

Emma tilted her head to the side, taking in the canvas. "How so?"

Knightley paused, suddenly at a loss of how to articulate it. "This small girl that doesn't know she's small."

She turned to him, an eyebrow arched high on her forehead as if she was offended.

He chuckled. "I just mean . . . she commands the room. The confidence . . . Klimt didn't shy away from it. He celebrated who she was, proved how being confident and bold was something beautiful."

Emma's gaze returned to the painting.

"I wonder if he painted her again as an adult," Emma said, more to herself than to him.

"Why?"

She shrugged, staring at it a moment longer before continuing on to the next room.

They wandered for a few minutes in silence. It wasn't until they were leaving the European gallery and heading toward Modern Art that he spoke again. "I talked to Ben earlier. He told me you took Nadine to go look at apartments for her in the Village."

Emma hummed in affirmation.

"Can she afford that?"

"Well, not right now, obviously. But once she gets a job at Christie's, she'll need a place. We found the cutest one down on Charles Street—"

"Does she have a job at Christie's yet?"

"Of course not. She's still in school. But there's no harm in looking. She has to know what's out there."

His fingers went to the bridge of his nose. He was getting a headache. "And her boyfriend is okay with all this?"

"Hmm?" Emma asked with feigned innocence.

"Her boyfriend."

"Um. I don't think that's an issue anymore." Emma was avoiding his gaze, staring up at the Rothko nearby.

Something was up.

"Why not?" he pressed.

She shrugged. "I'm pretty sure she's breaking up with him."

Knightley raised his eyebrows. "That's sudden."

"What do you mean?"

"Just last month she was at Sunday dinner telling us that she missed him."

"But did she miss him?" Emma's head cocked to the side as she studied a row of charcoal sketches. "Or was she just feeling guilty?"

"I don't follow."

"I just mean, was she upset because he wasn't here, or was she upset because he made her feel bad that *she* was? That she came here to follow her dreams and he got left behind."

"I think that's for Nadine to figure out."

Emma nodded. "Exactly. That's what I told her. She has to trust her instincts. And honestly, she came to New York City to build a new life, so she deserves someone who fits that new life. Preferably someone gorgeous and who I get along with, but we'll figure all that out as we go."

He stopped in the middle of the gallery. "Wait. Did you tell her to break up with her boyfriend?"

"I didn't *tell* her to do it," she said, rolling her eyes. "But the fact that she took to the idea so easily is pretty much proof that I was right and the relationship needed to end. She even said it wasn't her forever relationship."

He blinked. "Her what?"

"Her *forever* relationship. You know, the guy she's going to be with forever."

"That's not a thing."

"It's absolutely a thing. And she knows he's not it." Emma shrugged. "And honestly? She's right."

"How could you possibly know that?" he asked, his voice louder than he intended.

"Shhhh!" An older woman glared at them.

Emma smiled at her sweetly before turning to Knightley. The smile flattened. "Because she is smart and gorgeous and funny and she moved *here*. I mean, it's obvious that she could have her pick of anyone in New York."

Knightley sighed, keeping his voice to a murmur. "That doesn't give you the right to fuck with her life."

"Why do you think that I have?" she hissed.

His eyes widened. "I'm sorry. Didn't you just admit to it?"

"So you're assuming I did something wrong by pointing out the obvious? That I somehow manipulated her just by suggesting—"

He let out a harsh chuckle. "I've known you since the day you were born and trust me, you never just *suggest*."

Her arms were crossed over her chest now and she was looking at him like he had grown a second head. "Why are you so mad about this?"

"Because . . ." He stopped himself, closing his eyes and raking both hands through his hair as if it would somehow restore his patience. "You treat the world like it's your personal playground, Woodhouse. Like everything is here to amuse you until you find something better to do."

Her mouth fell open. "That is not true."

"No? What about this?" He motioned around the gallery.

"You mean *art*?" she said, wide-eyed. "I love art. You know this! That's why I'm here! It's my passion!"

He scoffed. "It's easy to have passions when it takes no work to maintain them."

She reeled back as if he had slapped her, and while he immediately regretted his words, he didn't take them back.

"You can't go through life jumping from one thing to the next," he continued. "Not everything is fun all the time. Some things take work and time and are not about you."

"Is that seriously what you think of me?" Her voice grew louder with every word. "That I'm some flighty, selfish—"

"No, Jesus," he seethed, shaking his head.

"Then what are you saying?"

"That caring for someone doesn't mean you get to dictate how they live their life."

She laughed, humorless and sharp. "Oh my God, I can't believe you of all people just said that to me!"

Other people in the gallery were staring at them now, but he didn't care. "She needs a friend, Woodhouse."

"I am her friend!" she practically shouted.

Another "Shhh," this one coming from a man on the other side of the room. They ignored it.

"This isn't some fun way to pass the time. This is someone's life. At your age you should know that." His voice was deep and ground through gritted teeth.

Her eyes narrowed. "At my age? Are you kidding? I'm an adult, Knightley. Just like you! I know how the world works!"

Her face was flushed and her chest rising quickly as she stared up at him, her chin high. His stomach tightened again with some hot, heavy feeling deep in his core. It was anger but something else, something he didn't take time to contemplate as he took a step forward, his face inches from hers.

"You think you know how the world works, Woodhouse?" he seethed. "Then do us all a fucking favor and start acting like it."

And then he turned and walked out of the gallery, down the stairs, and out of the museum.

CHAPTER 7

Emma spent the car ride down to her sister's apartment the next day coming up with names for George Knightley. Most were merely variations on "asshole" and "prick," so by the time the car stopped at Perry Street and Greenwich, she had made a mental note to research new curse words.

"It's me," she said into the video intercom when she buzzed her sister's apartment. Margo appeared and made a funny face at her before pressing the buzzer to unlock the building's doors. Emma walked straight into the elevator and went up to the fourth floor, where her sister's door was propped open at the end of a short hall.

The apartment was a converted loft space on the top floor of a historic building, which boasted exposed brick and whitewashed walls with sleek, black-lacquered wood floors and huge windows. An oversized kitchen island was the focal point of the main room, and off to one side sat a dining table made of reclaimed wood. On the other was a deep blue velvet sofa and two mismatched lounge chairs.

Emma dropped her purse on the table and sank her entire body into the soft sofa with an exhausted sigh.

"Do you think you're in therapy or something?" Margo asked, emerging from the kitchen with two glasses of water.

"I walked, you know."

"From where?"

"Just the corner, but these are four-inch heels."

"Spare me." She put one glass of water down in front of Emma and took a sip of the other. "So, why do you look so miserable?"

Emma rolled her eyes. "You have no idea what Knightley did yesterday."

Margo pursed her full lips.

"What?" Emma asked.

"I was wondering how long it would take for you to bring that up. Let's see, a solid thirty seconds."

"He already told you."

"He told Ben."

Emma grabbed a pillow and covered her face to muffle a scream. When she was done, she let the pillow fall. "He's the worst."

"Oh yes, he's just awful," Margo said with mock-condemnation as she sat down on the other end of the sofa.

"I'm serious, Mar. He was so out of line. Telling me I was manipulating Nadine—as if I would do that!"

"Hmmm."

"As if I somehow plotted to make her break up with her boyfriend or something."

"How *is* Nadine?"

Emma blinked. Oh, right. This was really about Nadine.

"She's fine. I mean, she's a little sad, but we'll find someone better for her. The city is full of eligible guys, and she's gorgeous. Should be easy."

Her sister raised a skeptical eyebrow. "So, you're playing match-maker again?"

"First off, you're welcome," Emma said, gesturing around her sister's marital home. "And second, I'm hardly doing anything. Just sharing some gentle guidance after class."

Margo leaned back. "Right. How's school going, anyway?"

"Really well. The one course I'm taking is a breeze, so I'm mostly focused on my thesis and polishing up my application for the Met internship."

"You're still doing that?" Margo's nose crinkled with confusion.

She tried to ignore her sister's tone. No doubt she thought this was just another one of Emma's short-lived hobbies—just like Knightley did. "What do you mean?"

Margo shrugged. "I don't know. I assumed grad school would be like when you tried to start your own fashion line in high school. Or the event planning business you and I thought up when you were at FIT that never panned out. You would still be really good at that, by the way."

Emma worked to keep her annoyance in check. "You know I've always loved art."

"Yeah, but I thought that meant, like, drawing pictures and visiting museums on the weekend."

Emma turned to look out the window so Margo wouldn't see her scowl. Just because she didn't talk about art—just like she never really talked about their mother, a topic that was almost always off-limits—didn't mean that she wasn't serious about it.

"The application deadline is in January, and I should hear about an interview pretty soon after that," she said, ignoring her sister's comment.

"And have you asked Dad to put in a good word yet?" Margo replied. "You probably wouldn't even need an interview once he calls."

"I'm *not* asking Dad for help. I can do this on my own."

"You do realize you might not get this thing without him though, right?"

"Thanks for the vote of confidence," Emma mumbled.

"Come on, you know I think you're amazing, but every graduate on the East Coast with a master's in fine arts wants to work at the Met. Meanwhile, Dad is one of their biggest patrons. Why not use him?"

Emma took a deep breath and replied as calmly as she could, "I'm going to do this myself, Margo."

Her sister threw up her hands. "Fine. Whatever. Just promise you won't completely rule it out?"

Emma softened. "We'll see." Despite her harsh words, she knew Margo's heart was in the right place. It always was.

"Good." Margo smiled, triumphant. "Now tell me how much you miss me."

"Not even in the slightest."

Her sister laughed.

"Seriously, though, it's fine," Emma continued. "I miss having you down the hall, but we're adjusting. Dad is keeping busy. And Nadine is over all the time now."

Margo nodded. "I'm glad you two found each other."

"Me too."

"So . . . are you going to apologize?"

Emma blinked. "To Nadine?"

"No, to George."

She rolled her eyes. "Why should I? I haven't done anything wrong."

"So if you see him at home, you'll walk away?"

Emma's head fell back against the pillows. "Maybe."

Margo scoffed. "You realize he's probably forgotten all of this, right? He's got other stuff going on."

"Like what?"

"I mean, he's thirty now. He's busy running a successful business, and he's single. He's probably getting serious about settling down."

Emma frowned. "What does that mean?"

Margo seemed to consider. "I think he's lonely. I mean, he's in that house all by himself, and if he's not there, he's in the office. Sooner or later he's got to fall for someone, even if it's just to give his mind something else to think about."

Emma curled further into the sofa cushions, ignoring the hot curl of possessiveness in her belly. Seriously, how long could this disagreement possibly go on?

The front door opened suddenly and Ben appeared, his long arms laden with shopping bags.

"Sorry I'm late! But I have brunch!"

Margo stared at him. "You don't have brunch. You have groceries."

"Ah, groceries that will *be* brunch. Give me ten minutes."

Margo groaned and brought her attention back to Emma. "Never marry a chef."

Emma shrugged. "Okay."

"I mean, someone in the restaurant industry is fine, but just, like . . . not a chef."

"That's . . . oddly specific."

"Is it?"

Emma narrowed her eyes on her sister. "What's going on?"

"I'm just offering more sisterly advice," Margo replied, eyes wide with feigned innocence.

"Okay."

"And, you know, Montgomery Knox is back in town in a couple of weeks."

Emma's head fell back against the sofa again. "Very subtle, Mar."

"I just think you two would be perfect together!" her sister exclaimed, immediately dropping the act.

"So what's your evil genius plan?" Emma asked, resting her head in her hand and getting comfortable.

"I want you, me, Ben, and Montgomery to go out, something casual. Maybe he could even come to Sunday dinner! Less pressure."

"Yes, no pressure at all when a woman's entire family is there on your first date."

"It's not a date. It's just dinner."

"Is he actually coming this time? Or is there going to be a dessert crisis in Marrakesh or something?"

"He is! I think. He's just got so much going on. But wait until you meet him, you'll *love* him."

Emma sighed, resigning herself to Margo's plotting as the smell of bacon and chives wafted in from the kitchen. It felt like her sister had been trying to get her and Montgomery together for months to no avail. Emma could never understand why she didn't just give up. But now, as she watched Margo get up and wrap her arms around Ben's waist, and Ben lean down to place a kiss on the top of Margo's head, it suddenly wasn't that hard to understand at all.

CHAPTER 8

"And then he hung up on me!" Nadine exclaimed, her arms flying out so wildly that she almost spilled her glass of pinot grigio all over Emma's linen duvet.

Emma listened from her perch on the armchair next to her bed, mentally patting herself on the back for choosing white wine, while also looking appropriately shocked by Nadine's retelling of her breakup with Marty. The anticipation had grown over the past two days between the actual event and when Nadine had time after class to come over to relay the full story, but Emma had the wine ready, as well as an array of post-breakup essentials: chocolate, tissues, and her Beyoncé playlist.

"Oh, very mature," Emma said, rolling her eyes.

"That's not even the worst of it. Apparently, he showed up at my parents' house afterward to see if they could get me to come home!"

"Stop it."

"Then my parents thought he looked hungry and asked him to stay for dinner!"

"Oh no."

"Thank goodness Nana sent him on his way with some of her

apple crumble." Nadine took one of the chocolates and shoved it in her mouth. "Like . . . I can make my own decisions about my life, you know?"

"Completely," Emma said sympathetically. "Are you okay?"

"Yeah . . . I actually think so." Nadine sighed as her anger seemed to dissipate.

"You seem to be handling it all rather well."

Nadine managed a weak smile. "You think?"

Emma nodded.

"Honestly, I'm just over it. I'm over him second-guessing every choice I try to make."

Emma huffed loudly. "Sounds like Knightley."

Nadine paused. "It does?"

"Totally. We were having a lovely time at the museum the other day, when he decided to start this huge fight and then he stormed out!"

Nadine sat up taller and scrunched up her nose. "Well, that's a little dramatic."

"Right?" See, Nadine understood. This was the reaction Emma needed: shocked indignation. And she knew her friend would provide it.

"And he hasn't talked to you since?"

"Absolutely nothing."

"Wow." Nadine grabbed another chocolate. "What were you two even fighting about anyway?"

Oh.

"Well . . ." Emma darted her eyes around the room, trying desperately to find the words that left her innocence infallible and also ambiguous. "He was implying that I insert myself into other people's lives and create more problems than I solve. Which I do *not*."

Nadine's eyes went wide. "Totally not!"

Emma nodded firmly. Nadine's reassurance was all she needed. "Thank you."

"I mean, look at everything you've done for me!"

Emma worked to maintain an impassive expression, even though her voice went up an octave. "Right."

"You helped me get the best job ever. Everyone at the salon is amazing, and Mateo has been so patient teaching me the whole inventory system. He wasn't even mad when I accidentally ordered a hundred extra bottles of semi-permanent toner."

Emma blinked. "Really?"

Nadine nodded, then her eyes lit up again. "*And* you're the one who helped me realize that I needed to break up with Marty."

Oh God. This was veering too close to the truth.

"I never would have done it if it weren't for you," Nadine barreled on. "And you're helping me with my thesis topic too!"

Yes, school! That was safe.

"Right! Your thesis topic. That's the perfect way to get your mind off all of this," Emma said, her voice loud and a bit overzealous. "Do you have your laptop with you?"

Nadine nodded.

"Great. But I think we need a change of scenery. You know, to help us focus." Emma smiled. "Grab your bag—I know the perfect spot."

They arrived at Vicarage Coffee ten minutes later, finding it almost empty except for an elderly couple perusing the menu at the counter. Zane stood on the other side and smiled as Emma and Nadine entered, nodding to Emma's usual table near the window.

"Who's that?" Nadine asked, staring over her shoulder at Zane as he started up the espresso machine to make the couple's drinks.

Hmmm, interesting.

"Zane," Emma said, removing her coat. "He's new, but it's like he's worked here for ages."

Nadine nodded, still staring. Emma couldn't blame her. Zane was cute, albeit in a predictable way: tall and lanky with light brown hair and a half smile permanently on his lips.

The spurt of the steamer seemed to startle Nadine out of her stupor; she darted her eyes away and surveyed the small room, its black-and-white checkered floor crowded with mismatched chairs and its dark walls covered in vintage coffee ads.

"This place is so cute," she said.

"It's great, and they have the *best* coffee," Emma replied with a nod. "Knightley and I meet up here all the time."

"Oh?" Nadine asked, a tinge of something unfamiliar in her voice. "Did you want to call him? He could join us after work, or maybe—"

"No," Emma scoffed, feeling indignant all over again. "No way. He hasn't even apologized yet. Besides, he probably has plans or something. Apparently, he's *so* busy with his job and his social life, he can't even—"

"Two beautiful ladies in my coffee shop this afternoon?" Zane purred as he approached the table. "To what do I owe the pleasure?"

Emma smiled up at him, stifling the last of her annoyance at Knightley to present Zane with a serene expression. "A looming thesis topic deadline. Thought we'd grab a cup of coffee in the hopes of getting some inspiration."

"Yes," Nadine said, smiling up at him. "Fill us up with some hot inspiration, please!"

Zane chuckled even as Nadine's cheeks flushed, as if she only just realized what she said.

"And what kind of inspiration are you looking for?" he asked, sliding his gaze to Emma.

"The usual for me," Emma said, nodding his attention back to Nadine.

"The same," she replied.

He turned back to the counter and was barely out of earshot when Nadine let her head fall into her arms.

"I can't believe I said that!" she said, her voice muffled by her sleeves.

"It's fine," Emma assured her. "He thought it was cute."

Her head lifted, her expression hopeful. "He did?"

"Totally. Did you see how he smiled?"

Nadine not-so-subtly stole another glance at Zane as he worked the espresso machine.

"He is so hot."

Yes. Why hadn't Emma thought of it before? Zane and Nadine— it was perfect.

"He is," Emma said, leaning forward. "I'm pretty sure he's a musician, too. He always brings a guitar case in and hides it behind the bar there."

That cinched it. Nadine sighed, no longer trying to hide the fact that she was now leering as he returned with their drinks.

He placed a mug in front of each of them, then turned his attention to Nadine.

"I didn't catch your name."

She stared up at him and smiled. "I'm Nadine."

He held out his hand. "It's a pleasure to meet you, Nadine. I'm Zane."

Nadine shook it, the motion so subtle that for that brief moment it looked to Emma as if they were just enjoying each other's touch.

This. Was. Fate.

And then it was over. Zane released his grip and turned back to Emma. "Sure I can't get you anything else?"

"No, we're fine. Thanks though," she replied, taking a sip of her latte.

He nodded and then turned to wink at Nadine before heading back to the register.

Emma wanted to squeal. The electricity between Nadine and Zane was palpable. She knew the cues.

"You know, I think he's single," she said, pretending to find the sugar packets interesting before stealing a glance to gauge her friend's reaction.

Nadine blushed. "Oh, I don't know if I'm ready."

"Maybe you just need to go on a few dates to get you back out there."

"I wouldn't even know where to start. Marty is the only guy I've ever been on a date with."

Emma's mouth fell open. "Really?"

Nadine nodded, her eyes drifting down to her lap.

"Well then, I have the perfect idea." Emma reached across the table and grabbed her friend's phone. "It's time to get your profile online."

"My profile?"

"Your profile for dating apps." Emma barely looked up from Nadine's screen as she continued with her train of thought. "We'll get you set up on Kissmet. And maybe Frolick. And you are practically a career woman now, so you have to be on YesBitch."

"Oh, I don't know . . ." Nadine hesitated. "Are you sure?"

"Absolutely. I set people up all the time! I have a great track record." Emma nodded confidently. Yes, the only couple she had truly set up was Margo and Ben, but that ended in marriage, so she obviously had an innate talent for it. And besides, how hard was it to swipe right? "First, we need a few photos of you."

"I don't think I have any."

"Are you serious?" Emma asked, truly perplexed. "Why not?"

She shrugged. "I hate getting my picture taken. Makes me self-conscious."

"Nadine, you're gorgeous. You have the bluest eyes I've ever seen, and I know people who would pay a fortune for those cheekbones. And your hair! God, Mateo is a genius." She lifted Nadine's phone and pointed its camera at her. The late-afternoon sun cast a soft light through the cafe and the photo captured its diffused glow on Nadine's skin and hair. Emma smiled proudly and turned the screen to show her friend. "See? You're stunning."

Nadine blushed again.

"Okay, now you try," Emma said, handing the phone back to her. "Flip the camera around and hold it just . . . like . . . that." She carefully positioned the phone in Nadine's hand and then elevated it up at a forty-five-degree angle. "Now tuck your chin . . . yes . . . look up at the lens . . ."

SNAP.

Nadine turned back to Emma. "Okay, what now?"

"Keep going. You have to take a lot to find the perfect one."

"How many is a lot?"

"Hm, I don't know. Maybe a hundred?"

Nadine's eyes went wide.

Emma proceeded to direct an impromptu photo shoot, instructing when to pout, to smile, to turn or tilt her head, until Nadine finally dropped her phone on the table and groaned.

"Please say we're done."

"Almost," Emma said as she picked up her friend's phone and scrolled through the pictures. "Now we just have to fill out your profile and tell all these guys why you're so amazing."

Nadine's face blanched. "I don't know how to do that."

"That's why I'm going to help you." Emma downloaded the

Kissmet app, filling in Nadine's information until it got to the profile questions. "Okay, here are a few prompts you need to answer to get a guy interested. So first one, 'After work you can usually find me . . .'"

Nadine shrugged. "Studying."

Emma's lips pursed. "Hmmm, how about 'wandering a museum or reading about the neo-impressionist art movement.'"

"Oh, I love the neo-impressionist art movement!" Nadine replied, her eyes lighting up.

"Right. Exactly." Emma quickly moved on. "Okay, next one: 'As a child, I really loved . . .'"

Nadine thought about it for a minute, then replied, "Dressing up Mr. Mittens."

Emma's fingers paused above the screen's keyboard as she looked up at her friend.

"Oh, Mr. Mittens is our cat," Nadine explained. "That's where Mom got the idea for The Posh Pussy, I used to dress him up in all my doll clothes. He only had one eye, so there was this one outfit for my Pirate Barbie that I—"

"How about: 'taking care of injured animals,'" Emma said as she typed. "Okay. Last one: 'The biggest way my life has changed . . .'"

Nadine laughed. "That's easy. Moving to New York."

Emma smiled. "Perfect." She typed in the answer and handed the phone back to her friend. "All you have to do now is complete the rest of your profile and pick a main profile pic."

"And then what?" Nadine asked, looking down at her phone as if a man was about to manifest out of the screen.

"Then guys will swipe right if they want to chat. And we can swipe right on them, too. It will be fun, I promise."

Nadine let out a decisive breath. "Okay, I'm in. My nana is

always saying you miss a hundred percent of the shots you don't take."

"What are my two favorite customers up to?" Zane was suddenly standing next to the table, leaning over Nadine's shoulder.

"Still studying," Emma replied, even though she was aware that they hadn't taken their laptops out of their bags yet.

Nadine let out a nervous laugh, moving to hide her screen against her sweater, but Zane still caught a glimpse.

"You're on Kissmet?"

"Oh! Um . . . yes . . . I . . ." Nadine stammered as her face turned a deep shade of crimson.

"That's cool. I'm on there too," he said, a sly grin curling up his mouth. "It looks like you still need a photo, though."

"We were about to pick one," Emma said.

"Need help? I have a great eye." He winked at Nadine.

Oh my God. It was *happening*.

Emma tried to bite back her smile as she stood up.

"You two go ahead. I'm going to pop to the ladies'," she announced, and quickly started toward the hallway in the back of the cafe.

She made sure the bathroom door was locked before she turned to the mirror to congratulate herself. Nadine and Zane . . . it really was perfect! Nadine needed flirting and compliments and mind-blowing sex. She needed a new love interest, and Zane was it.

Emma smiled proudly at her reflection. See, this was yet another example of how wrong Knightley was about her. Setting Nadine up with her hot barista? She was the picture of selflessness.

When Emma returned to the table a few minutes later, she found Zane still scrolling through pictures beside Nadine, who had a broad smile on her face.

"So, have you narrowed it down?" Emma asked as she took her seat.

"It's between these two," he said, holding up Nadine's phone so Emma could see. One was a selfie, and the other was the photo Emma took.

"Oh! Emma took that one!" Nadine announced proudly. "I think that's my favorite."

"Yeah?" Zane smiled. "Well then, I guess that settles it." He tapped on the photo and attached it to Nadine's profile before handing the phone back to her. "I told you I had a good eye," he purred. Then he turned his attention back to Emma. "So, what's your deal?"

"My deal?"

"Are you single too?"

"Oh, I'm not dating."

Zane laughed. "Right now or . . . ?"

"Well, I'm graduating in the spring and trying to secure this really competitive position at the Met before then, so . . ." Emma shrugged. "I'm on indefinite hiatus."

"What if the right situation came along?" Zane asked, his voice lowering a bit.

"I think the right situation is no situation." Emma took a sip of her latte. "But that's just me. What about you?"

"Hmmm . . ." He glanced between Emma and Nadine. "I'm really open to anything."

Emma looked at Nadine. Her friend was biting back a smile, and for once, Emma was at a loss for words.

"I was thinking, we should all go out sometime," Zane continued.

"Oh yes!" Nadine said.

Emma winced. *Too eager, Nadine.*

"Cool," Zane said. "My buddy is having a party in a couple of weeks in Brooklyn."

Emma's heart dropped. "Brooklyn?"

"Yeah. It's at a bar, but there's a performance beforehand."

Oh God, no. This was just getting worse.

Emma turned to Nadine, to somehow psychically transmit the awfulness of this suggestion, but Nadine was still staring up at Zane, her wide doe eyes transfixed.

"That sounds so amazing. What kind of performance?" she asked.

"It's like . . . how can I explain it . . ." He looked out the window as if deep in thought. "It's like an avant-garde interactive art experience with these glass bridges over water."

Emma closed her eyes to avoid rolling them. None of those words were appealing. She had been to her fair share of black box high school theater, thank you very much. But when she opened her eyes again and caught Nadine's unabashedly hopeful expression, she could only sigh.

"We'll be there," she said, forcing a smile. "Sounds . . . fun."

No one else came into the cafe for the next hour, so Zane hung out at their table until it was finally time for him to close. He locked the door behind them as they all left, a guitar case slung over his shoulder.

Emma took a small step toward the curb, using the excuse of hailing Nadine a taxi to leave the two of them alone for a moment. When one pulled up, she smiled brightly.

"Here you go, Nadine," she replied. "Are you headed downtown, Zane? You two could share a cab."

"I'm good," he said.

Emma's smile faltered as Nadine slid happily into the waiting car.

"See you later!" she exclaimed. Then she slammed the door closed and waved goodbye through the window as the cab turned down 82nd.

"I could have sworn you told me you lived on the Lower East Side," Emma said.

"I do," Zane replied, staring intently at her face. "I don't mind taking the subway though."

"Oh."

He took a step toward her. "Thanks for sticking around tonight. I think you two are hands down my favorite customers to hang out with."

"Oh, Nadine and I had a great time."

"Me too."

Emma darted her eyes around the street, trying to find something to say, anything to break the awkward moment that had suddenly landed between them.

That's when she saw him. Across the street, coat wrapped tightly around his body, Knightley walked toward home. But he wasn't alone. There was a woman walking beside him. She was tall with long black hair, her stature helped by the stiletto heels on her feet. She smiled at Knightley and said something close to his ear. His head was down, his gait wide, and he didn't look up at her as she spoke; for a moment Emma thought she had gotten away unnoticed. But then, as if he had sensed her presence, he looked over and their eyes locked.

It was just a moment, but her stomach lurched and her mouth went dry. Then Knightley's gaze snapped to Zane, who had taken another small step toward her. Knightley's expression hardened, and he locked his eyes with the concrete again, continuing home with the gorgeous woman beside him.

"So, what do you think?"

She blinked, realizing Zane had asked her something.

"I'm sorry?"

"You're down for Brooklyn in a couple of weeks?" he repeated, his grin widening.

"Yeah," she said, forcing a smile onto her face. "Definitely."

~

Emma took her time walking back to her house. She was angry and embarrassed and annoyed and . . . God, she couldn't even pinpoint all the feelings rushing through her veins. But by the time she opened the front door, she was only tired. Tired of fighting and being mad and just . . . all of it. So impossibly tired that she barely made it up the steps to the second floor.

Her bedroom was dark, but she didn't bother with the lights. She just sat on her bed, staring out her window at the now dark sky.

Knightley's kitchen light turned on across the yard, snagging her attention. The break in the trees meant that she could see the scene playing out in the room: his broad shoulders by the island; the slight, tall frame of the woman by the windows. A heartbeat later, the woman opened the sliding glass door to the garden and wandered outside, her laughter suddenly audible. Emma rolled her eyes; he wasn't that funny. Of course, that never stopped his dates before. The same manufactured giggle as they not-so-subtly surveyed the house, the same flick of their hair as Knightley offered them a glass of wine.

How many nights had she sat here at her window and watched a similar scene play out? Enough that she knew exactly how it would go from here. They would talk for a few minutes, slowly getting closer until the woman found a reason to touch him—a hand on the chest, her head on his shoulder. Emma recalled how as a teenager, one with little experience with boys, she had watched Knightley and his dates from this same perch. It was like an intensive tutorial on what to expect from dating: the wine, the laughter, and then . . .

As if on cue, Knightley's hand went to the small of the woman's back as he guided her inside.

This was usually the time Emma would close the curtains and laugh to herself at how predictable he was, even as her cheeks flushed. But right now, she couldn't bring herself to look away as the sliding door closed behind them and the kitchen light went out again.

What happened when he brought his dates back inside? Did he call them a car and kiss them good night? Or did he bring them upstairs? Emma had never spied a woman in his bedroom before, but his house was huge. Plenty of rooms to choose from. The different guest rooms, the different beds . . .

She usually didn't let her imagination go there. But now she couldn't help it. How he touched them, how he peeled off their clothes . . .

She blinked. What was she doing? This was Knightley. *Knightley.* Her mind had no business delving into this new territory, especially with him. But then, everything with him felt unwieldy lately.

It was as annoying as it was scary.

Another light turned on across the yard and caught Emma's eye, halting her thoughts. This one was on the second floor; Knightley had turned on his desk lamp and he was now standing in the middle of his bedroom. Alone.

His crisp shirt was unbuttoned, revealing the hard plane of his stomach, and he had a drink in his hand. His jeans hung low on his hips, so impossibly low that, as he slowly walked across the room, she thought she caught a glimpse of the trail of dark hair that ran from his navel. She wanted to dart her eyes away, but then he placed his glass on the nightstand and began unbuttoning his jeans.

Oh my God.

She held her breath as he slid them down his legs, then picked up a hanger lying nearby and folded them neatly over it. *Who hangs up their jeans?* she thought. *Of course he does.*

He disappeared into his walk-in closet with them. When he reappeared, he was wearing a pair of sweatpants and no shirt at all. His broad chest was just . . . there, his tanned skin on full display. She knew she should look away, but she didn't. Instead, she let out her breath, relieved her light was off and he couldn't tell she was watching.

He picked up his glass and took a long sip as his gaze wandered to his window. He stared out at the darkness for a long moment, then his head fell forward as he ran his hand through his hair. Her eyes couldn't help but track his movements, the tension in his arms, the line of his stomach down—

She shook her head. No. This was wrong. She needed to slink down to the floor and crawl out of her room and never think about this moment ever again.

But before she could do anything, he turned and stalked out of the room.

She closed her eyes and exhaled. What was wrong with her?

She got up, shaking out her limbs and taking a deep breath. This was ridiculous. She was ridiculous. And it would never happen again. As if to seal the promise, she turned on her own desk lamp, illuminating her room.

Nothing to see here, she thought to herself as she turned back to Knightley's window.

And then her mouth went dry.

Knightley was back in his room, looking up at her window

and registering her for the first time. There was no doubt he saw her; their eyes locked.

Oh God.

She gave him a small wave, the same she had done years ago when saying good night. Then she smiled: an olive branch.

He took a sip of his drink as he stared back. A long moment passed before he moved, and when he did, it was only to reach over and shut off his desk lamp.

His room went black.

Emma's eyes narrowed at the darkness, the storm of feelings in her chest replaced quickly by righteous indignation.

Fine, she thought. He wanted to stay pissed? No problem. But he couldn't ignore her forever. After all, Sunday dinner was just a few days away.

He would never miss Sunday dinner.

CHAPTER 9

Knightley missed Sunday dinner.

For Mr. Woodhouse, there had been a phone call with apologies that something had come up, and for his part, Mr. Woodhouse seemed unbothered. He assured Knightley that he would be missed, but that he hoped the lady keeping him from them was worth it. From where Emma sat across from her father in the study, she heard Knightley's laugh on the other end of the phone. She had also heard how he didn't refute her father's assumptions. Only some more pleasantries before both men said goodbye.

For Emma, there had been nothing at all.

Of course, she didn't care. She didn't even think about it. Not while she sat around the house, waiting for Thursday and class with Nadine. And not when she stared out her bedroom window each night, making sure not to look across the yard to the house that sat just beyond it.

Nope, she was fine. Knightley barely occupied her thoughts at all.

Not until the following Sunday, anyway. But that was only because she spent most of the day convincing herself that he wouldn't show up for dinner that week either. Which was why that evening, as she poured herself a glass of Chardonnay at the kitchen island and listened to Mrs. Pawloski rave to Ben and Margo about their father's new juicer, she was so surprised to hear the French doors to the garden open and a familiar voice say, "Hello there."

The wine bottle was still midair as Emma looked up to see his entrance. Knightley didn't seem to notice her as he peeled his coat off his shoulders and laid it over the back of one of the chairs, nodding to her father at the other end of the table. He hugged Margo and Ben, and it was only after he laughed at something Mrs. Pawloski had said that his amber eyes looked up to meet her gaze.

And it was at that moment, as they stared at each other from across the kitchen, that she had to remind herself that she wasn't supposed to care about him at all.

"Emma, bring over that white for George, will you?" her father said, motioning her back to the table.

"Of course," she said, recovering quickly. After years of Sunday dinners, she knew that Knightley hated Chardonnay—he preferred Viognier—which is why she donned a smug smile as she brought the bottle over to the table.

Knightley was seated at the end, opposite her father and next to her. It was where he had always sat, ever since the Sunday night dinner tradition had begun before she could even form complete sentences. Tonight it felt so different though, like a layer of familiarity had been replaced by something stiff and awkward. She tried to ignore the sensation, but it was only made worse by his blank expression as she set the bottle down in front of him with a loud thud and took her own seat.

Knightley didn't say a word to her, and everyone else was too busy listening to Mr. Woodhouse list all the fruits he had discovered he could now juice, to notice anything amiss. But Emma knew. She could feel it.

She and Knightley had gone almost twenty-four years without an argument. Sure, they'd had disagreements, but an eye roll or a well-timed barb usually solved it. Nothing that lasted more than a few minutes. Nothing that ever made her feel like the foundation of their friendship had fundamentally altered. Not until now.

This is ridiculous, she mentally chastised herself. They should be able to weather one little argument. Nothing had to change, she would make sure of it. With new resolve, she forced a smile and turned to him.

"So," she said, her tone light. "Hot date last week?"

He dragged his gaze to her and raised a questioning brow.

"Last week when you missed dinner," she continued.

Again, he didn't answer. Instead, he reached for the wine bottle Emma had brought over and poured himself a glass.

She frowned and stabbed the tuna steak on her plate. Leave it to him to carry a grudge, to sit there and ignore her like—

"No Nadine this evening?" Knightley murmured, interrupting her thoughts.

"We don't spend every waking moment together, you know," she replied.

"Ah. That's good."

He moved to turn away from her and panic set in, as if her window of opportunity was closing.

"Are we okay?" she asked, biting her bottom lip.

He paused. "I'm sorry?"

"It's just . . ." She let out a long sigh, trying to organize her thoughts. "I hate feeling like we're fighting, when really it was just a stupid disagreement. One fight shouldn't be the end of the world, right?"

A small grin crept onto his lips. "Indeed."

"So . . . friends?"

"I'll always be your friend, Emma," he said so softly that only she could hear, and something in her stomach tumbled.

She ignored it and smiled brighter, taking a deep sip of her wine. "Good. Because no one was really at fault or anything."

"Is that so?"

"Yeah. At the end of the day, we both want what's best for Nadine, right?"

His expression grew tired, and he leaned back. "Okay, Woodhouse."

She nodded. "All that's left to do is find her a new guy to take her mind off the breakup. I already have her on all the apps, so now it's just a matter of helping her pick the right guy. Preferably someone who can show her the city, you know? And someone ridiculously hot because she's gorgeous."

"You have a checklist?"

Emma smiled. "Oh please, everyone should have a checklist."

"We can't always get everything we want."

"Why not?"

He chuckled to himself. "Because in the real world, no one is spoiled enough to think that way. Except maybe you."

It hurt, like a slap that's over quickly but still leaves a sharp sting behind.

"Right. Of course." Her smile faltered and she tried to cover it with a laugh, but the sound came out thin and fragile.

The humor in Knightley's expression fell away as he watched her reaction. Then he leaned toward her, his brows knitted together. "Emma—"

"Attention, attention!" Margo announced from a few seats down. She was standing up, a huge smile on her face as she held

Ben's hand. "We have some news. And since you're all the most important people in our lives, we wanted you to be the first to know. We're—"

"Pregnant!" Mrs. Pawloski screamed. "You're pregnant, aren't you?"

Margo's expression deflated. "Yes. Yes, we're pregnant."

Mrs. Pawloski jumped up with a squeal, and suddenly the entire table erupted in cheers and hugs and congratulations. Knightley left his seat to go give his brother a pat on the back, Mr. Woodhouse kissed Margo on the cheek, and Fran stood by the island, tears welling in her eyes.

Emma watched it all from her seat. She was smiling too, but it felt brittle. A fragile mask forced on as the scene unfurled before her; something she watched with joy, all while feeling very much alone.

~

The news of a baby was almost enough to distract Emma from the otherwise awful dinner. Things continued to look up when Zane texted two days later to reschedule their weekend plans in Brooklyn after an audience member fell off one of the suspended bridges at his friend's art show and almost drowned. The show closed immediately. Of course, this now meant that Emma needed to come up with a different activity for Saturday night to bring Zane and Nadine together—something that would also keep her mind off Knightley. So she made an executive decision: they were all going to a karaoke bar downtown.

"I'm so excited!" Nadine squealed as Emma held up another top—this one a light green, silk blouse—to Nadine's small frame.

The bed was littered with different outfit options for her friend, and Emma wanted to make sure they picked the perfect one. After all, tonight was about Nadine. How spoiled could she be, putting the needs of others in front of her own?

"I love this for you," Emma said.

Nadine turned to the mirror. "Not too much?"

"Definitely not. I bought it at Saks a few years ago with my friends Lulu and Haydie and haven't worn it in ages, so you should just keep it. It's made for you."

Emma paired it with a short brown suede skirt and her favorite gold Lanvin necklace, the one with the little lipstick pendant on the end, to pull the entire outfit together.

Nadine stared at her reflection, eyes wide and voice suddenly timid. "I've never done karaoke at a bar before . . . In front of people."

"No?" Emma asked, straightening her new pale pink Rixo minidress. It was covered with little red rosebuds that she just adored. "Well, you're going to love this place. I used to go all the time when I was younger since they never carded."

"Are you a good singer?"

"Pretty good," Emma said as she lightly dabbed on some lipgloss. "It's all about confidence, Nadine. Commit to your song. Own it. You *are* a rock star."

Nadine laughed. "No pressure."

"You'll be great." Emma linked her arm with Nadine's as they started downstairs. "Zane's going to be even more obsessed with you after tonight."

Nadine's steps faltered. "You think he's obsessed with me?"

"Oh, definitely. The more time you spend with someone, the more you start to read the signs," Emma said as they reached the foyer. "He's meeting us down there at ten, so if we leave now, we should be a casual twenty minutes late."

"God, Marty used to hate it when I was late."

Emma let the sentence sit between them for a moment as she slipped on her silver Stella McCartney cropped bomber jacket.

"He called me the other day, you know," Nadine continued.

"Oh?" Emma replied, trying to sound nonchalant.

"Yeah. I was at work ringing someone up, so I asked Mateo to grab it. But when Marty heard a guy pick up my phone, he got pissed and hung up."

Emma whipped around. "He hung up?"

"Yeah. I tried calling him back a bunch of times, but he never answered." Nadine shrugged, her eyes looking dangerously glassy. "Mateo was really sweet about it. He bought me a cupcake from around the corner and told me I was too good for him anyway, but . . . I don't know . . ."

"Mateo is absolutely right. And that's what we're going out to celebrate," Emma said, grabbing her friend's hand and heading toward the door. "New freedom and new opportunities and the entire catalog of nineties pop music!"

∼

Their cab arrived at the nondescript hole-in-the-wall location right at Emma's calculated time. It was on a dark street on the Lower East Side, and barely drew any attention until the doors opened and the slurred lyrics of "Oops! I Did It Again" wafted out. Inside, people were packed tight, illuminated by the red Christmas lights on every surface. Everyone's attention was on the low stage in the back, where a group of women, clearly part of a bachelorette party, did their best Britney impressions.

Emma and Nadine maneuvered their way through the crowd to where Zane was already at the bar halfway through his drink. He looked like he had just come from work, or maybe that's just how he always dressed. Today it was a threadbare Joy Division T-shirt and a pair of well-worn jeans.

"Aren't you both adorable," he purred, greeting them with hugs. "What do you want to drink?"

"Gin and tonics?" Emma suggested. Nadine nodded.

Zane ordered and the drinks appeared a moment later, followed by three shots.

Zane smiled at Emma's confused expression. "Kamikazes. See, karaoke is usually where you end the night, not start it, so we've got some catching up to do."

Emma was not a shot person. She usually pulled the throw-it-over-your-shoulder trick when forced to participate, but he was right. Karaoke required some liquid courage.

"If you insist," Emma said, forcing a smile as she grabbed her shot and tossed it back. Nadine promptly followed, wrinkling her nose.

A table opened up near the stage and they grabbed it, along with a song book. Zane began looking through the long list as a man dressed in a cowboy hat and chaps sang Garth Brooks.

"*I've got friends in low places!*" he crooned, dancing to the beat.

"This is Marty's favorite song!" Nadine exclaimed, clapping along and swaying to the beat.

Oh no.

"You and Zane should do a duet!" Emma blurted out, grabbing the song book from Zane and fanning through it. "I'll go first while you both decide."

She jotted down the number next to her song pick and gave it to the very bored-looking DJ running the karaoke machine. He took it and nodded without bothering to look up from his phone.

Emma made her way back to the table, smiling to herself at how Zane and Nadine leaned in together over the song list.

"Any decision yet?" Emma asked, taking her seat again.

"Okay, okay. We've got it." Nadine giggled, looking at Zane. He winked and then got up and walked over to drop off their choice to the DJ.

When he was out of earshot, Emma turned to her friend. "Oh my God, he's so into you!"

"I know! I mean, I think I know? Ugh, he's so hot!"

"Do you think—" Emma cut herself off when she saw Zane coming back to the table. She smiled at Nadine as he took the seat next to her.

"So, what did you two choose?" she asked.

"Oh, it's a surprise," Zane said, shooting Emma a lazy grin.

Garth Brooks ended and the next song appeared on the television screen above the stage: "Pour Some Sugar on Me" by Def Leppard. And below it, the performer: Emma W.

Emma downed the last of her drink and hopped up to the stage, grabbing the mic as the lyrics appeared before her.

"*Step inside! Walk this way!*" she sang, her voice echoing through the speakers around the bar. Nadine was out of her seat, jumping up and down and cheering her on. Zane was still seated beside her, watching Emma with a smirk on his face. Then he reached over and put his arm over the back of Nadine's chair.

Yes!

Emma smiled to herself, closing her eyes and losing herself in the timeless words of Def Leppard until the final note rang out and a few patrons clapped. She gave a bow before stepping down from the stage and returning to their table.

"That was amazing!" Nadine exclaimed.

"It was . . . something," Zane concurred, then he leaned over and put his hand on Emma's knee. "I'm going to get us some more drinks. You in?"

Emma smiled as she politely moved her knee away from his hand. "Sure."

As he disappeared into the crowd lining the bar, Nadine squealed.

"Oh my God, Emma!" she breathed. "He had his hands all over me while you were singing!"

Emma blinked. She hadn't seen that. "Really?"

"Yes, he put his arm over the back of my chair, and when I sat down he did this back rub thing!"

Emma beamed.

It was *happening*.

Zane returned to the table with more drinks just as the TV screen changed to the next song: "Don't Go Breaking My Heart" by Elton John and Kiki Dee with performers Zane/Nadine.

"It's your song! You're up!" Emma exclaimed, pushing Nadine out of her seat. She shot Emma a nervous look as she and Zane walked up onto the stage, situating themselves side by side in front of the mic as the song started to play.

For a moment, as Zane sang off-key and Nadine mouthed the words, Emma doubted whether karaoke was the best choice tonight. But eventually they got the rhythm down, relaxing and smiling at each other as the song went on. Soon the entire bar was cheering and singing along, erupting in applause when they were done. Zane took a bow, while Nadine jumped down and hugged Emma.

"I can't believe I just did that!"

Zane smiled. "You were awesome."

"The perfect team." Emma beamed, not even trying to hide her smug grin.

There were more drinks and more songs, and Emma didn't even know what time it was when Zane finally suggested they call it a night. It didn't matter anyway. Her body was loose and her mind was riding the high of yet another successful match. She finished her drink—*what was this again? rum?*—before heading outside into the cold.

"Zane, why don't you share a cab with Nadine?" Emma suggested as they made their way to the corner.

"I'm heading uptown, actually. You and I should share a cab," he said, stepping into the street and lifting up his hand to hail the next taxi.

"But Nadine is so close!"

"Oh, I'm just going to walk," Nadine replied, barely suppressing a yawn. "The dorm is only a few blocks away."

"Wait, Zane, why don't you walk with Nadine?" Emma insisted. "Make sure she gets home okay?"

A cab pulled up just as Zane turned to look at Nadine over his shoulder. "I'm sure she'll be fine. Right, Nadine?"

Nadine nodded, oblivious. "Totally fine. You guys take the cab!"

Emma couldn't think fast enough. What was happening? Why was Zane blowing this opportunity?

"We could drop you off? It's cold," Emma blurted out.

Zane sighed. "Emma, the cab isn't going that way, plus that's a lot of stops. There's other cabs if she wants to take one."

"He's right," Nadine added with a drunken smile. She didn't seem to understand what she was giving up here, either. "And this is nothing compared to the cold back in Ohio. I like it."

Zane opened the taxi door and looked at Emma expectantly. "You see, she'll be fine. Come on."

Emma looked at Nadine. Didn't she want Zane to walk her home? Why was Emma the only one who was following the script here? After a few more awkward seconds, she finally gave up, giving her friend a quick hug before turning to the cab.

Nadine waved goodbye as they pulled away and turned down 6th Street toward FDR Drive.

"That was fun," Zane said, spreading his legs out across the seat so his knee grazed hers.

"Yeah," Emma said, trying not to sound annoyed. "I thought you would have wanted to walk Nadine home, though."

He shrugged. "She said she was fine."

Emma nodded and looked out the window across the East River. The cab went over a pothole, causing them to jolt forward and back again. Suddenly, Zane seemed to be right next to her. She tried to subtly move closer to the window, but he filled the gap.

"Emma . . ." he started.

"Yes?" she asked, leaning away from his body so much that she was almost flush with the car door.

"I was wondering something."

She waited. He only stared, as if expecting her to read his mind.

"What were you wondering?" she finally asked.

His hand moved to her thigh as he leaned forward, his lips getting dangerously close to . . .

Oh my God. He was trying to kiss her.

"Zane!" she said, putting her hand against his shoulder and forcing him away. "What are you doing?"

He smiled. "We should do this. See what happens."

"We?" she said incredulously.

"Yeah. You and me." He leaned in again, as if that cleared everything up.

"You don't mean you and me," Emma said, pushing him back harder.

His eyebrows pinched together. "What?"

"You're drunk," Emma stated, trying to compose herself. "You don't know what you're saying."

"So, what, you were all hot for me and now you're not?"

"I'm sorry?" She couldn't believe this. "What about Nadine?"

"Nadine?" he asked, looking genuinely confused. "She's cute and all, and I'd definitely hit that, but she's not here. If she was, we could all party."

Emma's eyes went wide. "What the hell are you even talking about?"

Zane lurched forward with puckered lips just as Emma turned her head, causing his mouth to land clumsily on her ear. She tried to push him away again, but he grabbed her arm and pulled her toward him instead.

"Get off me!" she screamed. "I am NOT interested."

"What the fuck is your problem?" he snapped back.

Emma couldn't believe this. She used all her might to shove him away from her. He fell forward just as the cab turned sharply into the next lane, sending his head into the Plexiglas console between the driver and the back seat.

"Fuck!" he yelled, cradling the side of his head. "Shit!"

"Serves you right! You're supposed to like Nadine!"

He scoffed. "Fuck Nadine. You and I have a thing. You can't deny it. Why are you suddenly being all ice bitch about it?" He grabbed her again and pulled her toward him.

"You're an asshole!" She couldn't fight the fury building in her. She freed her arm and reared back, sending her fist right into his face. She had never punched anyone before, but apparently she was very good at it. He flew backward, hitting the opposite side of the car.

"WHAT THE FUCK!" he cried, holding a hand over his right eye.

"Pull over!" Emma yelled at the cab driver.

The cab swerved to the side of the road.

"Get out!" she spat at Zane.

"What?"

"Get out of this cab right now!"

"We're in the middle of the fucking FDR!"

"Out!" she screamed, shaking with anger. Her fist was poised in the space between them, ready to punch him again.

He threw open the cab door and stepped out.

"You spoiled little bitch!" he snarled, and then slammed the door shut.

"GO!" she yelled at the cab driver, who did not miss a beat, accelerating and driving off uptown.

Her heart tripped against her rib cage as a wave of nausea came over her. She closed her eyes and forced herself to stay calm. "Thank you," she said to the cab driver.

He only nodded back.

She stared out the window, willing her hands to stop shaking in her lap as her shock quickly turned into an all-consuming rage.

How could she have misjudged the situation so badly?

She had never given Zane any encouragement. And even if she mistakenly had, his actions were unacceptable! Couldn't you be kind to someone without them thinking it meant more than that?

"Can't you?!" she shrieked.

The cab driver looked back at her in the rearview mirror.

Emma ignored him, squeezed her eyes closed. Poor Nadine! She was going to be devastated. And Emma was going to have to be the one to tell her.

When she finally opened her eyes again, she found the cab driver turned around and staring at her. She blinked, only then realizing they had stopped outside her house. With an apologetic smile, she swiped her credit card and got out, walking slowly up the steps to her front door. The cab drove away, and she paused to watch it disappear down the street.

She took a deep, cleansing breath, letting the cold air fill her lungs. Fuck Zane. She was Emma Woodhouse. No one treated her like that, and both she and Nadine deserved better. As awful as the night had turned out to be, it was better that she learned who he was now rather than later.

It was another moment before she pulled the keys from her bag and unlocked the front door. The house was dark and quiet as she dropped her coat in the foyer and headed downstairs to the kitchen, where she pulled a sparkling water from the refrigerator. She sat down at the island, staring at the French doors while she drank it.

She was fine. It was all going to be fine. Still, her body didn't feel ready to accept it; her pulse still raced, the adrenaline had yet to ebb.

She wasn't ready to go to bed just yet.

CHAPTER 10

Knightley woke to the sound of glasses clanging, the shuffling of feet, and the opening of drawers downstairs. The sounds were swimming in his head before he was even aware of them, working into a dream until something in his brain clicked and his eyes shot open.

He listened for a moment until he heard the unmistakable sound of one of his kitchen barstools skidding over the concrete floor, as if someone had walked into it. "Goddamn it!" a familiar voice cursed softly.

Emma had used her key again.

He threw his covers off and grabbed a T-shirt before starting down the stairs, pulling the white fabric over his head just as he entered the kitchen. The freezer door of the refrigerator was open, its light the only source of illumination in the darkened room.

"Hello," he murmured, his voice gravelly with sleep.

Her head popped out just enough that she could meet his eyes from behind the freezer door. "Did I wake you up?"

He was about to say something sarcastic, like how hearing someone rummaging through his house in the middle of the night might do that, but the words tasted sour on his tongue, and he swallowed them back. Because the truth was, he was glad she was there.

They hadn't seen much of each other this week, not since that awful Sunday dinner. He had tried to move on—spending too much time at the office, adding extra miles onto his runs—but his mind kept returning to what he had said, to her reaction, and to the residual guilt that still plagued him. It was new, something he wasn't used to feeling, especially not with her. So tonight he had a whiskey. And then another. And then forced himself to bed.

He had expected the guilt to return when he awoke, just as it had done every day this week, but as he stood there, staring at her wide eyes, he realized it was gone.

"It's not your fault." He ran a hand down his face. "Sound carries in here since the renovation."

"I hear taking out a bunch of walls will do that," she said.

He smiled as she disappeared back behind the freezer door. "What are you doing?"

"Looking for ice cream."

"Why are you looking for ice cream?"

A moment later she reappeared, a pint of chocolate in her hand and an eyebrow cocked high up her forehead. "Is that a trick question?"

She closed the freezer and made her way around the island, opening the cutlery drawer.

"Last time I checked, your kitchen had food," he said, leaning back against the opposite counter and crossing his arms over his chest.

"You think Dad lets us keep ice cream in the house? Have you seen the refined sugar content?"

She turned around with a spoon in hand and a triumphant smile on her face. Her cheeks were slightly flushed, and he guessed from her outfit that she was just getting home from a night out. Probably a little drunk, too. Usually he would call her out on it. Instead, he turned toward the refrigerator.

"Don't you want some?" she asked as he opened the stainless steel door.

He didn't answer, just grabbed a beer from the shelf.

She rolled her eyes and walked across the room to the long sofa facing the kitchen and slumped into it. Her short dress rode up as she tucked her legs underneath her body and took the lid off the top of the chocolate pint. He sat down on a stool at the island across from her, twisting the cap off his bottle. For a moment, it was silent.

She was one of the few people who he could do that with: sit together in silence without needing to fill the space with small talk. But right now it felt like there was a weight there, a thousand things he wanted to say, even more than he knew he should. Instead he took a sip of his beer.

It was another minute before she spoke. "You were right, you know."

Her voice was barely louder than a whisper, and when he looked up to see if he heard her correctly, he found she was still focused on her spoon, the ice cream on it untouched.

"About that barista," she continued, finally meeting his gaze. She smiled, but it was like the smile from dinner: so forced and fragile that he half expected it to dissolve.

"What happened?"

"It's nothing."

"Then tell me."

A sigh. "I went out with Nadine tonight and we met up with him. I was so sure he was into her, and for a while it seemed like I was right . . ." Her voice trailed off, her eyes darting back to her spoon.

"And?"

"And I wasn't."

His grip on the neck of his beer tightened. "Tell me what happened."

"It's fine, I swear," she said with another smile, this one a touch more sincere. "He just . . . called me a bitch after he . . . well, he tried to force himself on me . . . in the cab."

"He did *what*?" Knightley's anger made the question sound sharp and biting.

"Oh my God, don't go all big brother on me, please. I took care of it."

"You took care of it?"

She shrugged. "I punched him in the face and kicked him out of the cab."

He blinked. "Seriously?"

"Yeah." She raised an eyebrow at him. "Why are you looking at me like that?"

"I'm just . . . impressed." He let out a breath, his adrenaline subsiding a bit, but not completely. "Are you okay?"

She sighed dramatically. "Yes, I'm okay. I promise. It's just . . ."

"What?"

"My hand still really hurts."

He barked out a laugh and it forced her to do the same even as she chided him. "It's not funny!"

"I beg to differ," he replied, still smiling as the tension in his body released and he took a sip of beer.

"He's wandering down the FDR somewhere right now! I feel awful."

His humor dimmed at that, watching her expression change, the mix of humor and guilt and sadness playing under the seams of her smile. "You shouldn't."

"I probably gave him a black eye!"

"And he deserved it," Knightley said, leaning forward so his elbows rested on his knees. "Don't put this in some moral gray area. No one deserves to be treated like that. Least of all you."

"Oh really?"

"Really."

She seemed to consider, taking a bite of the ice cream before glancing back up at him. "When I kicked him out of the cab he called me spoiled. Did I deserve that?"

Fuck. He knew his words at dinner had bothered her. But her stare now wasn't critical; her green eyes were locked on his and there was a small smile still on her lips. She was giving him a chance, an out.

"When I said you were spoiled . . . that doesn't mean . . ." He stopped himself and ran a hand down his face. "I didn't mean that, Emma."

She laughed. "Yes you did."

"But I shouldn't have said it. It's not something you should feel bad about."

"It's fine."

"It's not," he said. "Especially when some asshole uses it against you."

She sighed, letting her head fall back against the sofa pillows. "I just don't understand why this is so complicated."

"What?"

"Men. Relationships. All of it."

"It isn't."

Another laugh as she lifted her head to throw him a patronizing glare. "That's easy for you to say."

He was about to take a sip of beer but paused with the bottle poised at his lips. "What is that supposed to mean?"

She rolled her eyes. "It's not complicated the way *you* do it."

"What way is that?"

"Without strings," she said. A smile was still teasing her lips.

This suddenly felt like dangerous territory, but he didn't want to stop. He didn't even know if he could. "And how would you know that?"

She maintained his gaze, even as her smile slowly faded. It was like she felt it too, the pull of this unexplored territory. The creeping feeling they wouldn't ever be able to turn back.

"You never introduce us to anyone, but I see you sometimes," she said, and swallowed. "When you bring them home."

A jolt of adrenaline shot through his body, though he kept still, his eyes steady. He had always been careful with the women he saw, as if keeping them relegated to his side of the yard shielded her somehow. He had told himself it was because she was young, she wouldn't understand, but now, with her green eyes locked with his, it felt so much heavier than that.

"What have you seen?" he asked.

She shrugged a little, her eyes falling to the ice cream to avoid his stare. "In the summer you open the doors out to the garden. And you bring them out there with a bottle of wine. It's usually late, so I always assume it's where you're ending your night. There's conversation, maybe some laughter . . ." She let her voice trail off as her cheeks flushed. "I can't ever see much through the trees, but sometimes I hear things. Laughing. Whispers. That's about the time you go inside and turn the lights off."

Jesus. He had no idea.

Her eyes were on him again then. "In the winter you still open the wine, but you both sit here." She ran her hand along the cushion of the sofa, as if she somehow knew about the women he had bent over its arm. "I can't see or hear as well, but the script seems to be the same. Wine, laughter. And then . . . lights out."

"Is that all?" he asked. His voice was so deep, barely above a whisper.

"Yeah." Her tongue darted out to wet her lips. He ignored his reaction to it, the warmth that spread deep in his chest.

He didn't move. He'd never felt guilty about his love life before, the various women he saw once or twice and never again. It was what suited him. It kept him from getting too attached, and he comforted himself with the fact that he was clear about what he wanted before anyone set foot in his home. The perfect arrangement.

But now guilt crashed into him like a wave, dragging him down even as he stared at her.

"Do you sleep with them?" she asked. From anyone else the question would have been intrusive, but the matter-of-fact way she asked it felt strangely intimate, sending a jolt through his veins.

"Sometimes."

"And are they still here in the morning?"

He shook his head. "No."

Her head cocked to the side. "And do they all know that ahead of time?"

A nod.

"See," she murmured, a lazy smile returning to her mouth. "Not complicated."

His eyebrows knitted together. He didn't like how that sounded like an accusation. "It's not complicated if you're open about what you want."

She sat up a bit straighter, leaning over her ice cream with genuine interest. "So tonight, then, after Zane told me he didn't want anything serious and he just wanted to fuck me—that was fine because he was open about what he wanted?"

"No . . . Jesus." Knightley ran a hand through his hair. "Being open about what you want also means you listen to what the other person wants too."

"And what if you don't want the same things?"

"Then you both know that before anybody gets hurt."

She scoffed, digging her spoon into the ice cream. "That's impossible."

"How so?"

"Because that's not a relationship."

"That's why it works for me."

"Okay, that works for you, and maybe the women you sleep with, but I don't know if that would work for me."

"Did you change your mind about being single? Do you want a relationship now?"

A lock of hair had come loose from her ponytail and fallen across her face, dancing along her cheek as she considered. He had to stop himself from walking to her and brushing it away.

She finally sighed. "I don't know."

"Then what do you want?"

She thought for another moment and then offered a small shrug. "To be there in the morning."

He blinked, the words like a blow against his chest. He leaned back, taking a long sip of his beer before answering. "Then it won't be complicated."

"How can you know that?"

"Because the person you decide to be with will know what he wants too."

"And what will he want?"

"You. All of you."

She swallowed, her lips parted slightly as she stared at him. "What does that mean?"

"He'll want all of it. To take you home and sleep with you,

yes. But make love to you, too. Wake up next to you. Go out for brunch. Argue over what color to paint the bathroom and who should load the dishwasher. You'll know what he wants because he'll tell you. And he'll know what you want because you'll tell him that's what you expect."

He could see her pulse point in her neck, thundering as the rest of her body stayed stone-still.

"So," she said, nodding once. "Not complicated."

His gaze fell to her mouth, her bottom lip now trapped between her teeth, and it occurred to him that right now it would taste like chocolate ice cream. He wanted to kiss it. The thought was like a lead weight falling in his chest. He should have hated how it turned him on, but he didn't; all he could think about was kissing her. Fuck the conversation, fuck whatever this dance was that they found themselves in lately, he just wanted . . . her.

And that's when it hit him. He wanted Emma.

The realization was so startling that all he could do was sit there and take another sip from his beer. The bottle was empty.

"It's late," he finally said. "You should head home."

She blinked. "Right. Yeah."

She stood, abandoning the ice cream on the countertop as she made her way to the sliding glass door. She stopped there and turned back to him, waiting for him to escort her home as he usually did. But if he stood up, she'd see the full evidence of his thoughts. So he stayed seated and only nodded goodbye.

There was disappointment on her face, but it stayed only a moment before she forced another smile and walked out the door. He watched as she made her way across the yard, disappearing between the trees. And he kept watching for a few minutes after that.

CHAPTER 11

By the time Monday arrived, Knightley had come to an executive decision: he was over it. He wasn't even sure what "it" was, only that it had taken up residency in his brain, occupying a corner of every thought, every moment. It whispered the wrong things at the wrong times and flooded his mind with images that should decidedly not be there, so much so that he had made an excuse to miss Sunday dinner again last night, just to ensure that no one saw his face, in case they could read his thoughts.

But he was over it now. The decision was made in the car ride down to his office, and by the time he sat down at his desk it was settled. Emma Woodhouse would stay firmly planted in her position as a friend, and that was that.

He threw himself into work then, already powering through the files on his desk before his computer had time to wake up. When Kate arrived at nine, he was pacing his office, asking to go over the day. Will and his team from Hampshire M&A would be here to meet about the Wentworth Hydroponics acquisition at eleven, and he wanted to go over any outstanding issues, review every printout. When she left with a list of things to do, he made phone calls and set up meetings for later in the week . . . but he could still feel it. That energy, that tightness in his muscles like if he stood still for too long it would burst forth and this decision would fall to pieces at his feet. So he kept moving.

"You look like shit," Will said when he walked into the conference room at eleven, taking a seat at the other side of the table. Per usual, his gray suit was impeccable, his dark blond hair was brushed back. Even his signature frown was in place.

"Good to see you too, Will," Knightley replied wryly, leaning back in his chair and unbuttoning his jacket. Will's comment wasn't an insult; Will didn't insult people. He was just brutally honest.

The rest of Will's team filed in, with his partner Charlie bringing up the rear. His usual smile was in place as he came around to shake Knightley's hand before taking the chair beside Will.

Charlie's excitement was palpable from across the table. Despite working in mergers and acquisitions, Charlie was still a science geek at heart. And while Will saw the long-term potential in Wentworth's business structure and revenue model, Charlie reveled in the chance to spend the next hour talking electrical conductivity and hydroponic fertilizer.

The rest of Knightley's team arrived and introductions were made before the lights were dimmed and Charlie began a Power-Point presentation outlining the prospective acquisition of Wentworth Hydroponics by Blaxton Agriculture.

Wentworth had been one of Knightley's first investments, back when the hydroponics start-up was just a recent college dropout who was growing microgreens in his parents' basement and selling them to Ben's restaurant. Now they had over three hundred people on staff, offices in New York and Los Angeles, and a prospective acquisition by the third largest agricultural company in the country.

Knightley should have been ecstatic. He should have at least been listening. But as they flipped to the next slide and Charlie began to review Wentworth's technical advancements, his eyes glazed over and his brain flooded with Emma's breathless voice.

Do you sleep with them?

The question pulsed in his brain, as if she were sitting there next to him, whispering it in his ear.

Jesus. He pretended to find something interesting on the papers in front of him as her words bounced around his brain, hitting the corners and returning at a new angle. Had he imagined her reaction: the flush of her cheeks, her wide eyes? Did he need it to justify his own?

And just like that, the energy was back like a live current, causing him to tap his foot and count the minutes until the meeting finally, blessedly, ended.

He was on his feet before Charlie had time to ask if there were any questions and out of the room before Will could ask if they were still on for lunch.

Back at his office he locked the door and collapsed into his chair, spinning to face the wall of windows behind his desk. The city was there laid out in front of him, the sun glistening off steel and glass. But he only stared straight ahead, not noticing any of it.

He was fucked.

~

Ford's Cafe was around the corner from his office so it only took him a few minutes to get there, but Will had still beaten him, taking up residence at the back booth, away from the sprawling front windows that faced Union Square Park. His attention was on the phone in his hand.

"You all right?" Will asked as Knightley sat down across from him.

Knightley forced a smile. "I'm fine."

"You sure? You had that same look during Charlie's presentation earlier."

"Shit, I'm sorry," he murmured, his head falling to his chest.

Will waved him off. "He was talking about the mineral composition required for lettuce plants. He was so happy, we could have all left the room to get coffee and he wouldn't have noticed."

Knightley laughed. He had been friends with Will and Charlie since Columbia, back when all three men barely knew how to do their own laundry, let alone what to do with the rest of their lives. But as much as Will and Charlie differed, they were as close as brothers. It was why Hampshire M&A was one of the most successful mergers and acquisitions firms in the city.

"I read the proposal he sent beforehand," Knightley replied. "It's a solid deal."

Will glared at him. "Of course it is. Otherwise we wouldn't have brought it to you."

"Then why are you looking at me like that?"

Will nodded to the table. "Because I ordered you that beer before you got here and you still haven't touched it."

Knightley smiled warily, bringing the pint glass to his lips and taking a long sip. "Thank you."

"You're welcome. Now, what's on your mind?"

"It's nothing, I'm just distracted," Knightley said, glancing down at his menu without bothering to read it. They went to Ford's enough that he had it memorized.

"Is it the LA office?"

"No, unfortunately. I haven't had to go out there for months. It's running like a well-oiled machine. Although if this deal goes through, I'll probably have to be out there more."

Will frowned. "Why?"

"Because Blaxton Agriculture is based in LA."

"And?"

"And we need someone in LA full-time for at least the first six months to oversee the transition."

"Which is why you have staff out there. Well-oiled machine, remember? You have to learn to let go," Will said, then arched an eyebrow at him. "Unless you want to go out there."

Knightley scoffed. "God, no. I hate LA."

"Then why the hell were you out there so much over the last couple of years?" Will asked, his attention already back on the menu.

Knightley paused, suddenly aware he didn't have an easy answer. "I was renovating the house," he answered lamely.

"I thought you did that because you were already going to be in LA."

It was true. Why the hell *had* he spent so much time at the LA office? Yes, it had been important to the business, but he had missed so much, too. Ben and Margo had started dating; he had known that marriage was inevitable. And then there was Emma. The girl who had been his shadow for so many years was gone, replaced by a woman who he was still getting to know.

"I just needed to get away," Knightley finally murmured.

"From what?"

He let out a long breath, letting his eyes wander to the windows and the park beyond. There had been a huge iron sculpture there just a few days ago, all hard angles and oppressive lines, but it was gone now; workers were putting up a tall Christmas tree along with stalls where holiday shoppers would be buying their hot chocolate and gifts in just a few weeks.

"I don't know." Images of Ben and Margo and Emma flashed in his mind again. "A lot of things were changing here," he finally said. "I guess I needed something that I could control."

Will stared at him for a long moment, his eyes narrowed. "Is this about a woman?"

Jesus.

Knightley shook his head. "Will—"

"If you're in a relationship, congratulations. But if you go out to LA for this deal, it's got to be for this deal. Any other reason will be a distraction."

"And I'm not in a relationship. So don't worry about it."

"Good," Will said, motioning across the room to their waiter. "Now let's order some food."

~

Knightley returned to the office after lunch but only stayed another hour before closing his laptop and directing Kate to send all calls to his cell. He felt restless.

So he walked. He went up Fifth Avenue, past the apartment buildings and the churches and the bus stops. Through Rockefeller Center, under the spires of St. Patrick's Cathedral, to the corner of Central Park, where bare trees lined the avenue that looked like it would go north forever.

He hadn't walked home from the office in ages. It was only a couple of miles, yet there was always an excuse. It was too late or too early, too hot or too cold. But right now, with a slight chill in the air and his wool coat wrapped tight around his body, it was fucking perfect. The sharp wind around the buildings cooled his skin and stung his lungs, and suddenly he wasn't thinking about Emma at all, just the momentum forward.

He began to meander down random streets until he stopped

at a red light at the corner of 83rd and Madison. His block was ahead, his house just a minute or so further down the street. But instead he looked right, toward the row of shops and restaurants nearby, and the tension in his muscles slowly returned.

The light turned green, but Knightley didn't move. Then he turned and headed toward Lexington Avenue.

There was normally a line out the door at Vicarage Coffee, but that was also usually in the morning, when everyone was looking for that final caffeine fix before heading to work. Now it was late afternoon, and the small cafe was empty except for the guy behind the counter.

He was wearing his usual stained apron over a faded Nirvana T-shirt. Even if Knightley didn't know Zane from his regular visits with Emma, the guy's eye gave him away: it was black and blue and almost completely swollen shut.

"Hey man, what can I get you?" he asked as Knightley approached the counter.

He didn't recognize him. Good.

Knightley gave him a tight smile. "A coffee."

"You sure? I make a mean latte." His voice sounded so casual, so relaxed, as if they were friends.

Knightley's fingers curled into a fist at his side as he said, "Just the coffee."

The man shrugged as if he doubted Knightley's choice, but he still turned and poured the contents of a nearby carafe into a to-go cup.

"What happened?" Knightley said, motioning to Zane's black eye when he turned back around.

Zane laughed, a lackadaisical sound that was so fucking irritating that Knightley pretended to dig for his wallet to keep from looking at his face.

"Man, you don't even know. Let me just offer you some advice: don't stick your dick in crazy."

The rest of the room seemed to fall away as the sound of Knightley's pulse rushed into his ears. It took a lot to get him angry, but right now he was almost blinded by it.

"Or, like . . ." Zane contemplated, completely oblivious as he handed the coffee to Knightley. "Don't *try* to stick your dick in crazy."

"Sounds like words to live by," Knightley coolly replied.

Zane let out a long breath and rested his elbows on the counter. "You know how it is. These girls beg for it and beg for it and then when you're like, 'Okay, let's fucking do this thing,' they turn all frigid."

Knightley forced another smile; it felt sharp across his face. "Really?"

"Especially these rich bitches up here," Zane said, motioning to the neighborhood around them. "Think they're better than you and do everything to make sure you know it."

"Is that so?"

Zane nodded sagely, as if they had formed some sacred bond in the last two minutes. "Girls like that, they're not worth it, man. Trust me, I know what I'm talking about."

Knightley cocked his chin toward Zane's black eye. "They're bound to bash your face in, right?"

The barista laughed. "Right? Exactly."

"And then a girl like that might tell her friend what happened. And her friend, well, he might get pissed off. Really pissed off. Maybe even more pissed off than the girl who gave you the black eye to begin with."

Zane stared at him, his smug smile slowly dissolving into a thin line across his face.

Knightley casually poured a packet of sugar in his coffee and stirred it slowly. "You have to watch out for a friend like that. Because that friend, he could make your life a living hell. He could get you fired. Make sure you can't find another job anywhere, in fact. Call every coffee shop and restaurant in the city. And then..."

Knightley put the lid back on his cup and took a slow sip. Zane watched, his face ashen and his one good eye wide.

"And then," Knightley repeated, "a friend like that could fuck you up even worse."

Zane finally blinked, leaning back a bit. "I don't know what she said, man, but—"

"Hey, I'm just offering you some advice," Knightley said, pulling a couple of dollars from his pocket and throwing them on the counter. "Trust me, I know what I'm talking about."

Then he turned and left without another word.

Outside it was already a bit darker, the air a bit cooler. Knightley took a deep breath, releasing the tension from his muscles as he started walking back toward home.

He felt better already.

CHAPTER 12

Every year it seemed like Christmas arrived in New York just a little bit earlier, and this year was no exception. By Thanksgiving there were already elaborate decorations popping up on every corner, a seasonal soundtrack playing on repeat at Bergdorf's, and incessant calls to Emma from Margo about ideas for the Woodhouses' annual Christmas party. She also ended each conversation with more hints that Montgomery Knox might even be in attendance. Despite Knightley's skepticism—he referred to him as "the ghost of Christmas past"—her sister assured her that the elusive restaurateur would be in the city very soon to help firm up plans with Ben. Emma didn't hold her breath.

Besides, she had much bigger things to worry about. Namely the fact that it had been exactly ten days since the Zane incident, and she had yet to tell Nadine.

At first the issue had simply been timing. Obviously, this wasn't news that you broke to someone over the phone. It was delicate; Emma had to tell her in person. But the week after karaoke was Thanksgiving, and while she and the rest of 83rd

Street celebrated around the Woodhouse dining table, Nadine flew home to Ohio. So, of course, Emma had to wait until she arrived back in New York. Unfortunately, Nadine was almost immediately busy with school and work and helping Mateo with some sort of hair competition, so by the time their shared class arrived on Thursday, Emma still hadn't had an opportunity to tell her the truth.

Emma spent the long walk from Bloomingdale's in Soho to campus rehearsing every possible explanation in her mind.

I'm so sorry to have to tell you this, Nadine, but Zane's a sex fiend.
Remember that guy Zane? Let's just never talk about him again.
Zane tried to take advantage of me, and I feel awful about it.

By the time she walked into the classroom, she had a script memorized. But then she saw Nadine already sitting in the center of the room, waving her over to the seat she had saved, and her mind went completely blank.

"God, I feel like I haven't seen you in ages!" Nadine embraced her in a warm hug, then released her enough to look down at her feet. "Oh, I love those shoes! Are they new?"

Emma blinked, looking down at her Fendi boots. "No. They're last season."

Nadine nodded. "Mateo was trying to convince me to go to a sample sale in Soho this weekend, but—"

Professor Goddard cleared his throat, shooting a hard glare in their direction as he approached the lectern. Emma offered Nadine an apologetic smile and wrote on the top of her notebook: *Chat after class?*

Nadine took her pencil and wrote just below it: *Yes!*

Emma sank deeper into her chair, not feeling like paying attention as Professor Goddard went through different slides, alternating between long monotone descriptions of each photograph and student questions. Normally, Emma had her hand raised to participate, but today she just stared at the clock until class finally ended and everyone began filing out.

Nadine stood too, already talking as she shoved her laptop into her bag. "I haven't even told you about Thanksgiving yet! It was so weird. I mean, it was the first Thanksgiving I haven't spent with Marty since ninth grade! And then Nana decided to announce that she never liked him anyway, and . . ." Her voice faded when she looked down and found that Emma hadn't moved from her seat. "Are you okay?"

"I'm fine, I just . . . I need to talk to you," Emma replied, her attention on her notebook.

"Right." Nadine sat back down. "Is it about Marty?"

Emma blinked. "What?"

"I just mean, do you think I should have invited him to Thanksgiving?"

"Um . . ." Emma murmured. "No."

"Good. I think you're right. I need to focus on my life here, don't you think?"

"Yes. Probably," she said without any confidence.

"Nana always says when one door closes, another one always opens; it's the hallways that can get your knickers in a twist." Emma nodded, trying to follow Nadine's train of thought as she continued. "But I feel like I'm in this exciting, multi-colored hallway and all these doors are about to burst wide open, you know?"

Nadine watched her, waiting for a response.

Emma looked down at her hands in her lap. "Nadine, I have to talk to you about something."

"Is everything okay?"

"It's about Zane. He's . . . he's not the guy we thought he was,"

Emma said carefully. "I'm so sorry . . . I really believed he liked you, and he did! But . . . well, it turns out he liked us both."

"What?" Nadine's face skewed with confusion.

Emma took a deep breath. "He made a move on me in the cab ride home after karaoke."

"He made a move on you?" Nadine murmured.

"It was awful and aggressive and . . ." Emma squeezed her eyes together like it might help dispel the memory. "He's an asshole. A really bad guy. All he wanted was a quick fuck . . . with either one of us, apparently."

"Oh my God." Nadine stared at the far wall for a moment. "Did he . . . did he hurt you?"

"No! Well, he almost did, but I . . . I punched him."

"You . . . punched him?" Nadine turned to Emma. "Really? You don't seem like a punching type of person."

"Exactly! It's not something I'd like to make a habit!"

"Are you okay?"

Emma sighed. "It's not about me, Nadine. I'm just so sorry. I feel like I pushed him on you. He seemed . . . well, he turned out to not be what he seemed."

"Oh, it's not your fault, Emma. Zane was out of my league anyway." Nadine offered a weak shrug. She was trying to put on a brave front, but Emma could see how her cheeks were flushed with embarrassment, how she couldn't meet her eyes.

"You're insane, Nadine," she said, dipping her head down to meet her friend's downcast gaze. "He is so far below you it's not even funny. I can't believe I didn't see it sooner."

Nadine smiled meekly. "I can't believe you punched him."

"Neither can I," Emma said, laughing dryly. Then she leaned over and grabbed her friend's hand. "You're amazing. And there are so many great guys in this city. We've only just started!"

"I'm so lucky to have you," Nadine whispered, then leaned forward and embraced Emma. After a long moment she leaned back and sighed. "Should we go get a coffee at another cafe and never go to Zane's dumb place again?"

"Nadine," Emma said, a broad smile blooming on her face. "That is the most brilliant idea you've ever had."

CHAPTER 13

On the long list of Woodhouse Christmas Traditions, a mid-afternoon screening of *It's a Wonderful Life* at a small independent theater in the West Village was one of Emma's favorites. She looked forward to it every year, even calling ahead to ensure they still had Milk Duds at their concession stand.

Unfortunately, due to slightly unforeseen circumstances (a particularly bad bout of morning sickness for Margo and an extended trip to LA for Knightley), Emma was on her own this year. At least, she would have been if she hadn't confessed as much to Nadine while getting manicures after class.

"Oh my God, I've never seen that movie!" her friend exclaimed with so much enthusiasm that the nail tech smudged Tutti Frutti Pink across her thumb.

This obviously couldn't stand. So it was settled: Nadine would meet Emma outside the theater on Saturday at 3:45 on the dot.

Of course, when Saturday arrived, and despite weeks of planning, Emma was still putting the finishing touches on her outfit when she was supposed to already be out the door. To make matters worse, the wait time for a car service claimed to be over an hour.

She'd have to try transportation plan B. Hopefully the taxi gods would be smiling down upon her today.

She threw on her black cashmere knit hat, zipped up her new winter moon boots, and grabbed her black Canada Goose puffer jacket before rushing out the door.

It had snowed heavily the previous day, and what had been a beautiful white blanket was now a gray sludge that overwhelmed the sidewalks and curb. Emma leapt over it, trying to maintain the pristine condition of her boots. She finally managed to get to the street, but even with her arm raised, cab after cab passed by.

"Damn it," Emma murmured to herself. She could take the subway, but that would mean walking further east. How much was a trip these days? Were buses still a thing? She mentally calculated her options just as a taxi rounded the corner with its light on. It was a Christmas miracle.

She extended her arm further, smiling broadly as it stopped just a few feet ahead.

"Taxi!" she yelled, running toward it. The passenger got out and, seeing her, waited with the door open.

"Hold up," he said to the driver.

"Oh, thank God," she said breathlessly as she finally reached them. "Thank you."

"It's my pleasure," the man replied, leaning against the open car door like he had all the time in the world. "You're clearly in a hurry."

His smile caught her so off guard that she paused. A crooked grin crinkled the corners of his clear blue eyes. Strangers didn't smile like that. Not in New York, anyway.

"Just a bit," she replied, hoping he would attribute the blush rising in her cheeks to her recent sprint.

"Well, I don't want to keep you," he murmured, stepping back from the car door to give her room to get in. A few strands of his long blond hair fell in front of his face, but he made no move to push them away. Despite the cold, his dark shearling fur coat hung open, revealing a black shirt unbuttoned just enough to expose a hint of his chest.

She found herself hesitating a moment before slowly brushing past him and sliding into the back seat of the cab. "Thanks to you . . ." she said, pausing to look up, ". . . I think I might make it."

"Have fun," he winked, slamming the door shut and hitting the top of the taxi with two gentle knocks before walking away. Emma sat there for a moment and realized she was holding her breath. She exhaled.

"Where to?" the cab driver asked as they started down the road.

"Oh, um, West 4th and Sixth Avenue, please," she mumbled, turning around to watch as the handsome stranger disappeared from view.

~

As her cab sped downtown, Emma texted Nadine to tell her she was running just a few minutes late. She pressed send, then began to idly scroll through her contacts until she came to Knightley's name. She usually dragged him to this every year, but he was in LA this week and wouldn't be back until tomorrow. That didn't mean she couldn't make him feel bad about missing it though, right? She smiled and began typing.

EMMA

I know you're not a big fan of It's a Wonderful Life, but you didn't have to fly all the way to LA to avoid watching it with me this year.

She pressed send and slid her phone back in her bag. She knew he was busy, so she didn't expect a reply.

Nadine was waiting outside the theater bundled up, hood on, in a long pink puffy coat that made her impossible to miss. She looked like a marshmallow, and Emma wanted to squeeze her.

"I need that coat!" She laughed. "You look so cozy!"

"I'm from Ohio. This is nothing." Nadine smiled, and the pair went inside.

After getting some refreshments, they found their seats in the center row of the old theater and sat down. Emma put her phone on silent, then carefully positioned their popcorn, drinks, and Milk Duds while Nadine shook off her coat.

"Wow, the perks of working at a salon are paying off: How does your hair always look fantastic?" Emma whispered as Nadine pushed the hood from her head. "Is Mateo sharing all his styling secrets with you?"

"Thanks! He really is the best," Nadine agreed, reaching into the Milk Duds and throwing a few in her mouth. "He showed me how to do this thing with a round brush where you kind of twist it as you blow dry it? But it's hard to pay attention because he has this tattoo on his bicep that kind of flexes every time—"

"Shhh!"

Emma turned to look at the row behind her, where an older gentleman eating his own box of Milk Duds was glaring at the two of them. The theater was practically empty and the movie hadn't started yet, but she still offered him an apologetic smile.

After a minute of silence, Emma leaned over to Nadine again. "So, have you had any matches on those dating apps yet?"

Her friend nodded, keeping her eyes down on the candy in her hand. "Yeah . . . got a couple of messages."

"That's amazing!" Emma said, her voice a little too loud, and she made sure to soften it as she continued. "What did they say? Do you have pictures?"

"Well . . . I didn't exactly write them back."

Emma's brow furrowed. "Why not?"

"I don't know." Nadine shrugged. "I was hoping to meet someone in a more . . . traditional way, you know?"

"What, like getting invited to a ball so you can sit in the corner and wait for someone to ask you to dance or something? There is no such thing as traditional anymore, Nadine. Everyone is online. Here, let me see your phone."

Nadine handed it over and Emma quickly opened the app, expertly navigating it until she found the inbox.

"This first guy is hot," she murmured, looking over his picture. Then she clicked on his profile. "Wait. Never mind. There's something sketchy about his answers, and I don't think that's his actual job. Okay, let's see the second one." She deleted the first message and moved on to the next. "He's cute, but . . ." She pulled up his profile picture, examining it closely. "There's no way he's twenty-five. It looks like this photo is from the nineties."

Nadine looked deflated. "Oh."

"Don't worry, this is just the first two," Emma said encouragingly. "Here, why don't you let me go through them later and swipe on a few that I think could be great. Then we can go from there, okay?"

Nadine offered her a watery smile and nodded.

Emma smiled back. "We're going to find you the perfect guy, I promise!"

"Shhh!" The man behind them leaned forward, his finger poised in front of his mouth.

Emma and Nadine stifled their laughs as the lights dimmed. A moment later, the screen lit up with the black-and-white opening credits. Emma had no idea how many times she'd seen

It's a Wonderful Life, but she had every word, every expression, memorized.

Nadine, on the other hand, hadn't seen it at all, so Emma was almost as excited to watch her reaction as she was to see the movie itself. But just as the credits faded into a snowy scene of Bedford Falls, she noticed her phone light up in her Balenciaga shoulder bag. She automatically reached for it, covertly shielding the screen so as not to distract Nadine, and looked down to see a text from Knightley.

KNIGHTLEY

> If a business trip was all it took to avoid that movie I would have opened an LA office years ago.

She smiled and unlocked her phone to reply but noticed three dots, as if he were typing another text. They danced on her screen for a while, then disappeared only to reappear a moment later. She stared down at them, waiting for whatever was taking him ages to articulate. But then the dots disappeared again.

Huh. She started to respond but hesitated, not wanting to be that person who texts at the movies. Milk Dud man was already annoyed.

She turned her screen off and put her phone back in her bag.

Emma tried hard to focus on the movie, but her mind wouldn't shut off. A text from Knightley was a rare occurrence, even more so when he was in LA. But that wasn't the only reason it nagged at her.

To be honest, things had felt off between them ever since that night she snuck into his kitchen to steal ice cream after the whole Zane incident. She was surprised by how she had articulated all her thoughts to him like that, open and honest and . . . real. They had such an open relationship normally, but this conversation felt different. Two adults just trying to figure it out.

She had been afraid it would feel awkward the next day, but it never did. Well, at least not for her. Maybe for Knightley. Until now it felt like he was avoiding her like the plague, but she had to remind herself that not everything was about her. Work was busy for him right now, as evidenced by this trip. Everything would be back to normal soon.

Her mind dwelled on their conversation, though. No strings, not complicated . . . it sounded so easy. And suddenly images of the stranger who had given her his cab floated in her head. His smile, his confidence.

That man looked like someone who had his pick of women, and Emma realized she would have still given him her number if he'd asked. And maybe that was okay. Maybe she was going about this the wrong way, and Knightley was right: no strings was the way to go.

Emma was brought back to the movie again when Nadine sighed as George Bailey told Mary he'd lasso the moon and a neighbor insisted he should kiss her instead. Emma watched her friend's profile, the grin on her face and the hope in her wide eyes. She smiled. Yes, she might be coming around to the idea that no strings could be a good thing, but it was clear that Nadine was still looking for true love. And Emma would help her find it.

After the movie, Nadine and Emma headed outside to the bustling city streets.

"That was *so* good," Nadine said, zipping up her puffy coat. "Except, why did they make it seem like Donna Reed was suddenly sad and ugly just because she was unmarried and wore glasses and worked at a library!?"

Emma laughed. "I have no idea. She's a spinster at, like, thirty!"

She was about to suggest they grab a hot chocolate at the Italian bakery around the corner when Nadine's body went rigid, her face ashen. Emma followed her gaze across Carmine Street to a couple walking past on their way to the park benches in Father Demo Square. She was so distracted by the woman—how she was plastered against the guy's side with her hands buried in his jacket and her lips locked on his neck—that it took a moment for her to realize that the guy was Zane. It was dark and he was looking away from them, but Emma would still recognize that mess of hair anywhere.

"It's him." Nadine's voice was barely audible.

Emma turned to her friend, blocking her view. They had to get out of there before he saw them. And before Emma clocked him again.

"Oh my God, do you think that's his girlfriend?" It was like Nadine was choking on the words. "Did he have a girlfriend this whole time?"

"Just forget it, Nadine. He's not even worth our attention."

"Was I trying to be the other woman?"

"Absolutely not!" Emma worked to think up something to say. "Maybe that wasn't even him!"

Nadine's pained expression turned incredulous.

Emma bit her bottom lip. *Damn it.* Then she had a brilliant idea.

"Let's go to Margo's!" she said, smiling brightly.

"What?"

"She lives a few blocks away on Perry. Just wait until you see her apartment—it's gorgeous." Emma pulled her friend up to West 4th Street in the opposite direction of Zane.

Nadine reluctantly let herself be led several blocks through tree-lined, cobblestoned streets before getting buzzed up to Margo's apartment. Emma exited the elevator and rang the bell, barely greeting her sister as she pushed past her into the apartment with Nadine in tow.

"How was the mov—" Margo started but was interrupted.

"Hi! We need drinks . . . and food." Emma tried to telepathically communicate the dire situation.

"Right. Got it," Margo replied, not missing a beat.

She guided them over to the kitchen and they sat down at the island, where Ben was cooking dinner.

Emma couldn't help but notice how beautiful their new apartment looked. A freshly cut Christmas tree decorated with white lights and silver balls stood tall in the living room. There was a fire lit in the fireplace and a Tiffany's glass bowl of real pine cones set on the large dining table. It was perfect.

"Try this," Ben said, not letting Emma even say hello before a huge spoonful of the most perfect flavors hit her tongue.

"Oh wow, what is that?"

"My mushroom risotto. Oh, and try these—they're mojito slushies. Not exactly the right time of year, but I wanted to make them. I had so much mint . . . not sure about the ratio. There's red wine too. Here, sit." In typical chef fashion, Ben communicated through his food, pouring drinks and setting out plates for them all.

"I want about a hundred of these," Nadine mumbled around a mouthful of mojito.

"So how was the movie?" Margo repeated, watching Nadine as she downed the rest of her drink.

"Amazing, as usual," Emma replied with a contented sigh.

"I'm glad you two went. I probably would have puked through the whole thing." Margo collapsed onto the couch and wrapped a furry blanket over herself. "I can't drink. I can't go out. I don't move from here. It's awful."

"I'm sorry," Emma said. "But at least you have a chef to cook for you."

"Ugh, I can't eat." Margo stared at the stove as if it had personally insulted her.

"Here try this one," Ben said, his dark brown eyes sparkling, oblivious to his wife's moaning as he put a plate of food in front of Nadine. "I added more cream sauce. What do you think?"

Nadine took a bite and slowly perked up. "That's really good."

"Have some more slushie, too."

Ben's food was the answer to everything. Nadine ate and drank and as her cheeks started to flush, Emma relaxed, finally seeing her friend's mind distracted.

"Did you tell Emma the news?" Margo asked Ben.

"Oh, right!" He turned from the stove to wag his eyebrows at Emma. "Knox is in town. Stopped by the other day to talk about the restaurant."

"So he's not your imaginary friend!" Emma shot him a wry smile.

Ben flipped her off and then went back to his risotto.

"You haven't heard the best part," Margo said. "He's right on 83rd! He's renting Mr. and Mrs. Crawford's old place."

Emma's mouth fell open. "You're kidding."

"You should stop by." Margo flashed her brightest smile at her sister. "Just go introduce yourself. Invite him to the Christmas party."

"Assuming he'll still be in town by then," Emma murmured, taking another bite of food.

"Be nice. He's interesting and charming—"

"As you've mentioned, like, a thousand times." Emma rolled her eyes. When Margo shot her a glare, she sighed. "All right fine, I'll stop by."

She would stop by Montgomery Knox's home and play nice. She might even forgive him for avoiding them for so long, but she wouldn't pretend to be blind to what Margo was up to. Leave it to her sister to decide that Emma needed to be in a committed relationship just as Emma realized that she didn't.

CHAPTER 14

Emma decided to go see Montgomery Knox the next day. It was like a Band-Aid, she reasoned: better to just rip it off and get it over with. Besides, it was Sunday, which meant that if she timed it right, she wouldn't have to stay long because of Sunday dinner. It was the perfect plan.

She put on a pair of leggings and an oversized V-neck sweater before throwing her dark hair into a messy bun, unbothered by the strands that fell around her face. Then she made her way downstairs, where her father was reading the morning paper in the kitchen. They sat in comfortable silence for a while as Emma looked out the window. Knightley's house was still dark; he was supposed to get back from California this morning. Maybe she would stop by after meeting the new neighbor.

Her thoughts were interrupted by a roar from outside, the sound of an engine and brakes echoing from the street.

"Is that a motorcycle?" she asked, craning her neck to listen.

"So unsafe," her father murmured, not looking up from his paper.

"Do they have to be so loud? I mean, is there a rule that if you have a motorcycle you need to announce it to the world?"

"Do you know that New Hampshire has no motorcycle helmet law? For anyone. None." Emma's father sighed, shaking his head.

"Just the worst," she mumbled.

Her father hummed.

"So," she continued, drumming her fingers on the table. "Margo wants me to invite that friend of Ben's to the Christmas party."

"Who?"

"Montgomery Knox. The one who missed the wedding. Apparently, he moved into the Crawfords' house."

Mr. Woodhouse stared at her like he didn't remember but was unbothered by the fact. Then he turned his attention back to the *Times*.

Emma continued. "Anyway, you're fine with inviting him, right?"

"Sure," he said without looking up.

"He's probably too busy to come anyway."

Mr. Woodhouse didn't reply.

"But we don't have to invite him."

Silence.

"Okay, I'm going over to invite him."

"Have fun," her father replied absently.

She nodded, cementing her resolve. Then she finished her coffee and started upstairs to the foyer to grab her black peacoat and her old Pajar après ski boots.

The bright morning sun had melted an almost circuitous path in the snow along the sidewalk and she took her time navigating it, trying to remember the last time she had been inside Mr. and Mrs. Crawford's brownstone. God, it had been years, back when Mr. Crawford was still running a rare book shop on Lexington. He and his wife Veronica had retired to West Palm Beach, but they had kept the house and rented it out occasionally in case someday, maybe, they wanted to move back.

Emma crossed the street, skirting around the conspicuous motorcycle chained up in front of the Crawfords' old home—seriously, who was going to steal that thing?—and walked up the steps to the looming front door.

There was a gold-plated lion-head knocker at its center, but Emma ignored it and instead pressed the doorbell. The chimes echoed in the house. Once they faded, there was no other sound at all.

She tried again. Still nothing.

"Quelle surprise," she huffed, and had turned around to leave just as the door opened. She spun back and stilled at the familiar face staring back at her.

"Well, hi," he said, his tone suggesting that he recognized Emma, too.

"Oh, it's you," Emma replied dumbly.

"And it's you." His blue eyes twinkled at her, and he leaned in before he continued. "Do you need me to get you another cab?"

They stared at each other for a moment before Emma remembered it was her turn to speak. "Oh, no. Not today."

"So . . . I'm not one to complain about a beautiful woman knocking on my door so early, but who are you?" he purred, bracing his hand on the doorframe.

"Oh, right." She blinked herself out of his breathtaking gaze. "I'm Emma Woodhouse. Your neighbor and—"

"No way." He laughed, flashing his bright smile. "I've heard so much about you from Ben."

"I've heard a lot about you from Margo. And here you are, Montgomery Knox . . . finally." She gestured at him.

"You know," he said, tilting his head to the side, his light eyes narrowing playfully, "I think your sister and Ben want us to get together."

Emma laughed and tucked a few fallen locks of her dark hair behind her ear. She wasn't expecting him to say what had been implied every time his name came up. *Oh, Emma, Montgomery is single. Montgomery collects art! Montgomery isn't too much older than you! Oh, Emma, Montgomery and you share a love of . . .* But at no point had it been mentioned that Montgomery was extremely, ridiculously hot.

"Do they?" Emma replied, feigning innocence.

His long, wavy blond hair fell to one side of his face, highlighting his blue eyes. Slight stubble framed his jawline as his smile broadened like he saw right through her lie. "Hmmm. Well, they couldn't stop singing your praises."

She could feel the trail of his eyes down her body. Emma offered him the same knowing smile when his gaze found hers again. He wasn't embarrassed, though: he seemed pleased that she was aware of his slow survey. She wondered how many girls fell for this, even as she suddenly found herself forgiving him for flaking on her sister's wedding, making them wait months to meet him, and apparently owning a motorcycle in the city.

"I'm sorry," he said, suddenly laughing. "It's fucking freezing out. Come in, let me take your coat. Excuse all the boxes."

He moved closer to her and gently took her hand, coaxing her inside. His skin was soft and warm and he smelled good, like leather and citrus . . . but then she remembered what she had thrown on before coming over. Her sweater was stretched out in all the wrong places and her hair was a mess on top of her head. She was lucky her black leggings could pass for actual pants. She was only supposed to be here to invite him to the Christmas party and run back home. This was *not* how she thought this would go.

"Oh, I really shouldn't," she said, slowly withdrawing her hand from his and taking another step back. "I just wanted to introduce myself and invite you to our Christmas party on Friday. It's an annual thing; everyone on the block shows up."

"I'd love to," he said, biting his bottom lip as if he was reluctant to continue. "But I have plans."

"Oh," she said, and blinked. She hadn't expected him to decline, and she was surprised by the dull pang of disappointment running through her chest. "Well, what about tonight?"

His eyebrows lifted. "Tonight?"

"We could have dinner. I mean, not you and me. Well, yes, you and me, but there will be other people there too." She let out a nervous laugh. God, what was wrong with her? "It's just that we usually have people over for dinner at our house on Sundays. It's a bit of a weekly tradition with . . . well, everyone. Ben and Margo will be there too—Ben's even cooking this week."

"Sunday dinner with the Woodhouses." Montgomery mulled it over, leaning against the doorframe. "I think I can make myself available. Should I bring anything?"

"Just yourself." She smiled. "Seven o'clock. Don't be late."

"Wouldn't dream of it."

She offered him a small wave and started down the stairs, but stopped when she noticed the motorcycle again. She turned back to him. "Is that yours?"

He nodded, never breaking eye contact. "It is."

"Those are really dangerous, you know."

His smile became almost carnal. "Not at all. They just need someone who knows how to handle them."

There was a warm hum through Emma's body as Montgomery stared down at her. Her mouth fell open and she knew she had to say something, had to actually *do* something, but her body wouldn't listen. He finally chuckled.

"See you tonight, Emma."

And then he closed the door.

Emma walked back home with a grin on her face. Suddenly the week was looking up. It was the holiday season. She had a Sunday dinner to plan. And they had a new neighbor on 83rd Street.

CHAPTER 15

Emma spent the rest of Sunday doing errands to distract herself from the impending dinner. She collected used clothes from their neighbors and brought them down to their church to donate. She stopped at the corner specialty Italian shop to pick up some appetizers for Ben. Then she got her father's dry cleaning from Gladys across the street. But she still couldn't escape her thoughts of Montgomery Knox.

He was . . . not what she expected. Not that she was complaining. He was everything she could have asked for: gorgeous and successful and flirty and confident . . . She took a deep breath as her cheeks flushed again. And clearly Ben liked him for her. He also had Margo's vote. Maybe this could be the no-strings relationship she was toying with. Maybe it could even grow into something more.

Montgomery wasn't some college student or barista: he was an adult who had traveled the world. He was putting down roots in New York. This had actual potential.

By the time she got home, Ben and Margo had arrived, and Ben was already busy cooking. Emma could hear them bickering in the kitchen below when she came in the front door, a familiar back and forth as he moved things around for easier access and ruined everything she had already organized. Emma avoided all of it and headed up to her room.

She descended the staircase a little while later—outfit changed and makeup freshened—and was surprised to see Knightley in the living room, pouring himself a glass of red wine from the brass bar cart. He was about to take a sip when he caught sight of her. He froze as she walked toward him, the glass hovering at his lips.

"Oh, you're back," she said in greeting.

His gaze stayed locked on her, but he didn't reply.

"Hello?"

Her voice seemed to jar him enough that he blinked, taking a quick sip of his wine as his eyes darted away. "I am."

"Did you just get in?"

"I've been home all day," he said, turning to pour a second glass of wine and offering it to her. *Shit*. She had meant to stop by, but the day got away from her.

"Oh, well, I didn't notice. I'm a very busy person, Knightley," she teased, accepting the drink even as her cheeks flushed. During all the long hours of pondering tonight's dinner, she completely forgot that Knightley would be there too. The realization sent a shot of adrenaline through her veins. "And how was California?"

"Fine," he replied. "How was the movie?"

"Good," she said. She took a sip of her wine, feeling it warm her throat. "Nadine came with me."

He hummed as if that were an answer. His eyes drifted down her body before he took another sip of his wine and met her gaze again. "Don't you look nice for a Sunday dinner."

Emma glanced down. She had gone through a few options before selecting a thin, white cowl-neck cashmere sweater and a short skirt that matched her black knee-high boots. She knew it was a little fancy, but not over the top for the holidays. She hadn't even put on much jewelry, just simple black pearl earrings, and let her dark brown hair down so it hung wavy over her shoulders.

"Oh, thanks." She hesitated. Was she trying too hard, she wondered? Knightley rarely complimented her on her appearance. "You look . . ."

He watched her search for the right word, narrowing his eyes. "Don't hurt yourself now."

"Sorry, you just . . . you look like you always look, Knightley." "And how's that?"

An eyebrow rose up his forehead as the question hung between them.

"You look . . . good. I mean, come on, Knightley, you always look good." She laughed and jokingly pushed at his chest. He did look handsome tonight, in his crisp white shirt and tailored pants.

His expression remained serious as her laughter subsided. She waited for one of his familiar witty replies, offhanded comments, or even a criticism, but instead he just stared down at her, and she swore his gaze shifted briefly to her mouth, then back up to her eyes again. Then he looked away and ran his hand through his hair to the back of his neck.

"Emma . . ." Knightley started in a low, raspy voice. She found herself inhaling sharply at the way her name sounded coming from his lips. It was different. Softer, like they were sharing a secret. "I—"

He was cut off by a loud knock on the front door.

"Hello! Anyone home?" A deep voice called out from behind it.

Emma turned just as Ben lumbered up the steps from the kitchen. "Coming!"

"He actually showed up this time," Emma said with a smile as she turned back to Knightley. But there wasn't any amusement on his face as his golden-brown eyes flickered from the door back to her. She couldn't decipher how he was feeling; that had never happened before.

Then the door swung open and Montgomery Knox appeared. He was wearing a faded leather jacket over a green sweater and dark-wash jeans, a bottle of wine in each hand, and a charming smile on his face.

"You made it!" Ben exclaimed, giving his friend a hug as Margo came up the stairs to greet him, kissing both his cheeks.

Knightley watched the three of them trade pleasantries. His lips became a hard line across his face.

"It's Montgomery Knox," Emma answered his unvoiced question. "We invited him."

"So he exists," Knightley murmured.

Emma was about to tell him to be nice, or at least try to be, but before she could say anything, Montgomery was walking to her, his smile so bright and gorgeous that the words dissolved on her tongue.

"There she is," he said, his voice like a purr. "Good to see you again, Emma Woodhouse."

She smiled back. "Good to see you too."

Knightley downed the rest of his wine and retreated back to the bar cart.

If Montgomery was offended, he didn't let on as Margo introduced him to her father and Mrs. Pawloski, who had emerged from the dining room. He didn't bat an eye at the moth holes along the sleeves of Mrs. Pawloski's sweater, only smiled as she lamented about how much they missed him at the wedding. And as he shook her father's hand, his smile widening, he complimented their home, particularly the Christmas decorations.

Of course, it was exactly the right thing to say. Emma spent hours every year choosing how to decorate the house for the holidays, and this year she had gone the traditional route. Thick crimson ribbons wrapped around garlands that lined the banisters. They matched the deep red bows on the Christmas tree, which towered over the piano in the living room. The fireplace still had the same hand-knit stockings hanging from the mantel that had been there every Christmas since Emma was little. Their green felt had faded a bit, but it only added to their charm.

Margo collapsed into the oversized couch in the center of the room next to Mrs. Pawloski while Montgomery took an armchair near the crackling fire. Mr. Woodhouse sat beside him and was explaining how he got special wood delivered from an organic farm upstate, when Knightley returned, his wine refilled.

"Ah, Ben's brother. Nice to finally meet you." Montgomery stood, walking forward and extending a hand.

"Welcome to the neighborhood," Knightley replied, offering a tight smile and a single, firm handshake.

"Ben tells me you're always out in LA. I thought we'd never meet."

Knightley's expression flattened. "Likewise."

Emma found her stomach in a peculiar knot as she watched the two men in front of her exchange words that sounded cordial but felt loaded.

"Drink? Who would like another drink? Whiskey sour?" she interjected with manufactured enthusiasm, motioning over to the bar cart as she looked back and forth between the two of them.

"What's a Manhattan dinner party without a proper whiskey sour?" Montgomery said. "I'd love one."

"Knightley?" Emma asked.

He stared at her a moment, then held up his full glass.

"All set here," he said slowly, a subtle finality in his tone. Emma forced a smile, then turned her attention to the drinks.

Montgomery leaned lazily against the bar cart and watched Emma pour the bourbon and fresh lemon juice Fran had prepared for the party.

"That's quite a lot of bourbon," he murmured so only she could hear. "Trying to get me drunk?"

She laughed, blushing as she tucked a wisp of hair behind her ear and handed him the glass.

After a few cocktails—and Mrs. Pawloski's oral history of all the ornaments on the Woodhouses' tree—Ben directed everyone down the hall for dinner.

They rarely used the formal dining room for Sunday dinner, and Emma could feel Knightley's gaze directed at her, but she ignored it as she took her seat. The large mahogany dining table was decorated elegantly with gold chargers underneath white china plates. Metallic-dipped candles cast a soft glow on the centerpiece of real pine cones. The entire scene was framed by the family's various oil paintings hanging on the fleur-de-lis wallpaper.

Ben was clearly in his element as he began to serve dinner: grilled coppa pork with chimichurri. On the side were roasted pumpkin wedges drizzled with maple syrup and a simple salad of soft lettuces with a shallot vinaigrette. As they ate, Ben explained their plans for the new restaurant. The menu, the decor, and how if it wasn't for Montgomery bringing in the investors and securing the space, none of it would be happening.

"We should have it up and running by summer," Ben added. "Maybe a soft opening even sooner."

"How exciting!" Mrs. Pawloski squealed.

"And you think Ben's restaurant is a good idea?" Mr. Woodhouse asked, his attention on his plate as he picked at a pumpkin wedge suspiciously.

"Dad . . ." Margo rolled her eyes.

"What?" Mr. Woodhouse asked, genuinely confused.

Montgomery smiled. "Ben has passion. And that is always the start of a good idea."

Ben raised his glass to Montgomery and they clinked them together, both laughing as if there was some inside joke the rest of the table wasn't privy to.

"I can't believe you had to miss the wedding!" Mrs. Pawloski lamented yet again. "You must have been heartbroken. Just heartbroken!"

"And the engagement party," Knightley added.

"Oh! That's right!" Mrs. Pawloski exclaimed. "You must be so busy! Where does your work take you?"

"Oh, too many places to count," Montgomery said with a sigh. "I wouldn't want to bore you all."

Mrs. Pawloski laughed. Only Emma heard the scoff that escaped Knightley's lips.

"But," Montgomery continued, "I really want to apologize for missing so much. I was in the weeds dealing with a few projects overseas. At some point, you just have to be able to walk away. I pride myself on that. I know when a deal is working and I know when it's time to cut bait."

"That sounds very stressful," Mrs. Pawloski said, leaning her head in her hand as she stared at him.

"It's part of the job. I have to make tough decisions daily."

"So how long are you staying?" Knightley asked, his tone flat.

The table's attention turned back to Montgomery. He just shrugged.

"I haven't decided. But New York has treated me well so far, so we'll see," he replied, stealing a glance at Emma as he took a sip of his drink.

"And how are you finding the new place?" Mr. Woodhouse asked. "The Crawfords are good friends of ours, you know."

Montgomery nodded. "It's beautiful. Just making some minor adjustments to go with all my things. Well, mostly my art collection. I'm still hanging it all up."

"Emma loves art. Don't you, Emma?" Margo announced, beaming. "She was always drawing pictures when she was little and getting lost in the Met."

"I'm also in graduate school getting my master's in art history," Emma added, trying to temper the annoyance in her voice.

Margo didn't seem to notice. "Yes, that too! I bet she would love to see what you have. We all would."

"Well, that settles it." Montgomery rapped his knuckles on the table. "I am going to have a party."

"Oh yes!" Mrs. Pawloski practically jumped out of her seat. "I love a good party!"

"How about New Year's Eve?" he asked.

"That's two weeks away," Knightley chimed in.

"Which makes it perfect." Montgomery turned back to Emma. "Unless you all have other plans?"

Like most New Yorkers, Emma never made big New Year's plans. It was always too crowded and loud in Manhattan and impossible to get a cab. Last year, she and Margo were home in their PJs and asleep by 12:01. Definitely not a party. But this . . . this was different.

"I think it sounds great," she found herself replying. Knightley gave her a disapproving look, but she ignored it. "I can even help plan it."

Margo clapped her hands, a huge grin on her face as if her

greatest wish was finally coming true. "Oh, this is perfect! Emma knows how to throw a party; she's the ultimate hostess."

Montgomery's smile widened. "Well then, I can't wait."

More wine flowed and more food was consumed, as most everyone seemed to be enjoying the newest member of their weekly dinner. That is, everyone but Knightley. As soon as dessert was served, he stood and excused himself with barely a goodbye. Emma almost missed it—she had been pulled into a long story about Mrs. Pawloski's foray into scrapbooking—but extracted herself in time to run downstairs and catch him as he was letting himself out the French doors in the dimly lit kitchen.

"Hey," she called after him. "You're leaving without saying goodbye?"

He turned, his hand still on the open door. He stared at her for a moment, as if he was debating what to say next, but in the end he only nodded to her and said, "Goodbye."

She took another step forward, folding her arms around her body as he started outside. "Wait."

He glanced at her over his shoulder. "Yes?"

She struggled to come up with what to say, if there was anything to say at all. There were words on her tongue that hadn't formed yet and they sat there, heavy and dumb, while he waited.

"Will you come to the New Year's party?" she finally asked. It felt like a cop-out, the lowest common denominator to keep his attention, but she didn't care. "You know . . . it could be fun."

He raked a hand through his hair. "Emma . . ."

It sounded tortured, like a plea.

"Give it a chance? Please?" she continued, suddenly worried he might actually say no.

Even in the dim light, Emma could see a muscle in his jaw twitch. "Is that what you want?"

"Of course that's what I want," she answered with a breathy laugh, then added more quietly, "What we all want."

He nodded. "I see."

Her wide eyes met his golden ones just as they turned dark, distant.

"Good night," he said curtly, and closed the door.

Emma watched him trudge through the leftover snow, striding off in the direction of his home until he disappeared into the darkness.

By the time she returned upstairs, the guests had moved back into the living room and were seated around the fireplace. More wine was poured, along with some whiskey, and soon Mr. Woodhouse retired for the night. A few minutes later, Margo insisted that it was time to go home, and volunteered Ben to walk a tipsy Mrs. Pawloski to her apartment a few doors down along the way.

Montgomery and Emma were alone.

Emma curled up in the deep armchair next to the fire and Montgomery sat opposite, his long legs stretched out on the ottoman between them. With only the soft lights of the Christmas tree and the fire's dying embers left to illuminate the room, dark shadows fell on his face. He had been staring at her for a while.

"Are you sure you want to throw this New Year's party?" she asked, trying to figure out what he was thinking.

"If you're there to help, I can't imagine anything I want more. Let's make this New Year's party unforgettable. Like an event. An experience. Great Gatsby–like."

Emma failed to dampen her smile. "Wow, sure."

"We need a DJ. There's this guy I know—I'll send you his Instagram—he's doing a residency down at Club Vibe and has a VIP following, too. We should go check him out together before the party."

A flutter made its way through her chest. "I'd love that."

"Maybe I can convince you to ride my bike down there?" He cocked his eyebrow at her.

She gave him a knowing smirk and shook her head.

He threw up his hands in surrender. "Okay. Okay. What else do we need?"

"I guess we should get a few bartenders? I worked with a company from Margo's wedding that was great."

"Yes. Perfect. Top-shelf only."

"If you say so." Emma laughed. "So you want this party to be big, then?"

"Big, but classy." He pondered for a minute. "An event that screams understated."

She tilted her head. Well, she had to appreciate his vision. It was clear that Montgomery wasn't used to hearing no when it came to anything he started. In a way, Emma could relate to that.

"We'll figure it all out this week," he continued. Then he pulled out a piece of Nicorette gum, maintaining eye contact as he chewed.

"Sounds great." Emma tucked her hair behind her ears and nodded to the wrapper still in his hand. "Are you trying to quit smoking?"

"I've been quitting for years. I'm addicted to the gum now."

"That's quite a vice."

"One of my tamer ones," he drawled in a low voice. "Unless you don't approve?"

"What if I don't?"

His gaze was intense as he took the gum from his mouth and put it back in its wrapper. Then he smiled.

Emma suddenly felt like she needed to move. She stood up and grabbed a few of the empty wineglasses from the mantel.

"Can you grab the ones on the coffee table for me?" she asked, already starting toward the doorway.

He stood slowly, unfolding his long body and stretching before picking up the glasses and following her as she made her way downstairs. The kitchen was dark, with only the light from under the cabinets to guide them as she lined up the glasses on the countertop.

"So this happens every Sunday night?" Montgomery said softly from close behind her. Very close.

She took a deep breath, trying to calm her rising pulse, then turned around to face him. His blue eyes were hooded as he took a step forward, backing her up against the marble counter. The French doors behind him were dark, their black windows revealing nothing that lay beyond.

"Well, this was livelier than a typical Sunday night," she admitted.

"Why do you think that?" he teased. Their bodies were only inches apart.

She laughed. "Do you want me to say it was because of you?"

"Well, I like a captive audience."

"I'm sure."

He leaned toward her. "I also like you."

She gripped the countertop behind her to steady herself as she gazed up at him—the slight stubble on his cheeks, the locks of untidy blond hair falling in front of his face. He reached for her free hand and intertwined his fingers in hers. Then his lips curled into a sly smile.

"Close your eyes."

"Why?" she murmured, his warm breath on her face.

He chuckled quietly. "You'll have to close your eyes to find out."

She hesitated before slowly doing as he asked. A moment, then his mouth met hers. The kiss was soft, then suddenly all-consuming, his lips and tongue tasting like the sugar and lemon from his drink. She didn't expect herself to respond so quickly and was surprised when a moan escaped her lips. God, it felt good, and she let herself get lost in it, weaving her fingers into his hair, pulling him closer. He pressed his body against hers, his kisses becoming more urgent.

"Emma," he breathed. It sounded almost desperate, and she suddenly realized it was the second time someone had said her name like that tonight. With Montgomery's tongue in her mouth, her thoughts drifted to Knightley. What had he wanted to say to her earlier? He seemed so serious. In fact, he seemed serious the whole night until he had abruptly left. Was he home right now? Sitting all alone in his house? What if he was at his back window, what if he could see—

Montgomery nipped at her bottom lip.

"You're so gorgeous," he murmured. The sound was soft, but it seemed to echo loudly in the space.

Her eyes snapped open, flicking to the dark windows that faced the back garden. Someone could be watching them right now. Right from across the lawn.

She pulled back in an instant, removing every part of her body that touched Montgomery, even as his fingers found her hips, trying to keep her close.

"You okay?" he asked, breathing hard.

"Yes, fine. I'm fine," she said, smoothing her hair and trying to avoid gazing at the doors a few feet away.

"Want to go to my place?" His lips floated over hers. "There's no one home there."

"Ah . . ." She wasn't sure what to say. Did she want to go to his place? He planted kisses along her jaw and neck, making it hard for her to think clearly.

"Right there across the street . . ." he whispered, bringing his mouth up to the shell of her ear. "We're neighbors now, remember?"

Her eyes widened. Oh God, she did not want to think about her neighbors right now.

As if on cue, the darkness beyond the window went from pitch-black to a familiar soft glow as the motion-detecting light in Knightley's backyard flipped on. Had he come outside? Did he turn the light on? Or was a cock-blocking squirrel simply ruining the moment?

Montgomery must have felt how her body tensed, because he paused. "You sure you're okay?" he asked again.

"Yeah, I . . . think I just drank too much tonight . . ." She sighed and rested a hand on his hard chest. "Rain check?"

He leaned in close and kissed her cheek. "Sure. We have a party to plan, right?"

"Right."

"Good." Then he took a step back, not hiding the fact that he was adjusting himself. "Come over early for it, too. I can't wait to show my art collection to someone else who appreciates beautiful things."

"Can't wait." She tilted her head to the side. "I'll see you before then, though . . . to meet the DJ."

"It's a date." Then he turned and left up the stairs.

Emma listened to the front door open and close behind him. She was still braced against the counter, her hands gripping the marble countertop. Why had she cut that short? Surely a porch lamp wasn't enough to make her send an attractive man home, right?

After a long moment, she exhaled deeply. Whatever the reason, now she felt hot and edgy. She grabbed a bottle of water from the refrigerator and took a deep sip. It wasn't like she wasn't going to see Montgomery again. They were planning a party together. And maybe that was the perfect time to make it official. She could start the new year with a new boyfriend in his new house; it was the ideal scenario. She should be celebrating. So why the hell wasn't she?

She looked up after a while, her gaze landing on Knightley's house. Her eyes traveled from the motion-sensor light, picking up no signs of life, only the tree branches waving in the wind. Then her gaze traveled up to his bedroom window. It was pitch-black; she couldn't see anything. But she still stared as her brain wandered. He probably hadn't seen anything; he probably wasn't even there. But the possibility still twisted her stomach as she turned off the kitchen light, the room matching the darkness outside.

CHAPTER 16

Emma slept in the next day. Even after she woke, she stayed in bed, staring up at the ceiling and wondering why she still felt so unsettled. Part of her knew she had to get up—there was a party to plan, after all—but even the prospect of that only made her want to hide under the covers. Thankfully it was Christmas break and there were no classes, so she could hide there forever—or at least for a couple of weeks. That was mildly comforting. But after a few minutes awake and alone with her thoughts, she got up and trudged to the bathroom. The shower hadn't quite warmed up by the time she stepped in, but she didn't care as she stood under the cool spray. The uneasy feeling was still there when she got out, so she tried to distract herself by concentrating on everything else: drying her hair and pulling it back, putting on a pair of black leggings and a long, cozy cashmere sweater, going downstairs to get some coffee.

She was concentrating so hard that she didn't look up until she walked into the kitchen. When she did, she almost jumped out of her skin.

"Jesus!" she exclaimed, staring at where her father sat at the island. And at Knightley sitting beside him. Because of course he was there. He was always there.

"Hello to you too," Mr. Woodhouse replied, taking a sip of tea as he continued to read the paper.

Knightley was watching her with an unreadable expression, and her stomach dropped. Had he seen her and Montgomery last night? Was he judging her? Angry at her? Her rib cage suddenly felt like it could barely contain her pounding heart.

"Morning," she mumbled, shuffling to the sink.

"It's almost noon," Knightley replied. He looked like he had stopped by on the way home from one of his runs around the Central Park reservoir. His face was flushed and a thin coat of sweat glistened on his skin, darkening the edges of his T-shirt.

She rolled her eyes as she filled a glass with water, hoping it would somehow dispel the flush in her cheeks.

"So, how was the rest of the night?" he asked.

There was no way to tell if the question was for her or her father, but Emma's pulse still tripped in her veins. "I . . . um . . ."

Knightley hadn't seen anything last night, she rationalized to herself. His windows were dark. He probably wasn't even home! But she still couldn't manage to look back over at him as she took a deep sip of her water.

"Oh, Emma, are you all right? You're not getting sick, are you?" Mr. Woodhouse asked, finally looking up from the *Times*.

"I'm fine," she replied, filling her glass again.

Knightley raised a quizzical brow at her. "You sure?"

She donned a feeble smile. "Everything is fine. The night was great. You just left early."

"Oh, I saw enough."

Oh God. She took another sip of water.

"You're probably not feeling well because you're not getting enough B6," her father interjected. "You should eat a banana."

Emma made her way to the other end of the island and picked up a banana from the fruit bowl. She could still feel Knightley watching her, but she didn't dare make eye contact.

"Fran's at the store, I'll have her pick up some buckwheat so I can make you some of my fortified porridge," Mr. Woodhouse continued.

"It's gruel, Dad."

He ignored her, standing up and ushering her to his stool. "Here, sit down. Let me make you a kale smoothie. Don't think I didn't notice all you did to make it enjoyable for everyone last night. Sit, sit. George was just telling me about his LA trip," Mr. Woodhouse said while he grabbed ingredients from the fridge.

"Oh, right. How was it?" Emma asked. LA was a safe conversation topic. She smiled, prepping herself to listen attentively like a true friend and feeling a bit guilty that she hadn't asked about it last night.

"Constructive," Knightley replied. She stared at him, waiting for more. He stared back. After a long moment, he sighed. "It was good, Emma. Our current deal is on track, and we don't anticipate any hiccups."

Mr. Woodhouse sliced into a mango. "And what is this deal exactly?"

"A friend of Ben's started a hydroponics lab a few years ago to grow microgreens for a lot of the city's restaurants. He ended up refining the technology in a way that meant he could mass produce these small self-sustaining farms, put them in shipping containers, and send them anywhere. We invested and now it's being acquired by a large agricultural company in California. I'm trying to stay on top of the transition."

"Is it going to see you out in LA permanently?" her father asked.

"I don't think so, but you never know."

Emma blinked. Wait, where was this coming from?

"It's nothing yet," Knightley continued, reading her expression. "But I'll let you know if it becomes something more."

She nodded. Her mind couldn't even comprehend what it would be like without him here permanently, and she pushed the idea far from her mind.

"LA . . ." Mr. Woodhouse shuddered, pausing as he dropped some ice in the blender. "Have you read about the air quality out there? The particle pollution alone could cause a stroke."

"Well, I guess that settles it. You can never leave. You're stuck with us," Emma joked, even though her voice sounded strained.

Knightly smiled. "We'll see."

"You *own* the company. Doesn't that mean you can do whatever you want at your office?"

"That requires actually being in that office, Woodhouse."

Relief spread through Emma's chest. It wasn't exactly the answer she was looking for, but at least their dynamic was returning to normal. Everything was as it should be.

"We were so busy welcoming the new neighbor we didn't get to hear anything about it. What was his name? Montgomery something?" her father pondered, throwing a handful of kale in the blender.

"Montgomery Knox," Emma replied a little too quickly.

Oh no.

"Huh," Mr. Woodhouse seemed to consider it for a moment as he added a banana, as if wondering why it sounded familiar. Then he gave up and put the blender on puree.

A deafening rattle filled the kitchen. Emma could feel Knightley's eyes on her and her pulse thrummed in her ears. Even if he hadn't seen the two of them in the kitchen last night, he must have seen how Montgomery looked at her over dinner. How she had smiled at him. The thought flushed her cheeks and she couldn't look back across the island until the blender fell silent and Mr. Woodhouse placed two glasses between them.

"Here we go, two kale smoothies," he said, pouring the thick green liquid into the glasses.

Emma grabbed hers and took a deep sip.

She immediately regretted it. The smoothie was awful, but Emma managed a smile and nod to her father as he started to make himself one.

"So are you going to bring that woman to the New Year's party, George?" he asked nonchalantly.

Emma almost choked on her drink.

"What was her name again?" her father continued.

Her name *again*? Had Knightley discussed this woman with her father before? Panic clawed its way up Emma's throat as she worked to maintain her composure.

"Davina Sundar," Knightley answered.

"Who?" Emma asked, aware that her voice may have gone up another octave.

"A friend. I met her at a fundraiser a couple of months ago. She's a human rights lawyer with the UN."

Oh God. Emma already felt intimidated. "And you're going to bring her to the party?"

"I wasn't planning on going to the party at all."

Her father scoffed. "That's nonsense. Emma's practically throwing it. You have to go. And bring your friend . . ."

"Davina," Knightley repeated.

"Yes, Davina. I'm sure everyone would love to meet her," Mr.

Woodhouse said, then paused. "But don't stay until midnight. No one should punish their body like that."

Knightley turned to Emma. "What do you think?"

"Oh." Her mind went blank, and it took her a moment to recover. "Well, you should. I mean . . . Montgomery told me it's an open invitation and . . ."

"Are you bringing someone?" Knightley asked.

"Well, I'm the hostess, so I guess . . . I'm going with the host."

"I see," he said, his expression darkening.

"And . . . you should . . . you know . . ." Knightley was watching her, his eyes narrowing as her tongue tripped over the words. ". . . absolutely bring a . . . someone . . ." Her stomach tightened and she couldn't finish the sentence.

He stared at her a moment longer. "Great."

Emma forced a smile onto her face. It felt ugly and wrong. "Great."

Mr. Woodhouse beamed at them as he threw some mango into the blender. "Great!" Then he pressed the puree button and the kitchen was again filled with the deafening sound of ice and fruit being crushed into a million pieces.

CHAPTER 17

"What about sequins? Are sequins too much?" Emma held the skirt up to her hips, moving from side to side in front of her mirror so the silver beads caught the light.

"It's New Year's Eve. I don't think anything's too much," Margo's disembodied voice said from Emma's laptop on her desk. She was on video chat, but when Emma looked over to gauge her reaction, she was staring at Margo's empty sofa.

"You're not even looking."

Margo's head popped back onto the screen, her hair disheveled and her eyes half open. "I'm right here."

"Doing what?"

"Resting my eyes."

Emma sighed. "Do you need to go take a nap?"

"I always need to go take a nap," her sister mumbled, adjusting her computer so she could lay her head on a pillow and still see the screen. "But I can also help you pick out your outfit."

"Then stop sleeping. I have to be over there soon."

"Why isn't Nadine helping you?"

"She's at work, so I told her I'd meet her there. I needed to finish up my application for the Met internship today, anyway. Sort of my New Year's resolution to start the year without it hanging over my head."

"I still don't understand why you're jumping through all these hoops. Dad can just call somebody over there and get you the internship tomorrow."

"I don't want to get an internship. I want to *earn* an internship," she said to her own reflection, and then frowned. Maybe sequins were too much.

"We're talking about a phone call to get your foot in the door. You can take it from there."

Emma closed her eyes and took a breath before turning back around to face the computer and change the subject. "So, what has Montgomery done to the Crawfords' place?"

"Wait, you haven't seen it?"

"Mar, I've barely seen him."

Margo rolled her eyes as if Emma was exaggerating. She wasn't. She hadn't seen Montgomery since the kiss after Sunday dinner two weeks ago. There had been texts, of course. Ideas about caterers and entertainment, all of which Emma had ultimately booked on her own. She told herself it didn't bother her, especially with those late-night messages from him about how he couldn't wait to see her again. Still, tonight would be the first time they would actually be face-to-face since their encounter in the kitchen.

"What about your date to go meet the DJ?" Margo pressed.

"It wasn't a date."

"Not officially, but—"

"No, I mean we didn't end up going. Montgomery had to cancel at the last minute. Something about dinner with a potential investor. I just went ahead and booked the DJ on my own. And the caterers. And the bartenders. And the photo booths. Montgomery just gave me his credit card."

"Don't take it personally. He's very busy. We're lucky he even has time for this." Then Margo sighed. "God, his parties are so epic. You're going to have the best time."

"Well then, you should come. It's practically my party anyway," Emma said as she turned back to the various clothing options she had pulled from her closet and laid out on her bed.

"Oh please. I'm pregnant and throwing up everything I eat. Let me live vicariously through you," Margo lamented, watching Emma peruse hanger after hanger. "What about that Richard Quinn dress you have? The one with the feathers?"

"Feathers are definitely too much."

Margo shrugged just as Emma's phone chimed. She looked down at the screen to see a text from Lulu. It was midnight in Paris, apparently, and Lulu had sent a photo of her raising a glass of champagne in what looked like a club with Haydie and Raquel flanking her on either side. "Happy New Year!!!" was the caption.

"Who is that from? Montgomery?" Margo said, her expression hopeful.

Emma gave her sister a look. "No. Just Lulu and the girls. They're all celebrating in Paris this year."

"Sounds awful."

She ignored her sister and texted Lulu back, promising to call next week even though she knew it would likely result in them playing phone tag for a month, and then began riffling through her clothes again.

"I love that you're the hostess of this party with him," Margo mused. "You're like the perfect team!"

Emma ignored the stab of annoyance that had been present all week as she planned this party entirely on her own. She picked up a hot-pink crepe one-piece. "What about a jumpsuit?"

"Well, it's gorgeous," Margo said, motioning at the screen as if her observation was obvious. "I'm not sure I can endorse a one-piece, though. Not as easy for him to bend you over a table for a quickie."

Emma turned back to the mirror, her brow furrowing as she considered.

"Oh my God, Emma, I was kidding!" Margo exclaimed, her eyes wide. "Wait, have you slept with him?"

"No, I haven't slept with him," she said, as if she hadn't been contemplating doing just that every day since their moment in the kitchen.

"Are you going to sleep with him?" Margo's face was so close to the camera now that Emma could practically see her pores.

"I'm going to hang up," she replied, moving to close the computer.

"I'm sorry! I'll shut up."

Emma withdrew her hand. "Thank you."

"You like him though, right?"

She studied the bright pink fabric of the jumpsuit as if it would buy her time.

Montgomery Knox. Yes, he was a bit flaky. And he had taken his time coming to New York to meet her in the first place. But still, now that she had a person to fit with the name, a face and lips and hands . . . her heart tripped in her chest.

"Well?" Margo's voice brought her attention back to the room.

"Montgomery is very nice and he's very cute and we'll see what happens," Emma said, as if it was a mantra to herself as much as to her sister.

Margo squealed. "You're totally going to sleep with him!"

Emma rolled her eyes. "Stop."

"Name your first baby after me!"

"Goodbye," Emma sang, already closing her laptop.

"Wait, what are you going to wea—" The audio went silent as the screen clicked shut.

Emma took a deep breath, turning back to the mirror.

She knew what Montgomery was expecting tonight. It was the same thing Margo was expecting, apparently. But it didn't help clarify what Emma actually wanted tonight at all.

Get a hold of yourself, she mentally chided as she straightened her shoulders. She had never been nervous around guys before, and she wasn't about to start now. It was fine, she was fine, and more important, she was in control.

She decided on the jumpsuit.

~

Montgomery had told Emma that the party started "when everyone showed up," which made his request that she arrive early a bit of a conundrum. Thankfully, since she had arranged for the caterers to arrive at six and the DJ to be set up by seven, she knew she could safely arrive at eight without cutting it too close.

The house was already buzzing with activity when she arrived. The front door was open for the caterers as they filed in and out with equipment, but she still rang the bell, holding her cashmere coat close to her body as she waited.

It was a long minute before Montgomery arrived, lazily approaching the entranceway. He was dressed up in a blue velvet tuxedo jacket and a crisp white shirt unbuttoned low to reveal his smooth chest. His black pants were tight and highlighted a pair of snakeskin boots. Emma tried to discern if it was perfect or entirely too much.

"Hello, gorgeous," he said, opening the door a bit wider so she could enter, but not wide enough that she didn't have to brush against his body to walk into the foyer.

She began to take off her coat, but Montgomery was there before she could finish, pulling it off her shoulders slowly before throwing it over his arm. He came around to face her then, smiling as his gaze went down her body.

"You look good enough to eat."

She laughed. The sound rang fake in her ears, a way to disguise her nerves as she stood there under his intense gaze.

"So, do you want the tour?" he asked.

"Not unless you want to give me one."

"Oh really?" he replied.

"Well, the Crawfords are friends of the family, so it's not my first time here."

"Ah." He offered her a lopsided grin. "But it's your first time with me."

Emma smiled back, her pulse thundering in her ears as he led her forward, his hand on the small of her back.

The foyer opened up into the living room, and Emma had to admit that Margo was right: Montgomery had transformed the place. The Crawfords had defined their home by how much they could fit within it—layered rugs and numerous sofas, coffee tables piled with books and walls covered with photographs of their extended family—but the space was now white and sparse, with only two black leather sofas facing each other. On the wall above them was a huge canvas crowded with every color imaginable, a patchwork of graffiti and dripping paint and a random stencil of JFK in the center. Wait . . .

Oh no. It couldn't be . . .

"It's a Max Betrug," Montgomery said, nodding to the canvas.

Oh God. It was.

Emma tried to smile, working so hard to bite her tongue, she thought she might taste blood. From the size of it alone, she knew it must have cost a fortune. It was also just . . . not good. A mess of color and paint by a street artist who was revealed to be fake, a persona created to be trademarked and licensed and . . . there was no way Montgomery didn't know that, right?

But when she turned back to him and saw how he was staring at it like he had impressed even himself, Emma realized that she was apparently very wrong.

Don't be a snob, don't be a snob.

"What about the rest of the house?" she said brightly, already moving toward the hall.

The dining room in the back of the house was buzzing with activity. Waiters with trays full of canapés were positioning themselves in the corners, with more coming up from the kitchen on the lower level. The dining table had been moved to the side and there was a bar set up, with bartenders preparing bottles and glasses.

Beyond them was the conservatory, a large glass cage that revealed the sun disappearing behind the building beyond the back garden. The room had been cleared except for a DJ booth, where a man with pink hair frowned down at a large board of slides and turntables, testing the speakers that had been placed in each corner.

The conservatory doors were open to the garden, as Emma had suggested, and everything there seemed ready, too. Tall heaters were positioned around different groups of chairs scattered across the yard with fairy lights strung above.

Emma smiled to herself. It was perfect.

She turned to tell Montgomery as much, but instead her gaze snagged on the double doors just to her left. They were open, and for the first time she noticed the freshly painted white room beyond. Emma remembered that room. Or at least a darker, more cramped version of it. When it had been Mr. Crawford's office, it was defined by crowded bookcases along the walls and heavy green velvet curtains on its tall window. He used to have a huge mahogany desk in the center, so large that she could hide beneath it while he and her father chatted, pretending not to hear the small secret spy giggling at their feet.

Now the room was practically empty. The bookcases were gone. So was the desk. Instead there was a glass coffee table in the center surrounded by four round chairs that sat low to the ground. They looked like they had been molded from huge pieces of pink plastic with no intention of anyone ever sitting in them at all.

Montgomery followed her line of sight and smiled smugly. "They're made from recycled bottles."

"They're . . . great."

He nodded as if this were a given. Then he glanced at a side mirror to adjust his long hair behind his ear.

She had to work hard to curb the desire to roll her eyes. God, Knightley would hate this. The pretension. The effort. All of it.

Emma shook her head, trying to dislodge the thought.

"Should I show you upstairs?" Montgomery asked, leaning in so his lips were close to her ear.

"Yes, upstairs," she said, a little too quickly.

It came out before she had time to think through what "upstairs" meant. But when she turned around and saw Montgomery waiting, the corner of his lips curled up as he held out his hand for her to take, her heart tripped over itself.

She took his hand. His fingers were soft, and she studied them as he led her back to the foyer and up the stairs, how loosely they held her own. His nails looked manicured, perfect . . . just like everything else in the house: too aware of itself, as if curated only to impress others. It was like someone's version of a museum, if they had never been to a museum before.

Oh God. Had Montgomery never been to—

"I'm going to assume you've never been in this room," Montgomery purred.

She looked up from his hand and found herself staring into a bedroom. He was right—she had never been in the master bedroom before, but she wasn't sure it mattered, anyway. There was no way this room resembled how the Crawfords had it.

The walls were painted a dark shade of navy and in the fading evening light they looked almost black, disappearing behind the looming bed in the center. And there, over the velvet headboard, was another painting.

Emma swallowed. *You have to be kidding me.*

It was a portrait of Montgomery. It was abstract and composed of different colors and crude shapes, but there was no mistaking the subject there at its center, staring down at the mattress.

"What do you think?" Montgomery's breath was warm against her ear, his body suddenly close against her back.

Don't be a snob. The mantra repeated in her mind again. *So he doesn't know art, big deal.* That didn't mean anything—in fact, it was probably a blessing in disguise. Did she really want to date someone who knew everything about her career? Someone constantly looking over her shoulder and measuring her knowledge against their own? Of course not. This was fine. It was *better*.

But somehow . . . she didn't feel better. She felt nervous and claustrophobic and . . .

Montgomery didn't wait for her to figure it out. He slowly moved to stand in front of her, his hand suddenly on her hip. His other hand traced up her bare arm, skimming across her shoulder, her collarbone, then slowly down her sternum, mapping a line down between her breasts to where the deep V-neck of her jumpsuit began.

The tall windows behind him revealed that it was almost dark outside and the house across the street had just turned on their light.

She wondered if Knightley was home right now.

Do not think about Knightley, her mind demanded as Montgomery's hand came down to meet her other hip, as he slowly pulled her closer to him. She let out a shaky breath.

There was no chance Knightley could see them here. There was no chance anyone could. It should have made her feel better, it should have shut off her brain enough to focus on Montgomery's body pressed against her own.

"You're so fucking sexy," he said, his voice low.

"Thanks," she replied.

Thanks? Did she just say "thanks"? And why did her voice sound like that, so high and so strained, a poor imitation of what she should sound like? Shouldn't it sound deeper, weighed down with lust or want or something?

The thought was interrupted as he cupped her jaw and leaned forward to kiss her. His lips felt soft as she closed her eyes, letting his tongue brush against her mouth. She leaned into him, trying to get lost in this, and it hit her suddenly that she was so preoccupied with telling her body what to feel that she wasn't feeling anything at all. She adjusted her face, turning her head to the side, and he took it as a sign to start kissing down her neck, pulling her tighter against him.

"Wait," she whispered, leaning back and creating a few inches of distance from his body.

"What's wrong?" he murmured, but he was already moving close again.

She put her hand on his chest before his lips met hers again. "I . . . I don't think I can do this."

He met her eyes, the fog of desire lifting slowly. He looked down her body, then to the bed only a few feet away. "Like, right now or . . ."

Something in his expression faltered, like this experience was completely alien to him. Was this the first time in his entire life he had ever been turned down? God, maybe it was.

"I'm just not sure . . ." She started then stopped, trying to find the words.

He blinked and then his lazy grin returned. "No worries. The party's about to start, I get it."

She let out a shaky breath. "Right."

He took a step back, looking down at her body again. "But let me know when you're ready. Okay?"

She opened her mouth, ready to explain that she wasn't sure she would ever be, but she was saved by the deep chimes of the doorbell. They both looked to the door.

"Well, I guess that's my cue," he said, unfazed.

She smiled. "I guess so."

~

Emma wasn't sure how it happened, but one minute the house was empty, and the next the party was in full swing. Bodies packed tightly into the dining room, lining up as they admired the questionable art, and piling high onto Montgomery's precious recycled chairs as the throbbing beat of the music vibrated through every bone of Emma's body.

She managed to find space at the bar, and as she waited for the bartender's attention, she scanned the crowd for Nadine. For Mrs. Pawloski. For anyone she knew.

In fact . . . Emma looked around. For a neighborhood party on the Upper East Side, this crowd was exceptionally young. Even more important, Emma didn't recognize anyone.

"Emma!"

She turned to find Nadine maneuvering through the crowd toward the bar. Her honey-brown hair fell around her shoulders, her cheeks flushed. She smiled broadly.

"Oh my God, I didn't think I was going to find you!" she said, her voice almost lost in the music.

"I can't believe you did," Emma said. "I have no idea who any of these people are."

"Well, I just saw Mrs. Pawloski in the living room," Nadine said, nodding back to where she came from. "She's doing shots with three guys in tracksuits, so I think she's okay."

Emma laughed, the tension slowly releasing her body as she gave Nadine a hug. "I'm so glad you're here."

"Me too," Nadine said. "Oh! I met Montgomery at the door! He's so hot!"

"Yeah." Emma's voice came out an octave higher than usual.

Nadine's eyes grew wide. "Did you hook up again?"

"No, not really . . ." She let the words fade and finally shrugged. "I mean, we were about to, but . . . I don't know . . ."

"Well, if it doesn't feel right . . ."

Emma shook the lingering discomfort off. "Doesn't matter. It's New Year's, it's a party, and you're here!"

"Exactly!"

Nadine began to sway with the music, her hips almost hitting a passing waiter. He dodged at the last minute, lowering his full tray of champagne to keep his balance. Nadine's eyes lit up as if it were an offering just for her and she grabbed two glasses. "Oh! Thank you!"

She turned and handed one to Emma.

"As Nana would say: here's to doing and drinking, not sitting and thinking," Nadine said, raising her glass in a dramatic toast.

"Hear, hear, Nana!" Emma concurred and laughed, taking a huge gulp of her drink.

Her head was swimming now, the champagne mixing with the humidity of the room, and she felt light, as if she could float away. As if none of this really mattered anyway, not the disaster with Zane, or the confusion about Montgomery, or even the awkwardness with—

"Knightley!" Nadine exclaimed.

Emma's eyes widened, her weightless heart suddenly falling like lead in her chest.

"What?"

Nadine waved toward the doorway behind Emma. "Knightley's here!"

She took a deep breath and turned.

There he was. Tall and gorgeous in a dark oxford shirt and scarf hanging around his neck. And on his arm was the stunning, dark-haired woman who Emma had seen through her window drinking and flirting with Knightley in the back garden. The same woman who was apparently his date tonight: Davina Sundar.

CHAPTER 18

He wanted to go home. Hell, if Knightley was being honest, he never wanted to leave his house to begin with. It made it worse that he could see the damn thing from a block away: the Crawfords' unassuming townhouse now draped in purple uplights, with music echoing from somewhere behind its massive front door.

He could still go home, he told himself as he and Davina ascended the front steps, but he knew that was a lie. Davina had been grinning ear to ear since he picked her up earlier, and now she was squeezing his arm as they entered the main room, her eyes surveying the crowd, the bar, the dance floor in the conservatory just beyond.

She was lovely, really. Beautiful and intelligent and perfect for him.

But he still just wanted to go home.

"Knightley!" He heard Nadine's voice over the music and looked over to the bar to find her smiling so broadly that he wondered if the drink in her hand wasn't her first. She jumped up and down, looking to her side where Emma stood.

Fuck. She looked gorgeous.

He ignored the thought, instead guiding Davina over to them. "Hello," he said blankly.

Emma mustered a smile, avoiding his gaze as she turned to Davina.

"Hello, you must be Davina," she said. "I'm Emma. I've heard so much about you."

Davina smiled back. "So nice to meet you too . . ." She leaned forward a bit, as if trying to hear over the music. "I'm sorry, what was your name again? Emmy?"

Emma's smile faltered. It only lasted a moment, but he saw it. A sudden wave of guilt flooded Knightley's chest.

"Emma," she answered. "And this is my friend, Nadine."

Davina smiled and nodded.

"I love your outfit," Nadine said, motioning to Davina's black velvet mini dress.

"Thank you. It's Alexandre Vauthier," Davina said, smoothing the front of her skirt.

Nadine nodded, though her forehead creased, as if whatever Davina had just said was a foreign language.

"You look lovely, Nadine," Knightley said.

Nadine held out her hands and gave a mock-curtsy. "Thank you. It's H&M."

He could see Emma trying to bite back a smile, a real one this time. She almost managed it, too, but as soon as Nadine turned to her, they both dissolved into laughter, leaning into each other as they tried miserably to stop. He looked down to Davina, expecting a look of disapproval on her face, but found her smiling too, like she was moments away from joining them.

The laughter died a moment later and suddenly the foursome was swallowed up in silence. The pounding music, the cacophony of conversation, nothing penetrated the bubble of awkwardness that they found themselves in. And it was only when Knightley met Nadine's gaze again, how she looked like she was waiting for something, how her eyes darted to Emma's outfit, that he realized why: she was expecting him to compliment Emma, too.

Of course he should compliment her. God, he wanted to. But the words became entangled in his throat, a mess of what he should say and what he wanted to.

You look nice, Emma.

You are stunning.

I hate what you're doing to me.

Emma was staring at him now, her eyebrow raised as if she was waiting for him to say something too. *Shit.*

He opened his mouth, not even sure what was about to come out, when a booming voice interrupted him.

"Ah, look at these beautiful people!" Montgomery appeared between Emma and Nadine, throwing his arms around each of them. "Everyone having a good time?"

He already looked drunk, his shirt unbuttoned down to his navel and pieces of glitter in his hair. A cliché of a cliché.

"It's amazing," Nadine gushed. "I am seriously going to drink all of your champagne."

"You better. I'll be disappointed if there's any still here tomorrow morning," he replied, leaning toward her as if they had some sort of secret. Then he turned to Davina. "I don't think we've met."

Knightley tried not to grimace and thought he got away with it, but then he caught Emma's gaze. She was watching him, a look of amusement in her eyes. Almost as if she knew just what he was thinking, as if she felt the same way. Odd.

He cleared his throat and nodded to Montgomery. "Montgomery, this is Davina Sundar. She's a colleague. Davina, this is Montgomery Knox."

Davina's eyes lit up. "Oh, so this is your house?"

"For a bit." He grinned, looking between her and Nadine. "Would you ladies like a tour?"

Nadine clapped her hands. "Yes please!"

"I would love that. I mean, if that's all right," Davina replied before looking to Knightley as if she needed his permission. As if he would care one way or another.

"Of course," he said, forcing a smile onto his face to mask his indifference.

Montgomery gave her a mock-bow and then offered his arms to both women. "Let's start in the living room. I have an original Max Betrug, you know."

The three of them disappeared into the crowd and the awful, ugly silence descended again. It had never been like this. Ever. What had once been so natural and easy was now hard. It felt like a living thing was taking up real estate between them, making it hard to breathe.

"Hello, Knightley," she finally said, bringing her eyes up to meet his.

"Hello, Woodhouse," he replied, turning toward the bar as he said it. He didn't want to have to look at her. He couldn't. She looked too fucking beautiful tonight, her cheeks flushed and her eyes bright. So instead, he waved to the bartender and pointed to a bottle of scotch.

"Fashionably late, I see," she mused.

He watched the bartender pour his drink, tempted to just grab the bottle, but he waited until the glass was offered before taking it and turning to her again. "I didn't know I could be late to something that didn't have an exact start time."

"And yet, with less than an hour before midnight, you still managed it."

"I have a reputation to uphold," he said, raising his glass in mock-deference. "And I didn't want to interrupt your date."

She rolled her eyes. "It's not a date."

"No? I could have sworn that's what you called it the other day." He took a sip of his drink. It burned as it slid down his throat.

"I'm surprised you were even listening," she replied, raising an eyebrow at him.

"Only barely."

"So, par for the course, then," she said. Her tone was nonchalant but somehow still earnest, like she was trying to steer them to familiar territory, their good-natured volleys of barbs and jokes. But neither of them knew how to get back there, and in the meantime, they had to settle for this cheap imitation, one marred by sharp edges and brittle foundations.

He took another sip of his drink.

After a long moment, Emma said, "Davina seems nice."

He nodded. "She is."

"She's very beautiful."

He nodded again.

"And *very* sophisticated," she said, as if prodding him.

"Yes, well. She's an adult."

The words rolled off his tongue before he could stop them, but it was too late. He saw their impact—how her smile fell, how her bare shoulders tensed, how she leaned back as if he had landed an actual blow.

"Yeah. Yes. That she is." She stumbled over her words, darting her eyes over the crowded room like there was a lifeline somewhere that she could grab on to. "You know what, I'm going to go check out the rest of the party."

"Emma, I didn't—"

"No, it's fine. Really." She smiled again, small and sad, but God if it wasn't genuine. "I'll see you later, Knightley."

It sounded so . . . final. She paused, staring at him a moment longer, and then turned and disappeared among the guests, leaving him alone.

CHAPTER 19

Emma wandered the party aimlessly, weaving through the crowd, not even sure what she was looking for. She finally made it to the living room and found a huge crowd jumping up and down as music pounded off the walls. Brightly colored glow sticks waved in their hands, and a few blow-up beach balls bounced overhead. The bartender had added plastic LED ice cubes to the night's signature drink, and now everyone's glasses lit up and blinked as they moved together on the dance floor.

The party was a success. And Emma had made it happen. That sort of triumph usually sent a thrill through her, a wave of excitement. Yet, as she surveyed the scene in front of her, it wasn't all that exciting.

She wanted to go home. But of course she couldn't. It wasn't even midnight yet, and she was the hostess, after all.

Still, she needed space.

There were heaters in the backyard, so she decided to head that way, down the hall toward the conservatory that led to the garden. Bodies blocked the way on every side as she started in that direction, and she was struggling so hard to get through them that she almost walked straight into a woman emerging from a side bathroom.

"Oh!" She caught herself before almost walking directly into Davina Sundar.

Davina seemed equally caught off guard, smoothing the front of her dress and giving Emma a nod. "Hello."

"Hi."

Emma waited, expecting Davina to say something, perhaps offer a compliment about the party, the decorations, the food. But by the time she realized a brief greeting was all she was going to get, the moment was bordering on awkward. So Emma broadened her practiced smile and asked over the music, "Are you enjoying the party?"

Davina leaned toward her. "What?"

"Are you enjoying the party?" Emma repeated, practically yelling.

"Oh, yes," the woman said, eyes darting over Emma's shoulder at the undulating crowd. "It's quite a scene, isn't it?"

Emma allowed herself a moment to beam. "Well, it was a lot to pull together, let me tell you. Especially on such short notice. Luckily, Montgomery is friends with the DJ and my brother-in-law knows the caterer, so the rest of it was really just logistics. But between you and me, I'm still surprised we pulled it off. I've learned that Montgomery is the worst at planning ahead."

Davina's brow furrowed. "I . . . I didn't know you two were together."

"Oh, we're not," Emma said. The words came before she had time to realize they barely affected her. "Not like that, anyway. I was just helping with the party since he's new to the neighborhood. He left it all to me, so it completely monopolized the past couple of weeks. I mean, who works between Christmas and New Year's?"

She released a tittering laugh and Davina smiled. "Just you and I, apparently."

"You were working, too?"

Davina nodded, scanning the crowd again. "There are usually a substantial number of asylum applications we need to submit to the government before the end of the year to ensure they're processed."

Emma swallowed. "Of course. Right."

Davina caught her expression and quickly added. "It is a fantastic party, though."

Embarrassment heated Emma's cheeks. God, she felt so small. She had spent the past week racing around organizing balloons and canapés, all while this woman had been saving actual lives.

"Yes, well," she replied, working hard to keep her tone unaffected. "It's still just a party."

Davina nodded again, her gaze sliding over Emma's shoulder. It looked like she was searching the crowd for someone.

"Are you looking for Knightley?"

"George? Oh, no. I'm actually going back upstairs. Montgomery wanted to show off the roof terrace," Davina replied. There was amusement in her eyes, but it dimmed when she saw Emma's expression. "Were you looking for Montgomery?"

"No," Emma said with a tired scoff. "No, after this past year I'm going to make a New Year's resolution to swear off men entirely."

Emma meant it to sound like a joke, but realized Davina wasn't smiling. She tried to manufacture one herself but it felt too strained. Too fake. She finally gave up and shrugged.

Davina's expression softened. "It gets easier, you know."

Emma frowned. "What gets easier?"

"Men," Davina said. "Especially once you learn that some of them are right for you and some of them are just for right now."

The words struck a chord somewhere in Emma's chest. "How do you tell the difference?"

Davina let out a soft laugh; the sound was lost in the music. "Don't worry. They find a way of letting you know." Then she turned and started toward the staircase. "Happy New Year, Emily."

"It's Emma," she corrected her, but Davina was already gone, her smooth movements disappearing up the stairs.

Emma watched her go and let out a deep breath. She needed some fresh air.

CHAPTER 20

Knightley was still at the bar finishing his second whiskey when they started handing out the streamers and hats and noisemakers. In the back of his mind, he knew he should find Davina. It was coming up to midnight, and even if they weren't exclusive, she would want to be there next to him. That was the reason you brought a date to a New Year's Eve party, wasn't it? The countdown, the kiss, all of it.

But right now, the laughter, the cheering, the music—it all felt stifling, a mess of fake revelry and cheer when all Knightley wanted was peace and quiet. He needed to think.

He headed out of the crowded dining room, through the throng on the small conservatory dance floor, and into the backyard.

There were tall heaters littered throughout the space that had melted the snow, so his feet treaded on brown grass as he walked across the garden. A few chairs were set up for guests, but they were empty, as was the stone fountain in the far corner that was partly hidden behind a large topiary bush.

He stopped next to it, letting his head fall back as the tension in his body released. Even with the heaters, the air was cold, and he welcomed the rush of freezing air into his lungs.

"Come here often?"

He stilled, not sure if the voice was in his head or right there next to him. But when he looked down to the fountain, there was Emma. She was perched on its stone ledge, champagne in hand, her high heels placed neatly beside her.

"Hello," he said. He was smiling. A real smile, for the first time all night.

"Hello," she replied. "Looking for your date?"

He shook his head. "I think she's with yours."

Emma sighed, leaning back. "He's not my date, Knightley."

Shit.

"Sorry, I forgot." He held up his hands in mock-surrender.

She stared up at him for a moment with pinched brows, as if considering her forgiveness. Finally, she nodded to the space on the stone ledge next to her.

He took it.

The music still throbbed, but it sounded distant. He looked around, only now noticing how hidden their spot was from the rest of the party. How the shadows and the hedge made them almost invisible.

"What are you doing out here?" he asked.

She shrugged. "I needed some space."

He nodded.

"What about you?" she asked.

"I fucking hate techno."

She laughed, the loud and uninhibited sound so surprising that he felt it in his chest. He tore his eyes away from her and focused on his hands. "Listen. I'm sorry. About earlier."

"It's okay."

"No it's not."

"No, I mean . . . this is how we work, right? I say something, you correct me." She sighed and shrugged. "It's fine."

She didn't mean it as an insult, but it still felt like one. Is that how she saw him? A man who was only there to highlight her faults? Jesus.

Before he could dwell on it, she shifted next to him, catching his attention. The lights from the house silhouetted her profile. "You look lovely tonight."

She rolled her eyes as she tipped her head back and drank the last of her champagne.

"I'm serious," he continued. "You look beautiful."

"Well, I went through, like, a million outfits. I think this is Lanvin," she said, running her hands down her legs. "Or maybe Rotate? I don't know."

"I'm not talking about the outfit, Woodhouse. I'm talking about you."

Her eyes darted away from him, finding something interesting in the grass at her feet.

"Thank you," she replied softly.

Silence filled the space between them again, but it didn't feel as foreign as it had earlier. This was familiar. Comfortable. Like here in this dark corner next to a bush and an empty fountain, away from the music and the crowds, was that lost nugget of what they once had.

"It was nice seeing you and Nadine earlier," he said after a moment.

She turned to him. "Was it?"

He nodded. "It made me realize I was wrong before. When I said that you were being selfish with her." He let his eyes survey the yard again as he considered. "It's been a tough year for you. Saying goodbye to Margo. Getting ready for graduation. Applying for this Met internship. It's good to see that you have someone there for you through all of it."

She cocked her head to the side. "What do you mean?"

He rubbed the back of his neck, trying to find the right words. "I mean . . . I'm glad you have a friend. I'm glad you have a best friend."

"Well, yeah. Nadine is an amazing friend," Emma agreed, glancing back to the party. "But she's not my best friend."

"No?"

"Of course not. You are."

He turned to her. She was staring down at the brown grass again, running her toes along the stiff blades. But he could still make out her expression in the shadows, how her bottom lip was trapped between her teeth. The slight flush of her cheeks. There was no hint of ego or defense. There was just Emma.

The thumping music faded and a slower song replaced it, filtering across the yard to where they sat. Knightley immediately recognized it as "Unchained Melody," but a modern cover, only a solitary woman's voice and a piano.

"Well, this isn't techno," he murmured.

She laughed softly. "Definitely not."

He stood and took a few steps toward the garden, then motioned her forward.

She froze, eyes wide, a small smile still on her face. "What?"

"C'mere."

"Why?"

"Because I'm asking you to dance, Woodhouse."

Her smile faltered, and she looked up at him like he had said something substantial. Something that mattered. Perhaps he had. There was a heavy weight somewhere in his chest that felt like it was constricting his breath, waiting for her reply before it snapped free.

Then she stood. Her smile had faded, but her eyes were still locked with his.

"Then ask me," she said.

He took his time walking back to her, stopping with only inches between them.

"Would you like to dance, Emma?"

She didn't answer, and for a moment Knightley thought she would say no. But then she put one hand on his chest and the other in his outstretched hand. With bare feet, her head barely met his shoulder, but she still fit against him perfectly as he pulled her close and began to sway with the music.

Knightley had never learned to dance, not properly, but then, this wasn't dancing. Nothing as choreographed or planned as that. This was his chance to just hold her, to feel her body against his for a few precious minutes.

A soft sigh and he felt her forehead rest against his chest. The rigidness of her body faded and she became pliable in his arms, molding to his planes and angles as if all resistance had been abandoned. Yes, he knew that feeling. This battle he had been waging, this struggle for the status quo, to keep them right where they had always been, it was exhausting. He didn't even know when it had begun, but he couldn't maintain it. And at that moment, moving together to the music, he could feel himself begin to give up.

There was a rise in the voices from inside, some cheering and yelling and suddenly the music cut out as the DJ's voice thundered through the night air. "Here we go, everybody! Get ready! 10...9...8...7..."

Knightley froze, his arms still around Emma as she pulled back enough to look up at him.

"...6...5...4..."

She was so close he could see the white tendrils of her warm breath in the cold air. He could just lean down; her lips were only inches away...

"...3...2...1! Happy New Year!"

Screams and cheers and laughing exploded from the house, echoing off the buildings around them. But it all sounded far away, so fucking distant as he stared down at her.

"Happy New Year, Emma," he murmured.

"Happy New Year," she replied. Her voice was raspy and deep.

He leaned down and grazed his lips against her cheek. But he didn't pull back. He couldn't. She smelled sweet, her perfume mixed with the warmth of her body, with *her*, and he couldn't help how his grip tightened, how he held her against his body as if she were about to disappear.

He turned his head slightly so his lips were hovering over hers, breathing the same air—a mix of champagne and whiskey and heat. She sighed and tilted her head up, pressing her body against his.

"Emma..." he growled, but the rest of his words became vapor in his throat, fading as he groaned. He wanted to kiss her, hold her, bring her home and worry about the consequences later. Nothing else mattered in that moment, nothing would if—

"Emma!" Nadine's voice cut through the air.

Knightley froze as Emma's body tensed under his fingers. Neither of them breathed as they heard her name again.

"Emma! Where are you? Happy New Year!"

It was instinct that made him step away from her, rake a hand through his hair and curse under his breath. He closed his eyes, trying to regain some control of his body in the few precious moments they had left. When he opened them he saw Emma still standing in front of him, her arms wrapped around herself.

Shit.

"I should go find Davina."

"Right." She stared at him a moment longer, the fog lifting from her gaze. "Happy New Year, Knightley."

He nodded, looking down her body one more time. That was it. That was his moment. That short, precious moment, and now it was gone.

"Happy New Year, Woodhouse," he said. And then he walked toward the house without looking back.

CHAPTER 21

Emma stared at the empty fountain for a long time. Somewhere in the periphery she could hear the party raging: the cheering and the celebration. She could hear Nadine still yelling for her. But nothing was louder than the voice in her own head.

I almost kissed Knightley.

Her fingers instinctively went to her lips. Was it the almost-kiss that had her so thrown? Or how the idea of kissing him hadn't thrown her at all? It felt so natural, like it should have happened. Like, in that moment, it *had* to.

But it didn't. He had pulled away, left abruptly. It was as if he had read her thoughts and tried to shoot her down in the kindest way possible. Now he was off somewhere with his gorgeous date and she was here, staring at the landscaping.

It hurt. A distinct, sharp pain in her heart that flared with the realization that, despite how things would have changed, she had wanted it. She still did. And he didn't.

"Emma!" Nadine's voice pulled her attention. She turned just as her friend rushed across the yard and threw her arms around her. "Knightley said you were out here! Happy New Year! Come on, we have to celebrate!"

Before Emma could reply, Nadine took her hand and pulled her back toward the house and onto the crowded dance floor. They were pressed in on all sides by undulating bodies, random new friends who dropped neon necklaces over their heads and threw streamers into the air. Nadine jumped and flailed and smiled under the flashing lights like she was in her element.

Emma tried to lose herself in the music too, the deafening beat that was vibrating through her bones, but every time she closed her eyes, she saw Knightley. The feel of his body against hers, his face inches away, that intoxicating mix of leather and pine on his skin.

When she opened her eyes again, she suddenly realized she was very tired. Of smiling, of pretending, of all of it. She was ready to go home.

Emma leaned toward her friend and yelled over the music, "I think I'm going to call it a night!"

"What? No!" Nadine pleaded. "This is the best party I've ever been to!"

"I'm just tired. But you should stay!"

"Are you sure?"

"Absolutely," Emma replied. "You have a key, right? Just text me when you leave and head up to the guest room."

Nadine nodded and lunged toward her to give her another hug, then turned back to the dance floor.

Emma sighed. It was time to go.

～

The cold night air was sobering as Emma stepped outside, the front door slamming closed behind her. The vibrations of the music ebbed as she held her coat tight around her body and descended the steps to the sidewalk.

She didn't bother turning on any lights when she entered her house, just headed downstairs to get a glass of water. She drank it all in one gulp and then filled the glass again, sipping more slowly this time as her eyes scanned the kitchen, finally falling on the French doors that led out to the back garden. To the townhouse there just beyond that well-worn path.

Knightley's windows were dark, just like they were the night Montgomery kissed her for the first time. He probably wasn't home yet. Would he bring Davina there afterward? Offer her a glass of wine before pulling her upstairs? Emma's mind began to churn out images of what that would look like, the view she would be privy to from her window, and she squeezed her eyes shut.

Don't go there.

Her phone buzzed in her hand and she looked down to see a text message light up the screen:

NADINE

> IM TALKINGG TO A GUY WHOS AN ARTIST AND HE KNITTS CONDOMS AND HE IS SO HOT COM BACK TO THE PARTTTYYY!!!

EMMA

> Already on my way to bed but stay as long as you can! The guest room is ready whenever you are :)

> AWW. OK. BTW KNGHTLIY GOT MEE SOMEtING CALED A FRENCH 75 IT IS SO GOOD!

Emma sighed. Even Knightley was staying longer than her. But at least he was still there. She didn't want to think about why that was comforting as she headed up to her room.

She took her time ascending the stairs to the second floor, slowly opening her door and turning on the light on the nightstand before sitting on the edge of her bed. A bit of the champagne was still swimming in her head, and she let her body go limp, falling backward and sinking into her comforter. She felt a bit guilty for bailing without saying goodbye to Montgomery, but the idea of staying . . . she shook her head. She would call and apologize tomorrow.

She yawned. God, she should wash off her makeup. At least put on some pajamas. Her body didn't listen, though, remaining planted in place as she stared up at the ceiling. After a long moment she sat up, ignoring the pull of sleep as she peeked out her window.

The house looming on the other side of the garden was still dark. Of course it was; he was still at the party. In fact, he was on a date with another woman at that very moment. A gorgeous woman who saved lives and walked like she was in slow motion. Why did Emma think he would even consider kissing her tonight when he had someone like Davina waiting to go home to his bed?

Regardless, he was still her best friend. And Emma was willing to bet she was his. After all, was there anyone else in his life who knew him as well as she did? Certainly not Davina Sundar.

She stretched her arms above her head and caught her reflection in the full-length mirror on the opposite wall and stared at the loose strands of her dark chestnut hair falling in front of her face, the slope of her neck down to her shoulders. She stood and took out her gold earrings, dropping them on her desk. Then she smoothed out the front of her jumpsuit.

She could be as sexy as Davina Sundar. That's what men liked, right? It was what Knightley liked, apparently. Surely Montgomery too. Someone who exuded sex?

Her reflection stared back at her as she stepped out of her heels onto her bare feet, instantly losing a few inches from her height. She pulled the elastic out of her hair, watching the dark locks fall over her shoulders. She studied her skin too, impressed with how nice her partly smudged makeup looked even after hours of partying. Her lips were still red, her cheeks naturally flushed, and her eyes were lined in black. She took her lip-gloss from her pink jumpsuit's hidden pocket and added more color and shine, pouting at her image.

There was no denying that she was pretty, Emma knew that. But sexy? Hmm.

Her head canted to the side as she reached behind herself and unzipped the top of her jumpsuit. It had a built-in bustier and was tighter than she realized, constricting and pushing up her chest. In one quick motion, she let her clothes fall to the ground and stepped out of them, standing in just her black lace strapless bra and underwear. It felt ridiculous.

She wondered if Davina Sundar ever had to work at being sexy. Probably not; she seemed to walk the line between sexy and sophisticated effortlessly. But did she know how Knightley took his coffee? How he hated loud talkers at the movies and was allergic to sunflower seeds?

Maybe none of that mattered, though. The heels Emma wore because she needed the extra height, the lace underwear she picked because of who might get to see it—all of it felt flimsy now, like she had decided to play a part tonight. She didn't want to play anymore.

Her shoulders slumped. She turned to the window and leaned her forehead against it, bracing her hands against the cold glass as she squinted to see into Knightley's room. Still dark, no hint of movement. Then her gaze traveled down to the brown manicured grounds, hibernating until spring. Without the leaves on the trees she could see the path to Knightley's clearly. She wasn't afraid of heights, but from this vantage point, she felt dizzy.

A thought hit her then: What if someone was watching her right now? Her heart tripped in her chest as she looked up at Knightley's dark window again. What if he was there? What if he looked out and saw her standing here in this underwear, not bothering to cover up? Not even wanting to? The thought made her pulse quicken. She stared into the darkness, pretending it was Knightley's deep golden-brown eyes staring back; that maybe his skin was still humming from her touch, her smell was still lingering in his nose.

But then a moment passed. And another. And she realized no one was there at all. Emma was all alone.

The beeping of her phone brought her back to reality. She turned to her bed, where she had dropped it when she first walked in, and picked it up.

NADINE

> JUST GOT IN! I"M INN THE GUEST ROOOM SEE U IN THE AM!

Emma blushed. God, she had been so lost in her own thoughts, she hadn't even heard her friend come in.

EMMA

She started for her bed, slowly reaching her hands behind her and unfastening her bra. It fell to the ground. Then she slipped on a sleep shirt, washed her face, and brushed her teeth, before crawling into bed and turning off her bedside lamp. Darkness fell around her as she stared up at the ceiling again.

It really was such a waste that only she got to see how sexy she looked tonight.

CHAPTER 22

Knightley was already on the fourth mile of his run as the sun came up. It crested the buildings along Fifth Avenue just as he rounded the reservoir, his breath already heavy and his shirt soaked through with sweat. It was cold and he could no longer feel the tips of his fingers or his nose, but he didn't care. Numbness was the point.

But it wasn't working.

Anger still prickled under his skin at how he had left Emma out there in the garden. He could have just told her how he felt. Hell, he could have kissed her. But he didn't. He walked away.

Afterward, he had wandered that ridiculous house until he found Davina in the dining room, chatting with a group of people he didn't know and didn't want to. All he cared about was that Montgomery was nowhere to be seen, and neither was Emma. It felt like a punch low in his gut.

"Ready?" he had asked Davina, leaning close so she would hear him over the music.

"Right now? The party's just getting started," she had said, offering him a playful frown. It hit him then that he didn't really care if she stayed without him or not. That he would rather go home alone tonight. But he didn't say it. Instead, he gave her a quick peck on the cheek and asked her to text him when she left so he could send a car.

It was only when he descended the front steps to the sidewalk, when he inhaled the sharp bite of the cold air into his lungs, that he realized he couldn't go home. Because Emma might be home too, right across the yard. Or worse, she might not come home at all. If he went back to his house, he would simply sit there and brood, stare at her dark window, and wait until she returned. So he had walked the empty streets of the Upper East Side, replaying the night over and over in his head. His own personalized brand of torture.

When he finally ended up back at home hours later, he had barely closed the front door before stripping off his clothes, leaving a trail from the foyer to the wet bar in the sitting room. Then he downed three fingers of whiskey and collapsed into one of the armchairs, waiting for the alcohol to do its job. But his mind refused to shut off, wandering back to the place he was trying to avoid: that window waiting for him across the yard, the one he could see if he went upstairs to bed. And after a few hours of fitful sleep in that chair, he went for a run to avoid it further.

Knightley picked up the pace now, widening his strides toward the reservoir's South Gatehouse as if it would erase the moment that had been replaying over and over again in his memory: those wide green eyes looking up at him, those lips slightly hovering near his own. The smell of her skin and the warmth of her body, how it had all made his blood hum.

Even now in the bracing cold, as he stopped to catch his breath at the park entrance on 85th Street, he could feel the mix of desire and guilt itching under his skin. But regardless of what almost transpired at the party, he should have known better. She had no idea how his feelings had changed, and instead of talking to her about it, he had almost crossed a line that would have made this all so much worse. He would have to admit everything, apologize, and try to salvage what was left of their friendship at the end of all this. Simple as that.

With new resolve, he headed back home, barely looking up as he crossed Fifth Avenue and started down 84th. He entered his house, headed upstairs, and turned on the shower. The water was scalding, but he needed it, staying in long enough for his skin to feel raw. Then he got dressed in worn jeans and a sweater, barely running a towel over his head before he started downstairs and out to the backyard.

He saw Emma through the Woodhouses' French doors as soon as he crossed the threshold to their garden. He paused at the door, watching as she poured a cup of coffee, idly stirring in some milk. Relief flooded his body, loosening the tension that was still holding tight to his chest. Perhaps she hadn't stayed at Montgomery's last night after all.

Her hair was pulled up in a messy bun and a robe hung over her oversized T-shirt and flannel pants. She must have just woken up, but she looked agitated. Her skin was flushed and her bottom lip was trapped between her teeth as if distracted by whatever thoughts were swirling in her mind.

He cleared his throat and knocked on the glass before opening the door, but she still jumped slightly, turning and facing him with wide eyes.

"Morning," he said.

"Hello. Hi," she replied, tripping over the words as she darted her eyes away from his. Somehow her cheeks became even more ruddied, and it took her another moment before she recovered enough to add, "Good morning."

"How was the rest of your night?"

"Great. Super," she said, trying to shrug and take a sip of her coffee at the same time. It caused her to almost choke on it.

Something was wrong. He opened his mouth to ask her what, but then he clamped it shut. This was about last night. He had almost kissed her and then hadn't even bothered to say good night. How the hell could she not feel awkward right now? Then another possibility snaked its way into his head: maybe it had nothing to do with him at all. She spent the night with Montgomery and had just come home afterward to find her neighbor awkwardly hovering at the back door.

"Can I grab some of that?" he asked, nodding to the coffee-maker.

She blinked. "You're asking if you can have a cup of coffee?"

"Should I not?"

"I just don't think you've ever asked permission."

He scoffed, grabbing a mug and pouring from the carafe as an excuse to avoid her gaze.

"So, how late did you stay out partying last night?" she asked.

"I wasn't out partying. I was at a party."

"Okay, then how long did you stay at the party after . . ." Her voice trailed off.

He took a sip of his coffee. It was hot and bitter, and he felt it run the full course from his lips to his stomach. "Not long."

"Oh," she said in the tone of voice she used when she was trying to sound nonchalant. "Does Davina live nearby or . . ."

Shit. Did she think he left the party and went home with Davina?

"No, she didn't . . . I didn't . . ." His words failed, and suddenly the silence between them was like a weight against his chest. "I need to talk to you about last night, Emma. I have to apologize and tell you—"

"Good morning, George," Mr. Woodhouse proclaimed as he entered the kitchen. "You already got a run in?"

Knightley leaned away from Emma, forcing a smile. "Yes, sir."

"Good man," he replied, opening the fridge and reemerging with a glass pitcher filled with green juice. "Nothing gets rid of a hangover like vigorous exercise. As long as you stay hydrated. Did you stay hydrated?"

"Yes, I stayed hydrated," Knightley assured him.

"That's what I like to hear. Emma, you should start running with George. It would be good for you."

Emma let out a nervous laugh, stepping back and walking around the island to sit on one of the cushioned stools. "I'll get right on that."

"Cold air in your lungs, the sun at your back. Just you and the open road." Mr. Woodhouse sighed, staring off into the distance.

Knightley nodded to him. "Sounds like you should come with me."

"God, no," Mr. Woodhouse scoffed. "The pavement is much too hard on my joints. I have the Pro-Fit TRM 8000 upstairs, remember? It has integrated shock absorption and a full biometric display. It measures heart rate and blood pressure."

Knightley looked over at Emma to find her staring at him. They shared a secret smile and for a moment it was like it always had been, two friends silently commiserating. But then her eyes darted to his lips. A new flush bloomed on her cheeks, and she quickly looked down into the depths of her coffee as Mr. Woodhouse continued undaunted.

"And the screen is HD. Thirty-two inches. I can stream any environment so it's almost like I am running outside."

"That's incredible," Knightley said with as much enthusiasm as he could muster.

"Incredible!" Mr. Woodhouse exclaimed, smiling as he poured himself a large glass of whatever the hell was in that pitcher.

Knightley turned back to Emma, who was still studying the bottom of her almost empty mug.

"Emma, do you think you and I could talk for a—"

"Please tell me there's coffee," Nadine moaned as she shuffled into the room.

Emma didn't reply, just stood and walked over to the coffeemaker, refilling her mug and then pouring another cup for her friend.

"Oh my God, I drank so much last night," Nadine croaked as she collapsed onto one of the stools at the island and let her head fall into her crossed arms.

Emma put one of the coffee mugs in front of her before she took another sip from her own. "I think that means you had a good time."

"The best time," Nadine's voice was muffled by her sweatshirt before her head popped up again. "Did you get a tour of his house? Isn't it amazing?"

"Yeah, I got there early and got a . . . tour," Emma said as she sat down beside her friend.

Knightley felt the revelation deep in his gut, like a swift punch that left him breathless. Of course, she had been there before he arrived; she had probably been alone with Montgomery for hours. *Jesus.* While he had been tearing himself apart all night over an almost kiss, it was likely a blip in her evening. A non-event.

"He didn't get rid of that toile wallpaper in the foyer, did he?" Mr. Woodhouse asked, looking up from the avocado he was slicing.

Emma cringed. "I'm afraid so."

"That's too bad. The Crawfords had to pay to have that shipped from London after Veronica saw it at Selfridges."

Nadine sighed. "Montgomery showed us all around. It's so insane. Just so gorgeous. I mean, I didn't know any of the names of the furniture designers he mentioned, but Davina seemed really impressed." She turned to Knightley then, her dreamy smile dimming slightly. "She seems really nice."

"George Knightley stayed long enough to introduce his date?" Mr. Woodhouse asked, eyes wide. "Alert the presses! Watch for hordes of flying locusts and frogs falling from the sky."

Knightley shifted his weight, suddenly feeling uncomfortable. "We're not together."

Mr. Woodhouse ignored him. "Emma, you should invite her to your birthday party." He announced it like it was a wonderful idea, rather than a thought that was like cold water over Knightley's head.

"That could be . . . fun," Nadine said, looking at Emma as if this were a question.

"Would ensure George didn't get bored either," Mr. Woodhouse added.

Emma smiled at her father, but it didn't touch her eyes. "I didn't realize Knightley might be bored."

He waved her off. "You know what I mean, darling. What do you say, George?"

They all turned to look at Knightley. He stilled, his coffee mug inches from his lips. "All right."

Mr. Woodhouse's grin widened. Nadine let her gaze wander to Emma. And Emma . . . she looked like it was taking all her strength to keep that smile on her face.

"Okay," Emma said, "I'll send you the details."

Knightley stared at her expression, at the feeble smile she was working to keep in place. And suddenly that fire in his belly that had driven him here dulled, as if the embers were being forcibly put out.

"Okay," he replied.

The kitchen became a flurry of activity then: Mr. Woodhouse started the blender on the counter as Nadine shouted over the clatter, asking Emma for details about the night before, and the cacophony was suddenly too much. Knightley felt tired, hollowed out. The need to apologize felt superfluous now. It was clear she had already moved on. And he had to find a way to as well. But for now, he had to leave.

He swallowed the rest of his coffee in one large gulp and put his mug back down on the counter with enough force that the sound caught Emma's attention.

"You're leaving?" she asked.

"Yeah, I have some things to do. For work."

He hated lying to her, mostly because he never had before. And he could tell she knew, how she trapped her bottom lip between her teeth as she watched him start for the door. "Do you still need to talk?"

He shook his head. "It's not important." Then he offered her a tight smile before turning to Mr. Woodhouse. "I'll see you tomorrow at dinner, Henry."

Mr. Woodhouse barely looked up from his grocery list. Knightley then turned to say his goodbyes to Emma. She was still staring at him with an unreadable look.

"See you later?" she asked.

"Yes, see you later," he replied. It felt like another lie, and he turned away before she could see the evidence of it on his face, heading out the door, his wide stride taking him back across the frozen yard.

CHAPTER 23

When Emma was little, the Woodhouse household had a saying: if there was an occasion worth celebrating, it should be celebrated at Tavern on the Green. Birthdays, anniversaries, graduations—they were all observed at the restaurant nestled in the middle of Central Park. It was cocooned by tall elms and fairy lights visible through the dining room's massive windows, and Emma had always pretended she was tucked away in an enchanted forest, dining on delicious foods that suddenly appeared as if made by magic.

The place had aged over the years, even closing for a short time, but it had reopened thanks to some new investors. When Mr. Woodhouse read in the *Times* that the recent renovation had revived some of the restaurant's shine and sparkle, he suggested they bring back the tradition and celebrate Emma's twenty-fourth birthday there at the end of February. Margo insisted it was the perfect idea—they could even get a private room—and Emma couldn't think of a reason to object. When her friends were in town, there would be parties and celebrations the entire month, but this year she had nothing planned. Plus, it would actually make her father leave the Upper East Side for once. But Emma did have a few changes to the tradition she was hoping her father would at least try to embrace.

"A brunch?" he'd said when she suggested it, looking over his paper.

"Yes. Brunch." Emma smiled at him.

"Not a dinner? Not even a lunch? Oh, Emma."

"You won't even notice the difference. It's essentially just a casual lunch anyway," she replied. "Which means we can really take our time."

He sighed, the closest she would get to an endorsement, so she took it, giving him a kiss on the cheek before heading upstairs and out the front door.

~

The cab pulled up at Tavern on the Green at precisely two o'clock, the time Emma was set to meet Margo and Nadine. There were still three weeks until her birthday, but decisions had to be made: the menu, the room, the decorations. Maybe they could even enjoy a mimosa or two with lunch while they deliberated.

Her eyes squinted under her Gucci sunglasses as she exited the cab. If she looked close enough, she could see where the twinkle lights were still wrapped around the trees. She imagined them turning on at dusk, how beautiful they always looked against the night sky. But today, the sun shone bright, highlighting their dark wires and dormant bulbs. Everything looked a bit harsher in the daytime.

Nadine and Margo were chatting away at the entrance when Emma walked in.

"We didn't want to get started without you," Margo squealed, hugging her sister, her burgeoning pregnant belly between them. Of course Margo looked elegant, even in her short black-and-white striped maternity dress. "This is going to be so fun. Just like when you were little, but with alcohol. At least for you two."

"This place is so beautiful!" Nadine gushed, her eyes wide as she looked around the massive space. "When I told Mateo I was coming here for lunch, he was so jealous! He told me it's classic New York, and that I wasn't allowed to come back again without him."

"Well, I'm glad you're here. We could use a fresh set of eyes to make decisions. And obviously you have great taste," Margo said, sweeping her fingers over Nadine's soft curls. "God, your color is amazing."

Nadine beamed.

The manager appeared then and introduced himself before leading them to the different private rooms within the restaurant that were available for parties. The final option was the Central Park Room, and as soon as the manager opened the doors, the trio gasped. The wood-paneled walls made the large space feel intimate, while natural light streamed in through the floor-to-ceiling glass windows.

"This is it," Margo said.

"Do we need this much space?" Emma replied. Though beautiful, the room was clearly intended for large parties, not a birthday brunch for just a dozen or so people.

"Oh please. This is an event. With one long table in the center, it will be perfect," her sister declared. Then she turned to the manager, explaining what she had in mind.

Not long after, they were seated in the main dining room, ordering lunch while poring over various binders full of table setting and floral arrangement options.

"God, this is crazy. My last birthday party back home was a take-out taco night at my friend's studio apartment," Nadine joked, taking a long sip from her mimosa.

"It's tradition," Emma replied, pausing over a selection of jewel-toned napkins as she considered. "Well, it used to be. When our father throws something, he likes it to feel like the old days, when people dressed up and made an occasion out of things."

"In those rare moments when he leaves the house." Margo winked at Nadine.

Emma abandoned the napkins and picked up the flower book, flipping through the pages before eventually deciding on simple yellow forsythias and branches.

"I love these," Emma said, holding up the picture. "We could put these in crystal vases on the communal table."

Nadine's eyes grew wide. "Those are so pretty."

"Hmm, not the white roses?" Margo asked, making a face.

Emma frowned. "Roses are a little formal, don't you think?"

Her sister shrugged—the same shrug that told Emma that she didn't agree but wouldn't argue—and jotted something down in her notebook. She kept track of the rest of their choices too, and after they had gone through every possible binder the restaurant had to offer, Emma wondered if Margo really needed her there at all.

"Now we just have to do the guest list," her sister finally said.

Emma wanted to groan. She was hoping to avoid this. "Okay."

"The usual Sunday dinner crew, obviously," Margo mused. "And the Crawfords are coming up from Florida."

"Right."

"Oh, and Davina Sundar. Dad said Knightley wanted to invite her, too, right?"

"Well—"

"He's really bringing Davina?" Nadine asked, her expression dropping slightly.

Margo didn't seem to find the question worth answering as she pored over her notebook. "So that just leaves the seating arrangements," she said, almost to herself.

Emma cocked her head to the side. "I don't know if we need a seating arran—"

"Montgomery can sit next to you," she said, pointing her pencil at her sister.

Emma blinked. "We're inviting Montgomery?"

"Of course we're inviting Montgomery. I mean, you like him, right?"

"I don't know," Emma started. "He's great . . . but—"

"Isn't he great?" Margo squealed, squeezing Emma's forearm before turning to Nadine. "Don't you think so?"

"Oh yes. He's . . . the life of the party." Nadine's eyes darted between them, and she took a sip of her drink.

"Oh my God, the *party*. That was weeks ago and you still haven't told me what happened," Margo said, turning back to her sister. "Don't think I haven't noticed how you've been avoiding the topic. Did you sleep with him? No judgments, pregnant lady just catching up over here."

Emma rolled her eyes. "No, I didn't sleep with him."

"You've kissed, though."

"Yes."

"And?"

"And it was good. He's fun." Emma's eyes darted around the restaurant. "He's very . . ."

"Very?" Margo repeated, leaning forward with her eyes wide, on the edge of her seat.

Emma laughed. "Oh my God, Margo. *You* should date him."

"Oh, stop it. I'm an old, knocked-up married woman. Let me live vicariously through you. Details please!"

Nadine laughed and almost spit her mimosa across the table.

"We had one very hot and heavy make-out session and then . . . I don't know. He's definitely smooth, and exciting . . . and gorgeous . . ." Emma shrugged. "But . . ."

"There's a 'but'?" her sister replied, incredulous. "Emma. He's a catch. We all like him. He's an adult with goals, and I can see a future there. Just give him a chance."

The waiter appeared with their lunch orders—grilled chicken salads for Emma and Nadine and a double cheeseburger for Margo—as her sister waxed on about Montgomery Knox and all his virtues: his career, his ambition, his looks. It was true, he had all those things. Yet, as Margo talked, Emma realized she didn't think about any of it when she was away from him. In fact, she barely thought of him at all.

"And . . ." her sister continued. "You're neighbors!"

"Are you done?" Emma asked.

"How's George?" Nadine chimed in abruptly.

"Knightley?" Emma hesitated, poking her salad. She didn't want to admit that she'd barely seen him since New Year's. It was almost like he was avoiding her, but she pushed that notion aside before it could take root. "Ah, I guess he's fine."

"I still can't believe he came to the New Year's party," Margo said, laughing.

"He seemed to have a great time, too. Didn't he have fun, Emma?" Nadine asked, her expression eager.

"I . . . think so," Emma said, her gaze darting to the windows. "He seemed . . . good."

The night flashed through her brain in a series of snapshots: the dance, the almost kiss, the look—God, the look he gave her just before he walked away. Her sister and friend watched her, waiting for her to say more, but she only lifted up her glass and took a long sip.

"He was all dressed up and he seemed like he made an effort to be there," Nadine continued, still watching Emma. "He looked so good, don't you think?"

Margo seemed to consider for a moment. "Do we like this Davina Sundar woman?"

Nadine and Emma hummed, nodding their heads in unison.

"Interesting," Margo replied. "Well, it's about time he brought around a date. This must be serious, right?"

Emma and Nadine only stared at her.

Margo rolled her eyes. "Come on, ladies, are they together? Please tell me you know something useful."

"I'm not sure it's *that* serious," Emma said.

"Probably not exclusive," Nadine offered.

"But she's lovely," Emma added.

Nadine agreed, "Yes, very . . . lovely."

"And beautiful."

"Yes, *so* beautiful."

Then they both took a bite of their salads, nodding again as if to further convince one another.

Margo's expression flattened. "Very helpful. Well, I guess I'll just have to ask him myself when I meet her at the brunch. We'll sit them on this end of the table," she said, pointing to the illustration she'd made in her notebook.

"Great," Emma said almost to herself. "Davina Sundar is coming to my birthday party too."

"God, he's so lucky to have us looking out for him. He'll be so happy," Margo said, around a huge bite of her cheeseburger.

They finished lunch and Nadine got ready to head back downtown to study for a test, while Emma and Margo stayed behind to go over final details. Emma walked Nadine to the door and gave her a hug before watching her leave. She really needed to get back to the table—Margo had cornered the manager again to discuss table linens—but instead she stared out the window. She had so many memories of walking up this restaurant path, so many birthday parties she and Margo had here as children, both dressed up in cute matching pink dresses with matching pink nails. Margo would make sure to apply the polish for them both the night before the big day. And then when they arrived, there were always an inordinate amount of balloons and entirely too many presents. It seemed so strange to be back here celebrating as an adult. Slightly awkward maybe, like it didn't quite fit anymore, almost how she'd feel if she put on a pink fluffy party dress right now.

Emma exhaled, looking down at her hands and realized they were shaking slightly. What was wrong with her? Why was the simple planning of this party leaving her so unsettled? Emma normally loved to plan events, and Margo would make sure nothing went wrong.

Maybe it was the Davina Sundar invite. After all, Davina hadn't even been invited to a Sunday dinner yet, much less a familial celebration. There was a required order of events that everyone knew to follow before you could just randomly be invited to a birthday party. This was New York, not lawless California! There were rules here. So why was everyone but Emma forgetting them?

She looked back up at the window and caught her reflection staring back. Her pursed lips, her flushed cheeks, the two harsh lines appearing between her brows. She had to stop her mind from spiraling. She took a long, slow breath.

Margo was probably right. They couldn't exclude someone Knightley was dating. And Emma would be next to Montgomery, the guy she was . . . what was she doing with Montgomery? God, she didn't even know.

"It's just a damn birthday party," she whispered to herself, trying to quiet the uneasy storm brewing within her.

She made her way back to the table to meet her sister, who was already standing to leave.

"Ready to go?" Margo asked.

"Yeah," Emma replied. "I should probably get back home to Dad."

"Walk with me around the park a bit? I feel like I never get to just hang out with you anymore."

Emma smiled, realizing she felt the same way. "Absolutely."

"I'm trying to get in as many steps as I can. I've already gained so much weight," Margo sighed as they left the restaurant and started strolling along the tree-lined path into Central Park. It was a pleasant day, the sun warming the cool air.

"You look great. Feeling okay?" Emma asked as the sprawling expanse of Sheep Meadow appeared before them.

"Now that the morning sickness is gone, I'm just so hungry . . . all the time," she whined as she eyed a nearby hot dog cart.

"Oh my God, Mar. We just ate."

"Maybe just a pretzel?" Margo was already walking over to the seller. She ordered two pretzels and offered one to Emma.

"Why don't you save that one for later." Emma motioned it away. "How are you feeling overall? Nervous?"

"Not nervous. Just working on the birth plan. We've managed to get it down to eighteen pages now."

Emma laughed. "It's going to be so wild having a little baby around."

"Yeah . . . I'm happy." Her sister smiled. "And what about you?"

Emma's eyebrows rose. "What about me?"

"How are you doing?"

"I'm fine," Emma replied, linking her arm into her sister's as they strolled.

"But are you happy?"

"Yeah, of course."

"I know I went hard on the planning back there, but I just want you to have the best birthday ever. Like we used to have, but a grown-up version, you know?"

"I do," Emma assured her, because she truly did.

"And I don't mean to push the Montgomery thing."

"No, no, it's fine. I know you're just looking out for me. And you're right, he's very charming."

Even as Emma said it, though, she found herself wondering what Knightley would think of Margo's pestering.

"So, what's going on with Nadine and George?" Margo asked.

Emma blinked. "What do you mean?"

"She kept bringing him up all morning. Does she have a crush on him or something?"

"What?" Emma scoffed. "You can't be serious."

"Why not? Nadine is so sweet. And it's not like she and George are strangers."

Emma's brain felt like it was shorting out, as though every thought she'd had, had been erased as she pondered Margo's words. Knightley . . . and Nadine? "I don't know . . . I just don't see them together."

"Oh, so you think he's serious about this Davina woman?"

"No," Emma said more firmly than she meant to. "*Not* Davina. That's not—"

"Okay, then what's the issue?"

"I mean, maybe . . . I just . . . Do you really think Knightley could like Nadine . . . in that way?"

"Why not? He's mentioned her enough times, and she brought him up plenty today. And thanks to you, they've been spending a lot of time together." Margo smiled slyly. "Stranger things have happened, right?"

Emma forced a smile. "Right."

CHAPTER 24

Margo's words were still ringing in Emma's ears three weeks later, as her cab sped across Central Park toward Tavern on the Green the morning of her twenty-fourth birthday. Nadine and Knightley? It was ridiculous. If anyone else had suggested it, Emma would have laughed. But it wasn't just anyone; it was Margo. And as much as she hated to admit it, Margo always seemed to be right.

It was like the first time Emma had ever tried to impress a boy. She'd fallen in love with David Goldblatt, who sat next to her in Mrs. Saltow's second grade class. There wasn't much Emma remembered about being seven years old, but she remembered him. How dimples creased his cheeks when he smiled, and he always smelled like crayons. She confided her feelings to Margo—who, at ten, was much more experienced with this sort of thing—along with her master plan of how to woo him: Emma would wear her ruby-red slippers from Halloween when she'd dressed up as Dorothy from *The Wizard of Oz*. Yes, they were a little uncomfortable, but they had a one-inch heel and she had never felt more beautiful than when she had worn them down Fifth Avenue with a bag full of candy on one arm.

Of course, Margo had laughed so hard she had almost cried. "Your feet are going to be covered in blisters before you even get to school, and then you'll be stuck in them the entire day! All because you want to impress a boy who won't even notice them?"

But Emma was adamant. David Goldblatt wasn't like other boys. He would notice.

Margo had been right, of course. Emma had barely navigated her way through the fresh snow on 83rd Street before her heels began to burn. By the time she walked into Mrs. Saltow's class, her toes felt like they were broken. Still, she sat down and waited for David to look over.

He never did.

To her credit, Margo hadn't reminded Emma that she had been right. She had simply helped bandage up Emma's feet when she returned home in tears and put on a movie while she made hot chocolate for the two of them.

Emma hadn't thought about that story in years, but as the car pulled up to the restaurant, it was there in the center of her mind, demanding attention. She wanted to blame it on her Loeffler Randall platform heels, the ones she insisted on wearing today even though her toes were already beginning to ache. Or maybe it was the possibility of Nadine's unrequited crush. But it wasn't until she walked into Tavern on the Green, when she saw the long table filled with family and friends all framed by the large windows and draped in yellow forsythias and branches and a few conspicuous white roses, that she knew.

Margo had been right yet again. The restaurant, the roses—everything was perfect.

And that was it, she realized. Margo was always right. It was a running theme throughout Emma's entire life. And if she was always right, then there was a good chance she was right about Emma's love life too. Her career goals. Even Nadine and Knightley. As everyone stood and cheered and she caught sight of Montgomery standing near the center of the table next to the only empty chair, the realization felt like a stone in her very expensive shoes. A nagging, unrelenting thing that was impossible to shake.

"I can't believe it. I just can't believe it!" Mrs. Pawloski exclaimed, coming around from the other side of the table to pull her into an embrace so tight, Emma's cheek was crushed against a faded stain on her jacket's lapel. "Twenty-four years old! I remember the day you were born! Honestly, I do! It feels like yesterday, but here you are, a woman, and I still don't feel a day over thirty. But I must be, right?" She laughed, a cackle that rang in Emma's ear as she forced a smile and moved further along the table, even as Mrs. Pawloski continued talking to no one in particular. "And doesn't the table look gorgeous? Absolutely gorgeous! I don't think it's ever looked this gorgeous before. I just can't believe it."

Nadine seemed positively giddy to be there. She looked beautiful—in fact, she looked like she had been to the salon even though it was her day off. Her golden brown hair was up in an intricate bun and her makeup was subtle yet impeccably applied, highlighting her light eyes and high cheekbones. Beside her, the Crawfords raised their champagne glasses Emma's way. At the other end Margo and Ben cheered, and her father at the head of the table next to them blew her a kiss.

And then she saw Knightley. He was seated on the other side of her father, between Davina and Mrs. Pawloski, the latter of whom had returned to her seat and was still talking. He was listening to her intently, not looking at Emma as he ran his hand through his hair and to the back of his neck. It was a motion Emma had watched him do hundreds of times, but now it was accompanied by an odd ache she couldn't quite place. If she could only—

"Hello, gorgeous," Montgomery murmured, his voice so close she almost jumped.

Oh, right. Montgomery.

She smiled up as he pulled out her chair and leaned in to kiss her cheek. She could feel him turn his head into her hair, as if he were about to whisper something illicit, when a shrill cackle erupted from across the table.

"Remember when you brought her home from the hospital, Henry?" Mrs. Pawloski was exclaiming to Mr. Woodhouse. Then she turned back to Emma and clapped her hands. "You were so tiny! I used to bring you back little birthday presents from all the places Burt and I would go! Chocolates from Switzerland, little baby clogs from Amsterdam, stuffed animals from every country. I bet you don't remember that, but we did!"

Emma's cheeks flushed with embarrassment. She opened her mouth to change the subject, but Mrs. Pawloski barreled on.

"We just loved to spoil you. But oh, did you cry! I swear we all thought you would never stop sometimes! The only one that could get you to stop crying was George! Do you remember that, George?"

Knightley smiled at Mrs. Pawloski before finally turning to Emma. He smiled at her, too, but it was a cordial smile: the same empty one he reserved for business meetings or small talk at one of Ben's restaurant openings. As if it were duty bound before he was allowed to continue on with his day, which he did, turning to listen to whatever Davina was whispering in confidence.

Emma looked away, pretending she didn't see him, like she didn't even care whether he was there or not. She almost got away with it, but then she caught sight of Nadine just a couple of seats away. She was watching Knightley and Davina, too, but she wasn't trying to look unbothered. Her expression was so dejected. Almost helpless.

Oh God. Did Nadine really have a crush on him?

Emma was about to lean across the table and ask her if she was okay, distract her with a glass of the champagne being passed around, but before she could do anything, Montgomery was at her ear again.

"What do you say after this we sneak off and go downtown for a real party?" he asked. She turned to find his face inches from hers and a glass of champagne in his hand.

She laughed uncomfortably, grabbing the glass and taking a deep gulp to avoid his intense gaze. Unfortunately, she found Margo's instead. She was leaning forward watching them, a wide and hopeful grin on her face.

"Oh, champagne!" Mrs. Pawloski squealed, her voice cutting through the air. "You know I love champagne! I just LOVE it!"

Emma let out a long sigh.

Maybe Margo was wrong, after all, because this entire party now seemed like an awful idea.

A team of waiters arrived with more drinks and pastries, and Emma finished her champagne then grabbed another one. It was fine, she reminded herself. All she had to do was smile and laugh and soon their meals would arrive and her father would give his toast and then they could go home. Easy. Simple.

She took another deep sip from her champagne flute.

"Maybe I should just get a bottle of that for us." Montgomery chuckled.

The hum of various separate conversations buzzed in her ears while the champagne bubbles seemed to fizz in her brain and she laughed again, this time so loudly that even Knightley looked over. His eyes were impossibly clear, almost golden today, and narrowed on her like she had done something wrong. Like she had somehow annoyed him.

She met his stare and raised an eyebrow at him. What the hell could he be annoyed about? Wasn't she being a perfect and gracious host? She had worked so hard to live up to his standards, done exactly what was expected of her, and still he found a reason to throw her that stare, as if she were a child again. As if she still had those ruby slippers on her feet.

"Excuse me, excuse me," Mr. Woodhouse said, standing and tapping his knife against his glass. "I hope you'll pardon the interruption, but I would like to say a few words. It is my little girl's birthday, after all. Although, she's not my little girl anymore, is she? As much as I hate to admit it, she's a woman. A beautiful, talented, kind woman who keeps our family running. Who keeps me running," he said, and smiled. "She helps everyone around her while going to school and planning a career and I don't quite know how she does it . . . I'm not sure anyone other than Emma ever could. She is perfection in every sense of the word. So, to our perfect Emma. Happy Birthday!"

There were cheers and glasses raised and Emma beamed, her annoyance ebbing thanks to the attention as much as the champagne.

"So, Emma, how's school going?" Mr. Crawford asked after her father sat back down.

"Really well. I'm graduating in May," she replied.

This snagged Davina's attention. "What are you studying?"

"I'm getting my master's in art history at NYU."

"Emma is going to graduate with honors," Nadine interjected proudly. "And she just found out that she's secured an interview for a postgraduate internship at the Met."

Emma blushed. She had gotten the email earlier that week and had only told Nadine the good news. It wasn't that she was trying to keep it a secret, only that she was hoping to avoid the inevitable question of—

"Oh! That's impressive! Did your dad pull a few strings?" Mr. Crawford asked playfully.

There it was. The familiar comment that turned her stomach.

"No, it was all me," she replied, working to keep her tone light.

Mrs. Crawford nodded. "So when's the interview?"

"Next month. Nadine is already helping me prep."

"And what's the backup plan?" Knightley asked as he took a sip of his water. He was staring at her over the rim of his glass with his familiar, bored stare. It was nothing he hadn't said to her before, but it felt different this time. Or was it just in her mind?

"I have a letter of recommendation from the dean and have been researching possible interview questions for weeks," she replied. "I'm going to get it."

Knightley nodded once, and for a moment she felt like it was a victory. But then it was over. He turned to Mrs. Pawloski like Emma had merely told him the weather. Like she had been dismissed.

Davina caught the motion too and glanced back to Emma. Her expression was almost apologetic as she offered her a small smile. "Congratulations, Emma."

Emma tried to smile back, but it faltered on her lips, so she let her eyes flit over the table, looking for something, anything, other than Knightley to focus on. That's when she caught sight of Nadine again. She was talking to Mr. Crawford now, but her eyes kept darting to Knightley as well, to how he leaned into Davina, how he nodded at whatever she was whispering in his ear. And Emma saw the sadness in Nadine's eyes, how hard she was trying to mask it with a smile.

The hum of conversation around Emma continued, duller

now. Her head felt like it was swimming, but she still reached for her glass and took another sip.

"So, what else do you have planned for your twenty-fourth birthday?" Montgomery murmured beside her, low enough so only she could hear.

"This is it," she said with a flourish of her hand.

"What?" he replied with mock-indignation. A few heads turned in their direction. "That's a crime, Emma. You deserve a full week of parties. Next year we'll go to Ibiza. Have you been?"

Emma shook her head, her cheeks warming.

"Then I'll take you. I can get us on the guest list at Freddie's."

"Oh, I love Freddie's," Davina mused from across the table.

Montgomery turned to her. "Well, well, Davina. You've been?"

She let out a breathy laugh, waving off the question even as she answered. "Years ago. One of my favorite DJs did a residency there, so it was a spur-of-the-moment trip."

"Those are the best kind," he replied, his mouth curling up in a lopsided grin. Then he turned back to Emma. "Well, that settles it. Birthdays in Ibiza from now on."

Emma laughed. She knew she was never going to Ibiza with Montgomery. She doubted he was even serious. But at that moment, she was glad he was here distracting her with thoughts of beaches and clubs far away from this table. "It's a deal."

"I guess you'll have to send me a postcard," Knightley murmured from a few seats down.

The words didn't seem to be directed at Emma in particular, but regardless, they still chilled the warmth in her chest. She reached for her champagne again and took another long sip before leaning into Montgomery.

"Well, this might not be Ibiza, but we have drinks and food. What else do you suggest?"

Montgomery hummed. "Maybe we should provide some enter-tainment? Have a dramatic lovers' quarrel that they can all gossip about later?"

The corner of Emma's mouth turned up. "Maybe you could tell me she didn't mean anything to you. It was just a one-time thing. And then I could throw the rest of my drink in your face."

He scoffed. "What a waste of perfectly good champagne. No, you should slap me and then stomp off to the bathroom. That way everyone can whisper about it until you come back."

"Yes, heighten the anticipation."

His smile broadened as he leaned closer to her. "Exactly."

Emma laughed again. She might not have fallen for him, but she couldn't deny that she was glad he was here today. "You're going to make some woman very happy one day, Montgomery Knox."

He winked at her. "Oh, I plan on making many women very happy, Emma Woodhouse."

She smiled.

"Oh my God!" Mrs. Pawloski exclaimed, waving erratically at Emma and Montgomery. "You two are just so adorable! Margo, where have you been hiding him?"

Margo shrugged, even as a smug grin turned up the corners of her mouth. Knightley smiled too, a polite, sterile smile. At least Davina didn't try to pretend; she looked embarrassed. Perhaps even a little annoyed. And suddenly that stone was back in Emma's shoe, refusing to budge.

A waiter arrived at the table with another bottle of champagne, and Mrs. Pawloski let out a shrill sound of delight.

"I adore champagne! Just adore it!" she announced again.

"I still think we would have been fine with sparkling water," Mr. Woodhouse murmured, eyeing Margo.

"No, Dad, you celebrate with champagne," she said. "After all, we have a lot to celebrate. Right, Emma?"

She looked to Emma and Montgomery then, a wistful expression on her face.

Emma suddenly realized she wanted to leave. In fact, at that moment, as all eyes turned to her, she couldn't figure out why she was there at all. It felt like she had been playing a part for so long now but didn't have the energy to maintain it. The facade was crumbling, and the strength required to repair it was too herculean. Or maybe she simply didn't want to fix it at all.

"Besides," Margo continued. "If I can't drink champagne right now, then I reserve the right to force it on everyone else."

"Oh, no need to force it on me!" Mrs. Pawloski said, laughing. "I think I would drink it with every meal if I could!"

Emma tried to smile, already opening her mouth to change the subject, but Mrs. Pawloski squealed again.

"My Burt used to say that he would buy me a champagne vineyard because I loved it so much! Can you imagine that? Me, on a vineyard? But he was adamant! He didn't even like the stuff, he just wanted me to be happy. And what can I say, champagne makes me happy! I only wish I had a higher tolerance. After just a couple of glasses I get drowsy and can barely string two words together!"

Emma could not resist. "Well then, I'm glad we reserved an open bar."

Even before the words escaped her mouth, she regretted them. The table fell silent for a long, painful moment as people darted their eyes away and their smiles faltered.

Mrs. Pawloski finally laughed, but it slowly faded to an odd, disjointed giggle as Emma's words seemed to register. "Yes, yes, of course. Exactly."

There was stiff laughter around the table until it was replaced by the hum of conversation again. But Emma still watched Mrs. Pawloski, at the embarrassment that rouged her cheeks and how she didn't touch her drink again. She was talking to Knightley now, and although there was still a smile on her face, Emma could tell by his look of concern that there was nothing light or trivial about their conversation.

The table was finally cleared, and people slowly began to stand and say their goodbyes. Nadine promised to stop by the house after her class on Tuesday, and Montgomery said he would text from the party downtown so Emma could meet him later. She already knew she would not be going.

Emma maintained her practiced smile through all of it until she found a moment to disappear down the hallway across the dining room to the restroom.

The mirror was waiting there for her as she closed the door and locked it. She stared at her reflection, her smile fading so her red lips made a harsh straight line across her face. Had she really said that to Mrs. Pawloski? Had those words really left her mouth? She had similar thoughts about the woman a thousand times a day, but the idea that any of them would escape into the ether made her cringe. Yet today it happened. Her frustration and anger had caused the worst to bubble up, and now there was no taking them back.

But maybe it wasn't so bad. No one else had said anything, right? The conversation had continued as normal, and yes, Mrs. Pawloski had seemed hurt, but she would probably forget it by the next Sunday dinner anyway.

It was fine. Everything was fine.

Perhaps if she repeated it to herself enough times she would start to believe it.

With that thought, Emma opened the door and marched directly into Knightley's back.

Her brow furrowed as he turned. "What are you doing creeping around down here? Davina isn't even in . . ."

The words dissolved on her tongue when she caught his expression, the hard planes of his face locked in anger.

"What were you thinking?" he growled, his voice low and so deep she felt it reverberate through her chest.

"Excuse me?"

"Your comment to Mrs. Pawloski."

She rolled her eyes, swallowing back the shame. "It's fine. I doubt she knew what I was talking about."

"Are you serious? She's been sitting next to me for the past twenty minutes and hasn't talked about anything else. How she's such an embarrassment, how lucky she is that you invited her at all."

"That's ridiculous! You know that's ridiculous. Of course she's invited, she's invited every year! She's like family at this point! But just because she's like family doesn't mean we can't acknowledge that she makes you want to scream half the time."

"You're right," he murmured, taking a step closer to her so she had to take one back, her shoulders hitting the wall. "And if she was still having lunch every day at the Carlyle or hosting fundraisers at her home every weekend, I would probably let it go."

Emma scoffed. His brow hardened.

"But she's not, Emma. She's lost almost everything. You get that, right? She has no money. Her husband died and left her with more debt than she'll ever be able to pay off. She's lived off charity for years. Even after breaking up that house of hers into apartments, she'll still have to sell it at some point. She has nothing, Emma. Nothing but you and me and the people that have been her family for years."

Emma lifted her chin, thankful for the darkness of the hall and how it hid the tears now welling in the corners of her eyes.

"Do you enjoy this or something?" she hissed. "Zeroing in on every mistake I make and calling it out just to make me feel bad?"

His eyes widened. "Make *you* feel bad? Jesus, Emma. Not everything is about you."

She wanted to tell him that she was aware, that this whole party—planned and executed by Margo—was a perfect reminder of that. But she didn't trust her tears to stay at bay if she admitted that out loud, so she just crossed her arms over her chest and stared at him.

He shook his head. "Every time I think you've stopped making yourself the center of the world, you go and do something that completely destroys any hope I have that . . ."

He tripped over his words, as if he caught himself before saying something else.

"Hope of what?" she asked, anger now mixing with her shame. "That I'll become an *adult* like you? So concerned with how not to live that you forget how to live at all?"

His eyes narrowed on her. "Excuse me?"

"You want me to be an adult, but only in the way *you* define it! And your definition has so much fucking baggage that I don't know if it's possible to ever fit in there!"

He leaned closer, his face only inches from her own. "What the hell is that supposed to mean?"

"You're not your dad! But when you try to police how exactly someone lives up to your expectations, you sure as hell sound like him."

The silence that followed was deafening. She could only hear their breathing, fast and heavy and intermingling in the space between them. Knightley didn't move, just stared down at her, anger and frustration and something else clouding his expression, something so dark and raw it was impossible to translate.

"George?" Davina's voice called down the hall. "Ready to go?"

He leaned back abruptly, standing straight and taking in a deep breath. "Yes. Ready."

He glanced back down at Emma. All the anger was gone now. His expression was flat, his eyes almost sad. And then he turned away toward Davina and the exit.

CHAPTER 25

"Well, that was nice," Davina said as their car pulled away from the restaurant. She was smiling but her tone suggested the opposite, as if revealing a long-withheld relief.

Knightley didn't blame her. The entire meal had been a disaster. The Emma and Montgomery show had stolen everyone's attention, which was surely the point. And as much as he tried, Knightley had fallen for it too, neglecting Davina most of the meal to steal glances at their shared smiles, ignoring the conversations around him to listen to their whispered flirting. Of course, Davina hadn't seemed to mind. She was distracted by the show as well, but seemingly not as entertained as everyone else.

It had only derailed once, by Emma's scathing comment to Mrs. Pawloski.

Well then, I'm glad we reserved an open bar.

He had recognized Emma's regret the moment the words left her lips. But she hadn't taken it back. She hadn't even apologized. And as Mrs. Pawloski crumbled into a mess of self-doubt beside him, everyone at the table moved on, including Emma. What should have been a capital offense was swept under the rug, as if it had never happened at all.

He let out a frustrated sigh just thinking about it, leaning back into the car's leather seat and watching the trees of Central Park give way to the high-rises of Midtown.

"So, Emma and Montgomery. What's going on there?" Davina asked, pulling him from his thoughts.

"I'm not sure," he replied, working to keep his voice even.

"On New Year's I got the impression they were just friends, but they looked very cozy today."

"They did."

"Does she like him?"

He kept his attention out the window as his grip on his armrest tightened. "Maybe."

She hummed, as if considering.

He turned to her. She was staring out her own window, though she didn't appear to be seeing the city passing by.

"It's too bad," she said. "He's going to break her heart."

"How do you know that?" He had meant to keep the same even tone, but the question came out biting.

She finally turned to look at him, a placating smile on her face. "Montgomery Knox is a player, George. He's there for a good time. Some phenomenal sex, maybe a brief affair, but he's not relationship material."

"And how do you know she wants a relationship?"

"She doesn't strike me as the type that's looking for a casual fling." Then she shrugged. "But maybe I'm wrong. And if not, she'll learn. Life experience, you know?"

She maintained his gaze, as if waiting for him to agree. The words were there on his tongue, but they felt bitter and wrong, so he turned away without saying anything at all.

The silence felt heavy as the car traveled downtown, through the congested streets of Hell's Kitchen to the rows of shops and brownstones in Chelsea. They turned onto 19th Street and stopped outside Davina's brick townhouse halfway down the block.

"Home sweet home," she said after a moment, looking up at her building.

Knightley nodded once, not moving.

She turned to him, watching his profile for a moment before her small smile returned. "And I'm going to guess you're not coming in."

It was both a question and a statement, and the tension that had been building in his body suddenly released.

"No," he sighed. "I'm not."

"Can't say I'm surprised."

"Davina, I'm sorry. I didn't—"

"Oh God, please. No excuses. Neither of us needs them," she said, rolling her eyes and offering him a wink before she stepped out of the car. "Besides, it was never going to work anyway."

"No? Why not?" he asked, a relieved smile on his lips.

She laughed, her hand on the top of the door as she turned to face him. "Because, George. You're in love with *her*."

Then she shut the door in his face.

~

The drive back uptown was a blur, the city passing in the periphery as his mind raced even faster, replaying Davina's words from every perspective, dissecting them from every angle. But as his driver pulled up outside his house, as Knightley avoided the front door and began to walk aimlessly down the empty sidewalk, he ended up at the same exact point.

You're in love with her.

That was it. No asterisk or disclaimer was necessary. He had spent so long trying to deny the truth that it was startling to have it presented so plainly.

He was in love with Emma.

It had been building for months. Maybe even years. Suddenly his retreat to LA and the months spent focused on the office there seemed like such an obvious excuse. Of course he wanted the office to be successful, but there was another reason he'd left. One who lived right there across the back garden. His childhood friend, his best friend. Except the girl he had grown up with was no longer the child who drew in his textbooks. She wasn't that teenager sneaking out on the weekends. She was a strong, independent woman now.

And she wanted Montgomery Knox. It was superficial, to be sure, but between the smiles and whispers at brunch, it was clear that it was what she wanted. That alone added to its weight. But regardless of how Knightley felt about her choices, she deserved the right to make them without his constant interference.

He had been trying to ignore that fact for too long, but the realization hit him in that hallway as she tried to defend herself. She held up a mirror to him just as he did to her. Jesus, she saw him more clearly than he saw himself. And it was a shoddy reflection.

And maybe that was it. Emma was trying to grow up and he was the one holding her back.

A resolution started forming in his mind. He knew now what he had to do. For him, and for her.

The wind picked up as he reached Third Avenue, and he tightened his coat around his neck. There was a diner on the corner and he headed inside, his skin warming from the heat as he sat down at the counter and ordered a coffee. Then he fished his cell out of his pocket. The phone number was there at the top of his contacts, and he pressed it.

Three rings and then it connected.

"George Knightley," Will said by way of greeting.

"Hey, Will. How are you?"

"I'm fine." That was Will's standard answer, an even tone that made it impossible to tell if he was being sincere or not. "What can I do for you?"

"Are you in the city?"

"No, I'm out in Montauk. Why?"

Knightley raked a hand through his hair. "Because I wanted to talk to you about LA."

He heard Will release a long sigh on the other end of the phone. "Of course you do."

CHAPTER 26

Emma woke up early the day after her birthday party. She sat up and an immediate wave of regret washed over her. She looked up at her closed shades. Whatever was waiting for her on the other side—the world, reality in general—wasn't anything she wanted to face right now.

She had been hiding there since she and her father took a cab from the restaurant back to 83rd Street. Emma went directly to her room and shut her curtains before climbing into bed to watch the light slowly fade from her window. Montgomery sent her a late-night text telling her the party downtown was not worth the trouble and he'd call her tomorrow. She didn't bother writing back, just turned over and forced herself to sleep. It was not her best birthday.

Unfortunately, the regret was still there in the morning. The light of a new day only made her mistakes more glaring, her embarrassment intensifying the more she replayed her words to Mrs. Pawloski. And then to Knightley. God, what had she been thinking?

It was a low blow to compare him to his father. The one man Knightley never wanted to be. But he had been just as harsh, hadn't he? The awful way he looked at her, the ugly disappointment in his eyes. It felt like they crossed some invisible line yesterday. And now all their hateful words slashed like deep cuts, personal ammunition deployed to hurt and maim. Why had they done that to each other?

She winced and pulled her down comforter over her head.

The plan was to stay in bed again today, but eventually her stomach started growling, so she headed down to scavenge the kitchen for food.

Her father was right where she expected him to be, reading the paper at the island. "Well, well. You're up early, birthday girl."

"Morning, but my birthday is over."

"Did you have a nice time yesterday?"

She nodded, grabbing a mug and pouring a cup of coffee.

"It was a good party." Her father paused, looking up from the *Times* as his brow furrowed. "I did want to say something, though . . . I couldn't just let it go . . ."

"Oh?" she asked, suddenly sure her father was going to reprimand her about what she'd said. She deserved it, too. Knightley often found fault in her actions, but her father rarely did. And now she was going to see that dreaded look of disappointment in his eyes as well. How could she have been so cruel?

"I wanted to say . . ." He put down his paper and looked her in the eye. "You were right."

She blinked. "What?"

"You were right, Emma," he repeated, smiling warmly at his daughter.

"I was?"

"A brunch was an outstanding idea. I'm sorry I doubted you."

"Oh." She let out a long breath. But the relief gave way to confusion. He wasn't going to say *anything*? Did he not hear the way she'd treated their oldest family friend? "Is that it?"

"I meant what I said in my speech. Everything."

"Even now?"

He chuckled. "Of course."

"You don't think I acted out of line at all . . . maybe to Mrs. Pawloski?"

"Oh, Emma, it was your birthday. She's a grown woman."

"But—"

"Who does like her alcohol." He gave her a knowing wink.

Emma forced a weak grin and took a sip of coffee. So he *had* heard what she'd said. And somehow he still saw his perfect little girl.

"I think I should maybe go see her," Emma mumbled under her breath.

"Whatever you need, darling," he said, turning his attention back to his paper.

She took her coffee and her phone and wandered upstairs to the living room. There weren't any lights on, but she barely noticed as she curled up on one of the armchairs flanking the fireplace. The watery morning light muted the colors in the room; the deep mahogany of the piano looked gray. The spines along the bookcase were dull.

Her eyes wandered to the wall above the sofa. There was a large black-and-white framed print there, one of the original architectural plans for the Chrysler Building that her father had gotten from Sotheby's a few years ago. It was lovely, but she couldn't help remembering what had been there before, vibrant and bright and bold: Pierre Bonnard's *Flowers on a Red Carpet*.

A sharp pain of sadness hit her chest so quickly she almost lost her breath. She missed her mom. She didn't even have any memories to miss, but she missed the paintings that she had hung to make this house a home. She missed feeling her mom around every corner, knowing that she was there even though she wasn't.

Would she have called Emma out for being so selfish and rude? Or would she have overlooked it the same way her father had? She hated the fact that she would never know.

Her phone began to ring in her lap, and she saw Margo's face on the screen.

"Hey!" Margo exclaimed. "I can't talk long, we're heading to a doctor's appointment, but Emma, that party was perfect! Did you go out afterward?"

Emma knew she meant with Montgomery.

"No, I was tired and called it an early night."

"Oh, that's too bad. But seriously, the whole thing was such a success. Ben and I were just saying!" Then her sister's voice became muffled. "I'm asking her if she had a nice time. Give me a second ... Okay, I'll tell her. Ben wants me to tell you that everyone had fun."

"I'm not sure about that," Emma replied, walking into her room and sitting on the edge of her bed. "I was so rude to Mrs. Pawloski."

"Oh, stop. You were just joking."

So her sister had heard her comment too.

"But joke or not, I—"

"Just got to the doctor's. Call me later, okay?"

And then the line went dead.

Emma stared down at her phone's darkened screen. This was insane. While she loathed the way Knightley confronted her, even she had to agree with him on some level. She was in the wrong. So why was he the only one calling her out on it?

This was one transgression even her family couldn't gloss over. She would have to fix it herself.

~

Wrapping a scarf around her neck and grabbing a light bomber jacket, Emma headed down 83rd Street to Mrs. Pawloski's brownstone a few doors away. It had been nearly as nice as the Woodhouse home when Emma was a child. Mrs. Pawloski and her husband had owned the entire three-story structure back then, and Emma had vague memories of a shiny black Rolls Royce always parked out front, elaborate decorations for every holiday cascading down the front steps. But that gleam had worn off now. The lush garden window boxes were gone, the black paint around each windowsill peeling.

Mrs. Pawloski was forced to sell almost everything after her husband died. She hadn't been aware of the millions of dollars of debt until his funeral, and even after she divided up the house into apartments, it hadn't been enough. Now she lived in the small one-bedroom apartment on the garden floor. Emma vaguely knew the details, but Mrs. Pawloski also never let on just how bad things were, so she had never bothered to ask.

Emma walked to the door, hesitated, and then knocked. After a long while, she heard the barking of a small dog and the unlatching of chains. The door opened slowly.

"Oh!" Mrs. Pawloski said, her eyes wide with surprise. "Emma!"

"Hello." Emma offered her a small wave. "I hope it's not too early."

"No! No, it's fine," Mrs. Pawloski replied. Her smile looked fragile.

"May I come in?"

"Oh." She hesitated. "Of course! I'm sorry, that's so rude of me! I should have invited you in. I'm just surprised to see you. I don't think you've been here in years. Come in and don't mind the mess. I never have visitors. Otherwise I would have tidied up!"

Mrs. Pawloski led Emma into the very small, very clean living room and asked her to sit.

Despite the drab exterior, the inside of Mrs. Pawloski's apartment had so much personality Emma wondered if the woman ran her own Etsy shop. All her old furniture seemed to have been repurposed and hand-painted with bright colors. It contrasted nicely with the fading wallpaper, which was covered with framed photographs of her and Burt's travels, and the numerous lamps with bedazzled shades scattered around the room. It was over the top and bold, but it worked. Mrs. Pawloski's home had a kitschy style to it that was just like the woman herself.

She insisted on making some tea and Emma waited while the little dog sat on the rug and stared up at her, silently judging.

"Here you go," Mrs. Pawloski said, returning from the kitchen with two mugs. She gave Emma one, then sat down in an armchair nearby.

They were quiet for a moment. Emma took a sip. She wasn't sure where to start.

"Oh, I remember Armani," she finally said, nodding to the dog. "He used to play in our back garden."

"Oh no, Armani died years ago! I've had this little angel for a while now. He is such a good boy. Aren't you, Mr. Peaches?" Mrs. Pawloski reached down to pet the dog's white fluffy head while he curled up at her feet.

"He's adorable." Emma couldn't believe Mrs. Pawloski hadn't mentioned him before, but then realized that she very well might have. Emma just rarely paid attention to her anymore. The guilt hit her again. "I . . . I really wanted to come over . . . and apologize for what I said to you yesterday. I shouldn't have acted like that."

Her voice wavered, and Emma suddenly felt like she might cry. Whatever pressures she'd put on herself over the past couple months were coming to a head at this inconvenient moment. Her career, her family, her relationships—everything that she had pushed to the back of her mind was now front and center.

"Oh Emma, you don't need to apologize," Mrs. Pawloski replied, her expression becoming concerned.

"I do. I really do," Emma admitted as tears started to pool at the corners of her eyes. She refused to let another person dismiss her behavior. "You're always so kind, and I was mean to you. So mean."

Mrs. Pawloski smiled slightly. "But you're kind, too. You were very kind to come here today."

"I'm really not." Emma choked back a sob. "I'm sorry. I don't mean to get so emotional. I just don't know what's wrong with me! I keep making the same mistakes over and over, even when I should know better. Knightley's right about that, you know, at least we can agree about that!" She threw up her hands as she now openly wept. "But I'm trying hard, so hard, to be mature, to make the right decisions. It's just never good enough." She shook her head, looking up at Mrs. Pawloski again. "And you're the one who has always been so nice to me. You never, ever judge. I'm just . . ."

Mrs. Pawloski's eyes widened in a rare moment of silence.

"So sorry," Emma finally whispered, wiping her wet face with the back of her hand.

Another minute passed before Mrs. Pawloski shimmied her chair closer.

"I've known you your entire life, Emma. Isn't that something?" She reached over and took Emma's hand in hers. "I've seen you stumble here and there, but you always get up. It's one of the things I love about you. One very small misstep does not undo all the good in your heart."

Emma could feel the tears falling down her cheeks again.

"You have to remember something else, my dear . . ." Mrs. Pawloski continued.

"What's that?" Emma sniffled.

"You're only, what is it? Twenty-four? Good Lord, you're

going to make so many mistakes. And you should! That's what makes life worth living. The mistakes lead you where you're supposed to be." Her smile became wistful, as if recalling a memory she had forgotten about. "Your mom was good at mistakes too, you know."

Emma's brow furrowed. "She was?"

Mrs. Pawloski nodded as if proud of the fact. "She and I were friends for a long time. Burt and I even introduced her to your father! It was love at first sight; we all knew it. But that first date shouldn't have happened at all. Cassandra had been planning to go to art school in Paris. Mailed in the application and everything. But guess what? She got the dates wrong. She missed the deadline by two days. Anyone else would have been devastated, but your mom just took it in stride. She even laughed! And then two weeks later we set her up on a blind date with your father. And I remember when she called me afterward. She said, 'Well, now I know why I messed up that application!' As if that had been the plan the entire time! Maybe it was destiny or something. Or maybe she just knew how to make the most out of her mistakes." Mrs. Pawloski shrugged slightly. "Everyone makes mistakes, Emma. And that's okay. In fact, that's good! They should. And I think . . . no, I know that your mom would be very proud of you and the woman you've become, mistakes and all."

Emma closed her eyes for a long moment, feeling the weight of Mrs. Pawloski's words deep in her chest.

"And when does anyone truly grow up, anyway?" Mrs. Pawloski continued. "You should have seen me in my twenties! I was wild. Oh, it was such fun! Even now I'm not perfect. No one is, my dear."

"Thank you," Emma whispered, squeezing the woman's hand.

Mrs. Pawloski smiled and leaned back. "Now, did you know that Mr. Peaches is two percent English Bull Terrier? It's true! I know he doesn't look it at all. But I did one of those DNA tests and that's what it said. Oh, do you want to see it? It's framed right over here."

For the first time in years, Emma forgot to look at the clock as Mrs. Pawloski talked, intent on listening to every word her old friend had to say.

~

The sun was disappearing behind the park by the time Emma left Mrs. Pawloski. As she walked back down the block toward home, she vowed to spend more time visiting her. Maybe bring Nadine, too. She pulled out her phone and was so busy texting the idea to her friend that she all but ran into Knightley coming down the front steps of her house.

"Oh," she said, taking a step back. "Sorry, I was on my phone—"

"Yes, I see."

They were silent for a moment as they stared at each other, the fire of their last encounter replaced by something cold and unfamiliar.

She tried to smile. "I don't think I've ever seen you leave our house from the front door before."

He nodded. It was only then that she noticed the leather duffel bag in his hand. Her stomach dropped.

"Were you here to see Dad?" she asked, trying to keep her tone light.

"Yes. He mentioned you might have gone to see Mrs. Pawloski?"

Emma took in a shaky breath. She hadn't planned on telling Knightley. In fact, she was hoping he wouldn't find out at all. So she didn't answer, but her silence was confirmation.

"That was very big of you, Emma," he said quietly.

She didn't reply. That devastating look of disappointment was gone from his clear, golden-brown eyes. She nodded slightly, trying to conceal how much his words meant to her.

After a long moment, Emma nodded to his bag, "Going somewhere?"

"Los Angeles." He said it abruptly, then motioned to a Suburban idling at the curb. "I came by to say goodbye to you and your dad."

Emma blinked. "Oh." A trip wasn't out of the ordinary, but something about his tone, the way he was looking at her . . . it was off. "When are you back?"

"I don't know. The deal is being finalized, so there's a lot to do. It could be a while."

"But . . . you are coming back, right?"

He hesitated. "Of course," he finally answered.

It should have been reassuring, but it wasn't. Nothing about this felt familiar or good.

"So that's it? You're leaving right now?" she asked, her voice rising.

A quick nod.

Panic and anger rose in her throat, leaving a hard tinge to her words as she said, "Were you even going to wait for me to get home before you said goodbye?"

He sighed, running his hand through his black hair. "Emma . . ."

He was cut off as her phone rang in her hand. She looked down at it as Knightley did the same; they both saw Montgomery's name and photo displayed prominently on her screen.

"You better get that," Knightley murmured.

"It can wait."

He nodded again, his expression tight. "I should go or I'll miss my flight. I'll let you know when I'm settled." Knightley started toward the car, pausing at her side. "Goodbye, Emma."

Her phone continued to chime, but Emma ignored it as she

watched him slide into the back seat. The door closed and the Suburban eased into traffic, disappearing as it turned down Fifth.

When had he decided to leave? Was Davina Sundar going with him? How could he not know when he was coming back?

She should have stopped him, told him not to go, not to leave her, at least get some clarity. Something. But she hadn't said anything at all.

She felt empty as she walked in her house, up the stairs to her room. As the sun set, she looked around the cold and empty yard and realized she already missed him. He left two minutes ago, and she missed knowing he was there. Even if they didn't speak for a couple days, just knowing he was inside his home a few steps away, it was the constant she needed. Now it was gone.

CHAPTER 27

March in New York was gray. Clouds took up permanent residence above while the last remnants of snow became a filthy, icy mess lining the sidewalks below. The trees in the park were empty, the colors of the buildings muted. It was a predictable pattern: after the best parts of winter were over, the city hibernated until spring.

At least, that's how it usually felt. Like you were going through the motions and then suddenly flowers were blooming and the sky was blue and you wondered how it had happened so quickly. Like the entire past month hadn't happened at all. But Emma felt acutely aware of it. Each day, each hour passed like there was a metronome inside her body. She felt it in her bones.

There was more than enough to keep her busy. She helped Nadine prepare for midterms. Nadine helped her prepare for her Met interview. There was a thesis to finish, Sunday dinner to plan, and Margo's baby on the way. But it still always came back to that metronome, back and forth, keeping a steady count of every second.

He had been gone seventeen days.

It wasn't that she was counting, yet it was impossible to ignore his absence. But why? He had spent time away from them before. For the past three years he had bounced back and forth between New York and LA, but this felt different. When they had their first Sunday dinner after he left, she looked at his empty seat and remembered that he had been gone exactly a week. And a few days later, when she stopped by the Met to take one last tour through their latest exhibit before her interview, she knew that it had been ten days. And then every night after, as she looked out her windows to the dark empty ones across the lawn, she would add one more to the tally.

Emma sat in the armchair by her bedroom window with a book in her lap. Her gaze drifted to those darkened windows now and she scowled. It was so selfish of him, leaving in the middle of March for sunshine and parties and beaches, while she was stuck dodging piles of gray snow and midterms and views of his abandoned house. The least he could have done was leave in the summer, when more of her friends would be back from abroad—if they decided to return. Or when she would have the internship to distract her, if she got it . . .

She slammed the book shut in her lap, suddenly angry. He could have at least waited until the leaves were back on the trees so they would have blocked her view! Of course he had to go now when she needed him most. All because of what? A little argument?

But after a few moments, the anger fizzled out as quickly as it had ignited. As much as she wanted to believe that she factored into his decision, she also realized that this was just the same selfish behavior he was always criticizing her for. This wasn't about her. He had a long list of responsibilities: his company, his friends, even Davina . . . and there at the bottom of the list was Emma. Silly, spoiled Emma.

Maybe that was the nagging feeling that wouldn't let her go. That while he had firmly planted Emma at the bottom of his list of people, she'd realized that he was at the top of hers. Amid all the friends and family, he really was her best friend. And as much as she wanted to say it was despite his constant chiding and correcting, she had to admit that it was because of it. He was never trying to be mean, he just wanted her to be ready for the world beyond 83rd Street. And just as she was beginning to finally understand what that even meant, he was gone.

"Darling!" her father called out from downstairs. "Nadine's here."

"Coming," she called back. But she didn't move for a long moment.

When she finally made it downstairs, she found Nadine seated at the island in what had become her usual spot, a notebook already open in front of her.

"I think I need to go back to the Cloisters for my Western Art paper," she said as soon as Emma appeared. Her face looked panicked. "I didn't take any notes on the unicorn tapestries, and I think that's going to be important. Do you think it's going to be important?"

"We've already gone to the Cloisters a dozen times," Emma said. "You'll do fine."

"But what if—"

"Just go online and watch one of the tours they've uploaded. That's how I passed almost all of History of Western Art last year."

"Work smarter, not harder," Mr. Woodhouse interjected proudly from where he sat at the kitchen table reading the *Times*.

Nadine stared up at her in awe. "You're going to do so well on Friday."

Emma winced just thinking about the interview. "I hope so. I'm still nervous that one of the curators might recognize my name."

"Work smarter, not harder," Mr. Woodhouse recited again, raising an eyebrow at her.

She rolled her eyes, picking a grape off the bunch in the center of the island and popping it in her mouth. "I think Knightley would take issue with that mantra."

"I think Knightley needs to remember it sometimes," Mr. Woodhouse murmured, already back to reading his newspaper.

"Have you heard from him?" Nadine asked. It was startling how her face lit up as soon as his name was mentioned. Emma ignored it.

"I don't know; I haven't checked my texts," she said. It was a lie, of course. She had checked her phone at least a dozen times since she wrote to him yesterday, prodding him with inane questions, like if she could go in and steal his ice cream while he was gone. He hadn't replied.

"Is he living in his house in Malibu, or did he find something closer to his office?"

Emma blinked. How did Nadine know if he was looking for a house closer to his office?

"I'm not sure," she admitted. "Did he tell you he was looking?"

Nadine nodded and laughed. "He said he was thinking of selling it and finding an apartment or something closer to work. I told him he was crazy. If I had a house right near the beach, I'd never move out. But he said traffic was awful."

"When did he say that?"

"At your birthday."

"I didn't realize you got the chance to catch up with him." Emma tried to keep her voice casual, but it still came out tinged with bitterness.

Nadine didn't seem to notice. "Yeah, just for a second."

Emma bit her bottom lip and worked hard to keep her expression neutral even as the anger began to curl in her stomach. Did Knightley really talk to Nadine about this before he told her? Emma's brain suddenly recalled every Sunday dinner, every random moment here in this kitchen when Knightley and Nadine were together, every time they shared a private laugh and whispered conversation.

"I've never been to LA," Nadine lamented, her notebook forgotten.

"Well, it's awful," Emma scoffed.

"You've been?"

"No. But it looks awful."

"Oh."

Emma's phone began to ring and she pulled it from her back pocket. Her sister's face illuminated the screen.

"Hi, Margo," she answered. Nadine smiled and waved at the phone. Emma gave her a curt smile back. "Nadine says hi too."

"Emma!" It was Margo's signature panicked tone, the one that made her voice go up two octaves because she was working so hard to make it sound like she wasn't panicking at all.

"What's wrong?" Emma said into the phone, catching her father's attention.

Margo went up another octave. "Something happened. Something awful."

A hole suddenly opened in Emma's chest, and she felt her heart fall through it, fear and worry rising up to take its place. "What happened? Is the baby okay?"

"The baby is fine."

"The baby?" her father exclaimed.

"The baby's fine," Emma relayed to him, then spoke again to her sister. "Is it Ben? Or Knightley?"

"No, they're both fine," Margo confirmed.

"Knightley?" Nadine gasped, looking stricken. Both she and Mr. Woodhouse were watching Emma now, hanging on her half of the conversation.

"It's not Knightley," Emma told her audience. "Then what is it?" she asked her sister.

She heard Margo take a deep breath, as if preparing herself. "It's Montgomery."

"Montgomery?"

Mr. Woodhouse turned to Nadine, whispering, "Montgomery is the gentleman staying at the Crawfords' house, right?"

Nadine nodded sagely.

Emma held the phone close to her ear, waiting for Margo to continue. When she didn't, she asked, "Margo, did something happen? Is he okay?"

"Oh, he's okay, all right." Margo's panic had shifted to a sarcastic anger usually reserved for ex-boyfriends or opposing counsel sitting on the other side of her conference table. "He's probably fucking fantastic!"

Emma was losing patience. "Margo, what—"

"HeisintheSouthofFrancewithDavinaSundar!"

Margo spoke so quickly that it spilled out like one long word, taking Emma a moment to process.

"Montgomery Knox is in the South of France," she repeated.

Across from her, Nadine's brow furrowed, confused.

"Yes," Margo replied.

"With Davina Sundar," Emma continued.

Nadine's eyes grew wide as Mr. Woodhouse turned to her again.

"Davina was that woman Knightley brought to Emma's birthday, right?"

Nadine barely nodded. At that, Mr. Woodhouse seemed to lose interest and turned back to his paper.

Emma could only stare at the wall ahead, her initial concern dissolving into an odd mix of confusion and disbelief. "Montgomery Knox. And Davina Sundar."

"I know, right?" Margo exclaimed, her voice going up yet another octave, so Emma had to momentarily hold the phone away from her ear. "What the fuck is that? He called Ben this morning and told him everything. I guess they hooked up for the first time at the New Year's Eve party. The party you organized! The bastard. He said it was only supposed to be a one-time thing, but then after your birthday they connected again. They've been seeing each other ever since! Can you believe that?"

"No," Emma said. Because she honestly couldn't.

"Did he mention it to you? Have you talked to him?"

Emma tried to think back to the last time she had spoken to Montgomery. He had called the day after the party, just as Knightley was leaving. But she hadn't picked up. And afterward, she hadn't wanted to talk to him, so they had just texted back and forth, but even that had fizzled a couple of weeks ago. To be honest, she had barely noticed.

"Not really," she admitted.

"He told Ben he'd be here to help with the restaurant, and now it looks like he's going to be gone until mid-June, and that's just ridiculous! Not to mention in breach of his contract! I think I could honestly kill him, just . . ." Her voice trailed off. "I'm sorry. This isn't about Ben's restaurant. This is about you. I know you and Montgomery weren't technically together, but it was clear that it was headed in that direction, and I know I pushed you to like him. And now he's left and broken your heart! It's so unfair. And it's my fault! I can't even . . ."

She kept going as if talking Emma off a ledge, as if she were about to crumble. But as Emma listened, she realized there was nothing even close to crumbling inside her. No tears pricking her eyes. No anger. No jealousy. And the lack of anything was a relief.

"He hasn't broken my heart, Margo," Emma assured her sister.

"Stop. You don't have to say that just to make me feel better."

"I'm not, I promise. I think I liked the idea of Montgomery more than I actually liked him."

"I don't get it."

"He was fun and I had a really good time pretending that there was something there, but . . ." Emma paused, the realization hitting her just as the words formed on her lips. "I think I tried to like him because you liked him. And you've always known what's best for me. I wanted you to be right."

"I don't even know what's best for *me* right now," Margo said. "I started crying last night because our stroller doesn't have a cup holder."

Emma smiled. "I will buy you a cup holder for your stroller."

"That's not the point," Margo said, her voice wobbling like she was about to cry again.

"You're right. The point is that your idea of perfect might not be my idea of perfect anymore."

Margo sighed. "So what's your idea of perfect?"

"A stroller with two cup holders."

They laughed. Nadine watched Emma and was starting to look confused.

Finally Margo's laughter faded and she sighed. "He's still an unbelievable prick though."

"Oh, absolutely," Emma agreed.

"And I still get to hate him."

"I would be disappointed if you didn't."

"Okay. Good." Margo took a deep breath. "I love you, Em."

"I love you too, Mar."

"I'm going to go read Montgomery's contract now and see if we can sue him."

"Have fun."

Emma hung up and turned to Nadine, whose mouth hung open.

"Montgomery and Davina?" her friend whispered.

Emma nodded. "Montgomery and Davina."

"But I thought they barely knew each other!"

"Apparently they hooked up at the New Year's Eve party," Emma said, and then paused. "Wait, you were with them both for the house tour. Did you see anything?"

"Nothing!" Nadine replied. "He showed us all his art and then some of the renovations on the second floor, and then he said we should get more champagne and asked me to go downstairs to get it while he showed Davina the view from the roof . . ."

As she said the words, Nadine seemed to be listening to the story for the first time, coming to the same conclusion as Emma. They looked at each other, mouths agape.

"Oh my God, they hooked up on the roof!" Nadine said, mortified.

"Who would hook up on a roof? It's freezing out," Mr. Woodhouse murmured from the table. Emma and Nadine had almost forgotten he was there and jumped at the sound of his voice.

"Montgomery Knox and Davina Sundar," Emma said.

He seemed to consider for a moment and then shrugged.

"You're not the least bit surprised?" she asked.

"Darling, I barely remembered their names five minutes ago," he replied, and then turned back to his paper.

"What about you?" Nadine asked, watching Emma carefully. "Did you really not like him, or did you just say that so Margo wouldn't feel bad?"

Emma considered for a moment. "I liked the idea of him. But I think he and I both knew it was never going to work out."

"Definitely not if he was hooking up with Davina," Nadine said. Then she paused, her face suddenly stricken. "God, what about Knightley? Do you think he's upset?"

Behind them, Mr. Woodhouse scoffed. "If he's upset by the loss of that woman, I'll eat a Big Mac."

It was an odd comment, and Emma's brow furrowed at it, even as Nadine's expression lit up once again.

"You think?" she asked him, her smile still directed at Emma.

"Absolutely," Mr. Woodhouse replied. "I've known that boy his entire life, and he's never been less interested in a woman."

Nadine looked like she was about to burst, bouncing slightly in her seat as she looked at Emma for . . . what? Encouragement? An endorsement? Emma only stared at her dumbly, watching her friend's smile widen across her face. It felt like the inverse of Emma's expression, the flat line of her lips turning down the more Nadine's grin turned up.

"I knew it," Nadine whispered triumphantly. "Maybe I'll get a chance to go to LA soon after all!"

And that's when Emma was struck by her second epiphany of the day: Nadine Pittman was really, truly in love with George Knightley.

CHAPTER 28

EMMA

3/20

Knightley. This is a text message. It comes through your cellular telephone. I know you probably enjoy strolling to the mailbox and reading your correspondences on paper like the olden days, but this is how people stay in touch. Write back and I'll tell you all the things you are missing in New York.

3/22

I read today that it hasn't rained in Los Angeles in one month. How boring. You would never believe what's happening here. Did you drop your phone in the Pacific Ocean?

3/31

Knightley - I found your stash of Thin Mints in the freezer. Am holding what's left for ransom. Write back or I'll have to resort to sending a carrier pigeon.

> Hey. Hope you're well. Wondering if you'll be back before the baby is born? Margo was asking. Take care.

Knightley's fingers hovered over his phone's illuminated keyboard. A litany of possible replies ran through his head, but his hands didn't move. They never did. It was a routine that was becoming a habit. His phone would ping with a new text from Emma, and then he would stare at it for too long before finally deciding to reply later. Later would come and he would convince himself it was now too late to reply at all.

Per usual, he abandoned his response to the latest message after another minute, letting his phone fall onto the glass top of his desk with a loud clang. Then he spun around in his chair and looked around his office. It was new enough that the smell of paint and plaster still tinged the air. The newly installed windows on the far side were still painfully clean too, highlighting the sharp lines of downtown Los Angeles just outside Knightley Capital. He stared out at the glass-and-steel buildings, trying to ignore the din of activity outside his closed door. Everyone out there was busy. Each person had their specific task and was doing that task well. It was good news. At least it should be.

He swung back around, pressing a button on his desk phone's intercom.

"Yes?" Nicole answered. She was his new assistant out here and sitting only a few feet beyond his door.

"Hi, Nicole, has Blaxton sent a redline of that contract to Legal yet?"

"Yes, it came through end of day yesterday. Legal reviewed

this morning and has a call to discuss with the Wentworth team tomorrow. Did you want me to add you to the invite?"

"No, that's fine," he murmured, mulling over whatever else could be outstanding. "And how about the final site visit to the new office space?"

"Still scheduled for Thursday afternoon. Our team has a meeting at four to review the lease." She hesitated. "Did you want me to add you to that invite?"

He ran a hand down his face. Did he? Of course not. He couldn't give two shits about the final details of an equipment lease contract. Or walking around an empty office building yet again. He already had a capable team handling both, along with dozens of others on hand to lend their support.

"No. Thank you, Nicole."

"Of course. Let me know if you need anything else."

He pressed the red button on his phone, hanging up, and allowed his eyes to slide to the window again.

What the hell was he doing here? He might as well be back in New York. He faced the same problem there, but at least he could wander over to Ben and Margo's if he got bored. Grab Emma and go to a movie or the museum. Walk through the park with her and hear about her day. Just go next door and see her face.

His head fell back against his chair. He missed home. He missed her.

Despite running away, burying himself in work, there was no escaping it: he was in love with her.

But this was for the best. Wasn't it? He had to get away, give her space without his constant hovering. The Wentworth acquisition gave him the perfect excuse; he had to be on the ground here to manage it. Except that after barely twenty-four hours it had been blatantly clear that the LA team had the acquisition under control.

Will had intimated as much when Knightley had called him before he left, but he didn't let that stop him from inserting himself in meetings, phone calls, approvals, anything to justify his presence. In the end, it was only a hindrance.

Why couldn't he let go? It seemed like he needed to control every element of his life, when all he really needed to do was take a step back. He knew this, so why couldn't he actually do it?

Emma's words came roaring back to him, a description of himself that had echoed in his mind since she uttered it in that darkened hallway.

So concerned with how not to live that you forget how to live at all . . .

It was true. He had spent so much time trying to define his life that somewhere along the way he forgot to live it. Yes, Emma made mistakes, but at least she had the courage to make them in the first place. That was better than sitting on the sidelines so there were never any risks to begin with.

He should have taken the risk of telling her that he loved her. He had the chance there in the kitchen that morning after New Year's Eve. Why hadn't he? The excuses were dwindling every day. So, she might not feel the same way, but was that really a worse option than this? An exile away from everything he cared about just because of a what-if?

It suddenly felt ridiculous that she didn't know. She deserved the truth, and he should take the risk of telling her. He needed to.

He had to go home.

Before he could think better of it, Knightley reached across the desk to his intercom.

"Yes?" Nicole answered.

"I need you to book me on the next flight from LAX to New York."

There was a pause on the other end of the line. "The next flight . . . today?"

Knightley was already on his feet, shrugging his suit jacket back on. He didn't have anything with him but there was no way he'd have time to trek back out to Malibu to pack a bag. He needed to leave now. "Yes, today."

"When should I book the return tr—"

"No return trip. This will be one-way."

Knightley was already in the elevator when Nicole called his cell to tell him the next available flight was in one hour and forty-seven minutes. He was in the back seat of his car directing his driver to the airport by the time she sent him confirmation for his ticket.

The Los Angeles skyline was behind him as they flew down the 110. He fired off a text to Will explaining, not that he thought his friend would mind, then tried to check his email but couldn't concentrate on anything but the time in the corner of the screen. So he shoved the phone back in his pocket. By the time his driver pulled them into the crawling traffic on the 105, he had nothing to do but stare out the window. His knee bobbed, his finger tapped the door, anxiety bleeding through every motion.

What will you say when you get there? He brushed the thought aside before it could take root. He couldn't let any of the hows or whys or what-ifs gain purchase in his brain right now. That type of overthinking was exactly how he had talked himself out of risks before. George Knightley, the poster boy for analysis paralysis.

He pulled his phone from his jacket pocket again, ready to check his email for the fiftieth time, when it began to ring in his hand. His brother's name was on the screen.

"What are you doing up so early?" Knightley answered.

Ben scoffed. "It's not that early in New York."

"It is for you."

"Fair." Then Ben cleared his throat. "So . . . how you doing? You doing okay?"

Knightley frowned. "What?"

"Margo wanted me to call and make sure you were all right. You know, with everything. She talked to Emma earlier. I guess she sounds okay, but you know Margo. She's still worried about her. Anyway, I know you and Davina weren't really a thing, but still. Lots of fish in the sea."

"Ben, what the hell are you talking about?"

There was a pause on the other end of the line. "Have you talked to Davina?"

"Not since Emma's birthday."

"Oh shit," Ben murmured to himself. "Um, okay. This is awkward."

"Ben, get to the point."

His brother let out a dry laugh. "Are you sitting down?"

CHAPTER 29

Emma pressed send on yet another text to Knightley that would likely be ignored and looked up from her phone to her bedroom window. His empty house seemed to mock her, the dark windows a glaring reminder of his absence. She missed her friend.

She sighed. She had to stop herself from ruminating, so she went through the usual excuses to justify his radio silence and decided that today he must be busy at work. He was living his life, right? She was too. It was just like every other time he was in Los Angeles while she was in undergrad. Emma had survived that; she could survive this. She was fine.

With renewed gumption, she stood up from where she was perched on her bed and walked to her full-length mirror, smoothing out the front of her black Diane von Fürstenberg wrap dress. She had a job interview today: *the* job interview. There wasn't time to obsess over Knightley. In just over an hour she would be sitting at the Met, wowing them with months of preparation. She had to concentrate on herself.

She was curious, however, if Knightley was keeping in touch with Nadine. If her friend knew he'd be going to Los Angeles before she did, there was no reason to think he wasn't keeping her abreast of what he was doing out there. Which meant he was probably looking at *her* texts, replying to *her* questions . . .

Stop it, she scolded herself.

Emma slipped on her Louboutin boots and put on a pair of sensible gold hoop earrings. No time to think about whatever connection was happening between her two friends. They weren't even in the same state.

But if he was responding to Nadine's texts, that could only mean he was purposefully ignoring her own. Suddenly possessiveness clawed at her chest. Knightley was her best friend, and yet there was a chance he had been keeping in touch with Emma's friend instead. How had she been so summarily cut out? She had introduced them!

But then . . . why was that wrong? They weren't being malicious or secretive, even if it stung somewhat. Emma had just been too wrapped up in her own world to notice.

"Focus," she said out loud to her reflection as she pulled the wrap tighter around her waist. Yes, Emma was fine.

~

An hour later, as Emma crossed Fifth Avenue, she found an unfamiliar flutter of nerves in her belly. She had been so confident for so many months, but now, as she stared up at the iconic columns framing the Metropolitan Museum of Art's front doors, she was suddenly worried. Maybe Margo was right; she should have enlisted the help of their dad. And perhaps Knightley had a point about the brevity of her experience. God, she was even questioning the choice of these boots with this dress.

Emma stopped at the curb and let out a shaky breath, adjusting her jacket and small leather bag. No, she was fine. They all might have her best interests at heart, but Emma was going to do this on her own or not do it at all. And with that final thought, her doubts fell silent and she started forward, up the steps and through the neoclassical facade of the museum.

Daylight flooded the main rotunda, breathing life into the dark stone walls and towering ceilings. The air was sweet, too, likely from the massive bouquet of jasmine branches that crowned the information desk in the center of the space. Emma made her way to it, weaving through the crowd of tourists and locals. The woman behind the desk smiled when Emma told her why she was there, asking her to wait just a moment as she made a call. So Emma waited, looking around the massive room as the minutes ticked by. All around her, couples and families milled about, studying maps and waiting in line at the different ticket counters that lined the area. Their conversations echoed off the stone walls, a cacophony of sound so loud that she almost missed her name being called behind her.

"Emma?"

She turned to see a tall woman in a white oxford shirt and tailored black pants approaching her. "Yes?"

"Inez Linde," the woman said, pushing her reading glasses up over her short black hair to shake Emma's hand. Her red lips were a straight line across her face.

"So nice to meet you," Emma replied, smiling.

"Apologies for keeping you waiting. Do you need to check your coat or anything?"

"Oh, I came museum ready," Emma joked.

Inez's expression remained neutral. "Let's take a walk where it's quieter."

She turned before Emma could reply, leading them past the information desk and through the atrium toward the Medieval

Art gallery. Emma followed her, trying to curb her pulse. Was this already going poorly? Or maybe Inez was just having a bad day? The questions flew through her mind as they passed across the crowded halls in silence.

The throngs of school groups and tourists thinned when they entered the sprawling sculpture courtyard at the center of the American Wing. The gallery was dotted with statues and stained glass, framed by a massive wall of windows that curved up to include the ceiling. Emma had been in this room a million times, but she didn't care. She was still in awe.

"This is my favorite part of the museum," Emma mused, almost to herself.

Inez stopped and turned to her slightly. "I'm sorry?"

Emma blinked, suddenly self-conscious. "Oh, it's just my favorite room here. I like to think about why things are where they are." She looked around, taking it in. "Like the Wall Street bank facade juxtaposed with the Tiffany stained glass windows. That decision was deliberate. You're being forced to have another conversation. It's not just about the art, but the relationship between the art and the space."

"And you find that interesting?" Inez asked.

"It's fascinating! Like, when I look at the gilded statue of Diana over there, there's the story of the artist, why and how it was made, and the journey it's taken to get here, but then there's the story the viewer brings to it, how it makes them feel. And then there's the curator's point of view. Why is it here specifically? What purpose does it serve?" Emma suddenly realized how much she was gesturing with her arms and pulled back. "I just find those connections and stories interesting, especially the less obvious ones. It's like a secret puzzle."

Inez was watching her, eyes narrowed in an astute gaze as if she were seeing her for the first time.

She let Emma linger for a moment more before continuing on, down a short hallway to an elevator that took them downstairs to the lower levels. When the doors opened again, they were clearly in the administrative offices of the museum. Emma followed Inez through the maze of hallways, the din of conversation wafting out from other offices until they reached a door sitting slightly ajar. Inez pushed it open and entered, not bothering to look back as Emma followed.

Inside was a large office. Its walls were lined with bookshelves, the contents of which looked to be meticulously organized. An L-shaped desk sat in the center, all papers and files lined up neatly across it.

"This is better." Inez sighed, settling in behind the desk and motioning for Emma to have a seat in the armchair across from her.

She did, trying not to fidget with the hem of her dress as Inez opened the file folder closest to her. Even from this vantage point, Emma could recognize that it was her résumé, though she couldn't make out what was written on the Post-it Note stuck to the middle of it.

Inez didn't bother to look up as she said, "Right. Well, this shouldn't take long. I think we know—"

Her cell phone came alive on her desk, buzzing and blinking and cutting her off.

Another sigh. "Excuse me for a moment." She didn't wait for Emma to reply before she answered. "What is it?" A pause while she waited for whoever was on the other line to reply. "Honey, I'll look at it as soon as I have time to check my email, but I'm in the middle of something right now. Can it wait ten minutes?"

Emma blinked. Ten minutes? Surely an interview for a position at the Met lasted longer than that. Or maybe not. Maybe this was all leading up to a polite dismissal, a "thanks but no thanks" moment that would fuel her nightmares for years to come.

"I will look, but I'm sure it's airtight. That's why you hired an attorney, right?" Inez continued, her tone soothing. "Okay, love you too." Then she hung up and turned back to Emma. "Sorry. My wife is starting her own business and it's consuming both our lives."

Emma smiled. She tried to sound unbothered. "What does she do?"

Inez leaned back in her seat. Her smile looked forced. "She's starting an art advisory firm. They connect artists and galleries with people looking for modern art for their homes: people who want art that speaks to them, not just expensive pieces."

Emma's interest was piqued. "Like art matchmaking."

Inez's smile changed. It wasn't the same curt smile as before—this one was more genuine, like she was pleased. Maybe even a little impressed. "Yes. Exactly. Art matchmaking."

"I had no idea that was a real job."

"It's a growing niche," Inez replied. "She used to work at the Whitney and started the company as a side project, but there's been so much interest that she's doing it full-time now. She needs to hire some staff, though, or I'm going to start invoicing her for these phone calls."

Emma laughed. "It's nice that you both work in the same industry."

"I suppose. But art in the home is different than art in a museum. Here we want to educate the public, preserve and study the work. But what she does . . ." Inez considered for a moment. "She says it's about finding pieces that make a house feel like a home."

Something deep in Emma ached and she let out a long breath. "That reminds me of my mom," she said, almost to herself.

An eyebrow cocked up Inez's forehead. "Oh?"

Emma blinked. She hadn't meant the words to come out, and her mouth fell open as she tried to think of how to explain them. "She . . . she died when I was young. I don't remember her, but I remember the art she collected. Where she hung each piece in our house, how she arranged the furniture around them. Those paintings felt as much like home as my actual home did. And then . . ." She let her voice trail off. She had been so close to telling Inez the rest of the story, about how her father had loaned those same paintings to this very museum. How she had come here after school so many times just to find a way to be close to them again. But it would reveal too much. So she just shrugged, careful to censure her words. "And then, when they were gone, it felt like she was gone too. Like I lost her again."

Inez's smile dimmed, but her gaze was still keen. When she spoke again, her voice was softer. "Art is about emotion. Many people forget that."

Emma nodded. "It's true. I know my mom because of the art she loved. And somewhere along the way it became something unique to me. Yes, I love art, but I also love what art means to people. How we interact with it. I mean, this is the Met. Thousands of people come here every day to see art. But do they really interact with it? Or are they just spending a few seconds in front of a masterpiece before moving on to another one?"

"Are they actually appreciating its perfection," Inez said, nodding.

Emma's head tilted to the side as those words rang in her ears. Inez watched her reaction. "You disagree?"

"It's just . . ." Emma's tongue darted out of her mouth, wetting her lips as she tried to grasp the realization still forming in her mind. "They're not perfect, are they? And that's kind of the point. Even the masterpieces have flaws. Mistakes the artist tried to fix or hide. But that's not a bad thing. Those flaws don't detract from art's value. If anything, they add to it. They make it more real. More human. And no human is perfect, just like no work of art is perfect. The mistakes and idiosyncrasies are what make them unique. It's what makes them worth something."

Like Nadine, she almost said.

Like Knightley.

Like me.

The thought landed squarely in her brain, so large and overwhelming that it took a few moments before Emma was aware of Inez's astute gaze on her.

Oh God. Why did she derail from her planned answer and say something so . . . personal?

Inez tapped her pen on her desk as if she was considering. "Very true." Then she cleared her throat, returning her attention to the folder in front of her. "So, Emma," she said, her voice returning to its sharp, professional tone. "Tell me why you're the right candidate for our Executive Internship Program."

They talked for a few more minutes, Emma answering Inez's questions with the rehearsed answers she had practiced for weeks. But just as she was beginnning to relax, Inez closed the folder again, as if she had an internal stopwatch counting down those predetermined ten minutes. Then she offered Emma that same tight smile from when they first met. "Thank you for coming in. I think that's all we need."

"Oh, sure. Of course." Emma nodded, her enthusiasm from only a few minutes before suddenly wilting as she reached down for her bag.

Inez leaned forward, keeping Emma's attention on her. "But I want you to know that I have truly enjoyed our conversation."

A smile returned to Emma's face. "I did too."

"The Executive Internship Program will be lucky to have you in the fall."

The flutter was back, making Emma's stomach feel like it could take flight on its own.

"Really?" Emma asked, eyes wide with shock.

Inez stood, offering Emma her hand. "Congratulations."

Emma took it, trying to bite back her wide grin but failing miserably. "Thank you. Thank you so much."

Inez let out a dry laugh. "It was my pleasure. To be honest, I don't think we would have picked your résumé out on its own, but thank goodness the folks in HR recognized your name and put two and two together."

Emma stilled. It was like the world had stopped on its axis and she was frozen in place. Her pulse thundered in her ears.

Inez watched the smile fade from Emma's face. "Everything all right?"

"I . . . didn't know," Emma managed to say.

"Well, it would have been hard to avoid it, I suppose." Inez shrugged one shoulder. "Henry Woodhouse is one of our biggest patrons."

The ringing in Emma's ears grew louder. "Yes. That's true."

She turned and started to walk to the door, her body on autopilot.

Thank goodness the folks in HR recognized your name and put two and two together . . .

And there it was: Emma Woodhouse had yet again been given what she wanted without having to do anything at all to earn it.

Her feet stopped in the doorway, and she slowly pivoted around to face Inez again.

"I can't accept the position." She said the words before she even had time to process them.

Inez already had her phone to her ear as if she were about to make a call, but paused. "Pardon?"

"I'm so sorry that I wasted your time," Emma continued, her hand going to the doorframe to steady herself. "I just . . . I came here to earn this position on my own. I've spent months preparing for it. I can't accept it if the only reason it's being offered is because of who my father is."

Inez put the receiver down slowly, her expression confused. "Emma, I'll be honest. This program is incredibly competitive. That said, you've proven yourself to be an exceptionally qualified candidate, regardless of how you secured an interview."

Emma offered her a sober smile. "Then I should have no problem obtaining a position somewhere else. I just . . . I need to do this on my own."

Inez watched her, the confusion dissolving from her face and replaced by a new understanding. "I want to give you something."

She reached down and opened her desk drawer. A moment later she pulled out a business card and extended it out. Emma crossed the office and took it from her hand.

The crisp white cardstock had the name Olivia Mason across the top, along with a phone number and email address. Below that was the name of a company: Casamentero Art Advisors.

"This is my wife's company. She's still early in the hiring process, but . . ." Inez nodded to the card. "You could be exactly the type of person she's looking for. If you're interested, you should give her a call."

Emma's mouth fell open, but it was another moment before she said, "I will. Thank you."

"She'd be lucky to have you." Then Inez gave her a smile. A real one this time.

~

Emma rode the elevator back up to the main floor of the museum in a daze. It was near closing time and the crowds had thinned, but she barely noticed as she wandered through the galleries and up the main staircase to the European Paintings gallery.

Did that just happen? Had she just turned down the internship she had been dreaming about for months? She meandered through labyrinthine rooms, passing random school groups and solitary visitors as she replayed every moment of the interview in her head. It had been going so well. The conversation was honest and real and . . . fun. Emma had enjoyed it. She had liked Inez and loved talking to someone about her passion without the added pretense of who she was or what anyone expected.

But that was before she knew they had recognized her name. After all Emma's hard work, all her preparation, her name was still what got her through the door.

Emma entered another gallery. It was empty, so she let herself collapse on the long bench in the center of the room. She expected the reality of her decision to hit her at any moment: the disappointment, the sadness, the anger. But as she sat there, all she felt was a budding sense of relief. A nascent calm as she studied the business card still in her hand.

You could be exactly the type of person she's looking for. If you're interested, you should give her a call.

Yes, she had turned down the job. But in its place had sprouted so much wild potential and promise that Emma couldn't help the smile that spread across her face. She looked up, grinning ear to ear, her gaze darting around the room and landing on a familiar favorite: Gustav Klimt's *Mäda Primavesi*.

How had she missed it before? It was hanging right in front of her, the young stubborn girl staring back at Emma's wide eyes.

She suddenly remembered the last time she had looked up at it. She had been with Knightley. He had told her how the girl in Klimt's painting reminded him of Emma. She hadn't said anything at the time, but the comment had bothered her. Not the comparison, but the idea that he saw her like that. Young and stubborn, naive and headstrong . . . but looking back, that wasn't all he had said, was it? In fact, he had almost made it sound like those traits were something to be proud of.

He celebrated who she was, proved how being confident and bold was something beautiful.

Knightley's words came back to her, ringing in her mind.

He would be so proud of her right now. Of course, he'd still josh her, but he would love to hear about her interview. How well she had done, how much she had prepared. And how she had turned it down. Margo might tell her she made a mistake, her father might roll his eyes, but Knightley would understand. And she wanted to tell him. She wanted to tell him everything.

Emma's brow creased and her mind swam. Knightley saw her imperfections, he watched her make mistakes, but he also knew it was what made her who she was. She wasn't perfect. And despite how he tried, Knightley wasn't either. They were both just trying to figure it out, but at least they had each other.

They would always have each other.

Sucking in her breath, the realization came to her like a thunderbolt and made her stand up, matching the strong posture of the girl in the painting, staring at her eye to eye.

"I love Knightley," she said aloud and froze, her words echoing in the quiet, empty space. Her hand went up to her mouth the minute she said it, but it was too late. It was out there. It was true.

Eyes wide, Emma gazed up at the painting like she was seeing it for the first time. The imperfect strokes forming her proud expression, her confident stance. Klimt's painting hadn't changed, but Emma's view seemed different now. So wild and new and terrifying that all she could manage to whisper was: "Oh fuck."

CHAPTER 30

The walk back to her house was a blur. Emma knew she must have done it, if only because she suddenly found herself staring at her front door. But she had no memory of the steps in between the museum and her house. No, her mind was consumed with one thought and one thought only.

She was in love with Knightley.

God, it was so obvious. Like a muscle that had always been there but she had only just realized she could flex. Now discovered, it trembled and tensed and ached, making her feel like the entire island of Manhattan had shifted and her body was getting used to a new center of gravity.

Her key somehow found its way into the lock, and she shuffled through the doorway to stand in the center of the foyer. She caught her reflection in the mirror over the entry table. Strands of her dark hair had loosened from her ponytail and her eyes were wide, unblinking, as if she were in shock. Maybe she was.

She was in love with him.

Slowly, her reflection revealed a small, secret smile. It was a relief to finally realize it, to be able to attribute this weight inside her to something tangible. Something real.

But then just as quickly the smile faded, leaving her lips in a thin line.

She may have been blind for ages, but surely Knightley wasn't. And if he felt the same, he would have said something. He would have *done* something. She recalled all the moments where there would have been an opportunity: the Sunday dinners, the morning coffees, even New Year's, how his lips had lingered there on her cheek . . .

And then she remembered how he had arrived to that same party, sullen and brooding, only smiling when he talked to Nadine.

Nadine.

Emma stilled, staring dumbly at the wall ahead.

Yes, she loved Knightley. But so did Nadine.

Her mind suddenly went into overdrive, cataloging every moment, every interaction. Introducing them at that first Sunday dinner, how Nadine had lit up when he arrived at that New Year's Eve party, how he had smiled and complimented her dress. How he had confided in her about Los Angeles. About Davina. About all of it.

And that was it. Her racing mind stopped suddenly. Everything stopped.

Knightley cared for Nadine, too.

He had given Nadine smiles that Emma had never received. Attention and affirmation that Emma didn't even recognize. Perhaps she could have laughed it off if he were someone else, like Montgomery. But Knightley wasn't a self-obsessed playboy—he wasn't in the habit of leading women on or being anything other than honest.

Maybe that was the reason he left. He would never just run off with her friend, but that didn't mean he didn't harbor feelings for her. And now he was avoiding Emma because he didn't know how to tell her the truth. Oh God. Is that what was happening?

She walked ahead like she was on autopilot, freeing her ponytail, then shedding her coat, her bag, her scarf in a trail that led downstairs to the kitchen. The room was silent, and suddenly the loss of him was immediate. She didn't know the next time he would be in this kitchen. He had moved on before she had a chance to realize what she had lost at all.

And she could never tell him. She would never do that to Nadine. She would have to swallow this and pretend.

Yes, she would just have to pretend.

Except that she couldn't pretend. Not with him. She had learned at an early age not to even try. He was probably the only person on earth who could see through her. So how could she possibly do this? How could she keep him from knowing?

Because he's in Los Angeles.

The thought came over her like a wave, cold and calming. Yes, he was gone. And as much as she missed him, at least he wasn't right there as a constant reminder. She could do this.

She let out a deep breath, lifting her chin as if it would steel her resolve. Yes, she could—

BAM BAM BAM

The sound of someone knocking on the garden glass doors filled the room and Emma screamed.

She gripped the edge of the island and turned around, ready to lunge for the knife block until she realized that the looming figure on the other side of the glass wasn't a murderer.

It was Knightley.

Her body was frozen in place, her eyes wide with shock as her heart tripped over itself. Meanwhile, he looked at her like she had grown a second head. Then he pointed down to the doorknob.

Oh. Right. It was locked.

She approached slowly and flipped the dead bolt, immediately hit by a blast of cool air and him: that familiar smell—a mix of pine and leather—and his body, tall and broad and inches from her. He was in a pair of worn jeans and that navy cashmere sweater she loved so much, the one that hugged his chest and arms and—

Oh God.

She tried to look away but there was nowhere to look. He consumed everything.

"Why is the door locked?" he asked, his voice hitting some deep part of her chest.

Pretend pretend pretend.

"Why wouldn't it be locked?" she countered, shrugging.

"Because it's never locked."

"It's never locked when you're here."

He seemed to pick up on the subtext. *You're not here now.* He only nodded once.

Silence fell and she realized again how close he was standing, his face near enough that she could feel his warm breath on her skin as she looked up to meet his gaze.

Too close, much too close.

She took a step back, and then another, trying to look like it was a natural movement, something she would just casually do, until she bumped into the kitchen table. It shuddered from the impact, and she turned just in time to catch the vase in the center before it toppled over and spilled its pink peonies all over the floor. She whirled back around with the vase still in her hands, a smile plastered on her face.

"Are you okay?" Knightley asked, narrowing his eyes on her.

"Fine. I'm fine," she said, putting the flowers down and flipping her chestnut hair away from her face. "I just didn't know you were back. From LA. You know, since you haven't answered any of my texts. Or emails. Or . . . anything. So, yeah, I didn't know you were back. When did you get back?"

God, she was so bad at pretending.

"Just now," he said. He was still staring at her intently. He also still hadn't moved from the doorway.

"Ah," she answered, working hard to maintain her smile. The sound of her pulse in her ears was almost deafening, drowning out any other thoughts that could have led her to say something else.

The silence expanded between them, so heavy that it felt like she might choke. Her eyes went down, away from his gaze, to where the sleeves of his sweater were pushed up just enough to reveal a hint of the roped muscles of his forearms. Damn it, she loved that sweater, how years of wear had made it so soft that she would sometimes steal it until he would catch her wearing it and demand its return. That had been back before he graduated college; now his broad chest stretched it more, tightened its seams against his shoulders, his arms.

God, she was staring. She looked away, darting her eyes to the table, to the wall, to the fridge. Yes, the fridge!

"Do you want something to drink?" she asked, walking over to it. His brow furrowed and she immediately knew why. She never offered him a drink. "I'm only offering because I'm getting something. Not because you're like a guest. Because you're not a guest. That would be weird, right? It's just that Dad bought these new avocado kombucha sparkling drinks, which sound awful, I know, but they're actually not that bad. Well, he says they're not bad. Anyway, do you want one?"

"I'm fine."

She grabbed the first bottle on the shelf and opened it as she turned back to the island.

Pretend pretend pretend!

She brushed her hair off her shoulder and took a deep sip as if she did this every day. As if the fermented soda wasn't burning away her taste buds.

"Good?" he asked, a wary smile tugging at the corners of his mouth as he watched her eyes water.

She swallowed, ignoring how her throat felt like it was eroding away, and put the bottle down. "Great."

Another pause.

His gaze slid down her body. "You're dressed up for a Friday afternoon."

"Oh." She looked down at her dress, smoothing out its wrinkles. "I had my interview at the Met a little while ago."

"That's right." He nodded. "I forgot. How'd it go?"

"Well, they offered it to me," she said with a slight shrug. There was a look of approval in his eyes, so much so that she almost had to look away. But she didn't. She maintained his gaze as she continued. "I turned it down, though."

His eyebrows bobbed up in surprise. "What?"

Emma lifted her chin. "The interview went really well. The woman I spoke with was lovely; by the end I think she actually liked me. But as I was leaving, she mentioned that the reason I was there was because they recognized my name. I didn't get the interview because of my grades or my hard work. I got it because I'm a Woodhouse."

His face fell. She could tell he was trying to work out what to say, running through the possibilities until he finally just sighed. "Are you all right?"

"I'm fine." She rolled her eyes. "I wasn't even going to tell you, since I didn't know if you were ignoring all my texts or just the mundane ones."

"None of them were mundane," he murmured.

"Oh, so you did read them," she said with a forced smile. Silence fell again and it was another moment before she continued. "Why didn't you respond?"

"I'm sorry. I should have."

Her brows knitted together. He rarely apologized, and Emma wanted to savor it, but anger still simmered in her chest, as if accepting it would be letting him off too easy. "So what are you doing back?"

He ran a hand through his hair and let out a deep breath. "There's something here more important than anything in LA."

Oh God. He was going to bring up Nadine. The room suddenly felt too small, like there wasn't enough air, and panic swelled in her throat. She couldn't talk to him about this. There was no way to listen and not reveal everything she felt. He would read it right there on her face. She had to change the subject.

"Oh, I have some good gossip for you," she blurted out.

"Is it about Davina and Montgomery Knox?" he asked, walking to the island opposite her.

She blinked. "You know?"

But even as the words left her lips she realized how. He had talked to Nadine. She had already told him.

"Ben called and told me."

Ah. Yes. That made sense too.

Emma studied his expression—the grim line of his lips, the concern creasing his forehead. He looked sad. Truly sad. And for the first time Emma felt awful at how much she had neglected to think about his feelings about Davina and Montgomery. How he could be heartbroken.

"Are you all right?" she asked.

He laughed, the sound humorless. "Funny, I was going to ask you that question."

She met his gaze, confused.

"You don't deserve to be treated like that, Emma," he continued. "By anyone. Least of all a guy like that. Someone who loves themselves more than they could ever love someone else. That isn't what love looks like, and I don't want you coming out of this thinking that it is."

It took her a moment to realize what he was talking about.

"Wait. Do you mean Montgomery?" She scoffed. "Oh God, no. No, it was nothing like that."

He stared at her grimly, as if he wasn't convinced.

She sighed. "I know it looked like there was something there—I even tried to convince myself that there was—but I was never in love with him. Not even close. We barely even dated." She bit her bottom lip, trying to find the right words. "We never have to talk about Montgomery Knox again."

Knightley seemed to consider for a moment before he murmured, "He gets everything he wants, then, doesn't he?"

She stilled. "What do you mean?"

"He swoops in, your attention already waiting for him. He's funny and charming and generous even when he's lying. Then he gets to run away and never face any consequences."

The words stoked her anger back to life. "Isn't that exactly what you did too?"

He blinked. "What?"

"You picked up and ran away and never bothered to tell anyone why," she said, crossing her arms over her chest. "Yes, okay, maybe work was busy, but that's no excuse. You ignored us, Knightley. You ignored me. And you never told me *why*. You just disappeared and wouldn't write me back, and I couldn't even ask you . . ."

He reached back and hooked his hand behind his neck. The movement pulled his sweater up to reveal a thin sliver of his taut stomach, a trail of hair leading under his waistband. She felt an ache that sent a flush to her cheeks, and she quickly looked back to the bottle in her hands.

"So ask me now," he said. It was almost a whisper.

Her heart stuttered as if it would explode at any moment, as if the fear and the tension would tear her apart if he even said Nadine's name. She had been so busy being angry at him for not telling her the truth that she hadn't considered what it would mean if he did.

After a long moment he nodded slowly. "That's probably smart. But I can't keep doing this. I can't stay quiet just for the sake of maintaining the status quo. And honestly—" He laughed bitterly again. "I don't care if you don't want to hear it. Because you need to. I need to tell you. Even if we both regret it the minute it's out there, I—"

"Then don't!" she exclaimed. Her grip on the bottle was so tight she thought it might shatter in her hands. "Don't say it. If it's going to change everything, please don't say it."

Shit. She had said too much. She caught her bottom lip in her teeth as he stared at her, his expression so pained she felt it in her chest. But he didn't reply, his eyes traveling across her face to her lips, where they lingered for a long moment. Then he seemed to remember himself and looked down.

A moment. A half second perhaps. That was all he needed to collect himself. Then he turned and disappeared out the French doors.

She stood there in the suffocating silence, staring at the spot where he had been standing.

What was she doing? This was her best friend. Regardless of how much it hurt, she had to be there for him. She had to go and hear whatever it was he had to say, even if it broke her heart.

And with that final thought she launched herself out the door and toward the house across the yard.

CHAPTER 31

"Knightley!" Emma yelled after him, but he was already inside his home, closing the sliding glass door behind him. She sprinted across the yard and threw the door back open, practically falling into the house.

He was at the kitchen counter, his back to her with his head hanging low.

"Please leave," he said firmly as she stood at the threshold catching her breath.

"No."

He turned around and his eyebrows shot up. "No?"

"I want to hear what you have to say."

"Do you? Do you really?" He crossed his arms and leaned back against the counter, watching her with a look of disbelief mixed with irritation.

"Yes! You're my friend. I want to be friends at the very least."

"Friends," he murmured to himself, shaking his head. "Right."

"Please, Knightley. Don't push me away again." She ignored the panic rising in her throat and lifted her chin. She could do this; she could handle whatever he had to say. What was the worst it could be? He and Nadine were in love and moving to California? The thought made her sick. But for him, she would hear it. She owed him that.

"Push you away?" he replied and scoffed, raking a hand down his face. "Jesus, you're impossible."

He turned his back to her, his head falling forward again as he leaned his hands on the counter.

Her mouth fell open.

"I'm impossible?" she cried, her voice high and loud, but she didn't care. All of her frustration was rising like the tide, her anger bubbling up to a white-hot rage. "You ignored me for weeks. You drop off the face of the earth. You left. You left *me*! Then you come back, acting like nothing has changed. Like you can still push me to live up to your ridiculous standards. And I'm the one that's impossible? You're the impossible one! You lecture me, you blame me, and I always take it! You tell me to grow up, when you're the one acting immature. You're pissed when I don't do things *exactly* as the perfect Mr. George Knightley would. I can't fucking win with you!"

She watched the broad expanse of his back, how his shoulders rose and fell with each angry breath. But he still wouldn't face her.

"Stop ignoring me!"

She grabbed whatever her hand found nearby, a small book on the coffee table, and hurled it at him.

It landed with a thud beyond his feet, and he whipped around. His brow was knit together, whether by surprise or anger, she couldn't tell.

"Say something, Knightley! Talk to me!"

He didn't respond at first. Just watched her, an icy glow in his golden eyes.

"You really think I'm horrible, don't you?" His voice was so low she could barely hear it.

"Don't you dare twist my words," she hissed. "I'm mad at you!"

"Yeah, I get that!" he shouted, the words echoing through the room.

She narrowed her eyes on him. "No, you don't get it. You can't just pretend I don't exist!"

"Believe me, I know!"

He clenched his jaw, breathing slow and deep. She waited, watching him struggle, like he was having an internal debate about what to do next.

"You want to know what I have to say?" His voice was deep and gritty as he pushed himself off the counter and began to walk toward her, one slow deliberate step after another.

"Yes," she said, stepping backward as he approached, lifting her chin higher even when she hit the wall behind her with nowhere left to go.

He stopped in front of her, leaving only a few precious inches between them.

"Even if it might change everything?" he murmured. His expression was almost pained.

"I'm your friend, Knightley. Nothing will ever change that," she said. Her heart tripped as her confidence wavered, her anger subsiding. There was no way he couldn't hear her pulse; it was thundering too loudly in her own ears.

With heavy lids, he inhaled sharply as he leaned forward, closing the small space left between them. She tried to match the fiery stare swarming inside the deep gold of his pupils, but her gaze fell to his bottom lip instead. So she closed her eyes.

"But that's the problem, Emma. I don't want to be friends." His voice was close enough that she could feel his warm breath on her skin. Then calloused fingers touched her face, and her eyes flew open again. His gaze was still locked on her, but the heat in his eyes had changed slightly as his thumb grazed her cheek.

"What do you want?" she whispered.

"I want you."

For a moment it felt like time had stopped.

Her breath hitched. Her fingers splayed against the wall behind her for balance, for reassurance that this was real as her mind replayed his words over and over again.

He waited, his face so close she could almost taste the sweetness of his lips on hers.

She blinked slowly, staring up at him through her thick eyelashes. Her mind and body reeled at his words.

I want you.

"You want me?" It came out like a question, as if saying it out loud might make it real.

His head fell forward. He braced his hands on the wall above her as his eyes closed, as if he were confessing his worst sin. "When I look at you, I can barely control myself."

It was only when those words left his lips and filled the small space between them that she realized this wasn't a dream. This was real. Knightley wanted her. And suddenly something ignited deep inside her.

"Then . . . look at me," she responded, her voice surprisingly low and steady.

A moment. Then his head slowly lifted, his expression shifting from surprise to triumph to something much more carnal as his hand came up to cup her jaw, holding her there, his eyelids heavy.

"Emma," he whispered, almost to himself.

God, her name on his lips. It was the best sound in the world.

"Yes," she whispered back.

He leaned in and kissed her. She gasped as his tongue gently teased her bottom lip, parting her mouth open, sending a shot of electricity to her heart, her head, her core. She didn't expect to moan so loudly, but when their tongues brushed together, when his hands bracketed each of her arms to pull her closer, she couldn't help it. Her body melted against his and she gripped at the fabric of his shirt for support, pressing him flush against her. A groan escaped his throat in response and a triumphant thrill ran up her spine. God, she never wanted this to stop. Never ever—

Then he pulled back suddenly, letting out a shaky breath as he rested his forehead on hers.

No, don't stop. Don't stop.

Their breathing was loud and erratic, their hearts pounding rapidly in sync. He opened his mouth as if he were about to say something, but all Emma could think about was his lips on hers again.

"Emma, I—"

She crushed her mouth to his, cutting him off as her hands pulled at his strong arms, bringing his body flush with hers once more.

Whatever anger or confusion had been weighing on Emma only moments before was redirected, fueling the spark. She wanted this, and so did he. George Knightley wanted her. She couldn't think beyond those words running on repeat in her mind. Every time they did, she could only feel the burning ache taking over her body, the heat quickly rising from deep within her belly.

"Fuck," he cursed under his breath. Then he pushed his hips forward to pin her to the wall, one hand securing her small frame while the other tilted her head back so he could kiss and tease her already swollen lips.

His nimble fingers moved, quickly untying the wrap belt of her dress. He kissed her bare shoulder before letting her clothes fall to the ground. Standing there in her boots and matching black underwear and lace bra, she should have felt exposed, vulnerable. But she only felt alive as he sucked in his breath.

"You're killing me, Emma," he whispered as his hands caressed the soft skin of her stomach. Then he leaned forward again, his lips grazing over her collarbone. She was barely aware of the whimpers escaping her parted lips.

She began to fumble with his belt and he chuckled, stepping back to undo it himself. Then he pulled off his sweater and stripped down to his boxers. A thin sheen of sweat was visible above his brow and on his torso, showing off his tanned skin as he stared at her, his breathing erratic.

God, he's so gorgeous, she thought, squeezing her legs together. Her hands acted on their own, reaching out to touch his chest. She skimmed her palms over his hard abs and downward, feeling him tense and inhale sharply. Unable to stop herself, her fingers went lower while her eyes followed. She heard him groan, his eyes locked on her, his breath coming out in short pants now as her thumb grazed over the skin just under the waistband of his boxers. She could see his hardness, thick and prominent underneath. She started to slide her hands under the material, but he was faster.

In one swift move, he grabbed her thighs and lifted her up against the wall, holding her in place with his strong body, her legs easily wrapping around his waist.

She gasped at the sudden change, taking a deep shaky breath. His mouth found hers again, devouring her soft moans while he rocked up against her. With every hard push, she shuddered. She could feel him right there, his length brushing against her sex in just the right spot, teasing her with only the thin material of her underwear separating them. She lifted her hips to push herself against him, dying for some friction to satisfy the insane thrill creeping up her spine and overtaking her senses.

"Christ." His hips jutted forward, like he was reading her mind.

Then his hand traveled firmly up her soft thigh, inching higher and higher to her core. She whimpered softly when his fingers stroked her underwear, her head falling back onto the wall with a thud. She could feel him watching her reactions, her parted lips, her furrowed brow. He slowly pulled aside the black lace seam and slid two fingers inside her, moving slowly at first, then increasing in speed as she tensed around his hand.

"Oh my God," she murmured, feeling the pressure building from low in her spine as he moved, setting an intuitive rhythm.

"You like that? You like when I touch you?" he whispered in her ear.

"Yes . . . yes . . ." she whimpered, trying not to lose it completely. "I like it."

His thumb circled her sensitive center as his fingers curled just so, working her deeper, harder. She shivered and her hips jerked forward, unable to hold back, surprised at how quickly he got her to the precipice.

"Knightley . . ." she breathed, panting and light-headed.

"I've got you," he whispered.

She gasped as the orgasm overtook her, her thighs trembling around his waist. He held her tightly against him, slowly letting her ride it out, kissing her cheeks, her neck, until she opened her eyes.

"You okay?" he whispered into her hair, nipping sweetly at her neck.

"Yeah," she breathed. "Holy shit."

She wrapped her arms around his shoulders and neck, desperate to get closer, to kiss him again, but he was already moving, pulling her down to the sofa. He fell back into the cushions, hands on her hips as he tugged her forward to straddle him. She knew he was trying to be gentle, but she could still feel him hard against her hip, and it sent another pulse through her bloodstream.

She brought her lips to his and his grip on her body tightened.

"Take your boots off," he murmured against her mouth. "The bra too."

She smiled. Part of her wanted to give him a hard time about telling her what to do, but a larger part loved it. She rose slowly, standing between his legs, and took off each boot, losing inches of height. Then she unclipped her bra, sliding it off.

"Fuck," he breathed when her breasts were finally exposed, nipples hard from the sudden exposure to the cool air. Then he leaned into her body, leaving a soft kiss against her belly.

His fingers found the lace edges of her underwear, hooking his thumbs on each side. He slowly dragged them down until they pooled at her feet. She held her breath as his gaze skimmed her curves like he was trying to memorize every inch of her body.

Then he tugged her toward him again and she fell back into his lap, her legs bracketing his hips.

He wasn't gentle now. His hands spanned her back and pressed her curves against the hard plane of his chest while he licked and nipped her lips, her jaw, her neck. His grip on her body was desperate, and Emma couldn't help the whimper that escaped her throat.

"Oh my God," she whispered, throwing her head back as his mouth journeyed across her collarbone, then down to her chest. Her fingers tangled in his hair and tightened as his tongue traced small slow circles around one of her hardened nipples, then the other.

"I've thought about this so many times," he said against her skin.

"You've thought about this?"

He nipped again and she gasped. "Yes, I've thought about this. I've thought about fucking you all over this goddamn house."

The ache in her core was building again as she imagined what he was going to do to her next. She tightened her thighs around his, grinding slowly against him, and he finally returned his mouth to hers. The kiss was demanding, and she could feel herself getting lost, every move threatening to engulf her.

"Need you, now," she murmured against his lips. She reached for the waist of his boxers, desperate to pull them down, to have him inside her, to dull that ache. But then he shifted, leaning back and lifting her weight up from his body so she was sitting on the sofa beside him. She let out a desperate whine, arching forward to keep her lips fastened to his.

"Shhh," he exhaled, peppering kisses along her lips and jaw before he reached down to where his clothes lay in a pile on the floor and pulled his wallet from the pocket of his jeans. A condom wrapper was in his hand a moment later. The room was suddenly so quiet; the only sounds were of their breathing and the distinct crinkle as he tore it open.

Somewhere in her mind, Emma knew she should feel nervous. Or self-conscious. But as she watched Knightley wrap his hand around himself and slowly unroll the condom over his considerable length, all she felt was hunger. Such a hot and overwhelming hunger that she had to touch him, ready to force his body to hers again.

"Wait, wait, wait," he said, a lazy grin on his face as he finished. Then he looked up and met her gaze. His eyes heavy and hard, mirroring her every emotion. "C'mere."

Those eyes stayed on hers as he gripped her hips, pulling her back to his lap and down onto him. She gasped at the feel of him filling her slowly, slowly, slowly until her hips met his and then he cursed, pulling her toward him and hugging her close.

It was all too much. Too intense. They held on to each other, as if they both needed a moment to adjust to the sensation.

She'd imagined this, but she didn't think he'd know exactly what to do, how to touch her, how to move. Then he started to shift, rocking her up and down on him, a slow intoxicating rhythm while he whispered with half-lidded eyes, "You feel so damn good."

Her eyes fluttered closed. He felt so perfect as he pushed into her again and again, slowly increasing his pace. His hands held her tightly as he lifted her up and back down, over and over as she leaned into the crook of his neck, breathless and dizzy. Sweat prickled along her brow as she chased the pleasure coursing through her with each deliberate thrust.

Her hands shifted from his broad chest to his neck to try to steady herself as her thighs began to tremble. He seemed to be losing control, too, pushing harder and harder, the deep ache in her core threatening to burst. She couldn't help the needy sounds escaping from her throat; all she could focus on was the orgasm barreling toward her.

"Come again for me." His words floated into her ear as his hand moved down her body between them to circle and press her sensitive bundle of nerves, the added stimulation making her eyes roll back.

She nodded slightly; she couldn't form words, only desperate cries as she tightened around him. She came hard, her back arching, the intense convulsions washing over her. He kept up his pace, transfixed by her face as she rode out the best orgasm of her life.

"Knightley," she breathed.

He kissed her desperately, gripping her until he was biting back a groan as he came.

"Jesus . . ." he panted under his breath, pulsating inside her. He held her tight as she fell forward, melting against his warm chest. Their skin was sticky and oversensitive, but she didn't care. She knew there was a conversation waiting for them, things to work out and define, but right now she pushed it all aside, closing her eyes and savoring every second in Knightley's arms.

CHAPTER 32

I t was the middle of the night when Knightley woke to the sound of glasses clanging, the shuffling of feet and opening of drawers downstairs. The sounds were swimming in his head before he was even aware of them, working into a dream until something in his brain clicked and his eyes slowly opened.

The wall of windows that faced the back garden was dark with only the watery light from the city sky revealing the outline of his bed. The indentation in the sheets beside him.

Emma.

The evening rushed back to him in an instant—the tension, the argument, and then the need, the fucking relief of having her. They had passed out afterward, waking up at midnight and stumbling up to his bed. He reached over and picked up his phone to see that it was now three a.m.

He lay there for a long moment, listening to the sounds coming from the kitchen, and suddenly a rush of panic shot through him. It had all happened so quickly; he had felt untethered, controlled only by the emotions that he had tried for so long to suppress.

But she had wanted him, too. That simple push, that give of

her lips and press against his body. That's all it took. This amazing woman that had borne the brunt of his criticisms and condescension and fucking baggage. This woman knew it all. And she still wanted him.

The thought faded as he heard footsteps lightly padding up the stairs toward his room. He sat up, pulling his legs free from the mess of sheets just as Emma appeared in the doorway. There was a pint of ice cream in one hand and a spoon in the other.

"Hi." Her voice was soft, almost a whisper, yet there was nothing tentative in her tone. In fact, there was nothing self-conscious about her at all. She stood in the doorframe, one hip leaning against it, with nothing covering her except the shadows from the hallway light. But even silhouetted, Knightley could make out every curve of her body. The swell of her breasts, the dip of her waist.

"You all right?" he asked.

"I was hungry." He saw the smile turn up the corners of her lips. "I was looking for Pop-Tarts or Lucky Charms or something, but all I could find was oatmeal and protein powder. Why do you buy so much ice cream but totally fail with really unhealthy breakfast foods?"

"Probably because I don't make breakfast for anyone except me." He had meant it to sound light, a self-effacing joke to get them back to familiar ground. But he realized his misstep as soon as the words left his lips and the smile faded from her own. How the statement alluded to others, women whose shadows loomed here in the darkness too.

Shit, he wanted to apologize. He wanted to start over and be the first to speak, to let her know how he felt, how *much* he felt.

"Emma, I didn't mean—"

"No, no, it's fine," she cut him off. "I didn't mean to make it weird. Or weirder."

He shook his head, maintaining her steady gaze. "It's not weird."

Silence stretched out between them for a minute as she studied his face.

She took a step forward, then another, until she was standing in front of where he sat on the edge of the bed.

"What is it, then?" she asked.

He reached out, putting a hand on either hip and pulling her to him. His fingers pressed into her soft skin as his thumbs grazed the rise of her hip bone.

I'm in love with you. The thought felt so natural and right that he almost said it aloud. But then he caught her expression. Her bottom lip between her teeth, the skin between her eyebrows pinched. It occurred to him that while he knew exactly how he felt, she might still be figuring it out.

So instead he said, "This is whatever you want it to be."

She ran a hand through his black hair, her nails tickling his scalp. "Is it?"

He leaned his forehead against her stomach, closing his eyes and nodding against her skin.

She laughed softly, but he could hear how it was forced. "Does that mean I can stay until the morning?"

Heat pooled low in his belly even as something in his chest tightened, making it hard to breathe. His past decisions, those women Emma had watched through her window—they left a veneer on this. He hadn't considered it, but now it was impossible to ignore. Did she really think he saw her like those other women? That she hadn't eclipsed them all even before last night?

His grip on her hips tightened. But he swallowed his frustration down. He'd let her take the lead here. And the morning was a good place to start.

"You better be here in the morning."

"Yeah?" she breathed, a tinge of relief in her voice.

He looked up at her. "Yeah."

She lifted one shoulder, a slight shrug like she was trying to be nonchalant. "Okay."

He laughed softly. "Are you done with that ice cream?"

"Well, it is really good," she mused. "And the carton is almost empty anyway so it's not really worth putting back in the freezer . . ."

He nodded, even as he took it from her and put it on the nightstand. Then he took her hand, tugging her back down onto the bed. She was trying to bite back a smile and failing, her dark hair spread out like a halo on the pillow.

He could feel himself getting lost in the moment again, but he didn't want to rush things. Last night was fast. It was fucking fantastic, but it was fast. She made him feel wild and delirious and it felt so damn good that he had given into it then, but now it felt too greedy. His body ached to move, to touch, but he held himself back, his face hovering just a few inches from her own.

"What?" she whispered.

"Emma Woodhouse," he hummed. "In my bed."

She laughed softly. "Pretty crazy."

"Is it okay?"

"Well, if we're really being honest . . ."

"We are." He brushed a few strands of hair off her forehead.

"Okay." She took a deep breath. "Then explain to me why you only have two pillows for this entire California King–sized bed? No decorative throws? Not even a nice embroidered lumbar pillow? What's wrong with you?"

He chuckled and rolled to the side, leaning on one elbow to look at her. "I'm sure you're about to tell me."

She huffed dramatically, but when she turned to face him again, her amused expression became more serious. A moment passed before she rested a hand on his cheek. He relaxed into her touch, letting her fingers caress the stubble along his jaw.

"Nothing," she whispered. "There's nothing wrong with you at all."

He offered her a wry smile. "I don't know about that. I've blamed you and lectured you."

"You've been honest with me," she corrected him. "And I've been honest right back."

"Don't ever stop, either." He turned his head enough to kiss her palm.

"Okay," she breathed. "I hate the pillows on your bed."

His smile broadened. "And I can't believe you turned down that job you worked months to get."

She pulled her hand away, mock-indignation on her face. "Hey! I'm proud of myself, actually!"

"You should be. That wasn't an easy thing to do. I'm proud of you too."

"Even though I'm about to be an unemployed graduate with no real job prospects?"

He leaned backward, resting a hand behind his head and stared up at the ceiling fan. "You'll figure it out. You always do."

She sighed. "But how do you know that?"

The skin between her eyebrows was pinched with concern again, like she was honestly asking. He reached over and pulled her closer to him. She came willingly, wrapping her limbs around his body and resting her chin on his chest. He looked down at her wide green eyes and hesitated before continuing. "Because you take more chances than I ever have and probably ever will. No matter what life throws at you, you face it with this unfailing belief in yourself. You refuse to shrink away. And I know I may second-guess you or make you feel like you're making a mistake, but that's only because I wish I was that brave. That's how I know."

She stared back at him and blinked. "Knightley, that is, by far, the nicest thing you've ever said to me."

He frowned. "Really?"

She nodded. A small grin teased her lips as she ran her fingers through his hair. "I think there was even an apology in there."

He laughed as he kissed her. "I'll apologize to you all weekend if you like."

He could feel her smile against his lips. "Good, because I've got nothing to do except . . ." Suddenly her body stiffened, her hand tightening on his hair. "Oh my God."

He stilled. "What?"

"It's Saturday now." Her eyes were wide, her lips a thin line across her face. "That means tomorrow is Sunday."

"And?"

"We have Sunday dinner. People will see us. People are going to know." She whispered the last word like it was a secret.

"Know?"

"About you and me."

"And that's a problem?"

"Of course it's a problem! They can't know! I mean, we hardly know. What do we even tell them?"

He wanted to laugh. He already knew what he wanted to tell them. Jesus, he wanted to shout it from the rooftops. But it was clear that she was still working it out in her head, and he wasn't going to be the one to push it. If she needed time, he'd give it to her. Still, they were lucky no one had picked up on the tension between them these last few months; he didn't know how they'd be able to hide it now.

"So you want to wait."

"Yes . . ." Her voice trailed off as she seemed to consider. "I mean, they don't even know that you're back from LA, right? So they won't even be expecting you. Maybe you should just pretend like you're not home yet. Like, keep the lights off and don't go in the backyard, and then next week we can figure out—"

"You want me to hide?"

"No! Not hide, per se. I just . . . I want to wait for the right time."

"And when is the right time, exactly?"

She rolled her eyes. "I don't know, Knightley. I don't have a calendar in front of me, so I can't tell you an exact date but—"

He bent forward to kiss her again.

"All right," he whispered, pulling back only slightly. "We'll keep it a secret from everybody."

"Not everybody," she breathed.

"No," he hummed. "Just your dad . . . Margo and Ben . . . Nadine . . ."

Her body stiffened again and her hand tightened around his hair so hard his scalp burned.

He winced. "What?"

Her face blanched as she stared back at him. "Nadine."

CHAPTER 33

Emma paced back and forth in front of the fireplace. The sun streamed in through the living room windows, revealing the warm spring day outside. Still, she felt a deep chill and would have loved a roaring fire. Or maybe she could just go curl under her blankets upstairs. Yes, she could go back to bed and avoid the day entirely.

"Do you need something?" her father asked as he passed the doorway.

"No, I'm fine," she said, barely offering him a smile as she continued her laps across the ivory Persian rug.

A minute later, Fran walked by. "Can I get you anything?"

"I'm fine," Emma said, a little too quickly.

Her pace increased as she stole another look down at her phone. 5:04 p.m.

Nadine always stopped by on Saturdays after she got off work at five. That meant that at any moment she would be at the door, smiling and completely oblivious to the fact that her heart was about to be broken. Again.

Emma let out a shaky breath. She had been trying to work out what to tell Nadine since she left Knightley's that morning. She had to break the news gently about what happened last night. But what *had* happened last night? God, Emma wasn't even sure. They had hooked up. She had a massive amount of orgasms. He let her demolish his ice cream. But that was it. Despite everything that had happened that night, all the vulnerability and honesty and, well, orgasms, he hadn't said anything about commitment or a relationship or love.

Meanwhile, she was in love with him. There was no denying it now. In fact, it felt ridiculous that she hadn't realized it before. But just because she loved him, just because this was real and true and permanent for her, that didn't mean it was the same for him. She knew his history; he had told her himself. He liked having no strings attached. And yet, she wanted strings with him. She needed strings. And their absence left her feeling lost.

She shook her head. Her mind was wandering again and she had to focus; this was about Nadine.

She decided to stick with the facts. The truth. She loved Knightley. And yes, she knew he didn't really do relationships and usually never saw the women he slept with after actually sleeping with them, but he also told her he wanted her there in the morning. He just hadn't specified which morning. Had he meant just today, or future mornings too? She really needed to talk to him, figure out what exactly this was before—

The doorbell cut off her train of thought.

Emma froze as she watched Fran cross the foyer to answer the door. A muffled greeting, a laugh, and then Nadine appeared, walking across the living room to collapse on the sofa.

"My feet are killing me!" she moaned. "Those marble floors at the salon are nice, but they're not made for people with high arches."

Emma tried to smile. This was it. But when she opened her mouth, nothing came out.

"Are you all right?" Nadine stared at her with concern.

"I'm fine! Totally fine," Emma managed to say, her voice a bit too loud. "Do you want a drink?"

"No, I'm good."

Emma nodded, then started pacing again, walking to the piano and back.

"Are you sure you're okay?" Nadine asked. "You're making me nervous."

"I'm great! I just think better when I'm moving, you know?"

Nadine nodded, even though the lines on her forehead didn't relax. "Okay. Well, I have some news. It's insane, but I have to tell you."

"So do I. In fact, I really need to—"

"I've met someone!" Nadine squealed.

Emma paused. "You met someone? Like, on one of your apps?"

"Oh yeah. No," Nadine said, brows knitting together. "I guess I haven't *just* met him since I've known him for a while. But it's only just become a thing, you know? I mean, I've thought he was gorgeous for *ages*, but I never thought he'd look at me like that, obviously." She laughed.

Emma swallowed. She could hear her pulse pounding in her ears, like she was on a roller coaster approaching its first free fall. "Obviously?"

"Well, after you introduced us, I just thought, why would he? But then I started to suspect maybe he did? It's like you said, the more time you spend with someone, the more you start to read the signs."

Oh God. Emma was going to be sick.

"And it's perfect because I'm pretty sure he's not even looking for a relationship, so—" Nadine caught her friend's blanched expression and her smile faltered. "Are you mad?"

"No." Emma shook her head, her tongue darting out to wet her dry lips. "No, I'm not mad. It's just . . . Nadine, I have to tell you something too."

Silence descended and Nadine's eyes grew wide. "Is it about the Met interview?"

"No, that can wait. I just . . . I have to tell you . . ." Emma closed her eyes to steel her resolve. "We . . . he and I . . . hooked up."

A long moment passed. When Emma finally opened her eyes, her friend was still there, her face contorted as she processed the information.

"You hooked up," Nadine repeated slowly.

"Yes."

"So . . . are you two together or—"

"I . . . I think I'm in love with him."

It was the first time she had said it out loud. The words came so naturally, so easily, it was like they had been there on her tongue for ages, just waiting to be set free. It felt good.

Then she saw her friend's expression. Nadine's usual smile was gone, her mouth slack, and her eyes were staring straight ahead.

"In love with him," she murmured to herself.

"I'm so sorry, Nadine." Emma sat down on the sofa beside her. She tried to push down the guilt, but it only came roaring back. "We didn't plan it or anything. It just happened."

Nadine swallowed. "I . . . I guess it makes sense. You've known him for so long. There's probably history there."

Her voice was so soft, so small. Emma bit her bottom lip, trying to keep her emotions at bay, but she was failing. "We were only ever friends. When I introduced you to him, we were still just friends."

"I believe you. And he's so gorgeous. And nice. And thoughtful. How could you not fall for him?"

"I never expected to, though. Honestly, I didn't."

Nadine made a motion as if to nod, but it died halfway through. "Right. Especially because of the whole gay thing."

Silence. Emma blinked, so taken aback that it took almost a full minute for her to find anything to say. "The gay thing?"

Nadine finally turned to look at her. There were tears in the corners of her eyes and her bottom lip was wobbling. "Because you thought he was gay."

Silence again. Emma's mouth fell open, but nothing came out for a moment. "Nadine. I don't think I've ever, in my entire life, gotten the impression that he was gay."

Now it was Nadine's turn to look confused. "But you told me he was."

"I did?"

"Yes, don't you remember?" Nadine turned her body to face Emma fully. "The first time we went to the salon. You told me he was gay."

Something clicked into place in Emma's mind and her eyes narrowed on her friend. "Nadine, who are you talking about?"

Her friend sighed sadly. "Mateo."

Relief flooded Emma's body, loosening every muscle, and she couldn't help but smile. "Mateo."

"I understand, though. And I won't stand in your way. If you want—"

Emma shook her head. "I'm not in love with Mateo, Nadine."

Her friend paused, confusion overwhelming her features again. "What?"

"I'm not in love with Mateo."

Nadine's nose scrunched up. "Then who are you in love with?"

The name was there on Emma's tongue, but she paused. The minute she said it, everything would become real. The truth would be out in the open and there would be no way to ever go back. Everything could change and the realization sent a slice of fear through her chest.

"Knightley," Emma said, releasing a shaky breath. "I'm in love with Knightley."

It was quiet for a moment, so quiet that Emma wasn't even sure that her friend had heard her. Maybe she hadn't said the words out loud at all. Emma made a move to speak again, but then Nadine's face broke into a wide grin as she squealed, "I knew it!"

Emma watched her, mouth agape. "Wait, what?"

Nadine's head fell back as she laughed. "I knew it! That first time I saw you two together, I knew there was something between you two!"

"What are you talking about?"

Nadine rolled her eyes. "Oh my God, Emma. From the minute you brought me to that Sunday dinner months and months ago, I knew. I just couldn't believe you didn't! I mean, you're so close and you find every excuse to spend time together and it was obvious you never liked Davina—"

"I liked Davina! I just didn't think she was right for Knightley. Which, considering how she ran off with Montgomery, was kind of prescient."

"Yes, but even before that."

Emma bit her bottom lip. "I just thought Knightley didn't like Montgomery."

"Are you kidding? He was so jealous! I mean, rightly so. Montgomery is a player. Hot and charming, yes, but still a player. I never liked him for you. And I didn't get why everyone was pushing you two together. Like, he clearly was not relationship material, so why—"

"Nadine," Emma said, trying to keep her friend on track.

"Right, sorry. I'm just saying he wasn't right for you. Knightley is. He always has been."

Emma turned, staring dumbly at the windows against the far wall. Nadine had only known them for a little under a year and *she* was able to see what they'd both been blind to for years? And if she saw it . . .

"Do you think anybody else suspects anything?" she asked.

Nadine snorted. "I think it's pretty obvious to everyone that *something's* going on."

Oh my God. A pit of worry opened up in Emma's belly as she imagined everyone already knowing her secret. The weight of it made her feel nauseous. They'd make assumptions. Margo would demand all the details. Mrs. Pawloski could already be planning the wedding. And what would her dad think?

"No. No way," she said, shaking her head.

"I don't know. You and Knightley are always flirting, and—"

"We're not always *flirting*," Emma interjected. "We argue all the time! And he's always throwing around his opinion even though no one asked. And yes, he checks in on me and makes it a point to hang out every weekend, but . . ."

Nadine had a smug smile on her face as she watched her friend begin to connect the dots.

"How did I miss this?" Emma finally whispered.

"Sometimes you don't see what's right in front of you unless someone hits you over the head with a frying pan. Well, that's what my nana always says."

Emma let out a breathy laugh. "Your nana is a wise woman."

Nadine shrugged.

"God." Emma sighed, pushing a few strands of hair from her face. "I've spent the past few hours eating myself up inside because I thought *you* were in love with him."

Nadine's eyes grew wide again. "Me? And Knightley. Are you serious? Why would you think that?"

"How could I not? You always bring him up and light up when he's around, and you said you wanted to visit LA, and you seemed so sad when he left! And I've seen you . . . talking with him. I just assumed!"

"Of course I felt all those things. Because *you* wanted to talk about him. *You* lit up when he came into the room. And *you* were sad when he left."

It was true. Emma did feel lighter when he entered the room. And it had felt like a crushing weight when he left for California. But she had barely been aware of those feelings herself, let alone that they were obvious to anyone who took the time to look. And meanwhile . . .

"You've been falling for Mateo this whole time and I never even noticed," she said as guilt swelled in her chest again.

"To be fair, you did think he was gay."

Emma couldn't help but laugh. "I thought he was!"

"Well, I mean, he's bi, so you weren't completely wrong," she said. "I didn't know that, though. I just thought he was this incredibly hot guy who was kind and nice and loved to flirt and also happened to be gay."

"So what happened?"

Nadine tried to bite back her grin but failed miserably. "We did it."

"WHAT?" Emma practically screamed.

Nadine nodded proudly. "Last night. After the salon closed,

he and I were cleaning up and I was just telling him how awful online dating has been and how hard it is to find a nice guy who wants the same things I want and . . . he kissed me. And he kept kissing me, and it was amazing, and then suddenly we were in the stock room, you know the one at the end of the hall where they keep all the developer and foils and . . ." Emma nodded quickly and motioned for her to keep going. "Right, so suddenly we were back there and it was . . ." Her smile widened. "It was *really* good."

Emma's mouth fell open again. "Are you serious?"

"I could not be more serious."

"So, what are you two now? Dating? Are you exclusive? Should we invite him to Sunday dinner or—"

Nadine held up her hand. "No. No labels. We're having fun. That's what I want right now. I deserve happiness on my own terms, remember? And so do you."

Emma's heart swelled. It seemed like a lifetime ago when she first introduced herself to Nadine, back when she was looking so lost on the street. Emma had felt she was doing her a service, that she was going to save her. Funny how the opposite came to be true.

She leaned forward and enveloped her friend in a hug. "I'm really so lucky I met you, Nadine."

"I'm lucky I met you too," she replied softly.

Emma sighed, releasing her and leaning back into the sofa. "I'm the worst. Let's be honest."

Nadine laughed. "Definitely not."

"Have you forgotten that I pretty much made you break up with Marty? Then I pushed you on some egotistical, womanizing barista. I missed every sign about Mateo while completely misreading your feelings toward Knightley. I'm an awful matchmaker."

"Maybe," Nadine said. "But you're an amazing friend. I am having the time of my life right now, and I credit a lot of that to you. You opened my eyes so much. It was only a matter of time before I broke up with Marty. And the Zane story just gets more and more hilarious as time goes by. But when it comes down to it, I love being single. I *love* living in New York. Yeah, I'm making mistakes, but that's okay. I'm figuring it out. And that's because you made me believe that I could. Without you I probably would have already crawled home to my parents' house. It's good, Emma. I'm *really* good."

Emma let out a deep breath. "I'm glad."

"Good. Now, when are you going to tell me every single detail of what happened with Knightley?"

Emma grinned. "As soon as we order some takeout and open a bottle of wine."

Nadine squealed and clapped her hands.

CHAPTER 34

For the fifth time in thirty minutes, Emma checked the progress of dinner. She paced the kitchen, watching Fran carefully stir the risotto. The roasted chicken was still warming in the oven. The spinach salad was prepped on the countertop. It was fine. Everything was fine.

Emma swallowed, repeating the mantra in her head. It all looked like the same preparation for every Sunday dinner that had ever happened before. That should have felt comforting. But it wasn't. Nothing was comforting right now as Nadine's words from last night clanged around clumsily in her head.

I think it's pretty obvious to everyone that something's going on.

In less than an hour everyone would be here and they would realize that she was in love with Knightley.

Of course, they hadn't said it. She told herself that was fine; he'd always cared about her and would never hurt her . . . not intentionally, anyway.

She swallowed. But that was the crux of it, the reason she was so hesitant to tell everyone about whatever this was. Knightley already told her he liked having no strings; who was to say he would feel differently now? And if that was the case, how could she move on from that? How could she see him every day and pretend that she didn't care? And have to placate her family on top of it? She couldn't even contemplate that.

So they would have to keep it a secret until they could talk about this. And that was fine. Totally fine.

With that resolution, she smoothed her sweater over her short wool skirt and looked over the dining table. It looked gorgeous, as usual. There was a bouquet of peonies in the center, and Fran was setting out the usual blue-and-white plates that were reserved for Sunday nights. Everything looked just as it should, so there was no reason to . . . wait.

"That's six plates." She barely realized that the thought was said aloud.

Fran looked up at her, waiting for her to continue.

Emma stared at her. "Why are there six plates?"

"Because there are six people coming to dinner?" Fran answered as if it were a trick question.

"But Nadine can't make it tonight."

"Yes."

"So that leaves five."

"No."

"Yes." Emma pointed at each plate, doing the math. "Me, Dad, Margo, Ben, and Mrs. Pawloski."

"And George."

Emma blinked at her. "Knightley's not coming."

"Why isn't George coming?" Mr. Woodhouse asked, appearing in the doorway, but not looking up from his book.

"He's in LA," Emma replied, working to keep her tone even.

"No, no, he got back a few days ago. Where have you been?" He walked over and sat at the kitchen island.

"But . . . his lights were off," she replied dumbly.

"I'll call ConEd." Then he saw her suddenly pallid complexion. "Are you feeling all right?"

"I'm fine."

Her father didn't seem convinced. "Well, I ran into him earlier and he said he was looking forward to it."

She rolled her eyes. "Unbelievable."

"What?"

"Nothing."

Fran looked between them. "Should I keep the sixth plate?"

Mr. Woodhouse said yes as Emma answered no, and Fran remained frozen in place.

They kept the sixth plate, and a few minutes later Fran began moving the food to the table. Emma could feel her face warming even as she tried to keep a calm facade, her eyes darting around the room to avoid her father's confused expression.

"You sure you're all right?" he asked, his forehead creasing.

"I'm fine. Totally fine."

He stared at her a moment longer, then shook his head and returned to his book.

Emma gnawed on her bottom lip. She had to text Knightley and tell him he was not in fact invited to Sunday dinner before—

The French doors opened with a thud. Her heart tripped against her rib cage as she looked up and saw Knightley standing on the threshold.

"Hello," he said.

He was looking at her and suddenly her whole body felt hot and, oh my God, she wasn't going to be able to do this.

"George, you're here early," her father said from the island, still engrossed in his book.

"Thought I would come by to see if I could help with anything," Knightley replied, not taking his eyes off Emma.

"Well, you can start by distracting that one," her father said, waving a hand in his daughter's direction. "She's been wandering around micromanaging everyone for the past three hours."

Knightley smirked. "I'll do my best."

"I'm fine," she announced before raising an eyebrow at Knightley. "I just don't know what you're doing here."

"It's Sunday dinner."

"I know it's Sunday dinner, but I didn't think you were coming because . . . you know, none of your lights were supposed to be on . . ." She widened her eyes, hoping to somehow telepathically communicate her point.

"You were serious?" he murmured, looking confused.

She let her head fall back in defeat. This was doomed.

Knightley gave her a conciliatory shrug, then said hello to Fran and inquired if there was anything he could do, as if this was the status quo and they weren't on the brink of a complete disaster. Emma wanted to scream. It felt like everything inside her was going to bubble over at once.

Then the doorbell rang and her father yelled for Margo to just come in before mumbling something about the house key she refused to use since she moved out. It all felt so normal, but it wasn't normal, and Emma didn't know if she could pretend much longer. She had to get out before she spilled everything she was keeping inside.

"I'm going to the bathroom," she announced.

No one seemed to hear her. Margo and Ben had barely entered the room and Mr. Woodhouse was already peppering them with questions about their latest doctor's appointment, while Fran was busy plating the asparagus. Emma took that moment to move toward the hallway off the dining room.

Knightley was near the doorway as she walked by. "You okay?" he whispered.

"I'm fine," she said through a tight smile and kept walking.

The bathroom was small, tucked halfway between the kitchen and the media room. No one ever used it, which explained the fact that it still had the same Laura Ashley wallpaper that her mother picked out in the nineties, but she was thankful for it now as she disappeared inside.

She took a deep breath and leaned against the sink before looking up at the mirror.

Oh God.

Judging by how flushed her face was, she was clearly either dying of scarlet fever or hiding the biggest secret she had ever kept in her life. She turned on the faucet and splashed some cold water on her cheeks, taking a few deep breaths to calm her racing pulse.

It was fine. Everything was fine. *Totally fine.*

The bathroom door opened suddenly. Before she had time to curse the fact that she'd forgotten to lock it, Knightley appeared, sliding into the small space and closing the door softly behind him.

Her eyes widened. "What are you doing?"

"I'm sneaking into the bathroom to check on you, unless you're referring to something else," he replied, failing miserably to subdue his smile.

"I said I was fine!"

He hummed, as if considering. "You want to talk about it?"

"Oh my God, I am not talking to you *here*," she hissed. "Someone could come in!"

"I've been coming over to this house since I was four and no one has ever walked in on me in this bathroom."

"They don't need to walk in. They could just walk by!"

"Then we'll just have to be quiet."

She huffed. "We'll talk later."

It was meant to sound final, a signal that he could go.

He didn't move.

"What?" she asked.

He took a step toward her, then another. The bathroom was small, so after just two steps he was already almost touching her, so close she had to crane her head up to meet his gaze.

"What are you doing?" she asked.

"Not talking."

She tried to laugh. It came out like a shaky sigh. "We're not having sex in the Laura Ashley half bath."

He paused. "I'm not looking to have sex with you, Emma."

A small bubble of tension burst in her chest. "Oh."

"Not right now, anyway," he added, cocking a playful eyebrow at her. "I just want to make sure you're okay."

The last bit of her defenses fell as she looked up at him. A few strands of his dark hair had fallen across his face, highlighting his golden-brown eyes. An intense warmth swelled in her chest, so overwhelming that her breath caught. She really, truly loved him.

She didn't even think before leaning up and kissing him. Her mouth pressed softly against his, a tentative motion as if testing the parameters of this new territory. She could feel his smile grow against her lips before he deepened it, swallowing the tight moan that escaped her throat as his tongue found hers.

"Shhh." He somehow managed the soft direction while never breaking contact. Then his arm reached around her waist, pulling her against his body as he leaned forward. Her back arched and she felt herself pinned against the cold sink.

When had her arms wrapped themselves around his neck? She didn't know and honestly, she didn't care. All that mattered was

Knightley: the taste of wine on his tongue, the feel of his cashmere sweater under her fingertips. He was warm and safe and the world seemed to melt away as he kissed her, licking and nipping as if they had all the time in the world.

Then Mrs. Pawloski's shrill laugh echoed just beyond the bathroom door.

"It was polyester! Can you believe it?" she exclaimed from somewhere down the hallway.

Oh God. They were still in the bathroom.

As if on cue, they both pulled back. Emma's hand went to her lips; despite the brevity of the kiss, they still tingled.

"Sorry," she murmured.

Knightley watched the motion, his gaze dark. "Never apologize for that."

Then he leaned forward, resting his forehead against hers. She closed her eyes, taking a deep breath and inhaling his scent, that familiar blend of leather and pine.

"I really do have something serious to talk to you about, you know," she whispered.

"Is it about forgetting this whole plan of not telling anyone?"

"The exact opposite of that, actually."

She couldn't hear his chuckle, but she felt it roll through his body. "So you never want to tell anyone?"

"Maybe. I don't know." She opened her eyes and leaned back, meeting his gaze. "I just don't want anyone to get hurt."

"Who is going to get hurt?"

Me.

But she didn't say it. Instead she sighed. "My dad, Margo, Ben, Mrs. Pawloski. They're all going to get *invested*."

He gently pushed her hair behind her ear, his eyes doing a slow survey of her face. "Okay. Let's talk about it tonight, then."

"Tonight."

"We should eat dinner first."

"Right." She stepped away from the sink and caught her reflection: flushed cheeks, wild hair, her lips slightly swollen.

Shit.

Her hands brushed through her chestnut hair and she took a deep, calming breath.

"You sure you're okay?" he asked, smiling.

She nodded. "Fine. Totally fine."

∼

As much as she had feared otherwise, they somehow managed to get through dinner without anyone mentioning that Emma looked like she had been thoroughly manhandled in the half bath. In fact, the conversation seemed to focus on everyone but her.

Margo complained about her swollen feet, her father insisted on sharing every detail of his new rowing machine, Ben wanted to know who could make it to the soft opening of the restaurant next month—at least, that's what she thought they talked about. Emma's attention was focused on maintaining a placid facade even as her heart raced. Knightley sat beside her at the head of the table, but she hadn't looked at him since their encounter in the bathroom. She couldn't.

He hadn't said anything during the meal either. Of course, he rarely did, but this time it was different. She could feel his amused look whenever his gaze shifted to her, even if she refused to face it. He was enjoying this. What a dick.

As he served himself a second helping of roasted chicken, Ben turned to his brother.

"So, how was LA?" he asked.

Knightley shrugged. "It was LA. Lots of traffic. Lots of work. The deal is on track, though. We're not anticipating any issues."

"That's lucky," Ben replied. "I would think trying to bring two companies together like that would have been a headache."

"Well, when you bring two things together, sometimes people focus on the possibility of problems more than the fact that there might not be any problems at all."

Emma's eyes darted from her plate to Knightley. He was still looking at Ben, but there was a sardonic grin on his lips that she knew was meant exclusively for her.

Ben scoffed. "Except if you work in restaurants. Then there's always a problem."

"Sweetie, your business partner running off before half of the investors could cut their checks is not a problem for all restaurants. Just your restaurant," Margo said.

"Hey, they all paid up eventually."

"Only because your wife is amazing at drafting iron-clad contracts," she replied with a saccharine smile.

"Oh, I remember when Burt and I almost got into restaurants. It was a disaster!" Mrs. Pawloski lamented. "The permits, the leases, not to mention that no one really wanted a Polish fusion restaurant in 1998."

Knightley nodded as he stole a glance at Emma. His smile broadened then, as if her look of pure rage was somehow attractive.

"God, I need something sweet," Margo said, leaning back in her chair so her swollen belly stuck out. "Is there any dessert?"

Mr. Woodhouse tutted. "No one needs dessert."

"Dad, I'm seven months pregnant and I'm telling you I need dessert."

"There might be some kiwis in the fridge."

She rolled her eyes and turned to Knightley. "Do you have any cookies over there or something?"

He shrugged one shoulder. "I had some ice cream, but Emma ate all of it this morning."

Emma coughed, almost spitting her wine across the table.

Knightley watched her, his eyes dancing with amusement as she struggled for breath. She was going to kill him. As soon as she could breathe again, he was dead.

Mr. Woodhouse looked at her as if he wasn't sure if he should be concerned or disgusted. "Emma. Saturated fats for breakfast?"

She was still coughing and couldn't answer, so Knightley leaned forward. "It was more of a midnight snack, I think."

Mr. Woodhouse still shook his head. "The lipids."

"Ugh, fine. We'll pick up some cupcakes on the way home," Margo said. "By the way, I'm coming by early tomorrow to go through those boxes of summer clothes from our closet. They're still up on the shelf, right Emma?"

Emma nodded, taking a deep sip of her water.

"You okay?" Knightley asked, loud enough so that everyone could hear.

She ignored him.

"Oh!" Margo said, eyes suddenly huge and a smile on her lips. "I almost forgot! There's this new associate at work, Jason. He just moved down from Boston. He is darling and so ridiculously hot, I can't even get into it." Ben looked at her pointedly; she didn't seem to notice. "And he's single!"

She turned to Emma, eyebrows raised and biting her lip as if she had just presented her with the gift of a lifetime. The entire table turned to Emma as well and waited.

"And?" Emma replied.

Margo rolled her eyes. "And I'm going to set you two up, obviously. I know the Montgomery thing was a disaster, but this is completely different. Jason is exactly the type of guy I see you with. Hot, but not super into his looks, you know? And so funny . . . He told this story at work the other day; it was hilarious . . ."

As Margo continued, Emma could feel the tension rising from the seat beside her.

"Oh my God, and your kids would be so gorgeous!" Margo exclaimed. "It's perfect. I'll organize a dinner next week. Like a double date."

"No," Emma said. Her voice came out so loud and high that everyone at the table turned. "No, I'm going to have to pass."

Her sister scoffed. "Don't be ridiculous. He's perfect for you. Seriously, don't even worry about it. I'll figure it all out and—"

"No, Margo." Her voice was stronger now, and she let out a long breath. Her anxiety was suddenly gone. Every fear and worry had just disappeared. "Really. I don't need you to figure it out. And I need you to stop thinking that you do. I love you but I need you to let go just a little. Okay?"

Silence enveloped the room. Margo looked shocked, her eyes wide as she stared at her sister.

"But don't you think—"

"Margo," Mr. Woodhouse cut her off. Margo turned to him, eyes wide. He offered her a soft, placating smile. "Pass the asparagus."

"Okay," she replied softly.

He nodded. Then he turned and gave Emma a wink. "Okay."

Under the table, she felt Knightley reach over and squeeze her knee.

She turned to him and found his expression had softened, a look of appreciation in his eyes.

She smiled back, mirroring his warmth as she mouthed, *I'm going to kill you.*

No one really understood why Knightley barked out a laugh at the end of the table. Or why Emma turned away without bothering to ask. And that was fine. Totally fine.

CHAPTER 35

Knightley pulled on his sweatpants as he sat down on the edge of his mattress and let out a sigh. He was ready for bed, but not at all tired.

He hated waiting.

Dinner had finished only a few hours ago, but he already missed her. He'd never experienced this type of gut-wrenching want with anyone else before. It was like his world had been fundamentally altered, as if the days before this had a slight gray tint to them now that everything was vibrant and colorful. This was more than just a passing infatuation. This was Emma.

He had loved watching her passion and strength on full display tonight. He had spent his entire life envying the Woodhouse family, but he also knew that while their love was unconditional, it could border on oppressive. Margo's meddling was a perfect example. There was no malice in it though, and while some people might have reacted with frustration or resentment, Emma had responded to her sister's latest scheme in such a calm, assertive way that even Knightley had been awed.

Of course, he couldn't help but prod her tonight, too. He flirted with her right there under everyone's noses and had already grown addicted to how her cheeks flushed whenever he caught her eye. Christ, he had barely gotten through the meal without reaching across the table and kissing her. And, if he was being honest about it, keeping this secret was turning out to be more fun than he thought. It was something only they knew.

It was the best Sunday dinner of his life.

But despite the playful edge to the evening, Emma's words from the bathroom echoed in his mind again.

I really do have something serious to talk to you about, you know.

No amount of stolen kisses or gentle teasing would erase whatever it was that still bothered her about this. About them. And that left an odd weight deep in his chest.

Across the yard her bedroom window glowed with the light from her bedside lamp. He could see the outline of all the furniture he was so familiar with from this vantage point, but the perspective seemed different now. He imagined her sitting cross-legged somewhere in there, tapping her nails, waiting impatiently until her father retired to bed so the coast was clear. Or was she staring at the clock in the living room, her type A personality choosing an arbitrary time she would allow herself to come over?

He leaned back, arms resting comfortably behind his head and closed his eyes, willing himself to relax. She would be over soon. Then they would talk. And whatever it was that was bothering her, he would make it okay. Whatever she needed from him, he would give it. He would give her everything. Because for the first time in his life, he felt happy. And it was all because of her.

Eventually, he heard the sliding door downstairs open and close. He sat up, ready to go meet her downstairs, but then he heard the soft sounds of her feet padding up the steps to his room on the second floor.

"Hello, Emma," he said when she appeared in the doorway.

She ignored him, walking past the bed to the desk. She sat down in the chair and turned it toward him, her back to the window.

"You're going to sit all the way over there?" he teased. When she didn't budge, he slowly turned his body, ready to stand up and go to her.

"Stay right there," she said, holding up a firm hand.

He stopped. "May I ask why?"

"Because we need to talk and I can't talk if you come over here with all . . ." She motioned vaguely at his bare chest. "That."

He smiled, leaning back slightly on an elbow. The full moon cast a watery light into his dark room, illuminating her features. God, she was beautiful.

"What would you like to talk about?"

She frowned. "Don't be cute."

"I'm being serious."

"Are you? Because you definitely didn't seem too serious at dinner."

Shit. He knew he had pushed it too far. "I'm sorry. I know you wanted to keep this a secret."

"Do you?"

"Absolutely," he replied.

"Wow." She shook her head.

"Emma, I got carried away."

"You think?"

"I don't think anyone picked up on it."

"But what if they did? All that talk about the ice cream? And the two companies? You made me so nervous! How could everyone not suspect something?" She let out a groan, shaking her head. "They could have asked what this is before we've even talked about what this is yet. I mean, are we dating? Are we in a relationship?

Are we just . . . sleeping together? This is all so complicated and there's just too much potential for people we care about to get hurt because we didn't think this through."

She glared at him, waiting for a reply. And God, when she stared at him like that, arresting green eyes full of fire, dark hair cascading down her shoulders, her arms across her chest—it gutted him. He suddenly realized that he had been so concerned with giving her space to work out her feelings that he hadn't considered the fact that he had kept silent about his own.

"I didn't think . . ." He let his voice trail off as he ran a hand through his hair. "That's it. I didn't think. I'm sorry."

Her mouth fell open as if momentarily stunned. Her shock made sense—Knightley could probably count on one hand the amount of times he'd ever apologized to her; now he'd done it twice in twenty-four hours. And suddenly all the other reasons he needed to began to clog his brain.

"And I'm sorry we didn't talk about any of this yesterday." He leaned forward, his elbows resting on his knees. "That you've spent the day wondering where we stand. I thought I was giving you space to steer this, but I wasn't clear about what I want."

She shrugged slightly as her gaze fell to the floor. "It's all right."

"No. It's not," he replied, his voice so deep and clear that her eyes snapped up to meet his again.

"I want you. I want to be with you. And I'm sorry if my past has ever made you doubt my commitment to this. To you. Because I am all in, Emma. Totally and completely. I want strings. With you."

She didn't reply, only trapped her bottom lip between her teeth as the last bit of frustration melted from her features.

"And I'm sorry that our lives are already so intertwined that this feels complicated. But it doesn't feel complicated to me. It feels like the easiest decision I've ever made in my life."

"Yeah?"

"Yeah," he murmured. "But I'm not sorry I can't keep my hands off you."

"Oh really?"

He slowly shook his head.

Her mouth twitched with a grin, mirroring the one on his own face. Then she stood up and made a move toward the bed.

He held up his hand. "Stay right there."

She sat back down slowly, her brows knitting together.

"Tell me what you want," he said.

She swallowed, keeping her eyes locked with his. "I want strings too."

Relief surged through his veins. "Yeah?"

She nodded. "Lots and lots of strings."

He smiled. "Okay then."

"I also want your hands and your mouth and orgasms and just . . . everything."

He stared at her for a long moment. "Ask nicely, then."

She scoffed.

He leaned back. "Ask. Nicely."

She met his gaze, all humor and pretense falling away.

"I'll give you anything you want." His voice was low and gravelly. "You just have to ask."

"Please," she breathed.

He stood up slowly and stalked toward her. He could see her holding her breath, watching his every move until he stopped to tower over her. Then he brushed his thumb along her jaw.

She let the breath out of her lungs then, a long sigh, and closed her eyes at his touch. She was still wearing the same outfit from dinner, a short wool skirt and V-neck sweater, which meant he could see the blush spread across her chest. He traced it across her skin, taking his time as his fingers skimmed her neck down to her collarbone. Then he knelt down before her. His hands rested above her knees and she jumped slightly at his firm grip before her body loosened again, leaning back. An invitation.

He slid his fingers up her smooth thighs under the edge of her skirt, the material gathering at her hips. He had spent so much of dinner imagining his hand reaching up this same way that he was already hard, straining against his boxers.

"What are you thinking right now?" she whispered, her chest rising as she inhaled sharply.

"Oh, so many things," he murmured, watching his fingers graze the thin cotton of her underwear. "First, I want to take these off."

His hands inched up further until he grasped the elastic waistband and slowly pulled them down and off, watching her expression as he did. Her breathing turned slower and heavier, matching his own deep inhales.

He leaned down and kissed the inside of her thigh. Jesus, he couldn't wait to taste her, feel her, make her say his name as she came. He wanted to savor it, too, draw it out so he could commit every moment to memory.

"Is there anything else we need to talk about?" he asked softly.

"I mentioned the orgasms, right?"

He chuckled. "Yeah."

"Then I think we covered it."

He took control then. A hand on either thigh, he spread her legs wide, revealing her to him. His chest tightened at the welcome sight of her, and he leaned down, slowly planting soft kisses up her thigh. His lips followed where his fingers had just been, his breath hot on her skin as he journeyed up until his tongue glided through her center. He was deliberate and slow with his pressure, licking, then sucking, as her hips jerked up to meet him. Her moans and sighs echoed in his ears.

Jesus, he could get lost in her forever. Each whimper, every shiver from her made him harder, and he had to adjust himself as he rolled his tongue, teasing her until he could feel her thighs start to shake under his touch.

"Oh God . . ." she gasped. He wrapped his hand around her leg and put it over his shoulder, his angle deeper, making her head fall back as she cried out.

Her body trembled and shuddered while his mouth, unrelenting, increased its pace. His fingers pressed into the soft flesh of her thighs the more she moved and lost control.

"Knightley . . ." His name was a cry. "So . . . close . . ."

One hand gripped the arm of her chair while the other went to his hair, tangling in his dark locks as her hips rose up to meet his rhythm, her breathing labored. Then he slipped two fingers inside of her, curling them just so until he could feel her tightening around him.

She gasped as she came but he didn't stop, his tongue tracing lazy circles around that most sensitive part of her until her body sagged, her muscles limp. Then he gently pulled back to look at her from under his brow, watching as she blinked her eyes open.

"We should talk things out more often," she murmured, a sated smile on her lips.

He smiled back and leaned forward, kissing her shoulder, nipping at her skin. "I'm going to remind you that you said that."

She laughed, a husky sound that sent a charge under his skin. One more kiss right below her ear, then he stood, gently taking her hand and pulling her up from the chair. He took his time undressing her, carefully pulling her sweater over her head and unzipping her skirt so it pooled on the floor. When he was done, she reached down and tugged at his sweatpants, working them down his legs so they joined her pile of clothes on the floor.

It took all his strength to stand there as she studied his naked body, as her fingernails traced down his arms and chest. It was like she wanted to try to memorize every inch of him. The thought made his pulse trip, and his hands became fists at his sides with the effort required to keep them in place.

Then she looked up, her green eyes meeting his, and it was like a tether snapped. She wrapped her arms around his shoulders, kissing him hard, and he groaned with relief, opening his lips and meeting her frenzy as she pushed him backward onto the soft covers of the bed. Her body was pressed close to him, her limbs tangled with his, but it wasn't close enough. Christ, it would never be close enough.

"You have no idea what you do to me," he whispered as his lips moved to her neck.

"*Knightley . . .*"

It was a soft plea, and he knew she didn't want to wait any longer. He reluctantly pulled himself back to hover over her, kissing her jaw once before he began to rise. "Give me a second."

"Where are you going?"

"Condoms are in the bathroom."

"Wait," she said. He was already on his feet when he paused. "It's okay."

He narrowed his eyes at her.

"I just mean . . ." Her voice trailed off and a new bloom of color rose in her cheeks. "I'm on the pill. And I trust you. I'm okay if you are."

He stared at her, momentarily stunned. "Are you sure?"

Her nervous smile faded, her expression becoming earnest. "I'm sure."

He never had sex without a condom. For obvious reasons, of course, but also because it had always felt too intimate. Another barrier to ensure his heart stayed isolated. Intact. But right now, with Emma staring up at him, her eyes drifting to his mouth, he couldn't imagine wanting anything separating them ever again.

His heart hammered in his chest as he nodded, leaning back over the bed and kissing her deeply. A moan escaped her throat and he devoured it, caging her in with his arms as she wrapped her legs around his waist.

She rolled her hips as if desperate for friction and he hissed, holding himself back even as he nudged at her entrance.

"You okay?"

She nodded, her tongue darting out to wet her lips.

Thank Christ, he thought. And then he pushed forward.

She gasped as he entered her and stilled, letting her body adjust to his size. But then she rolled her hips again and he bit the inside of his cheek, barely holding back a string of curses.

"If you keep doing that, this won't last long," he growled.

She released another breathy laugh. "Then we'll just have to do it again later."

He groaned, sliding out and pushing back in again. He kissed her open mouth, his tongue finding hers, sucking and biting at her bottom lip as his pace increased. She kissed him back, her low whimpers making it hard for him not to lose it completely.

He tightened his hold on her fingers and she squeezed his hand back in tune with each thrust of his hips. Her thighs were like a vise grip around his waist, even as they began to tremble, her hips rising to meet his.

"You feel so good." His words were hoarse with restraint. Fuck, he had to slow down. She was sending him over the edge way too soon.

"*Please . . .*" she panted. "Don't stop."

"Emma," he exhaled her name slowly. "You're so fucking beautiful."

He pulled almost all the way out and pushed back inside her hard, again and again, and she met every movement. Their bodies were so in sync it felt like a dream to him, one where time seemed to stop. There was nothing else, only this room. Only them.

Another whimper escaped her lips. He silenced it with a deep kiss, feeling her shiver as he quickened his pace. Her body was tightening around him, and he knew before she said the words.

"I'm . . . close . . ."

"God, I love watching you come apart," he whispered in her ear.

She didn't reply, just threw her arms out, wrapping her hands in the rumpled sheets.

"Look at me, Emma." His voice was desperate and commanding, his hand gripping the back of her neck as he continued his push into her. She met his gaze and he saw it; the moment the spark ignited her body and she exploded.

She cried out and the sound echoed off the walls as her orgasm rocketed through her. She arched up into him, but he didn't stop moving, pushing and pushing as he watched every aftershock coursing through her trembling body.

He cursed under his breath, drawing out her release, and quickening his own.

Then she opened her eyes again, so deep and green and sated, and *fuck*, he couldn't hold out any longer. His muscles tensed as he moved, spilling into her, groaning while his own climax hit him harder than anything he could ever remember before. He mumbled her name, slowed his pace, and finally crashed his mouth to hers—desperate to stay connected, unable to move away just yet. She returned his kiss as her hands combed through his thick hair. And he could feel the smile on her lips.

He wanted to say something, to find the words to encompass everything he was feeling. To tell her how his heart hurt when they were apart, how being with her made everything feel complete. He needed her to know. So he kissed her cheeks, her lips, her nose, then pressed his forehead to hers, and let their breathing meld together, fast and warm.

"I love you," he said. The words were there before he was even aware they had formed on his tongue.

Her breath hitched and her body tensed beneath him. He leaned back enough to meet her gaze and found her eyes wide, her swollen lips forming a little O. "You've never said that to me before."

He smiled, gently tucking a few unruly strands of her dark hair behind her ear. "Well, if I loved you less, I might be able to talk about it more."

Her brow furrowed, followed by a calm, blissful expression that spread over her face like a warm light.

"Does that mean you want me here tomorrow morning, too?" she asked, her lips curling into a lazy smile. But he could see it was tentative, like she was still testing the waters of this thing between them.

"Emma," he whispered. His hand moved to cradle her jaw, ghosting her lips with his thumb. "I want you here every morning."

She gazed up at him, green meeting gold, his own eyes reflected in their depths as she seemed to register the gravity of what it meant for him to say this to her. Mr. No-Strings-Attached was breaking all his own rules. He wanted all the strings, all the messy tangled knots that came with whatever the hell this was or would be. He just wanted her.

"I love you too," she finally breathed.

His heart tripped in his chest.

"Yeah?" He cupped her face.

"Yes, Knightley. Of course I do." He could see her eyes misting up, quiet tears threatening to fall.

Her voice was soft, but the words . . . they felt like a revelation. A new source of gravity tethered to his sternum, grounding him to this place.

She always had been that for him, hadn't she? No matter where he flung himself, no matter how much he tried to erase history, to search for that something that seemed missing from his core, she was always here, waiting for him to return. No expectations or judgment.

It was never this house calling him home. Never this city. It was always her.

He found her hooded eyes staring at his lips, his jaw, his eyes. She could probably see the realization blooming across his face; every fucking emotion was there on display.

He didn't care. He already felt raw and exposed—there was no use hiding it.

He was so fucking in love with her he could barely breathe.

He wrapped his arms around her, pulling her against him, and they held each other. All this time, everything he was looking for was right there, right across the yard.

~

The mid-morning sun was already over the tops of the buildings by the time Knightley woke. He winced against it, turning over to find Emma lying on the other side of the bed, curled around his other pillow and watching him with a small smile on her lips.

"Hi," she whispered.

"Hey."

Over the course of the night they had spread out across the bed. Now Knightley's long, tanned limbs took up most of the space, while Emma hoarded all the covers.

"Sleep okay?" he asked, stroking her arm.

"Yes."

"You snore, you know."

Her mouth fell open. "No I don't!"

He shrugged one shoulder.

"I do *not* snore."

"Don't worry. It's cute."

"Oh my *God*!" She turned her head into the pillow.

"It's just nice to see you're not perfect," he teased, leaning his face on his elbow as he watched her.

She lifted her head and turned to him, working to curb the smile that threatened to return to her lips. "Pretty close, though, right?"

He nodded slowly. "Absolutely."

She trapped her bottom lip between her teeth and stared at him for a long moment before she said his name. "Knightley."

It sounded almost obscene, and he suddenly needed to kiss those swollen lips again.

"C'mere. I want to hear you say my name like *that* again and again . . ." he murmured, grabbing her hand to pull her closer. "And again."

"*Knightley . . . oh . . . my Knightley . . .*" She sighed dramatically as she slowly slid in the opposite direction, out of the bed.

He smiled. Even when she was being sarcastic, it still drove him crazy.

"Where are you going?"

She laughed. "I just woke up. Give me a second."

He leaned back and watched her as she walked the short distance to his bathroom. Then he turned to check the clock on his nightstand. Ten a.m. Damn, they slept in.

She returned a few minutes later. He was sitting against the headboard, and she curled up beside him, draping her body over his. After a moment, she propped her chin on his hard torso, staring out his window as her hand made lazy circles on his chest.

"It's so strange seeing my room from here."

He turned. The glass took up almost the entire wall of his room, framing the Woodhouse home like a piece of art.

"I love that view," he said, pulling her up closer to him. "Although we need to talk about the lipstick."

Her hand stilled and she lifted her head to look at him. "What's wrong with my lipstick?"

"Nothing. I just don't understand why it takes so long for you to put it on."

"Have you been watching me?"

"It's hard to miss when you're sitting there putting it on for an hour."

"Stalker."

His head fell back as he laughed, full and loud. She watched the motion, a broad smile on her face again. "You know, a better question is: Who hangs up their jeans in—"

He kissed her, cutting her off. She melted into it, letting his mouth move softly against hers for a moment before she pulled away.

"Don't you have to work today?"

He shook his head. "Do you have school?"

"Nope. Lazy schedule, remember?"

"Good, because I'm not letting you leave this bed." He pushed her dark chestnut hair away from her face.

"Oh . . . and you love me. Don't forget that part."

"Yes . . . that too." His hand moved down her neck to trace her collarbone. "Is there anything else you want to talk about?"

"I think we covered everything." She sighed. "You're madly in love with me. I get it."

He laughed again, but it faded as he saw her smile falter. "What's wrong?"

"You know how I told you I didn't want to tell anyone?"

"Yeah."

"Well . . . I told Nadine." She watched his face contort with confusion and quickly added, "But she already knew! Well, kind of. Anyway, don't worry. She won't say anything."

"I'm not worried," he replied. His fingers glided down her arm to her exposed hip, tracing small circles on her skin. They faced each other, their limbs tangling together, the warmth of her body making his own shudder. "I'm ready for everyone to know. Just say the word."

"Yeah?" She didn't look convinced.

He pulled her over him, her legs straddling his lap, the covers falling behind her. His hands traveled slowly from her thighs to her waist.

"I love you. And I'm ready for everyone to know that." He paused. "But I'm not the only one in this relationship. Tell me what you want."

She seemed to consider it, then let out a long breath and nodded. "I want to tell everyone."

His eyes locked with hers. "Are you sure?"

"Yes," she whispered, sweeping her fingertips over his bare chest. "I want them to know."

His hands wandered up, cupping her soft breasts as his thumbs teased her nipples, gently grazing them back and forth until they were pert.

"When?"

"I don't know. Soon," she hummed, her eyes rolling shut.

He smiled. That was good enough.

He sat up, taking her mouth in his and sucking on her bottom lip. He took his time, working her mouth open, twisting his tongue with hers. She returned his kisses, her hands framing his face as she rocked her hips back and forth. He was already hard between them, and he knew she could feel it when she moaned, her hands moving up to weave into his hair, pulling him closer.

Somewhere in the periphery he heard a faint chime and light vibration. Emma's cell phone was ringing on a loop on his desk. He continued to tease and suck at her lips, rolling his hips so he could slide into her, but the incessant buzzing seemed determined to interrupt them.

He tried to lean back, to say something, but her grip on his hair tightened.

"Ignore it," she murmured.

A moment later it stopped . . . only to immediately start again.

He opened his eyes to look over at it, but then his gaze shifted past his desk to Emma's bedroom window across the yard. He squinted, registering a figure jumping up and down frantically and holding up the glowing screen of a cell phone.

A pregnant figure.

"Oh fuck," he muttered.

Emma whipped around and made eye contact with Margo, who was now waving her arms in the air and yelling at the glass.

Emma screamed, trying to grab the sheets to cover herself as she struggled to get off Knightley, but instead ended up tumbling back and falling off the bed with a thump.

He leaned slightly forward, suppressing a laugh. "You all right down there?"

"OH MY GOD!" she shrieked from on the floor, her face contorted in a mix of shock and anger. "She saw *everything*!"

He chuckled as she tried to get up but tripped, tangling herself in the sheets until she finally found her footing.

"It's not funny!"

"Well, you said you wanted to tell everyone."

"I wanted to tell everyone at the right time! Not right *now*! Not like this!" She wrapped the sheet around her body and marched over to the desk to grab her cell phone, which was still blinking and buzzing. "What do I even say?"

"Nothing. She can wait," Knightley said calmly, ignoring Margo dancing around in the window across the yard.

Emma looked at the phone, then up at her sister's shocked face. Then she hit decline on her phone, shut it off, and then flung it on the bed.

Knightley turned to his side and pressed a button by his nightstand. Blackout shades descended over the windows, darkening the room and obstructing Margo's view.

Emma's mouth fell open. "When did you get those?"

"I've always had these."

"Really?"

"Really. Just never wanted to use them before. What if I missed you at your window?"

She huffed, blowing her hair out of her face. She looked disheveled and beautiful. "Could have used those earlier is all I'm saying," she muttered.

He chuckled softly as he pulled her back down to the bed.

She fell into his body with a sigh. "Everyone will know now."

"Is that so awful?"

"No, it's just . . ." She shrugged. "I wanted to control the narrative."

"You can't control everything."

She threw him a smirk. "Says who?"

He leaned forward and brushed his lips against hers. "Don't worry about everything else. We're in this together. That's what matters."

She stared down at him for a moment, cocking her head to the side as she surveyed his features. "Yeah?"

He nodded, pushing a lock of hair from her forehead. "You're my forever relationship, Emma Woodhouse."

A sly smile curled her lips. "I thought that wasn't a thing."

He grinned. "Oh, it is absolutely a thing."

She laughed and closed her eyes, letting her head fall into the crook of his neck. There was a mess of drama waiting for them outside his bedroom door: her family and his and every other friend in their neighborhood who would be hearing about this in the next ten minutes. And that was okay. This was 83rd Street, after all; there would likely always be drama. Nothing was perfect; he was beginning to realize maybe none of it was meant to be.

Then Emma sighed and her entire body relaxed against his, and he stopped himself. He leaned down and kissed the top of her head.

No, not everything was perfect. But sometimes that made it even better.

EPILOGUE

It was eight p.m. on Christmas Eve, and Knightley's house glowed. Fairy lights and garland hung from every surface, and clusters of perfectly decorated trees framed each corner. The guests to the Woodhouses' annual Christmas party gasped and smiled at their new venue while Emma stood back, champagne in hand, smiling at her victory.

"You're looking smug," Knightley said, coming up beside her and placing a soft kiss on her lips.

"Of course I look smug. Look around!"

He did, his gaze sliding from the growing crowd of friends and family to the decorations hanging from every available surface. "Did you hire Buddy the Elf?"

She rolled her eyes. "It's perfect."

"Whatever you say, Woodhouse."

She turned to face him, a biting comment on the tip of her tongue, but the words dissolved when she saw how he looked down at her, a lazy grin turning up the corners of his full lips.

"Do you enjoy winding me up?" she asked, working to curb her own smile.

"So much, you have no idea," he murmured. He leaned down to kiss her again, his mouth just inches from hers, but stopped as a shrill voice pierced the air.

"It's gorgeous! Just gorgeous!" Mrs. Pawloski exclaimed, emerging from the growing crowd, Mrs. Crawford in tow. "I was just telling Veronica—wasn't I, Veronica? It's like a winter wonderland!"

Mrs. Crawford nodded beside her. Like the rest of them, she knew better than to interrupt Mrs. Pawloski once she was on a roll.

"The garland—well, it's just magic! It looks like there's real snow on it! Real snow! And the tree!" Mrs. Pawloski placed a hand on her chest as if it were all too much. "It's perfect! Oh, I just love the holidays!"

Emma's smile widened as she stole a glance at Knightley. "Why, thank you, Mrs. Pawloski. I agree."

"And let me tell you, the men around here aren't too bad on the eyes, either!" Mrs. Pawloski cackled. "George, are these your friends, or did Emma hire a modeling agency?"

Emma had insisted that if they were hosting this year's Christmas Party at Knightley's house, Knightley had to invite some of his friends. So now the party wasn't only filled with the usual attendees from 83rd Street, but also young professionals from Knightley Capital and their other firms. All of them looked like they had just stepped off the runway at Fashion Week, instead of coming from the nondescript buildings downtown where they worked.

"Oh! Looks like Nadine is enjoying the view too!" Mrs. Pawloski said, nodding to the far corner of the room.

Nadine was laughing, a glass of champagne in her hand. She looked happy and confident, and her hair looked fantastic thanks to the fact that she was still seeing Mateo even though she'd quit the salon a few months ago to take a new part-time job at Sotheby's. The sight of her friend so at ease with herself almost made Emma completely miss who Nadine was talking to. But then her companion leaned down, whispering something in her ear, and Nadine laughed again. Another man stood a foot or so away, ignoring them and looking utterly bored.

"Who is that again?" Emma asked, leaning into Knightley. "The one talking to Nadine."

Knightley glanced over. "That's Charlie. I went to school with him and Will."

"Is Will the one next to him who looks like he's waiting for a root canal?"

Knightley laughed. "Yes."

"Oh, there's Margo and the baby!" Mrs. Crawford interjected, spotting Emma's sister over by the fireplace. "I have to give that niece of yours a cuddle."

Emma smiled. If anything could overshadow her party planning success, it was Cassandra Knightley, the latest—and smallest—addition to their clan, named after their late mother. Arriving into the world on May 2, a full three weeks early, Cassandra had thrown all of Margo's carefully crafted plans out the window. Instead of a natural home birth, Margo had had an emergency C-section at Mount Sinai, and Cassandra spent two weeks in the NICU to monitor a possible heart murmur and fight off the effects of jaundice.

For Margo and Ben, it had been terrifying. Ben closed the restaurant and slept at the hospital while Margo and Cassandra recovered, spending every waking moment ricocheting between their beds. For Emma, it had been a call to action. She was supposed to start working for Inez's wife, Olivia, as a sales associate with Casamentero Art Advisors right after graduation, but she immediately asked to push back her start date to mid-summer. Of course, her new boss had agreed, saying, "What's all this for if we can't be there for our families when they need us?" It also helped that Emma had already managed to line up a six-figure deal with the Crawfords before she'd even started.

With work settled, Emma moved into the guest room at Ben and Margo's apartment for two weeks, coordinating clean clothes and supplies for Ben, calling pediatric specialists in the city, keeping her father calm, and organizing deliveries of fresh groceries and meals for when the family arrived back home.

By early June, they had. Cassandra weighed an incredible eight pounds six ounces, Margo could finally stand up and walk around without excruciating pain, and when the family of three walked into their clean, well-stocked apartment, it was like the stress of the past few weeks had never happened at all.

It was only when Emma got back home that night, when she finally sat down in her dark kitchen and let herself stop for the first time in almost a month, that the fear and anxiety caught up with her. Knightley had found her there, sobbing over a contraband pint of mint chocolate chip. He hadn't said anything, just picked her up and carried her over to his house, curling up with her on his long sofa, and holding her as the tears flowed. She woke up the next morning still in his arms, his chin resting on the top of her head. She hadn't moved for a long time. And she hadn't really left his house since.

"You'll have to wrestle her away from Dad," Emma replied, motioning behind them. "He doesn't want her to get cold, so he's insisting she stay in his lap by the fireplace."

The women tittered and headed in that direction, still oohing and aahing at the decorations.

Emma turned to watch them go, and Knightley took a step closer, his chest flush with her back. He wrapped his long arms around her waist and she leaned back into him. It was her favorite spot, as if she were made to fit there under the crook of his neck.

She had a hard time remembering her hesitancy at making their relationship official. After Margo had seen them, when she had torn down the stairs, screaming the news to her father and Fran and the rest of the neighborhood, it had been welcomed by everyone who heard. It was as if everyone expected it, as if everyone already knew. Everyone except Emma and Knightley.

Emma and Knightley. She smiled to herself. It was exactly as it should be. Despite all the pitfalls of her matchmaking ventures, she had still succeeded. She'd found her forever.

It really would be a shame to let that sort of skill go to waste.

Her eyes found their way back across the room to Nadine and Charlie. She was animated, talking and gesturing and smiling, and he was hanging on every word. Yes, that particular pairing seemed to be setting off just fine. But then her gaze drifted over to Will. His brow drew a severe line across his face as he pushed his blond hair away from it, his withering stare locking with the far wall as if he was counting the minutes until he could leave.

There was no denying that he looked miserable. But there was also no denying that he was very hot.

"So what's the story with Will?" she asked.

Knightley leaned down to kiss her jaw. "Met him at Columbia. He runs a mergers and acquisitions firm with Charlie. Very smart. Blunt but fair. Doesn't suffer fools."

"Is he single?"

Knightley stilled. "Emma."

She turned to him, eyes wide. "What?"

"I know what you're doing."

"What am I doing?"

He smirked and shook his head.

She shrugged. "All I'm saying is that someone who's that attractive and successful should not be looking miserable at Christmas.

Maybe if he found someone, he could enjoy himself. Or *smile*, at the very least."

Knightley leaned forward so his nose was only inches from her own. "Woodhouse, listen closely, because this is important. I know you want to see the entire island of Manhattan happily paired off, but let me assure you: William Darcy will never, ever get married."

Cassandra let out a wail from the other side of the room, and their attention went to her just as Ben and Margo jumped up to take her from Mrs. Crawford's arms.

"Hmm," Emma turned back to Knightley and offered a placating smile. "And where have I heard that before?"

He chuckled and she let the sound swell inside her, warming her skin as she looked out at the guests mingling around her.

The party was very much like every other Christmas party, but something about it felt different this year. Maybe it was the fact that Emma wasn't bothered by Mrs. Pawloski drinking red wine with her salmon canapé. Or that Cassandra was ignoring the rules of polite conversation by spitting up all over Mrs. Crawford's silk sweater. Or how Ben laughed even while Margo yelled at him for a towel, and their father, who used the diversion to push her sister's piece of dark chocolate Bundt cake to the other side of the coffee table.

Because in spite of these deficiencies—or maybe it was because of them?—Emma wouldn't have it any other way. She released a satisfied sigh and rested her head on Knightley's shoulder. Here, among this band of true friends, she couldn't imagine a more perfect happiness.

ACKNOWLEDGMENTS

The fact that this book exists is a testament to love, wine, and the lengths two friends will go to keep each other smiling (and sane) during a worldwide pandemic. This little idea that was meant to see us through a very rough time in the world has eclipsed even our wildest dreams. We have so many people to thank for that.

First off, thank you to our wonderful agent, Joëlle Delbourgo, who believed in us from the very start. You had us at "absolutely delicious."

Thank you to our fantastic editor, Molly Gregory, who not only loved this book but loved it enough to make it so much better. Your enthusiasm and thoughtfulness are the stuff of legend; your notes are suitable for framing. And thank you to our copyeditor, Stacey Sakal, who cured us of our fear of commas; our cover designer, Sarah Horgan, and our interior designer, Hope Herr-Cardillo, who worked so hard to make us look so good; and to the rest of the incredible team at Gallery: Jennifer Bergstrom, Jennifer Long, Aimée Bell, Sally Marvin, Lucy Nalen, Tyrinne Lewis, Caroline Pallotta, Emily Arzeno, Lisa Litwack, and Jamie Selzer; as well as

Anthea Bariamis and Lily Cameron of Simon & Schuster Australia. We appreciate you so much.

Even before this book was a book, we had so many people behind the scenes cheering us on, starting with our husbands, Tom Harding and Mike Pierantozzi: How do we even begin to say thank you? We have no idea. Just know that we love you so much. And to the woman who has seen and read everything, Elizabeth Stoll Bellezza, for your unwavering enthusiasm and sheer joy for this project; to Whitney Tancred for your vision, constant support, and loyal friendship; to Molly Lyons for believing in us so early on; to Mason Pettit for your advice and insider knowledge of NYC's restaurant world; and to Nicole Page, Jessica Winchell Morsa, Jenna Helwig, and Zoran Zgonc: you have helped us, laughed with us, and kept us grounded—we can never thank you enough.

To Emily's friends and family, especially Tom: your unending love, encouragement, and patience made this whole thing possible. Thank you. I love you more xxxxx. To Poppy and Henry, for your laughter and hugs and understanding nods when you heard the words "Mommy's working"; to my parents, Kevin and Joan, for fostering my dream of becoming a writer before I could even hold a pencil; to my transatlantic family for your support and advice when it felt like I had no idea what I was doing—I'm so lucky to have you; to Erica Orloff for having faith in me even when I didn't have any myself; to Zack, Thomas, Adam, Karen, Christi, Chris, Cori, Zoe, Nola, Cat, Liz, Jason, Andrea, Rob, Zach, and the rest of ComicsXF team for the friendship, the Zooms, and the reminders of why I love writing so much. And, of course, to Audrey: thank you for being the kind of friend I can text after too much wine and suddenly we've decided to write a book together. There's no one else I would want to go on this insane journey with.

To Audrey's friends and family, especially Mike for your belief in me and this project from day one. I am forever grateful for your love and guidance, and for always, without fail, making me laugh like no one else can; thank you for everything. And to our amazing and inspiring boys, Bear and Dex, it's all for you; love you so, so much. To my parents, Elizabeth and Donald, for never missing a chance to cheer me on from the front row. The confidence you instilled in me made this book possible. Mom, thank you for being a constant source of inspiration and strength, and Dad, thank you for all your patience and love. To my brilliant, supportive siblings for making life way more fun: Veronica, for always being by my side, and Philip, for beating the final boss in Link for me; I got so incredibly lucky with you both. To my fearless cousister Diana—you inspire me daily with your creativity—thank you for being my first friend ever; and thank you to Ella, Yana, Mike G., Ellen and Thomas, Marie S., the Tancreds, my wonderful in-laws Mary and Mike, and the entire Pierantozzi family. To Whitney for sharing the same brain since we were two years old; to Katie S. for remembering every moment since first grade; and to Karen A., Amanda, Mason, Lindsay, Abby, Rachel, Katie K., Debbie, Sam, Meg, and Siu Ping, for always being there. All the words of encouragement from Mountainside, Fairfield, NYC, TBR, and SOMA mean more than I could ever express. And to Emily, the greatest writing partner and friend ever, I cannot believe we did this. Late-night texts can lead to the craziest ideas!

And finally, to Miss Jane Austen. We bow to you.